"Be careful what stories you let your head write in the quiet. It rarely authors the whole truth."

-K.C. Blackwell

ESCAPE

Book One of the

Darkness in Devotion Series

K.C. Blackwell

First published by Blackwell Ink Publishing, 2026

Main cover art design © L. V. Eldridge (@l.v.eldridge)
Back cover art design © PoisonBlackHeart (@poisonblackheart)

First edition

For My Children:
My three reasons for always getting back up after I fall, and trying again.
You are the greatest story I'll ever tell.

For Patrick:
My loudest laugh, my sharpest truths, and my forever platonic soulmate.
You'll live forever in every line of this book, even though you left us too damn soon.

And to all my Chaos Gremlins who live to hear those two simple words:
Good girl.
Now spread those pages - Kael is waiting for you.

Acknowledgements

To every beta reader who opened this book before it ever had a cover—thank you.

To my Discord girls, who showed up chapter by chapter, message by message, hype by hype: this book carries your fingerprints too. Your late-night reactions, voice notes, theories, encouragement, and unhinged enthusiasm reminded me why stories are meant to be shared, not written in isolation. You made this process louder, warmer, and infinitely more perfect.

Thank you all for your time, your energy, your curiosity, and your willingness to step into this world while it was still finding its shape. Your feedback, your enthusiasm, and your honesty mean more than you know.

This story was built in the dark. In the quiet moments, messy ones, and the ones that nearly broke me. You were the first hands to hold it. The first eyes to see it fully. The ones who helped me carve it into what it was meant to become.

I'm endlessly grateful you were here at the beginning, before the polish and the spotlight, when a book and its author are most fragile and most full of possibility. Thank you for helping *Escape* become something worth escaping into.

—*K. C. Blackwell*

~The Playlist~

Escape – Stray Kids

Red Lights – Stray Kids

Lose Control – Teddy Swims

Dopamine – Jackson Wang

Love Me or Leave Me – DAY6

Let the World Burn – Chris Grey

The Hills – The Weeknd

*Cl*oser – Nine Inch Nails

Gasoline – Halsey

Take Me Back to Eden – Sleep Token

I'm Yours – Isabela LaRosa

Unholy – Sam Smith

Like a Villain – Bad Omens

Friends – Chase Atlantic

Heathens – Twenty One Pilots

Play With Fire – Sam Tinnesz

Obey – Bring Me the Horizon

If I Had You – Chris Grey

Haven – Stray Kids

Dangerous Woman – Ariana Grande

A Note to the Reader;

This story walks through dark places.

Escape deals with trauma, control, survival, and the long, uneven process of reclaiming oneself after harm. Some of the language, situations, and emotional beats may be triggering, even when events are implied rather than shown.

At its core, this is not a story about suffering for shock value. It's a story about resilience. About choice. About finding safety where none seemed possible, and learning how to breathe again after holding it for too long.

I believe deeply in reader care. That's why you'll find content warnings ahead, and why I encourage you to read at your own pace, skip scenes if you need to, or step away entirely if something feels like too much.
Your well-being matters more than finishing a chapter.

Thank you for trusting me with this story. I hope that, even in its darkness, you find moments of strength, tenderness, and healing within these pages.

Take care of yourself. Always.

K.C.

Trigger Warnings

This book contains themes and scenes that may be distressing to some readers, including, but not limited to:

Kidnapping and unlawful confinement

BDSM club scenes and explicit sexual content

Physical violence and assault

Gun violence and the constructive use of various weapons

Implied and off-page sexual assault (Child)

Implied and off-page sexual assault (Adult)

Sexual exploitation and coercion

Trauma responses and PTSD

Emotional abuse and manipulation

Drug use and references to substance abuse

Human trafficking

Criminal activity and organized crime

Depictions of power imbalance

Death and murder – including off manual use of a wood chipper

Explosions and severe injury

Reader discretion is advised.

Content

Prologue

Ten Years Ago…

The night didn't feel different from any other night. They all bled together on this side of town. It was the kind of neighborhood that concealed more than it showed.

The air was damp as a cold drizzle fell around me. The streetlights flickered as if they were too tired to hold on but too poor to quit. I knew that feeling well.

My breath fogged as I cut through the alley behind O'Donnell's liquor store, my hands shoved deep in my jacket pockets to try to stave off the night's chill. My mind wandered as I walked; the homework I didn't care if I finished, and the double shift I just crawled out of, before my thoughts landed back on her.

Ariya.

Always Ariya.

Her bright laugh, her blue eyes that sparkled when she would see me coming, and the sweet fullness of her lips. She was perfect, every piece of her carved as if it were made just for me.

She'd texted me an hour ago, 'You walking home?' I got no answer when I replied with a quick 'yeah'.

She had probably just fallen asleep. Between work and school, there weren't enough hours in the day to get anything that resembled real sleep, but we didn't care. We would get out of this shithole, one way or another.

A loud noise pulled me from my thoughts, as my gaze snapped up from where I had been watching my shoes while I walked. A sharp smack coupled with a muffled cry had my feet moving before I could think twice. I ran toward the alley I'd heard the commotion coming from as my heart thundered against my chest.

"Please – stop!"

Her voice sliced through the dark like someone dragging a blade against stone. My boots hammered against the wet pavement, and my breath burned cold through my lungs. I skidded around the corner so hard I almost ate shit.

Three men had crowded her against the wall. Their leering grins set something ablaze inside me as I looked at Ariya. Her hand held against her cheek as tears streamed down her face.

One of the assholes wore a jacket I recognized as Irish mob. Fuck. The kind of low-level runners who earned their place by hurting people to gain favor within the ranks.

Ariya's mascara streaked down her cheeks as her lip bled, and it was all I could do to stop my body from rushing to her. She looked up at me, and I swear my heart stopped as I watched the hope spark in her bright blue eyes.

"Kael," she breathed in relief, even as her voice broke. "Please—"

The biggest one turned to look at me, his sneer growing as he looked me up and down.

"Aw, look at that," he smiled contemptuously. "She brought us a puppy to play with."

I didn't bother with an answer; I just moved and let instinct take hold as I rushed the one closest to me. My fist connected with the jaw of the one who called me a puppy. He let out a startled sound before his body hit the wet pavement and echoed around me.

The second man stepped forward and swung a bottle aimed at my head. I ducked quickly and twisted his wrist until he screamed, then rammed my elbow into his throat. He collapsed, choking on his words and air.

The third one stepped back, calculating both the situation and me. His hand reached into his jacket, and he pulled a large knife. The metal glinted in the street-lit alley. Ariya's hands covered her mouth to stifle a gasp, the noise making something inside me ache. The sound hit me like a fist to the sternum as I stepped toward them.

"Leave her the fuck alone," I growled, taking another step closer.

"Kid, just walk away. She's not worth dying for. No piece of ass is. Haven't you learned that by now?"

He didn't get it. I couldn't walk away from her. Not now, not ever. He lunged toward me and I caught his wrist. But he was stronger, older, and just fast enough to catch me off balance. The blade sliced across my forearm, and the sting of it burned hot and then cold in the air as the blood surfaced instantly.

His grin was filthy. "Told you—" he started, but was cut off as I slammed him into the wall. The sudden exchange caused him to drop his knife, and my free hand caught it by sheer luck.

The handle fit my hand like it had been waiting for me as he shoved me back, a litany of curse words falling from his lips. I sprang forward, my forearm pinning him against the brick and the knife pressed into his throat.

"You think you have the balls, kid?" he asked incredulously as I pressed the knife tip in hard enough to watch the blood bloom on his skin.

"For her? Yeah," I replied before slicing a clean line across his throat. His eyes widened in shock, then horror as the blood began to pour from his wound. His hands gripped uselessly against the flow as he sank to his knees. I stood over him and watched his eyes fix, glass over, and finally go cloudy.

A scream from behind pulled me from the macabre vision. I turned just in time to watch the one I'd knocked out drive his knife into Ariya's chest. I let out a sound of pure anguish and sprang toward the asshole as hands locked around my middle, yanking me backward, holding me like a wild animal fighting for its life.

"ARIYA! NO! PLEASE!"

I couldn't get to her. I couldn't move. The hands that gripped me were too strong, too big, too practiced at holding back grief and anger.

Ariya stood frozen for a minute before she looked down. Her eyes found mine once before her body crumpled to the ground. A pool of sickening red formed around her as I helplessly watched the life drain from her. I stopped struggling. I stopped breathing. The last thing I remembered was the sound of my jaw cracking before the world went black.

• • •

I woke up in a chair sometime later that night. My wrists and ankles were bound as the dull hum of voices filtered in from the distance. My neck ached when I lifted my head, and my eyes landed on the man seated in front of me. His expensive suit and look of mild amusement screamed too much money and not enough consequences.

"You killed one of mine." His voice carried an Irish accent, the kind that was born in the trenches and clawed its way out.

"And one of yours killed what was mine." The exhaustion and anger weighed heavily on my voice.

"Yours? Sorry lad. She was supposed to be mine, and you interrupted her being…acquired."

My jaw clenched as I stayed silent. He stood, circling me slowly, like a wolf appraising prey he'd already decided belonged to him.

"Was she worth it?" he asked with a smirk.

I swallowed past the lump in my throat, willing my voice to be stronger than I felt.

"Always."

Conor's smile sharpened. Cold, cruel, and amused.

"Feelings are a weakness, Kael. No woman is worth dying for. Not even her."

It would be the first of many lessons Conor would beat into me, because in the end, he didn't kill me. He recruited me. But something inside me broke apart that night. Not the part that killed for her, but the part that watched her die.

My failure took the only person I had ever loved. And I swore I would never feel that kind of hollow again.

If I ever found someone worth breaking for again… God help the man who tried to take her from me.

Chapter One

Seraphine

The red neon hit first, the "A" in Escape still stuttering in and out like it always had. The sign glowed like a heartbeat against the crumbling brick, faint and steady, daring anyone who passed to step inside.

The street around it was nearly empty, only the echo of traffic a few blocks over and the faint hiss of a train in the distance. This part of the city never really slept; it just dozed with one eye open. Steam leaked from grates, carrying that faint metallic tang that had never quite left the district. Old warehouses turned into clubs, and factories converted into lofts. All of it continued to wear its age, and on certain days, you could still smell the oil and iron beneath the exhaust and neon.

Most nights, I told myself I'd stop and really look at the old building that housed Escape, admiring the way it felt more like a warning than a welcome. Tonight though, I just pulled my leather jacket around myself tighter and hurried towards the front doors.

A laminated sheet was tacked to the wall beside the door, its edges curled from years of humidity and neglect.

No recording stage shows.

No hands without consent.

Safe word is posted behind the bar.

A second list hung lower, handwritten and framed by thumbtacks.

Check in with the DM before play.
Red means stop.
Yellow means slow.

People read it, nodded like saints, and then walked in and sinned anyway. These were the rules everyone had to learn before earning their wristband. Rules put in place to keep staff and patrons safe.

I tugged my jacket tighter around me as if to hide myself from the night, and pushed through the black-painted doors. The air inside the club hit like a wave. Thick with sweat and perfume, smoke and anticipation. The bass rattled up through the soles of my boots, my pulse synchronizing instantly with the sound as I stepped inside. The shadows clung to the corners while colored lights painted the rest of the room in blues, greens, and blood-warm red.

This place used to be a cannery. The steel beams still ran along the ceiling like ribs, blackened by an old fire Michael had once called atmosphere. To me, it was the club's spine, the only thing holding the place together. For most people, it would have felt like chaos. For me though, it was home.

The crowd had already gathered around the main floor, pressed shoulder to shoulder, eyes drinking in every sight the club offered. Laughter and gasps rang out around me, and the raw sounds of pleasure from booths along the back threaded seamlessly through the music. All of it belonged here, just like I did.

Wristbands glinted under the bar lights. Black for members. Silver for platinum VIPs. Red for subs looking for a new Dom. Green for the tourists. The curious ones. The kind of code that told you exactly what someone wanted if you knew how to look.

• • •

Jenny caught my eye from across the room, already grinning like she had plans for me. She always did. Before every set, Jenny and

I went over the night's program. We'd go over the scene, the limits, and our signals. Routine made it safe, but the trust between us is what made it art. The curve of her mouth told me everything I needed to know. I was not leaving work unmarked tonight, and a shiver ran down my spine in excitement and anticipation.

Benjamin, the club's regular bartender, looked up and gave me a nod as I passed the bar. "Cutting it kinda close, eh, Sera?"

"Relax. I'm here, aren't I?" I shot him a glare and headed for the staff hallway.

The hallway smelled like citrus cleaner fighting a losing battle against barley and leather polish. From somewhere above the lockers, a fan whirred, blowing around hot air that didn't help. I shrugged out of my jacket, tossed it into my locker, and slipped into my show clothes like armor.

Tonight's set was a deep wine leather corset that caught the light when I moved. The boning pressed tightly against my ribs just enough to remind me I was contained only because I chose to be. The matching harness crossed over my chest, with brass rings polished from use. The kind that gave a soft jingle when I walked. A pair of fishnet stockings framed my long legs beautifully, while my knee-high patent leather boots added two inches and all the attitude I needed.

A thin silver collar finished it. Something I had bought for myself shortly after I was hired. Not to signify ownership, but my own personal kind of branding. A constant reminder that the only person who owned me was me.

At five-foot-seven with a body toned, sharp and soft in all the right places, I knew exactly how to make a crowd hold its breath. My breasts filled the corset's line, just enough cleavage to show some skin, but not give away all my secrets. My long, dark hair was pulled back into a high, tight ponytail that fell straight down my back. I always kept my makeup minimal but deliberate. Smoky liner with a light brush of pink across my cheekbones, and I finished the look, as always, with a glossy red lip.

I gave myself a quick once-over in the dirty full-length mirror that was held to the wall with what I can only imagine was gum and a dream at this point, before turning and heading back into the club, ready to make the stage mine.

• • •

The moment my foot hit the stage, the crowd erupted. The show Jenny and I put on three nights a week always pleased the crowd, with half of them coming back regularly to see if we would top the last one.

The lights sliced through the haze, turning the smoke gold and red, washing everything else away. My pulse thrummed against my ribs as the opening, eerie notes of my signature track, "Taste" by Stray Kids, filled my ears. The pulse of the music hit like a second heartbeat, raw and sensual, igniting my confidence with ease.

I walked to the center of the stage, keeping every movement deliberate, and I let the noise swell and crash against me. Heat rose off the crowd, their bated breath and hungry eyes watching and waiting.

Jenny waited by the St Andrew's cross in the center of the stage, her presence a shadow wrapped in leather and confidence. Her eyes met mine, and the noise faded into static. This was our ritual. And while we had done this routine countless times, it never lost its charge.

The Dungeon Master hovered near the edge of the stage, his clipboard in hand, and kept a quiet watch like always. A sentinel making sure every scene stayed inside the lines while ensuring the spectators never got out of hand.

The leather straps of the cross hung open, waiting, and I stepped toward them and placed my hands against the wood. The grain was rough beneath my palms, grounding me instantly. One by one, Jenny buckled me in. The first strap closed around my wrist with a soft click, then another, and another. Each sound drew the crowd tighter, their attention narrowing until it felt like the whole room was holding its breath.

By the time she fastened the last strap at my ankles, my pulse lit up with the thrill of knowing each person was there to watch my undoing. Not only to see me, but to feel me break for them as well. The straps bit into my skin, sharp and reassuring. Anticipation coiled thick in the air. Mine, hers, and theirs all braided into one electric thread.

Jenny leaned in close, her breath warm against my ear. "Ready, baby?"

I nodded, as my voice had relocated somewhere between my lungs and my spine. She didn't need it, Jenny always knew. Cool air ghosted over my bare skin as she stepped back, while goosebumps chased the path her fingers had left behind. The music level dropped, letting the crowd feel and hear everything as we began.

The lights dimmed to a thin line carved over us, and at the exact moment came the first strike of her leather crop. It landed clean across my shoulder blade, a crack of sound that cut straight through the music. The sting bloomed bright and hot, and the crowd hummed with approval as my knees strained against the leather, but the straps held me steady.

Another crack, lower this time, across the curve of my ass. I cried out, my voice carrying over the swell of the audience, but Jenny didn't pause. She never did. The crowd fell into rhythm with it, as their gasps and cheers fell in time with the rise and fall of my chest.

She circled me slowly, her movements precise and graceful. Every gesture was a part of the choreography. Her control. My surrender. Their fascination. The room fed on the silence between each strike, breath held with anticipation of where her crop would land next. She leaned in again, her voice a low purr against the thrum of my pulse.

"Good girl."

Two words. Soft enough to make my whole body shake. Her praise made my back arch against the restraints as a needy moan slipped free before I could catch it. Jenny smiled against my skin. I felt it, wicked and satisfied, just before she delivered another strike, sharper this time, harder.

The pain bloomed brightly, but instead of breaking me, it shattered the last of my restraint. The club vanished at the edges. The crowd blurred, and the low bass faded into the background until all that remained was the ache that sang through my body and Jenny's voice tethering me to it.

The hits stopped, and a hush fell that was louder than the breaths pushing out of my chest. One moment, I was bracing for impact, and the next her fingers brushed between my thighs, tearing an opening in the crotch of my fishnets. Her movements were efficient and unhurried, as she shifted the thin fabric of my panties to the side with a touch that knew exactly how I liked to be handled.

A soft sigh slipped from me, my body already open and ready. She knew my limits and boundaries, and she made sure never to cross them. Every inch of me quivered with trust as her fingers glided along my dripping, engorged lips, coating them in my sticky arousal. All too soon, her fingers left me, leaving me aching and desperate for more.

Protest curled at the back of my throat, but before I could speak, something cold pressed against me, sudden and insistent. My eyes flew open as I turned my head to look at her. Jenny leaned in, lips brushing my ear, her voice low enough that only I could hear.

"Hold it," she whispered.

Then she pushed, and before I could react, I was full. I moaned as my muscles responded on instinct, trying to push the toy out. Years of practice pushed back, and I squeezed around the invading shape, thighs quivering as a line of sweat beaded along my forehead.

The slow stretch stole my breath. The toy filled me deep, and my legs trembled. The straps were the only thing keeping me upright, and the crowd's noise swelled as they realized what she had done. Jenny's hand lingered a moment, her palm flat against my stomach like she could feel it seated inside me. She drew back and left me with the impossible task she had set.

Hold it.

My mind raced as I realized this was going to take every ounce of restraint I possessed and all of my willpower to keep the toy exactly where she wanted it.

Another crack split the air, fire lancing across my skin. I cried out, torn between the sting on my back and the pressure inside me, between the humiliation of all those eyes and the way my body betrayed me with every shudder. Jenny circled again slowly, savoring it. The show wasn't just in the blows. It was in watching me fight not to fall apart.

She refused to give me leniency or time. Strike after strike rained down, each one causing me to pull the toy deeper, tightening the coil in my spine. My body turned into a taut wire pulled to breaking. I strained against the restraints. My hips rolled without my permission as I fought to keep the toy in. My moans stopped being soft or controlled. They tore free, raw and desperate. The crowd cheered as if my sounds belonged to them. And to be fair, they did.

Jenny's voice slid through the haze, hot against my ear, a velvet chain I had never wanted to escape.

"Break for me. Let them see how perfect you are when you shatter under my control."

And break I did. For her, for myself, and for the crowd as my release hit like a lightning strike. Violent and blinding. My body bucked helplessly against the straps as the sting from her handiwork and the fullness between my legs collided. Every nerve lit up, and my cries drowned under the bass and the hungry roar of the crowd watching me come undone. Heat and tension burst along my spine and washed through me in waves. My hips rocked with it, my thighs shook, and my fingers curled tightly around the wood.

When the last aftershock ebbed, my head fell forward, resting against the cool wood. Exhaustion and satisfaction filled my limbs as they sagged heavy and loose.

Jenny's hand smoothed down my side, steadying me as I sagged against the cross. "That's it. Make them remember you," she whispered, sealing my ruin with praise.

She slipped the toy from me with a practiced ease that made my whole body shiver. The sudden loss caused a whimper to fall from my lips as she smiled proudly at me.

She stepped around me as she eased me out of the straps, gentle and efficient, before she pressed a kiss to my temple. Together we turned and bowed to the crowd. The movement was practiced but never fake. My legs trembled, and my body still buzzed with slowing aftershocks. I blew a kiss toward the front row, then stepped through the back curtain of the stage with Jenny's arm firm around my middle. Her version of aftercare, and it's the part of our shows I savored more than I would ever admit out loud.

A cold bottle of water was pressed into my hand before I even asked. Condensation slicked my fingers, grounding me. I looked up and found Benjamin watching me with that smile he always wore that never quite reached his eyes.

"Great show tonight, Sera," he said. His voice was soft and gentle, pitched like I might break if he spoke too loudly. His gaze slid down my body, lingering a second too long on the marks he could see from where he stood, before he looked back up with that same uneasy grin.

"The crowd loved it. You really do keep them wrapped around your finger."

I let out a small laugh and took a sip, buying myself a second to breathe. "That's kind of the point, isn't it?"

"True." His lips curved into another almost-smile that he used when he wanted to be flirty. "Still… there's something about the way they look at you after. Like they'd sell their souls if you asked nicely."

The tone underneath his words scraped at something in me. Not fear, just awareness that bit, sharp and unwelcome.

I smiled politely. The kind of smile meant to end conversations, not start them.

"I gotta go change and clean myself up. I'll see you later, Ben." I turned on my heel and headed through the hallway that led back to the dressing room.

• • •

The hallway to the dressing room was darker than the main bar area, and the air always felt heavier here. The sounds of the club dulled behind the concrete walls. Not silence, just quieter and more forgiving.

I leaned back against the wall, the rough concrete cooling the welts along my spine. The building still carried its history everywhere you looked. Old factory bones that were dressed up in new sins instead of new paint. I closed my eyes and breathed in the familiar scent of this place until my pulse slowed.

For a few seconds, the quiet felt like mercy. The echo of the crowd still hummed in my bones. Their cheers, their gasps, and that low murmur of awe that always followed the break. It was never just about pain or just the showmanship. For a few precious minutes, every eye on me meant I existed. Meant that I wasn't a ghost or a mistake. That I wasn't the girl who flinched at shadows. Here, I mattered. Here, I was myself, unabashed and proud of who I was in ways I had never thought possible.

Every strike had been something I chose. Every sound, every gasp, and every shiver was pain on my terms and control in its purest form. Being a sub meant having more power than a dom ever would, and it fueled something within me from the moment I found this life I'd built.

Movement at the end of the hallway pulled me out of my after-show thoughts unwillingly. Michael barreled toward me, Escape's owner and manager. A professional asshole in a cheap suit. His bargain cologne arrived first, cloying and chemical, trampling whatever calm I had left.

"Sera," he said, slowing just long enough to give me a once-over. His eyes did a quick sweep, lingering in ways I was used to but still hated.

"Just getting dressed, Michael. Then I'll be back out there."

He waved a dismissive hand, already moving past me while muttering about numbers or inventory or whatever manic spiral he was riding tonight.

"Dick," I muttered under my breath as I pushed into the dressing room.

The light inside the room buzzed overhead, flickering like it was deciding whether to give up or keep fighting another day. My reflection stared back at me from the mirror. My cheeks were flushed, and my lipstick was smudged at one corner. A faint sheen of sweat along my skin as welts stood out sharply along my shoulders and thighs.

Most people flinched at the sight of welts and bruises. Not me. I smiled and turned to get a better view. Every mark left was a reminder that I had given permission. That I had chosen every strike, every sound, every second of it. Pain I could step into and step back out of whenever I said so. Control I could command.

I reached back and ran my fingers lightly over one of the raised lines, and a shiver slid through me. Not from pain, but from satisfaction. From being seen and still owning every piece of myself when the lights came back up.

I let the memory of the cross roll through me while I stripped and changed into a fresh outfit. This time, I chose a black corset dress that hugged every curve and barely covered my ass. Knee-high socks and heels that were sharp enough to qualify as weapons in certain states. I did a quick touch-up of my makeup and reapplied my red lipstick in a careful sweep. The collar stayed. It always stayed. Not ownership, but my declaration. I chose who touched me, who marked me, and who got to see me undone and most vulnerable.

I caught my reflection one more time as my hands smoothed the corset's seams, fingers brushing the beautiful constellation of welts along the edges. A small, satisfied smile tugged at my mouth as I opened the door and stepped back into the hall. The muted hum of the club slid back under my skin, familiar and insistent. It called to me like it always did.

The hallway looked empty, and I adjusted the hem of my dress and started toward the bar, my heels clicking against the concrete. Each step echoing off the walls.

I stopped as Michael's voice penetrated my thoughts. The sound was sharp and desperate even though it was muffled through the thin door to his office.

"I told you, I didn't know! Please—"

A second voice cut him off. This one was low and controlled. The kind of tone that crawled over your skin and settled there. I couldn't make out the words, but the sound alone made the hairs on my arms stand. That wasn't a voice you begged; it was a voice you obeyed.

Curiosity rushed through my chest, reckless and hot. It mixed with the leftover adrenaline from the stage until it felt almost the same. Rush and danger blur together, and the brain has no way of telling the difference.

I took another step closer, palm brushing the rough brick as if the wall could anchor me. Any sane person would have kept walking, but sanity had never been my strongest trait.

Michael's voice cracked as I listened through the door. "I swear, I didn't! Ah, fuck! Please, you have to believe me!"

The answer came quiet and unhurried, and while I still couldn't catch the words, the calm in it was worse than shouting.

A dull, heavy thud resonated through my chest. The sound of flesh hitting something solid, and a strangled cry that didn't belong to a man who liked to think he was in charge.

My breath caught, and every instinct screamed at me to move. I didn't need to know more. Whoever was in there, Michael had found the wrong kind of trouble, and it was something I didn't want to be a part of. My feet finally listened, and I turned and walked fast, heels skimming over the concrete.

"Not my circus," I muttered, pulse thundering in my ears as I made a beeline for the DJ booth.

• • •

Patrick glanced up as I slid onto the platform beside the booth, his ice blue eyes softening before cocking a brow. His fingers never stopped moving over the mixer, adjusting knobs with that lazy precision only he could pull off.

"Christ, Ser," he said over the bass, a smirk tugging at his mouth. "You look like you just saw a ghost."

"Close." I grabbed the edge of the booth for balance, shaky as my pulse refused to settle. "More like I think maybe I heard one."

Patrick leaned in, his voice pitched just loud enough to cut through the music. "You want me to kill the track and clear the floor? Send all these depraved souls scattering?"

I laughed, but the sound was shaky, even to my own ears. "Relax, Pattykins." I used the nickname that always made him roll his eyes. "Keep the music going. I don't need your hero complex tonight."

He flashed a wolfish grin, but never missed a beat. "It's not a complex if I actually *am* the hero."

He twisted a dial, and the track slid into something darker and heavier. "But if some asshole's hassling you, I'll stomp his face into the floor. Or at least have one of the bouncers do it."

The ridiculous image pulled a real laugh out of me, and the knot in my chest loosened a little. Patrick wasn't a fighter. While he was tall and lanky, and his long arms always wrapped around me for the most perfect hugs, he was a lover before he would ever be a fighter. He had a sharp tongue and sharper instincts, but always stayed soft enough that I could lean on him when the walls closed in.

For a moment, with the music vibrating through us and Patrick's grin keeping me anchored, I almost forgot the sound of Michael begging. Almost forgot the low, cold voice that had answered him. Almost.

I lingered there a little longer, waiting for my pulse to settle. Escape had a way of swallowing secrets, no matter how loud they resonated, but Michael's voice still echoed at the back of my mind. His words had been broken and pleading, tangled with another presence that was cold, patient, and dangerous.

"Hey, Sera?"

I turned to see Benjamin weaving his way through the crowd, bar rag in hand, with that too-bright grin plastered on his face. It still didn't reach his eyes. His movements were sharp and jerky, and he always looked like he ran on too much caffeine, even though I had never seen him drink a coffee in his life.

"Do me a favor?" he asked. He tried to sound casual but missed by a mile. "Cover the bar for a few minutes. I just need to check on something in the back."

I arched a brow, wiping a bead of sweat from my temple with my thumb. "Since when do you leave the bar mid-shift?"

"Since Michael's been riding my ass about inventory. Five minutes. I promise."

Before I could push back, he was already gone. His thin shoulders and nervous energy disappeared into the hallway that led toward the offices. Typical fucking Benjamin.

Still, something in the way he moved always made the hair on the back of my neck prickle. With a sigh, I glanced at Patrick. He gave me a mock salute and dove back into his mix. I rolled my eyes and headed toward the bar.

The crowd pressed in from all sides. Bodies swayed as the smell of nicotine and alcohol clung to the air. The music pulsed through everything, including me, making my hips sway to the beat as I walked.

I slipped behind the counter and into a pattern my muscles knew by heart. Bottle. Pour. Glass. Smile. Repeat. My hands moved on autopilot. Banter with the regulars, flirt where it helped tips, and deflect where it didn't.

The knot in my shoulders loosened with each drink I slid across the wood. Routine had its own kind of compassion, and for a few minutes, I almost convinced myself that the sound of Michael begging hadn't been as bad as I remembered.

Then I felt it. Eyes locked on me. Not the usual hungry kind I had learned to ignore. This one didn't roam. It stayed and settled somewhere deep. Goosebumps prickled along my skin before I even looked up. And when I did, our eyes met.

He sat perched near the end of the bar, half-shadowed by low amber light. Not moving, not speaking. Just watching. His attention didn't slide over me like everyone else's. It held me pinned in place for longer than was comfortable.

The kind of gaze that wasn't just looking at me, but actually seeing me. I looked away first, pretended to wipe the counter, and forced my breath to behave. Just another customer, I told myself.

I took another cleansing breath and moved down the bar toward him. I leaned in when I reached him, the bar lights catching the greys of his eyes. My voice came out steady, casual enough that I almost believed it myself.

"What'll it be?"

He didn't answer right away. Didn't even blink. His eyes locked intently on mine as his fingers tapped the bar in time with the music. He tilted his head just slightly, like I surprised him, and for a second the world narrowed to that single look.

Finally, after what felt like an eternity, he spoke. "Whiskey. Neat. Don't water it down, please."

The noise of the club dimmed under the weight of his tone. It wasn't a request, and something in me answered to it anyway as my hand moved before my brain ever caught up.

Chapter Two

Kael

The phone rang just as I killed the engine. Staring at the screen, I felt my jaw tighten. Conor never called unless there was something I wasn't going to like.

"Kael." My voice answered flat and automatic.

"You at the club yet?" Conor's Irish accent slid through the speaker, calm in a way that made my shoulders tense. Too calm. The kind of tone he used when he already knew the answer and wanted to remind you who was really in charge.

I dragged in a slow breath, watching the neon "A" stutter in and out like a dying pulse. *Escape.* Christ. What a name. The type of place that claimed freedom, but instead recruited people who begged to be collared.

"Just pulled up," I muttered.

"You know the drill. Michael's late. Again."

Of course he was. Michael always was. The man was all excuses and flop sweat, a guy who talked too much when he should've been running.

"Want me to make sure he remembers?" I asked, knowing the answer already.

A pause before he replied. "Remind him who he owes. You've got room to… improvise."

That earned a dry laugh out of me, the sound low and humorless. "Improvise. Right. Got it."

The line clicked dead. Conor was definitely a man of few words and even less patience. It made my job easier. The less small talk, the easier it was to get to the fucking point.

I tossed the phone onto the passenger seat and stared at the club for a moment longer. The rain hadn't stopped since dusk, and it slicked the pavement black, making the neon bleed across puddles like an open wound. The sign blinked and stuttered. Damn thing was almost broken, but still holding on. Much like everything else in this part of the city.

The city dressed its sins in neon and perfume, but underneath, it stank all the same. But work was work. And if Michael thought hiding at his club like this would make him harder to reach, he was about to learn otherwise.

I pushed the car door open and stepped into the night. The air hit cold and sharp, carrying the scent of old oil, wet asphalt, and something else underneath. Rot, maybe, or just the same trouble that always seemed to follow me.

• • •

The bass reverberated through the pavement before I even reached the door. It wasn't just sound. No, it was alive, pulsing, and crawled up through my boots. A rhythm that didn't just move people; it hollowed them out.

I scanned the street out of habit. Two alleys flanking the old factory, one half-lit, the other dead dark. A couple of drunks stumbled past, laughing as if the city hadn't already chewed them up and spit them back out without prejudice.

The bouncer didn't ask for ID. He gave me one look and stepped aside. I nodded once and stepped through the black-painted doors.

Inside, the air was hot and thick, laced with cheap liquor, latex, and the distinct ozone smell from the strobe lights. Heat clung to everything, slick and relentless. I watched as the crowd moved like one organism, all teeth and want, light slicing across their bodies until no one looked human anymore.

Places like this were always the same. People chasing release like it was salvation, when all they were really doing was rehearsing surrender.

I scanned the crowd, looking past them with an indifference that took years to perfect, until my gaze landed on her.

She was strapped to a St. Andrew's Cross at the center of the stage, her head tipped back, and her body arched; her entire being was lit by the stage lights like sin turned sacred. Every movement was deliberate and practiced. Every sound she made was swallowed by the music. She didn't look afraid, or even humiliated. No, she looked alive, and the crowd worshiped her for it.

The woman behind her raised a hand mid-swing, her eyes gleaming with command. The strike landed sharp, the sound cutting through the room like gunfire. The girl on the cross flinched and then smiled back at the crowd. That smile cut right through me. The look was somehow small, but also dangerous and devastating.

For a heartbeat, something unfamiliar coiled low in my gut. Something I'd been trained to tune out years ago. I didn't like how it felt, and I hated how it made the room tilt. I looked away, quickly adjusted myself in my jeans, and forced my focus toward the hallway that would take me to the job.

Michael was the reason I was here, not the woman bleeding beauty onto a stage. Still, as I cut through the crowd and around the stage toward the back hallway, the sight of her there, obedient and proud, stayed burned in my mind longer than I wanted.

• • •

Michael's office stank of mildew, cheap cologne, and the sour stench of old whiskey. The bottom shelf kind. I took a seat in his chair, tipped it back on two legs, and hooked one boot under the desk's lip. As I leaned back, I kept my fingers locked behind my head, waiting. Patience was one of the few virtues I had left.

I heard the crowd erupt back in the main bar. The show must have finished, and they went wild for her. Good, she deserved it. I tried not to let the image of her strapped down crowd my thoughts again as the door to the office eased open on creaking hinges.

Michael padded in, muttering to himself, his eyes cast downward as he shut the door behind him. He turned and looked up to see me, and I watched as everything in him drained away.

"Kael…" The name came out thin and fraying at the edges.

"You're late, again, Michael."

Fear marred his face before he quickly schooled it and plastered on a salesman's smile. The one that was always too wide and slick, the kind of smile that sold itself to drunk men and lonely wallets. It made my fingers twitch. I stood before he could finish as the chair thumped to the floor behind me. He took an involuntary step back.

"Listen, Kael, things've been… complicated," he stammered. "Business, you know how it is, right?" His voice squeaked on the last word.

"I don't care about business. I care about promises. Like the one you made to Conor."

He babbled, some bullshit about numbers, contractors, and missed payments. Useless cries of small men. Tiny scraps of panic thrown at a wall. I closed the gap in three calm, unhurried steps. My hand locked his wrist and twisted until the joint popped with a wet and obscene sound. He screamed as his knees gave out under him.

"You think you can hide behind flashing lights and smoke machines? You know how to blame the world, yet can't find the words to own your damn mess. Bad form, Michael."

I hauled him deeper into his office and tossed him aside like a rag. He hit the floor, and the cheap desk rattled.

"You've got two weeks." I crouched, my face close enough to count the crinkled skin lines around his fearful eyes. My fingers hooked under his chin and lifted his face, forcing him to look in my eyes. "Two weeks to find what you owe. Two weeks to make it right."

The words landed like a hammer, and he begged, the sound filling the room like an animal's whine. "Please, Kael. I'll get it, I swear—" But his promise shredded under the weight of my stare.

His begging grated on my nerves, and I shut him up the way this city shuts loud mouths: fast, efficient, and permanently instructive. I grabbed the side of his head and slammed it into the desk. He fell backwards, landing on the cheap laminate floor like someone clawing out of a bad dream.

"You think you're clever," I said quietly, leaning down close enough that his breath assaulted my senses. "You hide behind the noise and lights. Weak men like you always get found, Michael." I let him fall back against the dirty floor and watched the sweat and blood bead at his temple.

He croaked out another promise, and this time I didn't answer. I just stood, my boots squeaking on the cheap floor, and fixed him with a look that let him imagine any worse fate he wanted. "Two weeks. Then I'll be back, and we can revisit how much you enjoy making Conor wait."

He finally stopped rambling, and his head fell back on the floor as the realization gripped him. I left him there, a mess in a cheap suit, and let his office door click shut behind me with a definitive sound.

• • •

There's a type of need that follows doing the job: a drink, a cigarette, hell, even fucking a stranger. Anything to take a moment to feel normal. Or whatever passes for normal in my line of work.

I came through the back of the stage and around to the main bar again. The heat slammed into me again. Lights, bodies, and the sharp tang of perspiration and cologne. People gathered like tidewater around the stage and bar.

I picked a stool with my back to the wall, one boot braced so I could move fast if I needed to. Always watch the exits, always know who's coming and going. That was the job. Everything else was just noise.

I leaned an elbow against the counter, scanning the room while I waited for someone to notice me. The air felt heavier here, dense like a sex-laden fog. Bodies pressed together too tightly, and voices that seemed to get lost under the bass.

It was a place that tried to hide what it was under colored lights and music, but the truth bled through in the corners: the desperate, the lonely, and the ones pretending they had control by giving it up.

Scenes like this always made me think of a crime scene before it happened. All the pieces were already in motion; most of the players just didn't know their roles yet.

I looked up when she moved into view, and for just a moment, I almost forgot how to breathe. Gone were the leather, the straps, and the stage lights that made her look untouchable. In their place was something more. Something rare in a world meant to diminish someone like her.

Behind the bar, she moved with the same control. Her motions were still deliberate and measured, but there was something more now. Her hair was loose, her face softer in the low amber glow, though her eyes carried that same defiance I'd seen when she smiled through the pain.

She poured a drink for a waiting customer, her lips set in a line of quiet focus, and the crowd seemed to lean toward her without realizing they did. Even here behind the bar, she drew them to her like gravity.

I told myself I was just observing, that it was simple pattern recognition. Nothing more than the habit of a man who noticed everything. But when her gaze flicked up, quick and sharp, straight into mine, the bar seemed to shrink around us. Nothing but the dull thud of the bass broke through.

Something in my chest tightened again. I'd spent years training myself not to feel that pull. Desire, fascination, or anything that blurred judgment. Weaknesses, all of them. But there was something about her that cut through the noise differently. It wasn't the outfit or the way her skin caught the light. It was her calm in the chaos. Like a fawn in a meadow, blissfully unaware of the wolves watching from the tree line. It made something inside me shift again, slow and unwanted, but this time I let it settle.

She came over and leaned in close enough that I caught the faint trace of perfume under the sweat and smoke. Patchouli and a hint of vanilla. The scent was warm, earthy, and grounding. An anchoring scent that didn't belong here but somehow ruled it anyway.

"What'll it be?" she asked, voice smooth and light, with just enough edge to pull me out of my own head.

For a heartbeat, I didn't answer. I just looked at her, taking in the curve of her lips when she flashed a small smile and the way the club lights caught in her eyes. Not fear or arrogance. Just *control.* My fingers drummed on the bar in time with the bass.

"Whiskey. Neat. Don't water it down, please."

She didn't flinch at the weight in my stare, or in the way my words left no room for refusal. She only tilted her head, like she was weighing the words. Like I didn't scare her.

She either loved the threat of danger that rolled off me or didn't recognize it for what it was. Both possibilities interested me. Both would be a problem.

I watched her move, my eyes following the slow, sure rhythm of her hands as she poured the whiskey. She slid the glass across the bar without flourish. No trembling or performance. Just quiet, efficient confidence. The kind that said the chaos around her would break before she ever did.

I wrapped my fingers around the glass, the heat of the room sinking through the chill that usually lived beneath my skin.

The liquor burned sharp and clean on the way down, control in liquid form. I let it sit on my tongue, scanning the room out of habit, and catalogued the faces.

Most of them looked the same. Desperate men pretending to be predators and women pretending not to notice. Everyone here was busy performing something. Everyone except her.

My gaze found her again. The way she moved through the noise like it couldn't touch her. My eyes traced the raw, red marks along her shoulders, half-hidden beneath the frame of her dress. Fresh and angry, yet deliberate and beautiful.

She hadn't hidden them, hadn't even tried, and that alone told me everything I needed to know.

The little smile she gave someone down the counter wasn't for me, but it hit somewhere deep just the same. Genuine and unforced. It was like she didn't belong here in a place like this. Or maybe she belonged more than anyone ever had. Either way, it made me sit up and take notice.

I shook my head, clearing the haze, and set the empty glass down harder than I meant to. The sound cracked through the low hum of music and chatter, earning a startled glance from the woman beside me. I didn't bother to apologize; I just stared at her until she looked away.

"Another," I said as she made her way back towards me.

She lifted a brow, but she poured it anyway. No words or hesitation. Just a small smirk as she placed the glass back down in front of me.

The second glass hit harder, and I leaned back, letting the whiskey sear its way down. I tried to remind myself it was just the job that brought me here. Just the debt. Just another night doing Conor's dirty work.

But my eyes still constantly found their way back to her, watching as she moved easily behind the bar. The way she laughed at something stupid a patron said, so soft and easy. As if she hadn't just burned on stage for them a little while earlier.

Something twisted in my chest again, and I didn't like it. I hated that her voice cut through the noise, and that I could still taste the faint scent she'd left behind in the air.

I drained the remainder of the second glass, letting the burn settle into something familiar yet entirely unwelcome. The whiskey was cleaner than the smell of desperation that filled the room. Cleaner than the thoughts I was trying to suppress about her, and all the ways I wanted to make her beg.

I'd done my fucking job. Delivered the message and left the mark. That should have been enough, yet when I stood, my gaze found her one last time. Maybe I was just trying to confirm she was real. That I hadn't imagined her standing there in that pool of light from above the bar, calm in a place built for chaos. And for another brief, dangerous moment, I wondered what it might feel like to touch her. To test that calm. To see how she would break for me, and maybe I, for her.

I set the glass down and turned, heading for the exit. "It was just the job," I muttered as I stepped into the night. It's always just the job.

Chapter Three

Seraphine

The door wouldn't open. No matter how hard I pulled, the handle slipped, its surface slick under my fingers, as if someone had greased the doorknob.

My hands looked all wrong. Whose hands are these? They can't be mine, and somehow, they were. Smaller and softer, with nails chewed to the stubs. My pulse hammered so loud in my ears that it drowned out my breathing. I yanked the door harder. The knob rattled in the frame, but the door wouldn't move. It never moved.

The air felt too thick to swallow. Every breath scraped down my throat like I was breathing sawdust. I pressed my ear to the door and listened to the voices just beyond it, and I covered my mouth.

Those voices. The ones I'd spent years trying to burn from memory, the ones with the same distorted and angry cadence crashing like waves against me. I couldn't make out the words, just the tones. The rise. The sickly-sweet cadence that stuck to the skin of my past. The sounds that were just heavy enough to crush a child's soul.

Something slammed, and the vibration rolled through the floor and up my legs, making me shake. My skin prickled, and my chest burned.

"No, no, no," I whispered, but it wasn't my voice. Too soft. Too young. Too fucking innocent.

The overhead light flickered as shadows all around me began to shrink and swell in some sick little dance. The wallpaper peeled in long, curling strips as shapes moved in the dark. Not faces, just outlines I knew too well and had desperately tried to forget.

The cold, almost-damp feeling of the carpet licked along my bare feet. This wasn't my apartment's hardwood. No, this was old, and threadbare, stained in places by things I refused to name. Nausea clawed up my throat.

"*Don't make a sound. You wouldn't want to get into trouble, would you? Don't forget, this is our little secret…*"

The whisper came from nowhere and everywhere all at once, and it brushed along the back of my neck like a hand I couldn't see. I flinched, spinning toward it, and the room tilted with me. The air swirled around me, smelling like old cigarettes and sour wine, as it wrapped itself around me like hands I'd known and feared all too well as a child.

I reached for the door again, my hands trembling so hard I could barely grip the handle. The metal burned this time, searing against my palm, but I held on anyway. I pulled, yanked, and begged until my voice cracked. Screaming for someone, anyone, to let me out.

The voices on the other side grew louder, overlapping, frantic, and mean. My name on their tongues was twisted and wrong. The walls pulsed with every syllable until I felt the sound in my teeth.

The light blinked once, twice, and then it went out completely. I was swallowed by the dark, and I sank to my knees, hugging them close to my chest as I hid my face.

Surrounded by darkness, an old feeling wrapped itself around me. Heavy and familiar, like a phantom weight pressing down on my chest. My body froze. I couldn't move, couldn't breathe, couldn't scream. My lungs clawed for air while my limbs stayed locked, pinned by something unseen. Muscle memory is a cruel fucking thing.

The smell of smoke wafted around me again. The faint creak of the door hinges. The sound of a footstep. My heart stopped. Then that familiar panic rose along my spine like ice.

"Please." My voice broke, smaller than I'd heard in years. "Please don't—"

The word shattered around me before I could finish. The door burst open and light flooded in, blinding and sharp. Something real tugged at me from the seams of my conscience.

"Seraphine!"

A warm and familiar voice tried to pull me out of the murky depths.

Bang. Bang. Bang.

A knock so loud and real, it punched straight through the haze and confusion.

The voice cut through my muddled thoughts so softly and carefully. So fucking familiar. I latched onto it before I even understood why. The dream fought to pull me back under, dragging me back toward the door, toward the shadows that whispered my name in all the ways I begged to forget.

"Sera, hey. It's Patrick. You're dreaming, sweetheart. Wake up!"

My eyes snapped open, taking in the room around me, and for a second, I didn't know where I was. My heart slammed against my ribs, breath tearing out of me in short, ragged bursts. The door. The carpet. Gone. In its place was my ceiling. My room. The faint glow of the city leaked through the blinds. Home. I'm home. I'm not back there. My throat burned as it had in my dream, solidifying my return to reality.

The cool air hit my damp face, and my bedsheet scraped against my legs, the sensation rough and real this time. Patrick's silhouette hovered in the doorway; his hands raised with his palms out. Our signal for *safety*. Even if I couldn't feel it, I could see it. *Safe. I'm safe.* The mantra repeated in my head.

"Hey, you with me?" he asked, voice low, steady, and almost painfully calm. "Can I come in?"

I tried to speak, but the sound broke on a sob. I could only nod as I pulled my knees close to my chest, hugging them as I had in the dream.

He stepped into my room, slow enough that I could've stopped him at any point. He'd learned how to move with my trauma. The way he maneuvered was like someone approaching a wounded animal. No sudden motions and no assumptions.

My sheets were tangled around my legs, damp with sweat. My hands shook where they clutched the blanket wrapped around me, my knuckles glowing white with strain.

"Easy," he murmured, kneeling beside the bed but not touching me. "You're safe. You're with me. It's only me."

His voice pulled the air back into my lungs, and I tried to focus on it. On the sound of him. On his steady cadence that never changed.

"In through your nose," his voice was calm and reassuring. Then, demonstrating, he slowed his breathing enough for me to follow. "Out through your mouth. That's it."

I mirrored him, shaky at first, with each breath catching in my throat. Every inhale scraped, and every exhale that followed trembled. But little by little, it all came back into focus. The shadows lost their edges, and the weight started to lift from my chest.

Patrick didn't reach for me until I reached out for him first. My fingers brushed his sleeve, and he moved closer, letting his hand settle gently on my shoulder. The pressure was light and grounding.

"You're here. You're home with me. They can't hurt you anymore. You've got the control now, okay?"

A tear slid down my cheek before I realized it, hot and silent. I nodded again, and my breath finally began to steady.

Patrick's smile was faint, sad around the edges, but real. "There she is." His hand gently cupped my cheek, soft and reassuring like always. For a long moment, neither of us moved. The hum of the city outside filled the silence, and my heartbeat slowed enough to stop shaking me like some obscene human maraca.

I swallowed hard, my voice raw and torn as I mumbled a low, "Sorry."

He shook his head immediately. "You don't ever have to apologize for surviving, Ser." His thumb brushed the back of my hand, light as static. It was enough to keep me here. *Safe. I'm safe.* I reminded myself again. As many times as it took to remember. We sat together in silence for a long while before he headed out of my room to give me the space he knew I needed after a nightmare like that.

• • •

The sky outside the blinds had begun to turn deep reds and oranges, as the canvas of early morning brought the city to life around me. My body still ached from work the night before and the nightmare, but at least the panic was gone, for now. Temporarily replaced by something dull and heavy, but manageable.

I pulled myself out of bed, draped my housecoat around me, and made my way to our kitchen. Counting my footsteps in my head and on my fingers to keep myself grounded.

I found my spot across from Patrick at the kitchen island. He had a mug in hand, his long purple hair a mess that said he hadn't gone back to bed either. He was my roommate, yes, but more than that, he was my platonic soulmate. Chaos wrapped in eyeliner who doubled as a DJ, confidant, and the only person who refused to flinch when I fell apart. He talked in sarcasm, lived solely on caffeine, and could mix a track that would make the dead dance.

The fridge hummed, stitching the quiet between us as I reached for the pack of cigarettes on the counter — his, not mine — and lit one before he could stop me. Patrick's icy blue eyes lifted over the rim of his mug.

"I thought you quit."

"I relapse on special occasions," I muttered, exhaling toward the ceiling. Smoke curled in the slant of morning light, a soft gray ghost between us, and he snorted.

"Nightmares count as special occasions now?"

"They do when they leave me shaking like a carcass underground in an earthquake. Besides, you owe me one after scaring the shit out of me with that knock."

He grinned. It was faint but there. "You were screaming loud enough to wake the dead, Ser. Knocking was a courtesy before the cops showed up, thinking my best friend was being murdered."

"Yeah, well, courtesy isn't usually your strong suit." I chuckled a little. "I've grown accustomed to the sarcasm mixed with your version of kindness. Don't go changing on me now, Pattykins."

He let that comment slide and leaned forward onto his elbows. "You back with me now?"

The question wasn't casual, it was code. His way of asking if I was safe inside my own skin again.

I nodded, taking another slow drag. "Eh." I gave a soft shrug. "Mostly yeah."

"Good." He took a sip of his coffee, watching me over the edge of the cup again. "Because you've got that look like you're about to start thinking too hard again."

"I always think too hard."

"Yeah, that's the problem." His reply was soft and gentle, but laced with concern.

For a while, we just sat there. The silence between us was never awkward. It was comfortable in the way only years of being each other's constant could make it. He drank his coffee and I finished my smoke. Outside, the city began to stir.

When I finally stubbed out the cigarette, he pushed his mug toward me. "You need it more than I do."

The coffee was still hot as I wrapped my hands around the mug, letting the warmth seep into my fingers, keeping me in the present. Patrick leaned back, stretching his long arms behind his head.

"You know, you don't have to do the strong thing every time."

I gave him a small smile that didn't reach my eyes. "I don't know anything else."

He studied me for a beat, then nodded. Not in agreement but understanding. "Alright then. Just… buy your own damn cigarettes next time. These are expensive."

A quiet laugh slipped out before I could stop it. "Asshole."

"Love you too, trouble."

The moment broke something tight inside my chest, and I exhaled a slow and steady breath. For the first time since waking, it began to hurt a little less.

• • •

By late afternoon, when the sun had climbed high enough to spill through the blinds, I'd convinced myself I was fine. The same lie I repeated most mornings and somehow always sounded better in daylight.

I went through the motions of a mundane life until the light thinned. Dishes. Laundry. Shower. Letting my hands work while my head stayed quiet. Lather, rinse, repeat. Patrick had crashed on the couch, snoring softly, one arm flung over his eyes, and I left him a note on the counter:

Thanks for the rescue, as always, DJ of the damned.

By dusk, I was back in front of the mirror in my room. The same ritual, different day. A corset, stockings, and boots. My makeup precise, and my hair tied high and sleek. The silver collar stayed, as always. Now as a habit with my self-made identity. My tether to sanity.

The marks from Jenny's scene last night left bright constellations painted across my back. I traced one with a fingertip over my shoulder, smiling as I felt the raised skin under the pad of my finger. It grounded me in a strange way. It was proof that I could endure. Proof that control wasn't something anyone could take from me anymore.

I left for work with my heart a little lighter, and the fog cleared. Patrick had left earlier to set up his booth, and the walk from our little apartment to the club was short, but enough to ease my mind.

When I arrived at *Escape*, the sign still flickered, with the broken "A" stubbornly refusing to die. The line outside was already wrapping around the corner. As I made my way inside, my eyes fell to the wristbands flashing in the lights: black, platinum, red, and green. A quiet pecking order that boasted exclusivity, but bordered just this side of pretension.

Benjamin was behind the bar as I walked in. His shirt clung damp to his chest, and his bright red hair was a mess from running his hands through it too many times. He looked up and grinned, that same one that always made my skin crawl.

"Look who's back. Our star performer here to slum it behind the bar tonight?"

I slid behind the counter, giving him a look that said *don't start.* "Shut the fuck up, Ben. Lord knows we can't count on you to keep the masses happy and drunk."

"Oooh. Touche. But you know you always make an impression when you're on stage. Half the room's been asking when your next show is." His gaze dipped to my chest, lingered a beat too long, then he forced his smile wider.

I moved past him, grabbing a bar apron, and kept my voice flat. "My shows are posted. They're just eager for everything they can't have."

He chuckled, low. "Sounds about right for the clientele we serve." Typical Benjamin. Always thinking his charm was a reward, when really it was just annoying and borderline creepy.

The night moved along as usual. Pour, drink, laugh at something not fucking funny, and repeat. Bodies swayed together as laughter rose and broke like waves. I was almost starting to enjoy the hum of normalcy. That was until I looked up in time to see Michael.

He was cutting through the crowd toward his office, his head ducked low, and the collar of his shirt pulled high. But as the light caught him just right, I winced at the sight of the bruise swelling along his temple and the faint split in his lip. His eyes caught mine for less than a heartbeat and narrowed slightly before he looked away.

He moved stiffly, like his body ached, as he sucked in air between his teeth when someone bumped into him. Something ugly twisted inside me, and my heartbeat kicked hard against my ribs. I watched for a minute longer until he adjusted his tie and disappeared behind the stage, heading directly for his office.

Benjamin followed my gaze. "Boss looks worse for wear, huh? Bet he's got another tab open somewhere he shouldn't." He smirked. "Man's a fucking walking cautionary tale."

I said nothing as my own anxiety crept in at the corners. I pushed it down with a hard swallow and poured another drink. The glass clinked a little too hard as I set it down on the bar. I tried and failed to push the sounds I'd heard coming from his office last night out of my head.

A hand brushed mine, pulling me out of my dark thoughts. The touch lingered too long, so I pulled my hand away and wiped it on a bar rag. I looked up as I did, noting the patron whose touch had set off all my alarms. I bit back the urge to roll my eyes, cause I knew this one. He was the kind who thought money bought privilege; his silver wristband gleamed in the bar light along with his too-white smile.

"Didn't know you worked the bar too…" His voice was smooth with the kind of confidence that only ever came from never hearing the word no, or choosing to ignore it entirely.

"You never asked," I replied as my voice took on a tone of simple annoyance.

His grin widened. "I heard you like giving private shows. I booked one of the rooms upstairs. Part of the benefits of being a platinum member. Means I get my pick of the performers, and as luck would have it, I chose you."

He set a black card on the bar like it was a badge, yet patient as a threat.

My jaw tightened. "You most definitely heard wrong."

He laughed like I'd told a joke. "Come on, sweetheart. Everyone here is for sale, for the right price of course."

Before I could answer, Benjamin's voice cut in, falsely bright. "Play nice, Sera. He's one of our *platinum* members."

The man's hand reached towards me, grabbing and holding my wrist as if I were a petulant child. I let him hold me and refused to move or break. My smile stayed cold as I narrowed my eyes.

"Platinum doesn't mean anything to me. Just another wristband in a sea of them. I said no."

He frowned but didn't let go. "Since when did a whore like you learn the word no?"

I smiled, and my teeth gleamed in the club lights. "Since I learned men like you prefer to fucking ignore it."

Then I moved, quickly. I slipped my hand out of his grip and grabbed and twisted his wrist just enough to make his breath hitch.

Benjamin swore softly under his breath. "Christ, Sera—"

I released him before it could become more of a scene, leaning in close enough for only him to hear. "You touch me or anyone else here without permission again, and I'll make sure your membership's revoked before the bruises have time to appear."

He pulled his hand back like he'd been burned. "You can't—"

"Fucking try me."

He stormed off, muttering something about sluts who didn't know their place. I just grinned and gave him a wave as he disappeared through the main doors.

Benjamin's smile faltered when the man stalked off, and his frustration turned to me. "You really gonna cost us a platinum member over a little handsy moment?"

I narrowed my eyes at him, my voice dropping to a deadly calm. "Without a second fucking thought, *Benjamin.*"

He scoffed. "You'll get yourself fired one of these days."

"Yeah, right. Michael wouldn't fire me for taking out the trash." I gave a nonchalant shrug and poured myself a shot as the adrenaline still rolled through me.

He glared but didn't answer, and the rest of the night bled into the usual rhythm. More drinks, more noise, and the same neon haze. But the image of Michael's bruised face lingered in the back of my mind, pulsing in time with the bass.

• • •

By the time the last drink was poured and the crowd had thinned to a slow, sticky trickle, my body ached in that familiar, bone-deep way. The lights had come up halfway, signaling last call and shining just bright enough to catch the curtain of smoke still clinging to the air.

Benjamin had already disappeared into the back with some excuse about inventory, which left me to close. Again. Fucking prick. I wiped down the bar, dragging the rag across the sticky counter, and listened to the low hum of the building settling. It was always louder when the people left. Like both the club and I got to exhale once the eyes were gone.

The bass had stopped hours ago, but my own pulse kept drumming in my ears, slow and stubborn. Like it didn't know when to quit. I let myself get lost in the tasks. The menial work gave me a chance to shut my brain off. I zoned out and eventually set the last chair on its table.

It was well after 3 a.m. when I flipped the last light switch, leaving only the red EXIT sign washing the room in blood-colored light. Neon leaked through the narrow window, painting the walls in faint pinks and blues.

I grabbed my jacket from the hook behind the bar and slung it over my shoulder, letting the familiar weight of it settle against me. I set the alarm, and as it beeped its countdown, I stepped outside the main doors. As the door shut, the comforting sound of the lock clicking into place relaxed me a bit more. There's comfort in routine, and I let myself take solace in another night survived.

I took the small step down to the sidewalk and froze as the feeling hit me. Not a sound, really. Just a shift. The kind of prickle that crawls up the back of your neck and makes the air feel heavier. Like the moment right before a storm breaks and the skies open up.

The street outside was empty, and the wind rustled what leaves were left on the trees lining the street as a piece of trash danced with the breeze down the sidewalk. I blinked, looked around again, then shook my head.

"Get a grip, Sera," I muttered under my breath, forcing a laugh that sounded too hollow. "There's no one fucking here."

Still, I double-checked the locks. Then tested them again.

The chill of the night hit hard as I put my jacket on and moved away from the large double doors of the club. The street stretched in both directions, empty except for the hum of a neon sign and the distant hiss of tires on wet pavement.

I pulled my jacket tighter and started walking toward the main street. My heels clicked against the concrete, each step echoing just a little too long.

Halfway down the block, I stopped. There it was again, that prickle crawling up my spine like a warning. I glanced over my shoulder and looked around. No footsteps. No voice. Just the uneasy feeling of a presence.

I turned again, scanning the shadows between the buildings, but there was nothing. Only the flicker of the club sign behind me. The broken "A" blinked twice, then went dark. I stared at it for a long moment, my pulse tapping out a rhythm that echoed in my ears.

A faint ribbon of smoke drifted in the air, and for just a second, I couldn't tell if it was real or a memory. I turned and shook my head, then kept walking. Just a little faster.

Chapter Four

Kael

I'd chosen the corner table for a reason. The spot wasn't overly close to the bar, but not too far from the exits if I needed to make a quick escape. Still close enough that I could see everything, and far enough to stay invisible. It was a habit. A survival instinct, really. The kind of instincts that end up carved into bone after too many years of watching rooms like this turn into bloodstains.

From here, the club broke into sectors: the bar to the left, the main stage dead center, and stairs that led to the private rooms on the second floor, climbing like vertebrae along the back wall. The stage sat empty, lights still haloing it like a crown no one dared to set down.

Heat and cologne hung thick while the fog machine pumped out ozone and mist. Every breath was a pulse, and every laugh a tell. The kind of place where people confuse chaos for freedom. I knew better. Freedom is quieter. The only true kind of freedom is final.

I wasn't here for a show tonight. Just a casual observer of Michael's biggest money maker. But fuck, she made it hard not to watch. She wasn't on stage tonight; she was behind the bar, and she somehow made it look like her own personal playground.

She moved as if she owned the rhythm around her. Never forcing it, not performing for it, just simply commanding it. The crowd bent around her in ways they didn't even notice, like she was gravity and they were all just trying to find the center. Calm in the middle of madness. It wasn't something you could fake.

I told myself I was only watching out of habit, even though I knew that was a lie. She was like a car crash; in the sense, I couldn't take my goddamn eyes off her.

Then *he* showed up. Some dickhead in a silver wristband and a tailored suit. One of the club's "platinum" assholes. The wristband bought them a code to the upstairs elevator and the illusion that boundaries were suggestions. House rules were printed everywhere, from behind the bar to the one on the entry wall, yet somehow men like him never learned to read.

He leaned too close to her, and his hand brushed hers, his fingers lingering like he owned the air between them. My jaw tightened as my fingers braced on the arm of my chair, ready to move the second he went too far.

Old reflexes kicked in: assessment, distance, and approach angles. My hand brushed the spot where my blade waited. It was just muscle memory, but my pulse still sped up. I could break someone like him before he blinked. Dislocate the wrist, and drive the edge of my blade under his chin. Quick, clean, and over before the music missed a beat. But then I looked at her. Really looked.

The shift in her posture and the stillness that meant she'd already made her choice. I couldn't hear what she was saying over the music pulsing through the club, but from the way she glared at him, I knew he was about to be disappointed.

Whatever she had said to him, it made the man frown like a toddler being told he couldn't have a piece of candy. And then he made the mistake of calling her a whore. I watched his lips as he made that familiar curl I'd seen too much as a child, and I felt my calm slipping into a rage I hadn't felt in years. Men like that always had the same mouth. The same sneer that looked down on me when I was the one bleeding.

I stayed sitting with every muscle tight, and waited for the moment I'd get to intervene, but I didn't get the chance to. She didn't need saving. Her hand pulled away, and her weight shifted, and I watched with fascination as she twisted his wrist hard. His arrogant grin contorted into pain before his brain had a chance to catch up.

She let him go, dropping his wrist like it was yesterday's garbage, and I let out a breath I didn't realize I'd been holding.

For a second, I almost smiled as the corner of my mouth raised just a little. Her control was fucking beautiful. The same kind of control I understood down to my marrow. The same kind that had been beaten into me, in another time and place. Fuck. In a whole other life.

She turned away and went back to her work like nothing had happened, and he slunk off, muttering and humiliated. I smiled and finished my drink. The ice clicked against the glass as I set it down on the table.

When the platinum asshole stormed out the front door muttering his displeasure, I followed. Not because it was the job, not this time. I followed because I was curious. And curiosity, for me, never ended well.

• • •

The cold bit into me when I stepped outside the club with the kind of chill that settled deep in the lungs. The city hummed with the sound of distant sirens, wet tires on pavement, and the pulse of neon that flickered off the puddles.

The platinum asshole wasn't hard to follow. Men like him never bother to look behind them. They were too used to being the predator to realize when they've become prey.

I followed as he cut down a side alley, probably heading for the parking lot. I slipped after him, quiet and unhurried. Patience is the job. You don't chase. Instead, it's easier to let the moment come to you.

He stopped to light a cigarette. I watched as the lighter flared bright against the dark, catching on his slicked-back hair, and waited for a beat until he exhaled.

"Rough night?"

He jumped and dropped his cigarette, as his hand immediately moved to his hip, where men like him keep weapons they don't know how to use. His eyes darted up, meeting mine. I saw the fear reflected in them and let my grin spread wide.

"What the fuck do you want?" he snapped, his voice shaky under his perceived bravado.

I took a step forward. "Just a conversation."

He barked a laugh that didn't quite land. "You one of Michael's cleanup boys or something?"

"Something like that," I lied. "But tonight's not about him. It's about you."

I let the silence hang as the alley stretched around us, narrow and dripping, and the sound of a nearby leaky gutter ticked like a clock.

"Do you make it a habit of touching things that aren't yours?" I asked, raising an eyebrow.

His expression shifted from confusion first, before turning into a sneer that told me everything I needed to know about who he was.

"Oh, the fucking bartender? Yeah. She's just a tease with a mouth on her. You want her, too? Go ahead, she's—"

He didn't get the chance to finish. I moved before he could breathe the next word. My hand caught his wrist mid-gesture and twisted it until it cracked. The sound echoed off the walls, small yet profoundly satisfying.

"Choose your next words carefully. Or don't. Either way, I'll enjoy myself."

He choked, eyes wide. "Jesus! What the hell is wrong with you?"

"Now that's too long a list for me to name tonight. I want to know who she is?"

"What?" He flinched as I wrenched his arm back again, and a fresh, raw howl bounced off the brick around us.

"The bartender. For fuck's sake." My voice was laced with impatience.

Sweat beaded at his temple; his knees wobbled. "I—I don't know. Sera, I think is her name. She's just some club girl. Michael's—maybe. Everyone knows—"

"Everyone knows," I echoed, tightening my hold until he whimpered, "you don't touch what doesn't belong to you. Consent is a line, and crossing it comes with a cost."

He shuddered, breath hitching, clawing at my grip with his free hand. "Please, I didn't mean—look, man, she's just—"

"A whore?" I asked, slow and cold. "You could never understand someone like her. To you, she's a conquest. You can't even see what she is underneath. Men like you are so fucking pathetic."

I let him babble for a moment, letting him spew apologies that were the same as always. I drew my knife, reveling in the way the leather whispered as the metal slipped free. He froze immediately, his bullshit excuses catching in his throat.

"Let me remind you exactly how to keep your hands to yourself."

Before he could react, I trapped his hand against the brick, and my blade came down in one clean motion through his index finger. His scream tore through the alley, echoing off the walls.

He crumpled, cradling his hand to his chest. His finger bobbed once in the puddle, then went still. The dismembered digit floated pale and useless.

"Consider that a lesson. Touch what isn't yours again, and I'll happily take more than your fucking finger."

His sobs bounced off the walls as he took off through the alley, and I let out a small chuckle, then wiped the blade on my sleeve before pocketing it.

I bent down and picked up the now useless finger from the puddle and wrapped it in a Kleenex from my pocket, then turned and headed to my own car parked on the main road.

• • •

Back in the car, I checked the rearview mirror once and caught a glimpse of my own reflection. I grabbed a handkerchief from the glove box and wiped at the blood that had splattered onto my face.

I should've left right then. Driven off, and found myself another bottle or a warm body to forget her. But the lights inside the club shut off, and my fucking curiosity piqued once more.

The door opened, and she stepped out, her jacket slung over one shoulder and her head bowed against the drizzle. Alone tonight with no bouncer and no backup. Just her and the echo of her heels against the wet pavement. I killed the headlights and watched.

Every instinct told me to look away. To leave and ignore her. She's a distraction. A complication in my already complicated life. Yet somehow, I couldn't take my eyes off of her.

She locked the door and double-checked it. The kind of habit that only comes from living with ghosts. I watched as she stopped and looked around. Her gaze roamed the dark corners and shadows, looking for danger. I took one last drag of the cigarette I'd been smoking and tossed it to the ground. The swirl of my exhale curled into the night.

She started down the street, and as her pace picked up a little, I caught the faint turn of her head every few steps. That sixth sense people get when they know they're being watched. I stayed half a block behind, quiet, unseen. Just shadow and breath. Old habits and all that.

She cut through a side street, toward the older apartments near the river. The kind of place where the rent's cheap and the neighbors don't ask questions. When she reached her building, she hesitated at the door, pausing again with her spine straight and her eyes scanning the dark. Then she disappeared inside, gone like smoke.

Only then did I let myself breathe easy again. With my hands shoved deep into my pockets, I walked the same path back to my car, as every thought became consumed by her. Fuck. She was the kind of trouble I didn't need.

Back inside my car, the silence hit hard, and my pulse refused to settle. I told myself I was just investigating one of Michael's assets. Professional interest on Conor's behalf.

The phone buzzed on the passenger seat, and Conor's name flashed across the screen as I read the message.

A cleanup job. Perfect. I could let myself get lost in routine and forget about Sera. Her name sounded like salvation and ruin in one, and I shook my head to clear my thoughts.

I looked back down at my phone, thumb hovering over the screen, then switched to my contacts. I clicked on a florist I used when I wanted to send a message. The kind of business that didn't bother with the annoying hows or whys when I included little gifts.

As soon as the owner answered, I cleared my throat and gave my order.

"Mid-morning delivery, please. A dozen black dahlias. A dozen white roses. And an… addition. Add in a card that reads:

For my Little Fawn. My apologies for how you were treated."

There was a pause on the line. "And the addition?" the florist asked carefully. I glanced at the glove compartment, where a small, white Kleenex sat waiting.

"It'll be in your drop box before you open," I finished, and hung up.

I started the car and let the engine idle. The lights of the city bled through the rain, and all I could think was that she'd looked more dangerous than anyone I'd come across in years. My Little Fawn.

• • •

Morning came too soon, gray and unforgiving. The city outside my window stretched out forever as steam lifted off the pavement like it was exhaling the night's sins.

My apartment was silent and clean to the point of being clinical. The coffee pot gurgled on the spotless counter as I looked around. Comfort was control. Everything had a reason and a place. Even the blood I'd washed from the blade last night had its place: down the drain where it belonged.

The smell of bleach hung faintly in the air. People said that type of scent meant sterile. To me, it simply meant I'd erased the sins of the night before. My phone buzzed on the counter, and Conor's name lit up the screen as I looked down at my phone.

Conor: *Dockside. Container 0801. 9 a.m. Bring your disposal kit.*

I gave a bit of a groan before finishing my coffee. The bitter taste reminded me of what the rest of the day would bring. I ran a hand through my hair, stood up, and rinsed the cup before putting it in the dishwasher. I had a routine, and it's how I'd survived this long.

I packed with the slow, reverent precision of habit. Taking stock of my tools, gloves, and plastic. Each motion folding into the next, catalogued and exact. For a small moment, I let my eyes rest on the folded newspaper on the table: a headline about corruption, the city eating itself. Same story, different day.

Her face slid into my mind uninvited. Red lights on her skin and her steady voice played like a song. Something warm and unfamiliar tightened again in my chest.

"Fuck," I murmured as my phone pinged again with a message from the florist.

Flowers By Meg: *Delivery complete. Recipient signed.*

Good. I let the idea of her finding the flowers, and the addition I'd included inside, sit there for a beat. A smile played at the corner of my mouth, wondering if she'd be horrified or intrigued.

I slid my knife into its sheath and paused at the mirror. My reflection looked willing, with a jaw set in stone, and a pair of stone-gray eyes that were always too calm. Someone who'd made peace with monsters by becoming one. It worked for me.

Outside, the air tasted of petrichor and exhaust. I lit a cigarette I didn't want and drew it into my lungs slowly. I packed my gear into my car and set out for the lakeside. The sound of the engine and the road ahead did little to clear my head of her.

The dock was quiet as I pulled up. Seagulls cried their song over the water; the kind of symphony nobody romanticizes. A man waited by a shipping container with his shoulders hunched against the cold. Another of Conor's low-level lackeys.

"You Kael?" he asked.

I nodded as he handed over a folder with twitchy fingers.

"Simple job. One body with minimal noise."

"Simple's subjective," I answered and took the file. He didn't argue. They never do. They just vanish back into the mist once the exchange is done.

I opened the folder and gave it a quick once-over. Male. Forty-two. Unpaid debts to the wrong people and peddled secrets that weren't his to sell. The kind of man who thinks money would buy an exit strategy. Everyone thinks they can buy their way out until they realize there's only one way out from the underbelly of this godforsaken city. And I was the fucking ferryman.

I opened the container, and the smell hit first: iron and rot folded in around me, demanding my attention. I pushed the door the rest of the way open and braced my palms on the cold steel. The body lay on the table like garbage. No showmanship or care. No pride in the work of whoever left him here. I scoffed. People didn't respect their craft anymore.

I set my tools out the way a surgeon lays instruments. Simple, orderly, and precise. I pulled out the gloves, sheeting, heavy-duty bags, and gorilla tape as a battered radio in the corner hummed a long-forgotten station. The sound filled the shipping container and kept me steady. There are noises that steady you when you do ugly things, and I've learned to enjoy them.

I draped the plastic and shut the container doors, turning on the construction lamp as I moved. Its white gleam carved a shadow into the corpse, his skin taking on a sickening, macabre glow under the reflection of the container.

I got to work and stripped him down, piece by piece, like taking apart a human puzzle I'd already solved a hundred times. The radio spat out a song I recognized, and I hummed along out of habit as the hours bled by.

I treated it like work because this was work for me. Clinical and practiced, just the way I needed it. The bone saw sang its steady, terrible song while I carved, wrapped, and tied. Each piece went into plastic, then tape, then twine, tied tight and numbered like a ledger.

When the surfaces needed cleaning, I used a mix of Oxi-Clean and water. The active agent ruined blood-detection; a neat trick I'd learned from a science magazine I'd kept after a dentist appointment. The cloth swallowed what it could, and the plastic folded and sealed around what had to be contained.

When everything was eventually bundled and sealed, I tested the weight, cinched another length of tape across it, and pressed down until I was sure nothing inside would ever see daylight again.

By the time I hauled my little packages onto the boat, the late-afternoon sun had turned the water to glass, making it too bright and unforgiving. I preferred the world around me to be dark and quiet. Always had.

I grimaced as I climbed onto the mid-size boat left for me by Conor's "organization". I stowed the bundles, untied the boat from the dock, and slipped out past the harbor. The city noise faded until there was nothing left but wind and the prop's steady churn. I killed the engine and watched as the wake erased itself.

One by one, I dropped each parcel into the water, letting the weights do their job. Each splash was swallowed fast as the bubbles rose once, twice, and then the surface smoothed over as if nothing had ever passed through it. I leaned against the gunwale and stared out across the flat expanse. The salt on my tongue tasted like erasure. Work done right leaves nothing behind.

A small, private ache followed. The kind that didn't belong to a man like me. I thought of her. The bartender. The way she'd straightened after he touched her, unbothered and unbroken. *Little Fawn.* I'd used it on the delivery card like a joke, but now I meant it. She was soft but fearless. A Little Fawn in a world run by wolves.

I wanted to know everything about her. Even the parts that didn't fit into my neat lines of work and silence. She consumed my every thought, and I couldn't wash her from my head any more than the sea could keep its dead forever. I shook my head and started the motor to head back in.

This was the part I liked best, the quiet after all the noise. But even then, she found her way back in. The bartender. *My* fawn. The only thing in that club that made me want to go back.

I lit a cigarette as the engine hummed beneath me. The smoke curled upward, vanishing into the wind as I pictured her again. Not on the stage this time, but against a wall, my hand around her throat. Her breath catching as her eyes locked on mine, and I could show her what it really meant to submit in ways she'd only ever dreamed of.

That dull ache came back and spread like a bruise beneath my ribs. A new kind of need. Her. I needed her. And I wouldn't stop until I had her.

Chapter Five

Seraphine

The knock came too early in the morning as the noise pulled me from a quiet, dreamless sleep. I blinked and opened my eyes. Another knock. This time, more insistent and incredibly annoying. The sound was too sharp to belong to a neighbor, and too polite to mean trouble.

I sat up slowly, grimacing at the sheets tangled around my legs like restraints. My head still throbbed from the late-night closing shift, and for a moment, I thought I had imagined it. Three quick raps landed against the outside door again, and I finally crawled out from the warmth and comfort of my bed.

Patrick's room across the hall was empty. Not shocking for this hour. Knowing him, he probably didn't even come home at all. I couldn't remember if I'd seen him when I stumbled in half-asleep last night.

I pulled my robe on, wrapping it around me like a blanket, and padded barefoot to the door. My reflection in the glass looked like hell. My eyeliner was smudged, mixing with the dark circles from too little sleep and hair that would give Beetlejuice pause.

"Package delivery," a muffled voice called through the door. I frowned as I unlocked the door. I hadn't ordered anything recently.

The man on the other side seemed barely awake himself, as I looked over his simple courier uniform and the clipboard in his hand. His eyes were glazed from too many early routes, and he held out a large white box, the kind used for flowers.

"You Sera?"

"Uh, yeah," I replied, confusion clouding my voice.

"Signature." He shoved the clipboard toward me, and I scrawled out something that might've resembled my name if you squinted hard enough.

He handed over the box and left before I could ask who it was from. I stood there confused as the morning air leaked in through the open doorway, and the smell of rain clung to the cardboard.

Flowers? At this hour? Patrick must've been playing a prank again. Except there was no note covered in glitter. No dumb pun taped to the side. Just *Little Fawn*, handwritten in neat, deliberate script.

I set it on the kitchen counter and slit the tape open with a paring knife. The floral scent was sweet and sharp, wafting out immediately. It was the kind of smell that demanded attention. Black dahlias and white roses. The bouquet was arranged with exquisite and clearly expensive care.

My eyes moved to the center of one of the roses, and there, nestled like some sick joke, was a severed finger. For a second, I thought it was fake until my eyes caught the roughly cut edge, and the blood dried along it, leaking onto the white rose it sat in, staining its petals a sick reddish-brown.

For a long moment, I didn't move. I could only just stare at the offending addition like it might vanish if I blinked. The world narrowed to the edge of the counter, the smell of flowers, and that obscene little piece of someone that didn't belong mixed with something so beautiful.

My stomach lurched as I recoiled, but the scream stayed lodged in my chest. I'd learned a long time ago what panic got you. The room swam a little as I processed what I was looking at. I tried to force my hands to steady, but they trembled harder as I sat down at the island counter. The finger lay in the center of the arrangement, pale and deliberate. Someone wanted me to see it.

"What in the actual fuck?"

The next thought made me look over at the door again. Whoever they were, they knew exactly where to find me. Someone had waited for me to finish work, followed me home, and sent me this… what even is it? A gift? A threat? The room spun as my brain frantically tried to connect the dots.

My eyes swept over the flowers again, pointedly trying to avoid the horrific appendage. They widened as I caught a flash of white tucked deep between the stems. A card.

"Alright, asshole," I muttered, reaching for the pristine-looking card. "Let's see who you are."

My fingers ripped open the envelope with little care for the clearly expensive paper, and my hands shook as I pulled out the white card with gold filigree around the edges.

For my Little Fawn. My apologies for how you were treated.

My eyes narrowed as I read the card. Something akin to anger simmered under my skin. Who the fuck was this psycho? And what was with that goddamn name again, staring back at me like some sort of twisted love letter from someone I couldn't pick out of a lineup. A chill crawled down my spine. Was this a sick joke? Had someone from my past finally caught up to me?

The thought sat heavy in my chest, pressing down until I could barely breathe. My pulse thudded in my ears, slow and uneven. I didn't even hear the front door open until it slammed shut again.

"Jesus, Sera—"

Patrick's voice hit like a bullet. I jerked so hard the chair screeched on the tile floor. He froze halfway to the kitchen, a paper bag dangling from his hand. The smell of coffee and sugar drifted in with him.

"You okay?"

I blinked up at him, still gripping the card so tight it bent between my fingers. "No? Yes? I don't fucking know. Maybe?" My brain was a mess as I tried to process everything.

His gaze flicked to the box on the counter, to the flowers, to the pale thing resting in their center, and the color drained from his face.

"Is that a fucking finger?"

"It would appear so," I said, my voice calmer than it ought to be when someone just sent you a body part with a love letter.

He set the bag and coffee down carefully, like any sudden movement might make the finger lunge at him, and crossed to me.

"Sera… is that real?"

I didn't answer. I just handed him the card. He read it once, twice, his jaw tightening.

"Little Fawn?" he muttered. "You know who that is?"

"No clue," I replied dryly, my fingers rubbing my temples as a headache started behind my eyes. "Maybe someone from my past is coming back to finish the job."

Patrick's eyes hardened as his lips thinned at the mention of my past, and the anger radiated off him.

"You really think one of those assholes would come looking for you again?" he asked, his normally calm voice taking on an edge I hadn't heard in years.

I looked up at him, my own eyes softening a touch. "Most of them are in jail. Or dead," I said, without a single ounce of pity in my voice.

"Whoever sent it, though, has a fucked-up sense of humor. And that's coming from me."

Patrick's lips twitched, the corner of his mouth threatening a smirk.

"You know, most people get chocolates or maybe a stuffed bear when someone's obsessed with them. You really know how to pick admirers, huh?"

"Yeah, my charm's fucking fatal," I muttered.

He barked out a short laugh that sounded suspiciously like a seal and ran a hand through his hair.

"Christ, Sera. Couldn't you just have a boring morning for once? Like, I don't know, breakfast? Normal people get breakfast delivered. You get a finger and a love note."

I shot him a look. "Since when have either of us been normal?"

That earned a snort from him.

"Fair point." His gaze drifted back to the box, and his voice dropped.

"Still, this is some next-level psycho shit."

He leaned against the counter beside me, close enough that our shoulders brushed. The warmth of him grounded me in a way I didn't realize I had needed, and suddenly I was more thankful than usual for his presence. For a while, we just stood there, the air thick with coffee, croissants, and the sickly-sweet perfume of the flowers.

Finally, he exhaled. "You think we should call the cops, or…?"

I gave a small, bitter laugh. "And tell them what? 'Hi, someone mailed me a finger with an apology note'? I can already hear them typing up the incident report under '*drunk prank gone wrong*'."

He cracked a grin at that, though the worry didn't leave his eyes. "You've got a point. They'd probably haul you in for questioning just because they could."

I looked up at him again, my face screwing up into disbelief. "What the fuck are we supposed to do with a severed finger?"

Patrick exhaled, dragging a hand down his face. "I mean… I'd say 'throw it out,' but something tells me that's bad crime scene etiquette."

I looked back down at the flowers and the pale, lifeless addition in the middle that seemed to mock me.

"Well," I muttered, "these flowers are too damn pretty to toss. Deranged psycho or not, at least they've got good taste."

I stood and rummaged through the drawer until I found a plastic baggie. Grabbing a wad of paper towel, I reached for the finger, trying not to think about how wrong it looked against the white petals. A visible shudder rippled through me as I dropped it into the bag.

"Ew," I muttered with a gag. "That felt exactly like I thought it would, and somehow I was still not mentally prepared."

Patrick snorted, half-horror, half-amused. "Congratulations, you're officially in your true-crime era."

I shot him a look. "Yeah, next I'll start a podcast. *Death & Lattes*. First episode: 'Things You Shouldn't Touch Before Coffee.'"

That earned me a real laugh this time, and his eyes twinkled as his whole body shook.

Patrick's laugh faded into a shaky sigh. "You're taking this way too well."

"I'm taking it the only way I know how to. Besides, these flowers didn't ask to be accomplices in a felony."

I grabbed a vase from the cupboard and filled it with water in the sink.

He raised a brow. "You're seriously keeping them?"

"Damn right I am. Might as well get something pretty out of this nightmare."

I filled the vase with water and started arranging the black dahlias and white roses, careful not to take the rose where the finger had been.

Patrick leaned on the counter, watching me like I'd lost it completely. "You know, this is wildly concerning."

"Relax. They're just flowers. The finger and this rose, however…" I opened the door and stood in front of the compost bin outside. I held up the plastic bag with a grin. "This is technically organic matter, right?"

His eyes widened. "You're not—"

"Oh, I am." I flipped open the lid, dropped the bag and the rose in, and dusted my hands off before stepping back inside. "Compostable. Circle of life, baby."

Patrick groaned, dragging both hands through his hair. "You're so fucking weird. You did not just compost a finger right outside our fucking kitchen!"

"Yeah, I did. But you love me," I laughed, blowing him a sarcastic kiss.

He didn't argue. He just stared at me, that same worried softness flickering behind his eyes. We didn't say anything for a while.

Patrick just stood there, eyes flicking between me and the compost bin like he couldn't decide which of us he wanted to hide from first. Finally, he reached for the forgotten drinks on the counter, brushing a few flower petals aside.

"You still want your coffee? I bought your usual."

The sweet gesture made my chest ache a little. "Yeah, of course I do. Thanks."

He handed it over without another word, then leaned against the counter beside me. The cardboard cup was still warm against my palms, and as the heat seeped into my hands, I began to feel almost normal again.

"You're not gonna lecture me?" I asked after a moment.

He gave a small shrug. "You seem like you've got it handled. My job's moral support and caffeine distribution."

A tired smile tugged at my mouth as I leaned my head on his shoulder. "You're doing great at both."

"Good. Now shut up and let me keep doing what I'm good at."

I chuckled softly, letting the warmth of the coffee flow through me, my eyes deliberately avoiding the shape of the compost bin through the window on the back door. The smell of the flowers lingered in the air, sharp and sweet, but I forced myself to focus on him instead.

"So you're performing on stage tonight," I said, arching a brow, a hint of amusement slipping through. "Are you nervous?"

Patrick snorted. "Me? Nervous? Please. I only throw up once before going on stage now. Total improvement."

I laughed, a real one this time, and he grinned as if he'd just won the lottery.

"Seriously, though, you'll kill it. You always do."

He shrugged, pretending not to care, but I caught the faint blush creeping up his neck.

"Yeah, well, someone's gotta be the pretty one between us."

"Ha. Funny."

"I try," he said, that lopsided grin softening his features.

Patrick glanced at the clock on the stove and groaned. "Shit, we've got like what, twelve hours before our shifts?"

"Something like that," I murmured, the exhaustion weighing me down now that the adrenaline crash was starting.

He pushed away from the counter, stretching until his shoulders cracked. "I'm grabbing a nap before the chaos. You should, too, unless you plan on explaining the finger incident to Michael after you fall asleep on the bar again."

I gave him a half-hearted salute. "Copy that, boss."

Patrick grinned and headed for his room. The door closed behind him with a softness I didn't know I needed.

I looked around the kitchen, as if taking stock of everything that had happened this morning. I finished my coffee, tossed the cup, and stood there for a long minute staring at the vase on the counter. The flowers were still perfect, too perfect, as their scent lingered in the air.

I couldn't decide what bothered me more: the finger or the note that came with it. A well-adjusted person would say the finger. I, however, am not a well-adjusted person.

Little Fawn, the name rang in my head again like a warning bell and a soft blanket rolled into one inconvenient package. Eventually, I made myself lie down, and before long, sleep pulled me under with a heavy, dreamless welcome.

• • •

By the time I woke, the light outside had dipped toward gold, and the city shone in that late-afternoon haze that made everything feel slightly unreal. Patrick was already gone. A note on the counter in his messy scrawl:

See you at the club. Don't be late, Little Miss Fingers-Are-Compostable.

I rolled my eyes and gave a short laugh.

After a quick shower, I dressed for work. This time, I chose a short black skirt, a tight white tank top, my signature silver collar, and a leather jacket. I pulled my hair back high and tight and ran the creamy red lipstick across my lips before smacking them together twice and grabbing my purse.

Locking the apartment door behind me, I stepped into the cooling evening air. The city hummed around me, alive and indifferent. The road, still slick from the earlier rain, shimmered under the fading light as I made the short walk toward Escape.

The club was already thumping when I arrived as the bass thrummed through the floor, low and steady. The air carried that familiar mix of anticipation, a kind of electricity that never really left me, even on my nights off.

I slipped past the bar, weaving through the tables until I found a spot near the stage. The lights were low and honey-warm, and the strobes flashed in the haze from the fog machine. People watched with that reverent silence unique to this kind of performance.

Patrick was center stage, shirtless and shining under the lights, the faint tremor in his hands visible only to someone who knew how to look. Across from him stood Jenny, dressed in all black leather and oozing ownership. Her tone was sharp enough to cut through the lowered music as she circled him, as the crowd remained utterly still.

It wasn't crude. It was a dance filled with trust and precision. When she caught his chin and tilted it up, he followed without hesitation. His eyes were soft and submissive as he gazed up at Jenny. Pride prickled warm in my chest. He was so fucking good at this. He always had been.

I let myself relax, letting the rhythm of the performance wash over me. The rise and fall of the crop against Patrick's soft skin. The way he obeyed her every command, as if it were second nature. I relaxed into myself a little, and the nerves I had felt for Patrick melted away with each perfectly obeyed movement.

I smiled softly, enjoying the moment, before a change in the air made my skin prickle.

Someone had moved in behind me. Not close enough to touch, but close enough that the space between us felt charged. I stilled, just as a presence settled there, quiet and undeniable. The company felt warm and steady.

A pair of hands brushed my hips, resting there lightly. Not a grab. Just a simple contact. A statement that he was there, and he wasn't going to be moved. My pulse jumped with instinct that screamed to turn, to shove, or to defend.

But then something about the touch stopped me. It wasn't forceful or demanding. It was calm and measured. Like the hands belonged to someone who knew I wouldn't say no. A breath warmed the shell of my ear.

"My name's Kael."

My body froze at the sound of his voice and the feel of his breath on my ear. It didn't startle me or unnerve me. It should have. But instead, I felt my body relax just a bit.

The music swelled as Jenny gave a sharp order. Patrick obeyed, dropping to his knees with theatrical grace before his mouth was on Jenny's perfect pussy, just as she'd commanded. I couldn't look away from the stage, but I couldn't stop thinking about the way Kael stood behind me, either. My entire being felt pulled in different directions as the show continued.

The second I let myself relax, even an immeasurable amount, Kael's fingers flexed once against my hips, as if he was trying to ground me and keep me locked in both moments. Patrick on the stage, and Kael like a sentinel behind me. And for reasons beyond my comprehension, I let him stay. Let him hold me as the room disappeared to just the stage, and him. Everything else faded into the background.

The stage lights shifted, washing everything in red and gold. The crowd murmured its approval as the climax for both the show and the performers became imminent. The bass of the track rolled through my chest. I tried to focus on Patrick, on the steady rhythm of the performance, but my body betrayed me. My awareness split itself clean down the middle, like I'd been cut in two.

Half of me was up there with him, counting each movement, every breath of the scene I'd watched him rehearse a dozen times. The other half was trapped in the stillness behind me, caught somewhere between curiosity and alarm.

Kael didn't move much. That was the most unnerving part. Most men who crowded too close at the club were obvious about it. Always loud in their breathing, eager to be seen, and desperate to test boundaries they didn't understand. He was none of that. His presence felt deliberate, like he was waiting for me to decide and give permission for what came next.

The weight of his hands stayed steady on my hips. Their touch was warm through the thin fabric of my skirt as his fingertips rested in that careful space between pressure and permission.

Jenny cracked the leather crop against Patrick's skin, and the sound was sharp enough to pull me back to the stage. Patrick's face was a sight to behold as his expression became the perfect mix of anticipation and surrender. Jenny's cum slicked Patrick's lips and chin as the crowd leaned forward as one, drawn to the tension the two of them spun like silk.

He wasn't nervous anymore. He was glowing under her attention, and his eyes were soft and reverent. Every line of his body tensed for the moment when control became release.

Kael's breath brushed the back of my neck just once. Soft enough that it might've been accidental. I felt myself tense once more as every cell in my body went on high alert. My mind screamed to move. To turn around, look at him, and say something. But the part of me that had lived through too many dark rooms and too many nights behind the bar understood something else. Power isn't always about movement. Sometimes it's about stillness.

So, I stayed still and watched the show as if my mind wasn't unraveling. Like it was trying to decide whether this was a fight-or-flight moment or something more. The scent of him threaded through the air between us, something dark, clean, and faintly spiced. Not anything I could name. Just something uniquely him.

On stage, Jenny stepped behind Patrick, her voice carrying clearly through the speakers. "You trust me?"

"Always," he breathed with the kind of sound that rippled through the room.

Her hand slid into his hair, lifting his head up to look back at her. She lifted the crop, paused, and checked his eyes. "Color?"

"Green."

The crowd hushed, and the music coiled tight as the anticipation built. She circled him slowly. A tap to his shoulder and a count under her breath that only trained ears heard. One. Two. Three. The final strike landed clean, the kind that leaves a perfect line and an afterglow you feel in your soul. Patrick's breath hitched, and the noise that escaped him wasn't pain. It was surrender and desire and need all wrapped together as one.

Applause swelled, and the lights flared warmer. Jenny held him there in the moment with her palm spread over his chest, claiming the moment without cruelty. The whole room leaned into it, a shared intake of breath at the crest of the act. Patrick would get his climax, and the crowd would feel every ounce of it.

My fingers tightened around the edge of the table. Kael must've noticed, because his thumb brushed just once over the line of my hip. It was barely contact, but it sent a shock straight through to the core of me.

I forced a breath out through my nose, steadying myself. This was my safe place. My domain. I'd built this life to be untouchable and untamed on my terms. Yet somehow, Kael had found a way to stand behind me and make every piece of me question my decisions.

He leaned in slightly, close enough that his words barely reached me over the music. "You're shaking, little bartender."

His tone wasn't mocking. It wasn't even flirtation. It was a simple observation. His voice was soft and quiet, like he knew more about me than I did. The kind that slips under your defenses and sits there, waiting.

"I'm not," I lied, my voice low, almost lost in the bass.

He hummed, unconvinced. "You force stillness when you're scared. Interesting."

That made my anxiety heighten. He was right, and I hated that he was. Years of learning how not to flinch, how to disappear in plain sight, and somehow he'd seen through it within minutes.

"Breathe for me, darling," Jenny called.

I exhaled slowly, like the command had been meant for me instead of Patrick.

Patrick moved on cue, precise and fluid. Jenny's hands worked him hard; his back bowed beautifully, like a string brought to its breaking point. The crowd reacted with that same breathless awe. I tried to stay with it. To watch the art of it and keep my balance as the club spun around me.

Kael didn't move away, and his presence didn't shift or demand. It was a gravity I hadn't realized I was orbiting until it was too late. A loud cry filled the air as Jenny brought Patrick to his release. His eyes were cloudy with ecstasy, and a wicked grin split his mouth. Jenny pressed a sweet kiss against his forehead as they both turned to face the crowd.

Applause. The height of a scene done right. Jenny bowed, pulling Patrick up with her, her hand tangled in his hair as she forced him to bow. Patrick bowed, his gaze lowered, the perfect picture of devotion.

As the show ended, the music kicked back up. The dance floor filled once more, and the club went back to its routine. I smiled at the normalcy I'd come to breathe for and let myself relax, just a fraction. Just for a minute.

As the music swelled around me and my heartbeat settled back into its normal rhythm, Kael's breath touched my ear, soft as a secret.

"Did you enjoy the show…Little Fawn?"

Chapter Six

Michael

My voice cracked as I paced the length of the office with the phone wedged to my ear.

"I said I'm good for it, Christ almighty, how many times—"

The office smelled like stale whiskey and bad decisions, and the blinds hung crooked, letting the city lights bleed into the room like an open wound.

"I told you. Business is turning around. Friday nights are packed. You'll have my payment by the end of the month." I paused, teeth grinding. "Yeah, I know what I fucking owe. You don't need to keep saying it like I forgot."

The answering laugh came through the receiver, low and humorless, with that clipped Dublin bite that always made my skin crawl.

"Don't laugh at me, Conor," I snapped, trying to stop myself from shaking. "You think I haven't already met who you send when things go sideways? I know exactly who Kael works for."

Silence. I swallowed. My throat felt too small, and the walls seemed to close in tighter. "He's not needed here. Everything's fine."

"Come up with the full payment, or we own the club, Mick." Conor's voice crackled through the line.

"No, don't! Listen, there's no need for that. I just need time. You don't send your fucking cleaner over a few late payments." I laughed, but there was no humor behind it. "Come on, you and I go back years."

"The money, Mick. Or I won't just have Kael deal with you. I'll burn the fucking club to the ground with you in it, and then move on to your wife and daughter, just for the trouble you cause me."

My knuckles whitened around the phone. "Conor, please..."

The line went dead, and the ceiling fan ticked overhead with its uneven wobble. The bass from the club bled through the floorboards, slow and steady. The pounding in my chest was anything but as I dropped the phone onto the desk and exhaled.

"Fuck."

Conor's voice stuck like smoke in my head. *You've had your time, Mick. Now it's ours.*

I grabbed the bottle from the drawer, poured a splash into the glass already filthy with fingerprints, and tossed it back. The answering burn felt like home.

The office door creaked open, and the sound of it cut through my thoughts like a sword.

Benjamin slid into my office, wiping his hands on a bar rag that wore the night's stains. His shirt clung to him, damp from lugging cases of beer from the cellar. "Arguing with Conor now? Guess that's why they keep you on a short fucking leash, huh?"

I didn't look up. "You're supposed to be running the floor."

"I was until the register came up light again. Thought maybe you'd want to know."

"Then fix it."

"That's what I do, isn't it? Fix your fucking problems." He laughed under his breath and leaned against the doorframe, pretending to look casual. "You look like shit."

"Appreciate the concern." I poured another drink and didn't bother to offer him one as I glared at him.

Benjamin watched me with that stupid, smug look on his face. "Conor wouldn't be threatening you if you'd stop parading your *dates* through the casino when you take them on *his* dime."

I froze for half a second before I caught myself. "You have a bad habit of knowing too much about my life outside the club. You know that?"

"Knowledge spends better than cash in our circles, Michael, and you're not exactly subtle." He shrugged.

I met his eyes and glared. "Keep your fucking mouth shut."

"For now." He stepped closer, voice dropping. "But if you're that far under, maybe let me know what the play is. If you start drowning, it pulls the rest of us under, too."

"You worried about your paycheck?" I asked.

He smirked. "Always."

We stared at each other long enough for the silence to sour. The kind that told me he'd keep his head down only because it suited him. Benjamin didn't stay loyal. He followed the money like every other asshole in these circles.

"Get back to work."

He lingered another beat, eyes flicking toward the half-empty glass on the desk. "You should slow down on those. They're bad for your liver. Kind of like making deals with Irish mobsters."

"Out," I growled, pointing toward the door.

He grinned, all teeth and smugness, and slipped out of the room. The door clicked shut behind him, and the closing door muffled the hum of the club again. Laughter, bass, and a hundred lives moving just fine without me all faded to a dull thud around me. I sat and stared at the blinds until the light blurred.

Conor wanted his money, and Benjamin was always sniffing for leverage. And Kael… Kael was a problem I didn't need to show up at my door again.

The memory of that night still weighed heavily on my bones. Ribs that ached when I laughed too hard and a wrist that throbbed at the threat of rain. He hadn't bothered to raise his voice. He just looked at me like I was already a ghost and went to work until I remembered the difference between the pain of consequence and the pain of a promise made.

I needed cash and fast. Conor didn't take excuses; he took collateral. And all I had left worth anything was Escape. Or the people in it. I leaned back as my gaze slid to the list of platinum members pinned beside the register reports. Men with too much money and not enough impulse control. I knew a few who'd pay obscene amounts for something they weren't supposed to have.

One name stuck out: Cameron Sykes. A hedge-fund creep with a taste for the rough stuff. He'd offered before, half-jokingly, after one of Sera's nights on the BDSM stage. "What's her rate off the clock?" he'd asked with that crocodile grin. I'd laughed it off then, but tonight the idea sounded like redemption wrapped in secrets.

"One weekend, no rules," I muttered under my breath, the phrase tasting like easy money on my tongue. "Outside club jurisdiction, and part of the debt could be paid."

The math lined up like a gift-wrapped solution. It could work. Conor didn't care where the money came from, so long as it was paid. The door creaked behind me again, and I damn near dropped my glass.

Benjamin again. Of course. Always hovering when the smell of blood hit the air. He smirked, catching the way I shoved the ledger half under a folder. "Plotting or praying, Mikey?"

"Neither. Just business."

He stepped closer, eyes flicking to the list on the wall. "Looks like the sort of business the local pimps would love to hear about."

I forced a laugh. "You keep your nose out of it, Ben."

He leaned in, voice low and snide. "Selling the help now? That's new even for you."

"Don't start."

"Not starting. Just curious what you'll tell her when she finds out you've been shopping her around like she's meat. That's not a good look, Mikey. Honestly? I kinda hope I'm around to see her tear you apart."

His words landed like a slap, and I glared, eyes narrowing. "What I do with *my* staff is none of your business. She gets paid to do what she's told. You could take a page from her book."

Benjamin eyed me carefully, as if he could read everything I was adding up in my head. He tipped his head like a man who'd been handed the map he wanted all along.

"Ya know, I could talk Sera into it. For a fee, of course."

For a second, I just stared, suspicion tightening behind my eyes. Nothing in this place ever came cheap, including the "help" offered by shitty bartenders with too much free time.

"How much?" I barked, annoyed by his audacity.

He pitched a number, and I let it settle between us. It was less than I expected, yet enough to pay part of my debt to Conor and still leave a little for the casino tables.

"Fine. But if any of it goes wrong? It's you who's getting thrown under the bus this time."

"Relax, man. Call it an *amalgamation* of great minds. I'll set it up with Sera. You get the money wired, Conor gets his payment, and we all go on doing what we do." He shrugged, looking like the cat who had caught the canary.

The plan snapped into place, and I could already see the exchange. Cameron would just be some businessman in town, needing a date for a couple of black-tie events he was attending. Money would quiet the rest.

"Alright. Go tell Sera whatever you need to in order for her to agree."

Benjamin's smile got sharper. "Sure thing, Mikey. Just remember, if I don't get paid, all your secrets get spilled."

I nodded in resigned agreement. Benjamin knew too much, and I wasn't about to let those skeletons get pulled from my closet. It sounded easy. Foolproof. The idea Benjamin described was an easy out stitched together with money and threat, but it was an out I needed. I was so far down the rabbit hole that morality was a luxury I could no longer afford.

I picked up the phone with hands that shook from nerves and whiskey, as I dialed the number Cameron had left once. Benjamin watched me compose the lie I'd have to tell to sell the only thing I still believed in: survival. He stared long enough that I could see the appetite in his eyes.

When the line connected, a voice answered brisk and rich. "Cameron Sykes speaking."

I steeled my resolve. If I sell the plan, I'd live another couple of weeks at least. I looked at the photo of my wife and daughter on my desk as I remembered Conor's threat. My voice immediately cleared.

"Cameron, it's Michael Stence from Escape. I have an offer for you. Exclusive to you alone."

Cameron laughed into the phone, his voice becoming smooth as silk. "Do tell, Mikey. Now you've got my attention."

The lie I fed him was polished and unpracticed, wrapped in euphemism and promises of discretion. When Cameron asked for a price, I gave him a number higher than I'd originally planned. Conor gets his payment. I get a weekend to myself with the tables and escorts, and everyone wins.

He accepted the offer without a moment's hesitation. By the time I hung up, I felt lighter. The money would be deposited into my account by the end of the day tomorrow. Everything was finally in motion.

I stared at the ledger until the ink blurred into a single black smear. The plan was on. I'd bought time for now, and I could almost taste the casino whiskey and my favorite escort on my tongue.

"Benjamin," I snapped, fixing him with a look. "Go tell Sera she has a date for this weekend. Make sure she thinks it's *just* a date. Otherwise, she won't go. Her fucking morals or some bullshit." I sent him off with a wave of my hand and swallowed what was left in the glass.

Benjamin left with a sly salute that might've been funny in another lifetime, and the office fell quiet the second the door shut. I leaned back as the chess pieces slid into motion. When you spend your life figuring out how to get out of tight spaces, it becomes second nature. The thing about tight spaces, though, is that eventually you find yourself stuck. But not me. No. I'd always been the rat that found the hole in the wall.

I poured another drink, and a smile crept in. Cameron was the kind of man who thought privilege was a physical thing he could wear. More money than brains, but he'd be a good scapegoat if anything went south. On the plus side, he'd pay upfront, and by the weekend, my payment to Conor would be handled. Anything that happened after that wouldn't be my fucking problem.

I finished writing up the contract and hit send on the email. I leaned back in my chair with the ease of a man who just bought his freedom. Yeah, it was at the expense of someone else, but in this city, you either eat or get eaten, and I had a hell of an appetite.

Benjamin texted me once while I drafted the contract:

Client wants specifics. Wants her as arm candy at dinner. Also requested a private suite. No staff around. Says he's willing to pay extra for "privacy".

The words "arm candy" made me raise an eyebrow. If Cameron had it his way, Sera would be far more than eye candy. I chuckled darkly. *Let it happen. She needs to be brought down a peg or two.*

• • •

The remainder of the night went off without any more calls. Sera was in a weird mood, but she always seemed to have some sort of bug up her ass these days. She and Patrick were huddled in his DJ booth when I came out to make my way around our platinum-level guests. Always gotta make sure the piranhas are fed, lest they come after me for their next meal.

At dawn, I drove to the hotel with a weight off my shoulders. The wire hit my account sometime overnight. I sent Benjamin his fees and transferred a large chunk to Conor. "Smart man," was all the text said. He'd received it, and now I had one less thing to worry about.

I met Cameron in the lobby, the man moving like a shark in fucking Versace. Yup, he definitely had too much money and not enough trouble. He oozed capitalism and entitlement, and I was pretty sure he hadn't earned either. He took the folder with the outlined information from the contract, the way CEOs take checks, bored and already counting the interest.

"Michael. You promised exclusive."

"It's exclusive," I told him. I used my smoothest voice, the one that'd gotten me out of knife-point situations in the past. "Black-tie. Your *arm candy* for the night." I used his words against him with practiced ease. "Sera will not be affiliated with Escape for the weekend. No work calls, nothing except being at your beck and call. As requested."

He scanned the contract quickly, his eyes flicking to the lines about his requests, then to the fee. "No cameras. No staff. I want privacy."

"You've got it. Just fucking sign here, and she's off the schedule for the weekend at Escape," I said as I slid the pen toward him, my hand shaking less today than most days.

He signed like a man who knew he was buying exactly what he wanted, and the grin on his face almost made me concerned for Sera. But I swallowed that thought down and ignored it. As of now, she wasn't my problem for the weekend. Cameron's purchase ensured that.

He asked once when she would be arriving, and that was it. Men like him assumed consent could be bought with bank transfers and signed papers. That the mechanics of payment were the mechanics of agreement. It was easier to beg forgiveness than ask permission, not that he would do either. I let myself picture him "correcting" Sera's mouth and grinned to myself. Not my problem this weekend, so long as she came back alive and unmarked where clients could see. Anything else was just business.

I walked out of the hotel feeling ten pounds lighter and twice as clever. The city was waking up, all that golden-hour bullshit spilling across the pavement like it meant something. I climbed into the Lexus, adjusted the mirror, and grinned at my reflection.

"See?" I muttered to myself. "Still got it."

As I left the hotel in my rearview mirror, I finally let out a breath that wasn't tethered to worry or rot. The rats always survive. No matter the cost.

Chapter Seven

Seraphine

My pulse pounded in my ears, drowning out everything else as the whole club faded around me. My body locked up so fast it felt like someone had yanked a cord inside me as his voice echoed in my head. *Little Fawn.* He used the name. It was him. And every stubborn, panicked part of me wanted to pretend it wasn't. To pretend the box with the fucking severed finger hadn't come from him.

Every instinct in my body begged me to run, but I didn't have to. Kael was already gone, vanished like smoke, and the cold his absence left on my skin was nothing compared to the terror and fury punching through me. Kael had sent me a finger. A fucking finger with the flowers. And then he'd whispered that stupid name like it was some sort of secret between us.

I forced air into my lungs and turned toward the bar, pushing through the crowd on autopilot. Someone laughed too loudly, and someone else brushed my arm. Every sound hit wrong. Too bright, and too close. I didn't remember asking for a drink; I only remember one appearing in front of me. Tequila. The burn as it went down did little to settle the panic threatening to explode out of me.

The tequila steadied me just enough to keep moving, to stop myself from unravelling right there at the bar. I made it to the stairs leading to the DJ booth, gripping the rail as if it were the last solid thing in the room, tilting to the side.

Patrick was there, thank God. Still in half his performance gear, his headphones around his neck, as he fiddled with wires he probably didn't even need to fix. He looked up as I climbed the last step, reading my face immediately.

"What happened?"

"Nothing. Or everything. I can't fucking tell right now."

"You're shaking, Sera."

I dragged a hand down my face, trying to sound like I wasn't unravelling. "He was here."

Patrick blinked. "Who?"

"The guy who sent the flowers."

That got his attention. He straightened as all the humor drained from his face. "You're sure?"

"I'd bet my life on it. He called me Little Fawn. Same as the note. Same as the box."

I tried to steady my hands, but they just kept fucking shaking.

Patrick swore under his breath. "Jesus Christ, Sera…" He dragged a hand over his face, rubbing it quickly like he was trying to wake himself up. "You really think it was him? Not some creep being, well, creepy?"

"I know what I heard. He said it like he wanted me to hear it. Like it was just between us."

Patrick's jaw tightened. "Did he touch you?"

"No. He was just… there. And then gone."

I couldn't bring myself to tell him that Kael had kept a hold of me during his show. Or that a part of me had liked his touch. That I liked how commanding he was without a word, and how he somehow felt like safety until he ripped the life jacket off with that stupid nickname and left me to drown.

I sank onto the stool beside the console, my hands gripping the edge hard enough to ache. "I didn't even see him leave."

Patrick swore again, louder this time, earning a few glances from the dancers below. "Okay. You're not going home alone tonight. I'll walk you out after we close."

"Pat—"

"Don't." His tone left no room for argument. "If this guy's been watching you, I'm not letting you step outside by yourself."

The weight of his words made something inside me twist. Watching me. He was right. That note, the flowers, the finger. Shit. This man knew where I lived. Where Pat lives. The dread crept back in, winding itself tightly around my ribs and settling. Kael hadn't found me tonight; he'd been waiting.

I swallowed hard. "Oh, good. Not only does the fucker know where we live, but where I work too." I sighed, rubbing my temples. "If he's been watching me, he's been watching all of you. You, Jenny, every other girl here. What if he decides one of *you* is next? I can handle myself, but they shouldn't have to deal with this."

Patrick's expression softened, the sharp edges of his usual sarcasm dulling for once. "Hey," he said quietly, resting a hand on the table between us. "You don't have to take all that on yourself. None of this is your fault."

"Yeah," I muttered, staring down at the floor. "Tell that to the psychopath leaving body parts with goddamn love notes."

The music shifted around us, and the bass slid into something darker and slower. My stomach twisted. The song was haunting, and left me feeling both exposed and more than a little on edge. A shadow flickered along the balcony rail in my peripheral vision. There and then gone. Fuck. Now I'm seeing things. Or maybe I wasn't.

The air felt heavier. Electric. Like he was still here, watching.

Patrick's voice cut through it. "You okay?"

"Yeah," I lied, forcing a breath. "Just thought I saw something."

"You gonna let me walk you home tonight?"

I nodded, smiling up at him. "Yeah, I'll hang around 'til close. My big, strong Pattykins can feel like the hero tonight." I winked at him, biting back a laugh.

"You joke, but we all know I'm your knight in aluminum foil, Ser."

I laughed and turned to leave, stepping down from the booth on my way to get a drink and try to make sense of the night. But as I turned to move, Benjamin appeared at the bottom of the stairs, like a sick cosmic joke, waving me down with that shit-eating grin he always wore when he wanted something. Just like that, whatever calm I'd scraped together shattered in an instant.

"Seraphine! Just the woman I needed."

I crossed my arms. "That's never a good sign."

He chuckled, the sound low and smug. "Relax, sweetheart. I come bearing good news. Michael's lined up a little… opportunity for you this weekend. Strictly appearances. You in?"

My brow arched. "Define appearances."

Benjamin spread his hands in mock innocence. "He's a regular here, platinum member. The guy just needs a date for a few black-tie things. Charity events, dinners, the usual boring rich-people crap. Smile, drink champagne, look pretty. That's it."

I eyed him warily. "Michael signed off on this?"

"Please," he scoffed. "He's the one who recommended you. Said you were the only one who could pull off classy and dangerous at the same time." He grinned, knowing the compliment would land just right. "Five grand for the weekend. All expenses covered."

I hesitated. Five thousand dollars wasn't pocket change, not even close. Still…

"What's the catch?"

Benjamin's grin widened, wolfish now with my interest on the line. "No catch. Guy's clean, vetted, platinum account, the whole thing. Think of it as good PR for the club. You get a mini vacation, and everyone walks away happy."

I narrowed my eyes. "And by everyone, you mean Michael."

He shrugged. "When the boss is happy, the rest of us get to keep our jobs. Hierarchy, baby."

I sighed, glancing toward the bar. I could feel the tequila from earlier humming through my veins, softening the edges of my doubt. "Fine. But if anything goes sideways, he owes me ten grand, not five."

If I got out of town for a weekend, maybe Little Fawn's biggest fan would turn his attention somewhere else.

Benjamin laughed, the sound oozing satisfaction. "That's my girl. I'll text you the details tomorrow. The hotel, itinerary, all that jazz. Just make sure you pack something nice. The client likes… presentation."

"Right," I muttered, my skin crawling as he called me "his girl". "Tell Michael he owes me."

"Oh, I think he already knows," Benjamin called after me, his voice slick with meaning.

• • •

The next few days blurred together, calm on the outside, a raging storm underneath. But no more body parts were sent wrapped in flowers. No stalkers in the shadows. Just me on edge and waiting. Fuck, I hated the waiting.

I spent the afternoon picking out an outfit for the evening. Something that screamed high fashion, even though I couldn't tell you the difference between Fendi and Armani if my life depended on it. I put on just enough jewelry to look expensive without giving away that half of it was thrifted. Fashion, but make it cost-effective.

I settled on a sleek black dress. Low-cut enough to keep them looking, but long enough that I wouldn't be mistaken for a high-priced escort. Even though, in the grand scheme of things, I kind of was. I clasped a simple necklace around my throat, a far cry from my usual silver collar, but this one meant I could pay rent for the next couple of months without worry.

As I slid into the town car that the client had sent, my thoughts blurred together like the city lights outside. Just a couple of simple get-togethers, I told myself. Smile. Drink. Don't get murdered. Should be easy enough.

I looked up as we pulled up to the hotel, and my eyes widened. The place looked like it charged you just to breathe near it. The entire interior was all marble and gold trim, with chandeliers that probably cost more than my entire building, and a doorman who gave me the kind of look that said I didn't belong here, but wasn't paid enough to say it out loud.

I checked my phone while the car idled at the curb. Benjamin's text thread sat at the top.

Benjamin: *Car's on the way. Don't be late. The client likes punctuality.*

I rolled my eyes, Benjamin's tone already getting under my skin, and replied:

Seraphine: *I'm already here. And I'm unavailable for the rest of the evening.*

Another message came in as the driver opened my door.

Unknown Number: *Miss Seraphine? This is Cameron. I'm in the lobby. I'm glad you agreed to spend the evening with me.*

I stared at the text for a second, then typed back:

Seraphine: *No problem, but just call me Sera, please.*

I stepped out of the car, tucking my wrap around my shoulders against the cooling autumn evening. I smoothed a hand down the front of my black dress and walked toward the revolving door, plastering on the kind of confident smile I'd perfected behind the bar.

Cameron and I spotted each other immediately. He was a man who filled a room without trying. The kind that looked exactly like his name. Cameron. Daddy's money, wrapped in an expensive suit, and his smile just this side of too perfect. He carried the easy confidence of someone who had never had to work for any of it.

"Sera," he greeted, voice warm and practiced. "You're even lovelier than I remember."

"Well, aren't you charming?" I replied, smiling prettily before taking his offered hand. His grip was firm. Too firm.

He laughed lightly, the sound rehearsed but pleasant. "I do try. We have a banquet tonight, in the Regency Orchid Hall." He looked at me like I should be impressed by this information, and I made sure I pretended to be.

"Sure. Is this a charity event, or are all the rich people gathering in one place tonight to high-five each other?"

His lips tightened for half a second before he smoothed the expression away.

"Orphans, I think. Maybe coats for hairless cats. I honestly don't even look anymore."

He laughed and ran a hand through his hair, looking almost embarrassed. That earned a real laugh out of me, the absurdity of it cutting through the nerves buzzing under my skin. He chuckled along with me as he led me toward the hall, his hand resting lightly at the small of my back. Gentle enough not to alarm, firm enough to remind me it was there.

• • •

The ballroom was decorated with all white linen and dim lighting, as waiters moved like ghosts between tables, each one carrying something more expensive than my entire week's pay. Cameron grabbed two glasses of champagne off a passing tray. The kind of move men like him assume is irresistible.

"Tell me, Sera. What made you decide to work at a place like Escape?"

I raised an eyebrow. "What makes anyone? Money, mostly. The hours don't make me want to die, and I don't do mornings unless someone's actually dying."

His smile sharpened just a little. "I imagine the money has to be great to afford someone like you."

"This isn't something I do often. Usually, I work the stage or bartend. This is more of a favor than a job."

He hummed, pretending to be paying attention. I took a sip of champagne, ignoring the way his eyes lingered on my chest a second too long.

The time leading up to the catered dinner blurred together easily enough. He laughed in all the right places, complimented my dress, and played a perfect gentleman. Every conversation he participated in sounded like a competition to see who could say "market volatility" with the straightest face. Sharp suits and sharper smiles blended together around me while I played the part of the quiet, demure girlfriend perfectly. And for a while, I almost believed it myself.

Dinner began and later ended with a toast and the kind of applause that didn't sound real. Crystal clinking against crystal as perfect teeth flashing in dim light. I smiled when Cameron did, laughed when he expected it, and let the rhythm of it all carry me. For a few fleeting hours, it almost felt like a role I'd been born to play. The band began to play as the dinner was cleared, and Cameron held out his hand to me, bending slightly at his waist.

"Care to dance?" he asked with a smug smile, like he knew I couldn't say no, even if I wanted to.

I took his hand and let him guide me onto the marble flooring. As the music swelled, we glided across the floor. He kept one hand on the small of my back as the other held my hand against his chest. I made sure to laugh at all the right places and pretended to listen as he droned on about the markets and the best companies to invest in.

When the crowd began to thin, Cameron leaned close, the scent of expensive cologne mixing with the champagne hanging on his breath. "You were wonderful tonight," he said, his voice soft, intimate enough to sound like it belonged only to me. "Would you join me upstairs for a nightcap? Just one drink before you head home."

He said it like an invitation, not an expectation. Smooth. Harmless. Gentlemanly.

A tiny warning bell chimed in the back of my skull, quiet, but insistent. And like an idiot, I ignored it.

• • •

The elevator ride was quiet except for the soft hum of classical music. His hand found the small of my back again. Gentle, but with quiet pressure that said he expected me to stay exactly where he put me. The mirrored walls reflected his smile back at me a dozen times, and none of them looked real.

When the doors opened, I followed him down a short hallway lined with white lilies in crystal vases. The suite was exactly what I expected. Lavish and understated in the way that screamed money. The floor-to-ceiling windows looked out over the city as its lights glittered like a thousand eyes looking back at me.

"Champagne?" He asked, already pouring before I could answer. "You really were exquisite tonight. Poised. Elegant. I can see why the club keeps you so close."

I accepted the glass he offered and took a cautious sip. "I bring good money to the club." I gave him a grin and a wink.

He smiled, the kind that meant to charm and disarm someone. "I can see why."

We talked for a while about nothing. Musing about the weather, the hotel, and the band at dinner. Just small talk dressed up in silk. But there was a shift somewhere in his tone, subtle at first. The pauses between words stretched longer, and his eyes stopped matching his smile.

"You know. I almost didn't believe Michael when he said you were available for private work. You seem… a little too proud for that kind of work."

He stepped closer to me, closing the distance between us. The words landed heavily. Too casual to be harmless, and I set my glass down carefully.

"Private work," I echoed. "You make it sound like I'm on retainer."

His grin widened, predatory now. "Aren't you?"

The air in the room changed and thickened. I could smell the flowers in the vase and hear the faint rush of traffic outside. Everything else narrowed to the space between us.

"I think you've misunderstood the arrangement. This was a date. Dinner, polite conversation, good publicity. That's it."

He chuckled, a low sound that didn't reach his eyes. "That's cute, but I didn't pay for conversation and publicity, sweetheart."

The world tunneled in around me, and every sound fell away except his breathing and my heartbeat.

"Then you got fucking scammed."

He moved toward me, slow and deliberate, like a man who believed he was owed something. I stepped back, but his hand caught my wrist, his grip firm, but not yet cruel.

"Don't," I said. My voice came out steady, sharper than I felt.

Cameron's smile widened, his demeanor turning cold. "You don't mean that."

I twisted my wrist free, the motion quick and practiced. "You'd be amazed at what I mean."

For a moment, we stood there, eyeing each other, the tension building as we waited to see who would move first. I could see the anger building under his skin, something hot and spoiled that no amount of money could polish. He took another step forward, and that was his mistake.

I met him halfway, and my fist connected with his nose. The crack was sharp and sickening before he stumbled as his warm blood sprayed across my knuckles. He let out a pained grunt, his body wavering for a moment, and I followed with a shove to his chest that sent him crashing down onto his back on the floor. He looked stunned, then furious.

"You fucking bitch—"

"Why are men like you always so unimaginative?" I snapped, stepping forward again, heel pressing into his throat before he could rise. His hands came up on instinct, but I shifted my weight, adding enough pressure to keep him still without crushing. His face went red, then purple.

"No is a full fucking sentence, asshole," I hissed.

Cameron clawed at my ankle desperately, drawing blood, his eyes bulging as he glared up at me.

A knock at the door broke the spell. Three sharp raps. Then silence. I didn't move. Neither did he. The knock came again. Louder.

Cameron tried to call out, but I pressed the heel of my shoe harder against his throat, cutting the sound short as the mechanical lock opened.

The door swung open, and Kael stood in the doorway, his eyes dark and almost amused. He looked between us at Cameron pinned beneath my heel, to the overturned champagne glass glittering on the carpet, and a slow and dangerous smile lit his face.

Fuck, he was beautiful when he smiled. I pushed the thought down and shifted my weight, pressing my shoe harder against Cameron's throat.

"Didn't mean to interrupt." He smiled down at Cameron like he was watching a fish squirm on a hook. A predator admiring his prey.

His voice was calm enough to make my skin prickle. Everything sounded too loud as the quiet stretched while we measured each other. Kael's eyes took inventory with a calmness that was something like acceptance. It was fucking unnerving.

"Get your foot off his throat, love." His words hit me, soft but undeniable.

Love. The word slid its way under my ribs and nestled there, like it had always belonged. My body betrayed me and obeyed him before my brain had a chance to catch up. I stepped back, breath shaky. Cameron rolled onto his side, coughing, his eyes wild.

Kael crouched beside him, one hand resting on his knee. "You laid hands on her," he murmured, almost conversational. "That was a terrible idea."

Cameron tried to speak, but Kael's hand moved fast, a blur of control and warning. His fingers pressed against Cameron's jaw, forcing his gaze up. "Apologize."

"I—I didn't—"

Kael's voice dropped, all of his earlier patience gone in an instant. "Apologize."

Cameron stammered something that might have been sorry. Kael smiled, and the air around him calmed again.

"Good man."

Then he stood, straightening his cuffs, and turned to me. "You're bleeding."

I glanced down. A line of red traced my ankle where Cameron's panic and clawing had cut my skin. Kael stepped closer, crouching again.

His hand gripped my calf, steady and warm, as he inspected the cut. Without a word, he pulled a white pocket square from his tux and wiped the blood away. His touch was gentle and my hand found his shoulder, instinctively, just to keep my balance.

"You should go home now."

"What?" My voice cracked on the word. "You can't just—"

He looked up at me, eyes soft, and the dark, clean scent of him grounded me in all this ruin. Then he stood, towering close enough that I could count the flecks of black in his gray eyes. His hand came up, and his fingers brushed a strand of hair from my face.

"You don't want to be here for what comes next."

Something in his tone made my stomach drop. "Kael—"

"Go, Seraphine." His tone came out sharper. My name on his tongue hit like a command, and left no room for me to argue.

He held my gaze until I moved. My feet felt heavy, and my heartbeat was too loud as I grabbed my wrap from the back of the chair and backed toward the door. From his spot on the floor, Cameron whimpered, but Kael didn't bother to look at him.

"Kael. Wait. What are you going to do?"

His eyes met mine, unreadable yet calm. "I'm going to take out the trash."

I stood there a second longer, caught between fear and something else I couldn't name. Then I nodded, because there was nothing left to say.

I opened the door, stepping into the too-bright hallway. The door closing behind me echoed like a gunshot and felt just as final.

Michael owed me more than ten grand for this bullshit. And I was done being the one paying the price.

Chapter Eight

Kael

The night was still bleeding neon when she came out of the club. I'd been there for an hour already, with the engine turned off, as smoke curled from the cracked window and the rain turned to mist on the windshield. Escape sat, almost peaceful from a distance. It was just another warehouse turned club drowning in light and noise, but it was also the place I first saw her, and it meant more than it should to a man like me.

The door opened, and Patrick came out first, his head on a swivel like a man who knew trouble had been circling. Sera followed a few seconds later, jacket pulled tight against the light rain and cool air, her eyes darting toward the shadows like she could feel me there. She wasn't wrong. I was almost always there. Just out of sight.

I stayed still, just another shape in the dark, and watched as Patrick walked her down the block. They laughed at something I couldn't hear, and the sound didn't fit the night. It was far too bright and alive. I told myself I was only here to make sure she got home safe. That it was chivalrous and gentlemanly. The kind of due diligence that kept my Little Fawn out of harm's way. That's what I told myself.

Truth was, I couldn't stop looking at her and the way she carried herself. The way she kept her head held high even when the world pressed close. It did something to me I didn't have words for, like control recognizing control. There was something more to her, and I wanted to know exactly what it was that had her so deep under my skin I couldn't get her out of my head.

When they reached her building, Patrick lingered a second too long at the door. Protective, but not possessive. I respected that. When the two of them finally disappeared inside, I let myself ease, just a little.

The street was quiet, with puddles reflecting fractured light. My footsteps barely made a sound as I moved to my usual spot. Old habits and all that. The kind learned in alleys far less forgiving than this one.

Her building was nothing special, just another relic of better decades, brick mottled and tired. The second-floor light flickered on, and my eyes locked on her window, framed by thin curtains.

For a few minutes, I just stood there. Watching her silhouette cross the room, her shadow pausing like she could feel eyes on her. I took a steadying breath. This wasn't just lust. Not anymore. It was something heavier. Protective. Possessive. Both. I stayed until the light went out. Until I was sure she was safe, but even then, I didn't leave.

• • •

By the next night, the city had washed itself clean and pretended nothing ugly had ever happened. That's what cities do. Every day is a new beginning. The previous night's sins get washed away by sunlight and street cleaners.

I watched her from across the street again as she left for work. Same walk. Same jacket. The same guarded calm that made everyone else underestimate her. They didn't see what I saw, the strength in her stillness.

This was my new habit. Watching her nightly as she made her way to work. Some nights I watched her in the club. Her show had become my new favorite, and I was addicted. I couldn't look away from her, even when I wanted to.

I always stayed just far enough to stay unseen, close enough that I could end anyone who tried to touch her. It wasn't stalking; this was prevention. A necessary precaution to ensure Sera was as safe as she could be in this fucked-up city.

So when she came out of her building on Friday evening, I was back in my usual spot, watching. She was dressed in black silk that didn't belong to the world she usually moved through. This dress was elegant. And while Sera was beautiful no matter what she wore, elegance wasn't in her repertoire. This was new. I cocked an eyebrow as I watched her.

I'd already known she had plans. Michael's name had come up on a call earlier that afternoon, a favor owed, a contract settled, and Cameron Sykes' name buried in the fine print. I didn't need to read between the lines to know what it meant. Men like Cameron didn't pay for company; they paid for the silence after.

Like any good protector, I made my own arrangements. The tailored tux I wore fit like a glove, and I kept the invitation nestled in the pocket inside my jacket.

The car that waited for her outside wasn't one of the usuals; it was too polished. I tailed them easily, keeping two cars between us, with my eyes locked on the back of her car as they made their way downtown.

The hotel they pulled up to was all gold trim and white marble. The kind of place where money erased consequences. The kind of place you needed to be a certain caliber just to walk through the front doors.

I made my way through and into the ballroom. The entire fucking place was a shrine to excess. Chandeliers dripping gold, waiters meant to be rarely seen and never heard, and music far too soft to cover the secrets underneath. Every smile in that room had teeth, and hers was the brightest one there.

She walked in on Cameron's arm, her head held high, and that black dress catching the light like sin wrapped in silk. She didn't belong here, and that was exactly why every man in the room turned to look, including me.

I stayed near the back, half-shadowed behind a column, just another suit among dozens. Watching. Waiting. Cameron never stopped touching her the entire time, and it made my fucking skin itch. His hand at her elbow or the small of her back, guiding her like he thought he owned her. Every time he leaned close, my jaw tightened. She smiled when she needed to and laughed when she had to. Polite and composed, but I could see it. The distance in her eyes and the calculation. The kind of alertness that comes from surviving men who mistake kindness for invitation.

The jealousy that twisted inside me clawed at the back of my mind. She was mine, and this man was pawing at her like she was his personal plaything. Watching her endure his touch made it simmer at the surface like something feral. She didn't see me, but I saw everything. The way her fingers tightened on the stem of her glass when she was irritated, the faint arch of her brow when Cameron bragged too loudly, to the subtle shift of her weight when she was ready to leave.

When the band switched to slower music and Cameron's hand found her waist, I moved. Not toward her. Just close enough to remind myself I could. I watched as he whispered in her ear while he moved her around the pristine dance floor. My hands clenched into a fist, and I took a breath to keep myself from breaking his neck here and now just to prove a fucking point.

As the event died down, I watched as he leaned in, whispering something in her ear. My jaw ticked, blood simmering under my collar. My eyes followed them as they slipped from the dance floor and disappeared toward the elevators in the corridor. My feet followed, steady and silent, gaze locked on the curve of Sera's hips as she walked beside him.

Just as I reached the exit of the hall, a voice stopped me cold.

"Kael."

Arthur. Fuck.

He looked exactly like every hotel manager who'd ever learned how to weaponize his trade. From his round face, thinning hair, to that too-wide smile that never touched his eyes. A parasite dressed in hospitality.

"Long time," he said, stepping close enough that I could smell the brandy on his breath. "You're a hard man to track down."

"Not hard enough," I muttered. My eyes flicked past him toward the elevators, where Sera and Cameron disappeared behind the closing elevator doors. "Make it quick."

Arthur chuckled, low and knowing. "Relax. I heard you might need access to a room. Our mutual friend said 'You like to be… prepared'."

From his jacket pocket, he produced a sleek black keycard. Unmarked except for the gold stripe at the bottom. He twirled it once between his fingers before holding it out to me.

"This is a master keycard. It'll open any door in the hotel, including Cameron's penthouse suite. Consider it a professional courtesy."

I arched a brow. "What's the catch?"

Arthur smiled wider. "No catch. You've done good work for the right people. Let's just call this a favor that keeps the balance even."

"Appreciate it," I replied, already moving.

Arthur's grin didn't fade. "Try not to make too much of a mess this time. Replacing our carpets doesn't come cheap, Kael."

I didn't answer him back. My mind was already in motion. She was out of my sight, and a thousand scenarios played out in my head. Each one ended with Cameron's blood on my hands and a smile on my face.

The elevator doors opened, and I moved through the hall like a ghost. Every sound catalogued in my head. From the hum of the vending machine and the tick of distant heels to the faintest sound of laughter from behind a door. Hers. Then a crash. Glass breaking and muffled voices. I reached the suite just as the second shout broke off into silence.

I knocked on the door. Three heavy, loud raps, like a warning. The sound strangled into nothing. I knocked again while pressing the card against the mechanism.

I stepped inside, and the first thing I noticed was her perfect heel pressed against Cameron's throat, and her body coiled like she'd been forged in violence. Every line of her was a threat dressed as grace. I'd seen trained killers look less certain.

For a moment, I just stood there, watching her. Entranced by the calm on the surface and the rage that burned underneath.

"Didn't mean to interrupt," I said with a grin, looking at Cameron as he floundered under her hold.

Pride bloomed through my chest. My Little Fawn has teeth. I like it. I stepped closer, letting my gaze settle on Sera.

"Get your foot off his throat, love."

She obeyed before she even realized she had. The sound of her breath trembled against the silence as Cameron rolled to his side, coughing, and his eyes wild with rage.

I crouched beside him, resting a hand on my knee. Calm. Controlled. "You laid hands on her. That was a terrible idea."

He tried to talk, but I was already on him. My hand caught his jaw, forcing his gaze up. "Apologize."

"I… I didn't—"

"I said… apologize."

The words came out slow and final. He stammered something that might have been sorry, and I smiled. "Good man."

Then I straightened, smoothing my cuffs like nothing had happened, and turned back to her.

"You're bleeding."

A thin red line ran along her ankle where it looked like he had scratched her.

I hadn't even realized I'd moved until I was crouched again, one hand around her calf. Her skin was warm beneath my palm, and her pulse was steady against my thumb. I pulled a white pocket square from my jacket and wiped the blood away with a softness unbecoming of a man like me.

She steadied herself on my shoulder, and the second her hand lightly gripped the muscle there, I felt my cock stir, and my heart rate tick up.

"You should go home now," I answered quietly, ignoring every basic instinct to take her in the moment.

Her voice cracked. "What? You can't just—"

I looked up at her and inhaled the scent of her that hung in the air. An intoxicating blend of sweat and fear that mixed with the faint sweetness of patchouli. It crawled inside me and made a home there.

I stood close enough to her that the heat between us felt alive. I brushed a strand of hair from her face and let my hand linger for one heartbeat longer than I should have.

"You don't want to be here for what comes next."

"Kael," she started softly. My name on her tongue made something inside me break, and I knew I would make her say it again. But next time, I wanted her to scream it while I was buried inside her.

My jaw clenched as I fought back the urge to take her right here and now. In front of Cameron, just to make him watch. I rolled my head and cracked my neck, pushing those thoughts aside as my eyes found hers and narrowed slightly.

"Go, Seraphine."

She opened her mouth again to speak, and I shook my head once. That was all it took for her to understand. When the door clicked shut behind her, the quiet that followed was absolute.

• • •

Cameron was still on the floor, clutching his throat, trying to find air or courage. Probably both. I watched him for a long moment, letting the calm settle over me again. She was safe, and that was all that mattered. Now I could finish what he started.

I turned, my gaze finding Cameron's as he knelt on the floor. Not broken or begging. Not yet anyway. He still had that look in his eyes, the kind of fire men wear when they think they can fight their way out of consequences.

He swung the moment he stood upright, but his movements were sloppy and wild. The kind of movement that belongs to someone who's never been in a real fight. His fist cut through empty air, and my hand found his throat before he could swing again.

I made a tsk'ing noise at him and grinned. He clawed at my wrist and tried to speak. I loosened my grip just enough for him to wheeze out a curse.

"Fuck you."

I smiled wider and nodded my head eagerly. "That's the spirit."

He swung again, and this time, I let him connect. The punch landed against my ribs, solid but unconvincing. Pain flared and died just as quickly. It was almost disappointing. I caught his arm mid-swing the next time and twisted until something cracked. His scream broke through the quiet of the room.

"Do you know what it takes for me to not kill a man?"

He didn't answer, just panted loudly, as sweat slicked his temple.

"Discipline. Years of it. And then you come along and lay your filthy fucking hands on her. So, you don't get the mercy discipline brings."

My arm snaked around his neck, the crook of my elbow resting just beside his windpipe. His breathing hitched as I began to squeeze just enough to let him know he wasn't leaving here on his own two feet.

"Don't do this! You… whatever she's paying—"

"She isn't paying me," I cut in. "She's mine, and what's mine is untouchable by things like you."

His eyes widened. "She… she's yours?"

"Mine," I repeated, my voice a menacing growl. "And you touched her." I clicked my tongue in his ear.

He spat at my shoe, and I almost laughed. Still fighting, and still convinced pride could save him.

"You've got spirit, and I can respect that."

I tightened my hold, grinning as my muscles contracted like a snake, and he groaned low in his throat against the fabric of my suit jacket. He thrashed, kicked, and elbowed me. The struggle lasted seconds, but every one of them stretched, thick with the sound of his ragged breathing.

I didn't rush it. Control was the point. He needed to feel the world narrowing. I wanted him to know it was me closing it around him.

When his movements started to falter, I pressed my lips to his ear.

"This part is my favorite," I whispered, as a wicked grin ghosted across my mouth.

He jerked once sharply as my arm crushed his windpipe. My other arm wrapped around his face, and with one quick twisting motion, it was over. The sound echoed through the room as his body slumped at my feet.

The room went still except for the soft hum of the heater under the window. I wiped my hands on his jacket and stood, keeping my breathing slow until my pulse settled. The smell of him, sweat and expensive cologne, still clung to the air. Underneath it lingered the faint trace of her perfume. Patchouli and smoke. It pulled my attention back to the door where she'd stood.

For a moment, I could still see her there. The defiance in her eyes and the tremor in her hand when she touched me. That feeling crawled through me again, slow and unrelenting. It wasn't lust exactly. It was recognition. A claim of her that had nothing to do with ownership and everything to do with inevitability. She'd changed something in me, and now the world would have to adjust.

I stood over him and watched the stillness settle as the quiet hum of the elevators down the hall and the low buzz of the city outside gave me a soundtrack for what came next. It all came back slow, like the world had been holding its breath.

Arthur had said to keep it clean, and this time, I did.

• • •

Outside the door sat a luggage cart, gleaming under the hallway lights. Someone had draped a crisp white hotel sheet across it, the kind used for room service deliveries. Arthur's handiwork was efficient as always.

I slipped the sheet from the handle, rolled Cameron onto it, and hoisted him onto the cart, hiding the evidence with a second sheet over the whole thing. The wheels squeaked softly as I pushed it down the corridor, and no one bothered to look twice. No one ever does when you look like you belong.

The service elevator waited at the end of the hall, unmarked and louder than the others. I swiped the card Arthur had given me, and the doors opened with a low rumble.

The ride down was silent. My reflection stared back at me, warped in the polished steel, as my cufflinks caught in the faint light. My pulse stayed even as the metal box descended, and I thought of her. I let her wash over me for just a minute. My Little Fawn…

The elevator gave a small jolt as it stopped in the sublevel garage. Dim light greeted me with the smell of oil and exhaust as the doors opened. I wheeled the cart across the concrete, past neat rows of luxury sedans that gleamed under the fluorescent lighting.

My car sat in the corner, away from the cameras Arthur had turned for me. The trunk yawned open with the click of a button on my fob, and the plastic lining the space sat untouched and ready. I like to be prepared for any situation.

I lifted Cameron's body into the trunk, careful to keep him within the plastic. He landed in the space with a dull thud. A fitting sound for the end of someone like him. I adjusted a chain around his ankles, looped it around itself once, and locked it tight. The bag of weights I kept in the compartment went next, just enough to make sure he stayed where he belonged when I got him there.

I closed the trunk and stood there for a second, my palms flat on the metal. My reflection ghosted faintly in the dark paint.

"She's mine," I offered quietly to the empty garage. The words landed with finality as I got in and started the car. I ran my fingers through my hair before pulling out of the parking spot and out of the structure.

The drive to the river was short, and the city beyond looked washed out under sodium light, with the thinning traffic and the rising buildings skeletal against the mist. I rolled the window down, and rain drifted in, cold and clean. It reminded me of her. Fuck, everything did these days. My Little Fawn was etched into my skin, and I knew I would do whatever it took to be the reason she smiled. Not the kind reserved for patrons at that fucking club, but because I made her happy.

When I reached the bridge, I watched as the water below moved fast and brutal. I parked by the guardrail and got out. The night was empty except for the sound of the current rushing passed the concrete.

The trunk opened with a soft click, and the chain clanked as I dragged the bag out. The weight leaned against me, solid and grounding. I let him drop into the water below without another thought of him. The river accepted my offering with a hollow splash, then a hush.

Little bubbles rose to the surface, bursting one by one until nothing remained. The current closed over everything, black and final.

For a moment, I just stood there, listening. My heartbeat matched the river's pull. My hands rested on the railing, rain running down my sleeves. The air was colder now, but it felt right.

She filled my thoughts again; the only light left in this night. Her strength. Her laughter. The look in her eyes when she realized I'd be there, no matter how far she ran.

She wasn't a habit anymore. She was the gravity I'd been orbiting without knowing it. The reason behind every cleaning job, every body, every rule I'd broken, and every one I'd follow again if it meant keeping her untouched.

The world didn't know it yet, but it had shifted and bent around her. When I finally turned away from the river, dawn was beginning to scrape the horizon. The city blinked, pretending innocence. I drove back through wet streets until her building came into view.

Her window glowed faintly behind thin curtains. She was moving inside, soft shadows, the shape of her shoulder, the curve of her hair as she poured something into a glass.

I parked across the street and turned off the engine. Rain tapped the windshield in slow, uneven rhythms. I sat there watching her silhouette move, safe, unaware, whole. The world could burn if it meant she'd never have to know what it cost to keep her that way.

I stayed until the sun rose and the rain turned the world to glass. Until she was asleep behind those curtains, safe in a world that didn't deserve her. I didn't leave until I was sure the sun would find her before anything else did.

Chapter Nine

Seraphine

Everything felt too loud tonight. The bass hit wrong, and the tempo mocked me as if it knew I was itching to get out of my own skin. The sound felt like it was syncing to my pulse instead of the track. Even the lights felt heavier, catching on the metal fixtures and flashing too bright against the haze. The club was alive the way it always was, but it pressed closer now, like it could feel me unraveling beneath the surface.

Every shadow looked like him, and my eyes searched the club, waiting for the moment they would land on his. But they didn't. He wasn't here, and I couldn't tell if I was relieved or disappointed.

There was no reason to still feel the whisper of his voice brushing against my skin.

'Go home, Seraphine.'

I told myself I was fine. That I'd gone home and locked the door, and finally showered and slept. I'd done everything right.

But I could still hear it. I could still feel his hand wrapped around my calf as he gently wiped away the blood on my ankle. His touch had been so warm and so grounding. A contradiction to his steely gray eyes and the danger he kept locked behind them.

I shook my head and tried to clear it from any thoughts of Kael and Cameron. A shudder rolled through me, and for a moment, I wondered if another body part would end up being delivered to my house in flowers again. The thought almost made me laugh. Almost.

The tension in my shoulders eased a bit as I made my way to the dressing room of the club. Well, what we call a dressing room. It was a catch-all room, designed to hold everything we might need and everything that needed fixing, which took up three-quarters of the room. Michael didn't like spending money on the actual club, just on his appearance and the club's appearance.

Jenny was already in the dressing room when I came in, her blonde hair braided tight, hands gloved and clean, while she checked coils of rope like she trusted nothing but tension and fiber. Bundles of silken rope hung neatly from wall hooks, every strand oiled and soft from use. The faint scent of her jasmine perfume and rope oil clung to the air.

"You're late," she said without looking up.

"Just fashionably," I chuckled, peeling off my jacket, but the sound died in my throat.

Jenny's dark eyes flicked up, her gaze sharp and knowing. "You sure you're good for this?"

I nodded, too fast. "Yeah. I need something to keep my mind busy."

She didn't push, just tested the strength of a line between her palms, then clipped a carabiner through the loop with a satisfying snap.

"Then help me finish these anchors. I already checked the rig above the stage, but I want perfection. Can't have my favorite co-star falling from the ceiling mid-orgasm."

That earned a laugh from me, real and unrestrained. I let myself begin to relax, just enough to make it through tonight.

I crouched beside her, my fingers brushing the rope as I tied the familiar knots: single-column, double, clean and efficient. The ritual steadied me. The way the fibers flexed and tightened, the sound of the rope sliding against itself as it burned faintly against my fingertips. It was something real and solid. A small piece of me I could control. By the time we had checked every clip and backup line, the tension in my chest had calmed enough that I could breathe.

The rig would hang center stage tonight for our suspension act. Controlled lift and full-body restraint, the kind of act that blurred the line between beauty and surrender. Usually, the anticipation sent a thrill through me. Tonight, my pulse raced for a hundred different other reasons.

The bass thudded faintly through the walls, steady as a heartbeat. The murmur of the crowd seeped through the cracks in the dressing room door. Their voices sounded low, hungry, and waiting.

Jenny coiled the last of the rope over her shoulder and brushed a stray hair back from her face.

"Alright, little bird. Let's go fly."

I stood, my knees popping in protest, and smoothed my hands down the lines of my bustier. The motion was automatic. Center yourself and control what you can. The vinyl creaked faintly as I adjusted the buckles, testing each one, and grounded myself in the familiar tightness.

• • •

The corridor to the stage was narrow and hot. Every step toward the pulsing lights ahead pulled the anxiety higher in my chest. The crowd's energy hit me before I even stepped through the curtains covering the back of the stage. The red velvet did little to hold back the electric, anticipatory waves flowing through the club.

Patrick's voice crackled through the comm near the door. "Ready when you are, ladies. Lights on your mark, Jenny."

She gave me one last look, fingers brushing my shoulder. Her touch was light, reassuring, and commanding all at once. "Color check?"

"Green," I breathed, and it came out steadier than I felt.

Her hand lingered just a moment longer, then she smiled that wicked, familiar smile. "Then let's give them a reason to hold their breath."

The lights dimmed as I stepped into the center of the stage. The rig hung above me, ropes coiled neatly, glinting faintly under the spotlights.

Jenny's voice cut through the hum.

"Hands."

I lifted them without thinking. The first brush of rope against my skin drew a shiver up my spine. She moved with the same rhythm she always did: wrap, pull, tighten, check. Precision disguised as grace.

The pattern anchored me, and every knot was another thought pulled loose.

When she hoisted my arms above my head, gravity shifted. The creak of pulleys, the momentary loss of balance, then stillness. My toes left the floor. My body protested as it stretched taut, bound and balanced in the air.

Suspension always felt like falling in reverse. Being weightless and unanchored made every nerve feel alive but quiet.

"Good. Stay right there," Jenny murmured. "Let them see what beautiful looks like when it's suspended."

I obeyed. The tension that had lived in my spine since last night loosened, vertebrae by vertebrae. My heartbeat slowed until it matched the bass vibrating through the stage.

She moved behind me, the scent of her perfume threading with the rope oil. Each adjustment, each tug, pushed me a little further out of my body. The crowd blurred to color and pulse. Only the rope remained with its pressure, its promise, and the gentle ache where it held me.

Jenny's voice reached me again, lower now, meant only for me. "You're safe. I've got you." I gave a small nod, both to her and to our Dungeon Master, watching from the shadows.

I tensed slightly as she moved behind me, trailing her fingers along the curve of my ass. She grabbed another coil of rope and began to bind my thighs, starting just below my hips.

The ropes cinched tight, forcing my legs apart and exposing my already gleaming pussy to the audience.

She took her time, reveling in the way my breath hitched with each pass of the rope over my sensitive skin. As she finished the bindings around my thighs, she connected the ropes to additional pulleys, slowly spreading my legs wider until I was fully exposed. The cool air of the club did little to soothe the heated ache growing there.

"Too tight?" she asked, her eyes checking mine for hesitation.

"No, it's perfect." My voice was breathy and filled with desire.

Jenny smiled wickedly. She knew what I needed tonight. She had seen my body tense and full of anxiety in the dressing room. She leaned down, her lips brushing the shell of my ear.

"Shhh," she cooed, her breath hot against my skin. "I know what you need. Relax for me, my perfect little bird."

Her words coaxed something inside me to let go. The noise of the club receded like a tide, leaving nothing but the sound of my breathing and the distant hum of the lights.

My breath caught in my throat as she moved to a spot near the back of the stage, picking up a belt with a large silicone cock attached to the front. She slipped it around her tiny waist, her eyes barely leaving mine as she buckled the belt around her. The sound of the leather sent shivers skating down my spine.

"Look at them," Jenny said with heated command, her hand waving toward the crowd. "I want them to see your eyes when you surrender."

My eyes closed for a moment as my lashes cast a shadow on my cheek. When I opened them again, I looked toward the crowd. My eyes gleamed in the lights, unfocused but full of capitulation.

I tensed as she stepped between my thighs. Her hands pressed my legs apart farther, holding me open and bare as the thick head of the dildo pressed against my opening, and my pulse quickened at the sensation.

With a thundering crack, her hand came slicing through the air, landing perfectly against the plump, rounded edge of my ass. Without warning, she pressed herself all the way inside me, seating herself to the hilt.

Every ounce of anxiety shattered. My mind blanked, and all that existed was the fullness and the promise of release. Every muscle relaxed. A relieved sigh fell from my lips as I sank further into submission.

Jenny's hands gripped my hips tightly, her touch grounding. My eyes, cloudy with supplicant yearning, locked on hers. Her pupils had swallowed the dark brown of her irises, leaving only hunger and want in their place.

My head fell back, hair spilling loose as the ropes held me steady. The world tilted with the motion, stage lights painting my skin in gold and shadow. I hung there. Every piece of me lay open and on display. Every ragged release of my breath was an offering to the crowd.

Jenny began to move, her hips slamming into mine, the sound a heartbeat the crowd couldn't ignore. Each withdrawal left a hollow ache, a split second of loss, before the next thrust filled me again, deeper, claiming back the air she had stolen. The rhythm built until I was nothing but movement and breath, strung up between pain and pleasure, worship and ruin.

"That's it, little bird," she whispered. "Don't fight it. Let us watch you fall."

Pleasure began to coil inside me like a snake, winding tighter with every thrust, every pull of the ropes against my skin. The inevitability of release dragged me toward it. Slow and merciless, until there was nothing left to hold on to. My thoughts scattered, and my breath vanished until all that was left was raw nerve and desire.

One of Jenny's hands coiled in my hair, bending my body back as she bared me to the room, every piece of me on display as I barreled toward the edge, my entire body tensing with the desperate need to let go.

The pressure inside me broke all at once. My body arched, trembling as a sound tore from my throat that didn't sound human. Heat flooded through me, violent and blinding, a storm ripping through every inch of me until I was shaking in the ropes.

"Mine," Jenny whispered, her fingers tightening slightly in my hair.

She slowed her pace, prolonging my pleasure as long as possible while her fingers skated along my skin. The aftershocks rolled through my body in time with my pulse. As she eased out of me, a full-body shudder raced through me. The sudden emptiness left me satiated, yet still longing.

The applause swelled, distant at first, pulling me back. My skin flushed, and my breath came in shallow, stuttering gasps. The ropes creaked as Jenny eased the tension, lowering me inch by inch until my toes brushed the stage.

The world tilted again when the last knot loosened, and Jenny caught me before gravity could. Her hands, always so warm and steady, anchored me against her chest. The smell of her wrapped around us like a cocoon.

"Easy, pretty girl," she murmured, her lips close to my ear. "Breathe, sweetheart. You did so good for me, baby."

Her voice was the first thing that felt real again. I nodded, muscles trembling, my head resting against her shoulder as she unbound the last of the rope. Each release left a ghost of pressure on my skin like a map of where I had been held. My body hummed, too alive and too weightless all at once.

Jenny pressed a cold bottle of water into my hand. "Small sips."

The plastic crackled under my shaking fingers. The water quenched more than just my thirst. It centered me once again.

The DM appeared at the edge of the stage, his presence a silent check-In. I lifted my hand in a small wave. Green. He nodded once and disappeared back into the crowd.

Jenny brushed her thumb along my jaw, tilting my chin up until our eyes met. "Back with me?"

"Yeah," I whispered. My voice sounded wrecked and honest.

She smiled softly, not her stage smile, but something real.

"Good girl."

The words hit somewhere deep, a final tether pulling me home. The noise of the crowd was just noise again. The ropes, the stage, the heat, all of it blurred behind the calm that came after the storm.

• • •

The dressing room felt too small when I stepped inside. The air was thick with body spray and rope oil. My hands shook as I braced them on the counter, the cool metal edge pressing into my palms. Makeup lights buzzed faintly above the mirror, turning every mark on my body into a confession.

The rope had left lines across my thighs, my ribs, and my wrists. Small testaments of where I had been held. I traced one with my fingertip, feeling the faint raised heat beneath the surface. It didn't hurt, not really. It burned in a way that had nothing to do with pain.

Jenny moved quietly behind me, the way she always did after a scene. No words, just presence. The sound of her peeling off her gloves, the faint creak of leather, the whisper of fabric. She came to stand beside me, close enough that our reflections blurred together in the mirror's haze.

"Still with me?" she asked softly.

"Yeah." My voice didn't sound like mine. It was hoarse, quiet. "Just… coming down."

Jenny nodded, eyes flicking over my reflection before settling on my face. "You hit deep tonight. Deeper than usual."

I swallowed hard, unsure if that was a compliment or concern. "Guess I needed it."

She hummed in agreement, reaching for a towel. "Here." She pressed the soft cotton into my hand, then started wiping at a streak of rope oil near my shoulder. "You did well. Clean scene. Well controlled. The crowd loved it."

"I wasn't thinking about them," I whispered.

Her hand stilled for half a beat before continuing. "No. You weren't."

The silence stretched between us as the hum of the club beyond the door seeped through the walls. Bass, laughter, and muffled voices that made my head feel hazy. The world kept moving, unaware that mine still hadn't found its footing again.

Jenny set the towel aside and met my eyes in the mirror. "You sure you're alright?"

"I'm fine." Too quick. Too sharp. Definitely not fine.

She didn't call me out this time. Just stepped back, giving me space, her reflection fading from mine as she moved toward the door. "Take a few minutes. Then come find me for the check-out, okay?"

"Yeah," I said again, quieter this time.

The door clicked shut behind her, and the silence was deafening. I stared at my reflection until my eyes blurred. My makeup was smeared, my lipstick was half gone, and my eyes were still glassy. I looked wrecked. Not from the show, but from everything simmering underneath. Kael's voice echoed again through the static in my head.

'You don't want to be here for what comes next.'

And God help me, part of me still wanted to hear him say it again. To feel his touch on my skin, and his breath in my ear.

Fuck.

My chest tightened, and the air felt heavier. I grabbed the water bottle from the counter and drank, each swallow grounding me a little more. I pressed the cold plastic against my cheek until the chill cut through the fog.

The reflection in the mirror steadied, but the turmoil under my skin was threatening to pull me apart at the seams.

"Get it together," I muttered, forcing air into my lungs. I slipped into my jacket, the leather clinging to my still-warm skin, and pushed away from the counter.

The hallway outside waited, dark and narrow, pulsing faintly with the rhythm of the club. I pulled on the dressing room door, and the heavy steel protested as I dragged it open. The sound hit me first, everything suddenly too sharp, too close.

"Fuck!" I growled, wrapping my arms around my middle as I made my way toward the back exit. The need for air and silence kept my feet moving.

Just as I reached for the handle, a hand slipped around my wrist. Instinct flared, and I yanked back hard, adrenaline cutting through the fog.

"Don't fucking touch me, asshole!"

I snapped, spinning toward whoever thought that was a good idea, and my entire body froze.

Kael.

My breath caught somewhere between my lungs and throat. His gray eyes met mine, steady and unflinching, with that same impossible calm that hid something dangerous underneath. He looked maddeningly composed, even here in the dim light, with shadows crawling over the sharp lines of his jaw.

"Shit. I'm sorry, Sera. I didn't mean to startle you."

His voice came out calm, barely carrying over the club's thrumming just behind the walls.

"You didn't startle me," I lied as my pulse kicked like a drum. "You shouldn't be back here. It's employees only. Not… whatever the fuck your job description is."

Kael's gaze flicked briefly toward the door behind me, then back.

"And you shouldn't be walking out alone after that performance you just gave," he said, ignoring my comment as he eyed me up and down, taking stock of the marks on my skin. "There are wolves lurking in the shadows, Little Fawn."

"Wolves? Please. I just spent thirty fucking minutes hanging from the ceiling, pretty sure I'm the scariest thing in this hallway."

Kael's eyebrow raised, the corners of his mouth twitching as he fought back a smile.

"Scary doesn't always mean safe," he deadpanned.

"Neither does the quiet," I shot back, crossing my arms.

The faint ghost of his smile vanished, replaced by that unreadable stillness he wore like armor.

"Come on. You need air."

He nodded toward the doorway, his eyes never leaving mine.

I should have told him to mind his own business. But my head was buzzing, and my pulse was still tangled in the leftover static from the stage. So I let him hold the door open and stepped into the alley.

• • •

The night hit like a shock. Cool air brushed against my skin, cutting through the film of sweat and perfume still clinging to me. I breathed in deeply, the first real breath I had taken all night. The city smelled like old buildings and ruin. This neighborhood's signature scent.

Kael stayed a few feet back, leaning against the brick wall, as if he belonged there. The glow from the club's backlight painted him in amber, softening the sharp lines of his face.

"You always play the knight lurking in the shadows?" I asked, my voice still rough.

He glanced at me, expression unreadable. "Only when the princess looks like she's about to pass out."

"Princess," I scoffed. "Wrong fairy tale, big bad wolf. Here we do nightmares and sin, not talking to animals and shit."

"Fair. But you're bleeding, Little Fawn. Doesn't take a wolf to notice it."

I looked down at the faint red smear near my wrist and rubbed it away with the edge of my jacket. "It's nothing."

"And yet, everything about you suggests otherwise."

That pulled my eyes back to his. He wasn't taunting me. He meant it, that quiet kind of concern that made something tight and unsteady curl in my chest.

The wind picked up, sweeping through the alley, carrying the distant hum of the city. For the first time all night, the noise felt almost bearable.

"I'm fine," I whispered.

He shook his head slightly. "You keep saying that like if you say it enough, it'll be true."

"It's worked so far."

Kael pushed off the wall, his steps slow, deliberate. He stopped just close enough for the air between us to change.

"You don't have to keep pretending."

"I'm not pretending," I murmured, but even I didn't believe it.

For a moment, neither of us moved. The streetlight flickered overhead, painting the ground in flashes of gold and shadow. He leaned in close, bringing his fingers up to push a stray lock of hair behind my ear.

"Get home safe, Seraphine."

His lips brushed the shell of my ear, and for an instant, my brain calmed and found its footing. He turned before I could answer, footsteps fading down the alley until only the hum of the city remained.

I stood there for a long time, breathing in the cool night air, and let it scrape the heat from my skin. The silence felt heavy and charged. Like his touch had rewired the air itself. I told myself I was steady again. But all I could feel was the ghost of his breath, still claiming the space between my ribs and the empty ache that needed more.

Chapter Ten

Kael

The smell of her shampoo lingered in my nose as I walked away from the alley. I ran my tongue along my lower lip, my mouth suddenly too dry as I climbed into my car and sat for a moment. A cold, misting rain made a mockery of the neon lights, turning them into colored starbursts across my windshield. I started the engine and drove with no destination in mind. No need for one when the only thing on my mind these days was her.

The wipers worked in a slow rhythm. My hand was steady as I navigated the streets, but my head was anything but. She was still everywhere. The way she sucked in a breath when the cool air hit. How her pulse kicked under the delicate skin below her ear when I told her to get home safe, her eyes lifting to mine, pupils blown and glassy.

She wasn't safe. Not at work, and not around me. The light ahead turned yellow, and I pressed the gas, driving through it. I could still smell the alley. The damp brick and old rot. I could still hear the low hum of the transformer on the pole. But under it, there was a ribbon of jasmine mixed with patchouli and sweat that didn't belong to the city. It belonged to her.

She quieted the worst of it, the noise in my head. Not all of it. Just enough to stop the voices from sorting every face into a problem or a solution. That kind of calm carried weight. It was a blanket thrown over a feral animal. And sooner or later, the teeth would still show.

I turned down a side street with no plan. My chest had that tight ache I never admitted to. It felt like a bruise you keep pressing, just to test the throb. My mind drifted again to the finger on the flowers, the way she whispered my name, and how she walked out alone because she would rather break than bend. All of it was cataloged in a place she had carved into my head.

My phone buzzed on the passenger seat, and the screen bathed the car's cab in harsh light. I glared at the offending rectangle. Conor's name lit up the screen as I let it ring twice.

"Yeah."

"Michael paid." Conor's voice always sounded amused, even when he was angry. Especially when he was angry. A man who liked watching other people suffer at his hand, smiling while they did.

"It was fast, Kael. Too fast."

The wet asphalt hissed under the tires as I kept my breathing even.

"Means he understood the lesson."

"It means he had a friend." Conor paused, just long enough to make me picture his smile.

"And when boys get help, they think that means they're safe." Paper rustled on his end. "So we adjust and make a new payment schedule."

"Adjust. Yeah. Sure. What's your plan?"

"Double, and the date moves up. Tell him he has five days." Another pause, and a small clink, glass against glass. "Make sure he believes you."

I watched the light ahead shift. Green to yellow. I stopped this time.

"Understood."

"Kael…"

"Conor?"

"Your little pet at the club? Make sure you keep your fuckin' head clear." He let the silence stretch. "Women like that make men do foolish things."

My jaw tensed, and I looked at my white knuckles on the wheel. "She's not yours to worry about, Conor."

"Good. Call me when the message is delivered."

The line went dead with no goodbye. Conor never needed one. I let the phone fall back to the seat. Five days. Double. Fuck. Michael would probably puke when he heard it. He would ask me for help he had no right to ask for. He would try to bargain with someone else's bones. That was his nature. Weak men always thought they could negotiate, right up until a man like me started pruning their edges.

A horn sounded from behind me. Shit. The light had turned green. I moved forward, then pulled into the first empty lot I saw. A closed liquor store. Bars on the windows and a hand-painted sign that said CASH ONLY. I parked under the flickering security light and killed the engine. Rain made a soft spray on the windshield that looked like static.

I closed my eyes and saw the knot patterns again. Rope biting into her soft skin, and the map it left behind. She had come down shaking. She had told me she was fine when I knew she wasn't. She was a beautiful liar.

I tasted the word on my tongue. Fine. The word was too small for her. People used fine to describe fine China patterns, silk ties, and decent whiskey. Fine was for things that sat still and behaved. Not for a woman who balanced control and chaos like a blade dancing on its edge.

She wasn't fine. She was precision and ruin wrapped in leather and red lipstick. The kind of danger that made you forget you were bleeding until you looked down and saw red.

The sky had started to pale, turning the wet streets to ribbons of dull silver. Dawn was always the ugliest hour. It stripped everything down to what it really was with no shadows left to hide behind. Just truth and hangovers and regret.

I drove while the city was still empty. The clubs had shuttered, the stragglers stumbled their way home, and the rain began to fall harder, blurring everything around me. I told myself

I was just taking the long way back, but my hands didn't listen. They turned toward her street without being told.

Her windows lay dark, as a thin line of light pollution cut across the curtains, and I slowed without meaning to. The habit was too ingrained. Assess, observe, catalog, control. No movement. No silhouette in the window. Nothing but the amber glow of the streetlight and the low idle of my engine. Good. She was home, safe. Or at least safer than anywhere near me.

I sat there long enough for my pulse to return to normal as my fingers tapped against the wheel, a rhythm with no song behind it. It was the kind of quiet that started to itch under the skin before I shifted into drive and left her street behind.

The city bled out in the rearview, all the color and noise drained from it. My apartment wasn't far, and I craved the concrete walls, deadbolt locks, and silence thick enough to choke on. Home, by necessity only.

By the time I parked, the sun had climbed high enough to stain the clouds pink. I didn't bother taking off my jacket before I sat on the edge of the bed, elbows on my knees, staring at the floor until the room blurred.

Five days, double the payment, and one message to deliver. Beneath it all was a woman who wasn't fine. And since finding her, neither was I.

• • •

The next night came too fast, and the sky was dumping rain again. Fall in this city was nothing but wet and miserable. Like it knew its inhabitants. The city wore it like penance, washing the sins off the pavement just long enough to make room for new ones.

The sign for Escape glowed like a wound on the block when I pulled up. The bass hit low and heavy through the walls, steady as a heartbeat. I killed the engine and sat for a moment, watching the line of patrons snake toward the door, people already pawing at one another like hungry puppies.

I told myself I was here for one reason. Deliver the message. Keep it clean. But the lies always sound better when you whispered them to yourself.

The bouncer gave me a nod on my way in. Jackson, I think Sera had called him. Built like a bear and twice as mean when he wanted to be. He didn't stop me, didn't need to. My face was already filed under don't ask.

Inside, the air was thick with smoke, sex, and the underlying barley-and-hops stink that clung to the walls. Red and violet lights bled through the haze, painting everything in sin and shadow.

My eyes scanned the interior before landing on her. She was behind the bar, with her hair pulled back again, and the dim light catching the amber in it when she moved. Her hands worked smoothly and efficiently, like choreography she'd memorized long ago. When her eyes lifted and found mine, the noise of the club faded.

Her smile was soft, careful, almost shy. It wasn't for the crowd. It was for me, and it landed harder than I'd ever admit. I gave her a nod, small and deliberate. A silent *I see you.* Her fingers hesitated on the shaker, just barely, before she turned back to her customer. Good, keep working, Little Fawn. Pretend I'm not here, and let me stay in the shadows.

The music came roaring back as I moved through the crowd. Patrick's voice floated faintly over the speakers, smooth and sharp in equal measure. I took the narrow hallway behind the stage — the one that led toward Michael's office. The air there was different. Thicker, quieter, like the soundproofing knew what it was protecting people from.

Michael's door was cracked open just enough for me to see the flicker of the monitor light against his face. He was alone. Perfect. I didn't need witnesses for this conversation, so I pushed the door open without knocking.

He looked up, startled at first, then annoyed when he saw who it was. "Jesus, Kael. You ever hear of knocking?"

"Not when I'm sent to collect."

His expression shifted. A quick flash of fear behind the smirk. He tried to cover it with a laugh, but it landed flat.

"I paid! Conor got his fucking money!"

"Yeah. That's the problem."

I shut the door behind me, the click echoing louder than it needed to.

He swallowed hard. "Problem? What problem?"

"You got that money too quick, Michael. Makes Conor think you're hiding cash. Makes him decide you're worth testing."

I stepped closer, slow and deliberate, the floorboards creaking under my boots. "So now you pay double, in five days."

"Five… Kael, that's impossible."

"See now that sounds like a you problem, Michael."

His hands twitched on the desk. "He can't just—"

"He can," I cut in, my voice low and unwavering. "And he did."

Michael stood, trying to look taller than he was. "You could talk to him. Tell him…"

I narrowed my eyes at him and let a small, cold smile slip. "I'm not your message boy or your savior."

He deflated a little, shoulders sinking. "What the fuck does he want from me?"

A short laugh escaped me.

"Everything."

The silence stretched between us as the low thump of the club's bass filtered faintly through the walls, a reminder of the world still spinning just outside this room.

"Five days," I repeated, turning toward the door.

"Kael. You could help me. You've got his ear."

I stepped back and walked over to him. I leaned over him, as one hand found the back of his chair, and the other closed around his throat. He choked as his eyes grew wide, his mouth opening and closing like a fish. My fingers tightened hard enough for him to remember what I was capable of.

"You could stop buying escorts and gambling away everything you have. But you don't. Actions have consequences.

I am not your fucking savior. I am your executioner when you inevitably fail." I repeated the words slowly, forcing them down his throat.

I released him, smoothed my jacket, and turned for the door.

"Five days, Michael. Otherwise, I come back. And next time I won't be so gentle."

The door shut behind me like a tomb.

• • •

The air in the hall felt thicker after the heat of the room. I needed distance from his cheap fucking cologne, his fear, and the wretched sound of his voice trying to bargain with his own mistakes. That kind of sound that lingered if you didn't find a way to drown it out.

I stood a moment longer, listening as the noise of the club returned: bass, laughter, the clatter of glass swirling together. All of it was muted by the concrete walls. I didn't head for the front. Instead, my feet turned the other way, toward the back corridor and the exit that led to the alley. The metal door groaned when I pushed it open.

The rain had stopped, but the pavement still glistened. The alley was the same as always. Damp brick, flickering light, and the faint buzz of the transformer overhead were all reminders of where I was. The smell of smoke hit first, sharp and clean.

She was there. Leaning against the wall, one ankle crossed over the other, a cigarette between her fingers. The ember glowed orange against the dark. She tilted her head back, exhaled slowly, and for a second, I just watched the smoke curl away from her lips like something alive.

"Didn't picture you as the type to take a break," I rasped. My voice came out rough.

Her eyes flicked toward me, a small smirk tugging at the corner of her mouth. "Didn't picture you as the type to send flowers."

I let the door close behind me as the corners of my lips lifted slightly. "Didn't picture you as the type to appreciate them."

She laughed quietly, the sound softer than the night before. "You here for business again, or pleasure this time?"

"Business, baby girl. Always business."

"Right." She took another drag, the tip flaring bright. "You don't strike me as the type who knows how to relax."

I stepped closer, just enough for her perfume to cut through the smoke. "And you don't strike me as the type who smokes."

She lifted a brow. "I quit." Her laugh was soft. "And I'll quit again tomorrow."

I nodded slowly, understanding what she didn't say. She flicked the ash, the ember falling in a lazy arc to the wet ground. "You don't talk much, do you?"

"I prefer actions over words. Leaves less to misunderstand."

She huffed a small laugh, shaking her head. "I should go back inside."

"You should."

My gaze stayed locked on hers. She didn't move, and neither did I. The silence between us wasn't uncomfortable. It was the kind that hummed at the edge of something neither of us were ready to name.

When she finally stubbed out the cigarette and brushed past me, the scent of smoke and patchouli trailed in her wake. I reached out, catching her wrist gently. Her green eyes lifted, surprise flickering in them.

She didn't pull away. Just looked up at me like she was trying to see the man behind the monster. Her pulse jumped under my thumb where I traced slow circles against her skin. Her eyes dropped to my mouth, then back to my eyes as her tongue swept across her bottom lip.

I leaned in, closing the distance slowly, giving her every chance to move, and my pulse pounded hard in my ears when she didn't. My lips brushed hers in a ghost of a touch. Her breath caught, and then her free hand slid up, fingers curling behind my neck to pull me in. Her lips met mine with more force than I expected.

The taste of cigarettes and tequila mixed with something sweet and dizzying caught me off guard, and for a heartbeat, I didn't move. I just let the shock of it settle in my chest and then let instinct take over.

The hand that had been on her wrist slipped to the small of her back, pulling her against me. Her skin was warm against the chill of the night, and she melted into me, chest to chest, her breath quick and shallow. My other hand found her waist, and I pressed my palm flat against the curve of her hip. She fit there like she'd been made for it. The smell of her clung to the air between us, softening everything about me.

When she kissed me again, it wasn't careful. It was the kind of kiss that came from wanting too long. The kind of kiss that blurred all reason and lines. Her mouth parted, a soft sound caught in her throat, and I felt it more than heard it. Her fingers fisted the lapels of my jacket, dragging me closer.

My tongue found hers, swallowing her moan. A low growl rumbled from my chest as I caught her bottom lip between my teeth, gentle but firm. Her soft body molded against my hard edges. My fingers tightened on her hip. Not enough to hurt, just enough to remind her I was hers, before she even realized it. I broke the kiss for air, resting my forehead against hers.

"This is a bad idea."

But I didn't move away. I breathed her in deeply, letting her scent settle deep inside me.

Her lips brushed mine when she whispered, "Then stop."

I couldn't. I kissed her again, slower this time, and deeper. Her fingers tangled in my hair, tugging until it hurt in the best way. The alley tilted around us. The world shrank to heat, breath, and the sound of rain dripping from the eaves.

When I finally pulled back, she was still holding my jacket with one hand, knuckles white against the leather. Her pupils were blown wide, and her voice was barely a whisper.

"Next time, I prefer Fuji mums to dahlias."

A laugh broke out of me before I could stop it. Low and real. "Noted, Little Fawn."

That earned another soft laugh. She stepped back first, smoothing her jacket, eyes still locked on mine.

"I really should go."

She smiled almost regretfully.

"Yeah."

Neither of us moved until she leaned in and pressed a chaste kiss to my cheek and slipped back through the door, leaving me with the quiet hum of the transformer and the scent of her lingering in the night air.

I stayed in the alley long after she disappeared inside as the quiet came back heavy. I could still taste her on my tongue, still feel the echo of her body pressed to mine. It was the kind of memory that didn't fade. It carved itself into my skin and left behind a scar shaped like her name.

The city hummed, and a car passed on the main road, headlights spilling briefly into the mouth of the alley before fading again. Somewhere in the distance, someone laughed too loudly. Life went on, unaware that mine had just veered off course.

I pulled a cigarette from my jacket pocket. A habit I'd promised myself I'd broken, and it hung from my lips unlit for a moment before I flicked the lighter open. The flame stung my eyes as it caught. Smoke burned low in my chest, bitter and grounding.

The rain started again, light enough that I barely felt it. It darkened the concrete around my boots, ran down the back of my neck, and cooled the heat still burning there. I stood in it until the cigarette was half ash, then dropped it and crushed it under my heel.

Control said I should leave. Distance, clean lines, no witnesses. But I wasn't built for clean anymore. She'd seen through that. When I finally went back inside, the hall felt different. The noise from the club came in waves, carrying laughter, clinking glasses, and the low pulse of the bass. I moved through the shadows, back toward the main room.

• • •

She was behind the bar again, like nothing had happened. Calm, professional, and untouched. She didn't look at me when I stopped at the edge of the crowd. Smart girl. Her expression never faltered, but the way her shoulders stiffened for a heartbeat told me she knew I was there. That tiny tell buried itself inside my memory.

I let my eyes trace the crowd instead. Faces all blurred together in a sea of strangers, regulars, and predators. All of them were looking at her. And that, more than anything, tightened something dark in my chest. She laughed at something a customer said, tipping her head back as the light caught her throat. The sound shouldn't have cut me open the way it did.

I turned away before the thought could finish, before I could start justifying the wrong kind of impulse. In my world, weakness had a cost. And she was my only weakness. One I would gladly pay for, without a second thought.

By the time I stepped outside again, the street was almost empty, and the rain had given up, leaving the air damp and cold. I unlocked the car and sat for a long minute, engine idling.

Through the windshield, the club sign glowed steady and red. Escape. The word looked like a warning. Five days. That was all Michael had. Five days to come up with 'double or die'-trying. I shook my head, not caring if he could manage the miracle Conor was asking for. It wasn't my problem. He would just be another mess for me to eventually dispose of.

The city stretched out in front of me, endless and unkind. I closed my eyes, and for a moment, all I could see was her. Smoke curling around her lips, eyes gone soft in the dark, the way she had whispered "then stop" like it was a challenge she knew I couldn't back down from.

I put the car in gear and pulled away from the curb. The reflection of the club's neon followed me in the rearview, shrinking smaller and smaller until it disappeared behind the rain. But the ghost of her stayed. And I knew, down to the bone, I'd crossed the line I drew for myself.

There was no going back from this. Not for me. Not for her. Not ever.

Chapter Eleven

Benjamin

Cameras never lie. They don't flinch or blink. They don't have the luxury of pretending something isn't happening, and that was why I liked them.

The feed from Michael's office flickered across the monitors, like a miniature world of smoke and fear. I leaned back in the cheap rolling chair, a coffee going cold at my elbow, and watched Kael move like a storm across the room.

Michael sat behind his desk, shoulders stiff, and his mouth running faster than his brain. His voice filled the air with useless noise, a distraction meant to disguise the sound of his own heartbeat. I turned up the volume just enough to hear.

"Five days."

Kael's voice was as steady as a surgeon's hands.

Michael's face drained of color. "Five… Kael, that's impossible!"

Kael didn't answer right away. He just stared the kind of stare that stripped a man down to his bones. When he finally spoke, it was quiet enough that the mic barely caught it.

"Sounds like a you problem, Michael."

I smiled. There it was. The threat. Precise, clean, and surgical. Conor would be pleased. Or not. It was always hard to tell with him.

Michael tried to bargain again, his voice trembling, when Kael leaned forward, one hand curling around his throat. The audio crackled at the sound of a choked breath. I tilted my head, studying the way the muscle in Kael's forearm flexed as he squeezed. Controlled and calculating. Perfect in its own violent way.

"Five days," Kael repeated as he released him.

When Kael left the office, the camera caught the door swinging shut behind him. Michael stayed slumped in his chair, one hand clutching his throat like he could hold his pride together through pressure alone.

I muted the feed, and silence rolled over the small office like smoke. Five days and double the payment. Conor's math was something to behold. Still, it would serve its purpose. Fear was the most reliable currency in this business, and Michael had plenty to spend.

I leaned forward, elbows on the desk, and watched the loop replay. My reflection ghosted faintly over the screen as a slow smile curled across my lips. Kael was slipping. I could see it in the hesitation at the door, the faint tremor of conflict under all that steel. Whatever had his attention was new, and it was dangerous.

The alley camera told me why when I flicked through feeds until I found him in the narrow strip of darkness behind the club, where she was out for her break. Seraphine. Fuck, she was beautiful. Michael's little prize, though he never understood what he had when it came to her.

She was smoking, rain streaking down her leather jacket, and Kael was watching her like she was oxygen. The angle caught just enough. A half-lit kiss. Her hand in his hair. His body bending toward her like gravity itself had changed direction. Leverage always looked the same. Two people, too close, with one of them forgetting who might be watching.

"Jesus, Kael," I muttered. "What the fuck are you doing?"

I cut the feed when the door closed behind her, leaving Kael alone in the rain. I sat back and ran a hand through my hair. Fuck. This was going to complicate things. He had crossed a line he couldn't uncross. And Michael. Poor, stupid Michael. He had no idea the woman he paraded around like a trophy was about to become the knife that cut him open.

I picked up the phone and dialed a number I knew by heart. It rang once before Conor answered.

"Talk."

"Your message was received. Five days and double the amount. That's quite the ask, Conor."

"And Michael?"

"Terrified. Exactly how you like them. But there's something else." I glanced at the frozen alley image; her hand pressed against Kael's chest. "Your attack dog found himself a new toy."

"Oh?" The intrigue in his tone was unmistakable.

"She could be a complication. A big one."

Conor laughed softly. The sound made my skin crawl. "Good. Distractions make monsters easier to leash."

He hung up before I could respond. The line went dead, leaving only the hum of the monitors as I stared at the alley feed and felt that familiar pull between loyalty and survival.

Kael was a weapon, sharp and unflinching. But weapons weren't meant to feel, and the moment they did, someone always had to pull the trigger. I had seen it before.

I walked back into the bar like a man who had only stepped out for a smoke. A smirk on my lips, and a bounce in my step. The room swallowed me without hesitation. Laughter, clinking glass, bass thudding like a heart that didn't care who bled. I moved through it on instinct, a shadow threading between bodies that never noticed the hand pulling the strings.

Plan-making was its own kind of intimacy. It was all about the details, patience, and a refusal to let sentiment take a back seat. I found a stool at the far end of the bar where the light was dimmer, and the faces didn't matter.

Seraphine was there, pouring like the whole room depended on her rhythm. She glanced up, caught my eye for half a second, and went back to work.

My mind ticked through the club's ledger like an accountant with a vendetta. Michael's debts. Conor's appetite. Five days ticking down like a timer I could hear in the walls. Cash fixed some problems, and this place ran on more than cash. Flesh was tradeable, loyalties were negotiable, and a clean story could bind harder than any contract.

The decision arrived like an instruction. Trade one of the girls to erase the debt. Brutal, sure. But also clean and effective. And it wouldn't be my job to pick. Conor always chose for himself. He had a taste for what he wanted and the patience to wait until a man presented it on a platter. Which meant my job wasn't to decide who went but to make the logistics invisible. Make it look inevitable. Make Michael wake up to a debt erased and a life rearranged without ever knowing the cost.

It would be easy to make one of these girls disappear without a trace. A little something extra in a drink before close. A walk out the back door while the camera conveniently went down. Conor loved finding new playthings and breaking them under his thumb. What Conor did with some whore wasn't my problem. If it cleared the debt, it was a solution.

I thumbed my phone from my pocket. The screen cast a glow that felt more honest than any face in this room. I opened Conor's chat and watched the cursor blink. Violence could be suggested without a single explicit word. I didn't type an offer or a threat. I typed something that felt like both.

Benjamin: *Tonight? Come by. Let's talk business.*

Simple and clean. Nothing that tied hands or names to the action. An invitation that left just enough room for appetite to fill in the rest. It let a man imagine the worst and decide whether he liked how it felt.

I hit send, set the phone face down, and finished my drink.

I'm a goddamn hero to this place, I thought as I slipped behind the bar again.

• • •

An hour or so later, as I wiped down the counter, the crowd shifted and parted like water pushed aside by the tide. Conor and his entourage walked in. Men like him didn't bother with lines or memberships. They arrived, and the room rearranged itself around them. I nodded toward the back rooms as he passed.

"Sera."

She glanced over.

"Watch the bar. I've got a meeting, and they don't like to be kept waiting."

I didn't wait for her answer; I moved through the crowd with purpose, a snake gliding through tall grass. The office door clicked shut behind me.

Conor sat in Michael's chair with his boots propped on the desk, and his eyes fixed on the monitors like he owned every inch of the place. His expression didn't flicker.

"What do you want, Benny?" His Irish accent rolled thick and unhurried.

"A trade. For the debt."

My voice stayed even, the same tone I'd use ordering a sandwich. Conor nodded, still staring at the screens.

"Alright, I'm a fair man. What do you think is a fair trade for Micky's debt to my boys and me?"

I glanced at his goons, a wall of muscle on either side.

"One of our girls. Take your pick. Plenty here who fit your preferences."

Conor's lips twitched into something that wasn't quite a smile.

"Any girl?"

"Not any girl. Pick one without consequences. No family that'll make a lot of noise. No men who'll come looking. I don't clean up loose ends I didn't create."

He hummed, sounding pleased.

"Interesting."

"Pick your poison. No returns and no second thoughts. You get a new toy, Michael keeps his club, and this meeting never happened."

Conor leaned forward and tapped the monitor glass, each tap deliberate.

"A new toy. I like the sound of that."

His gaze drifted to the bar footage as Seraphine poured a drink, her eyes lowered, and her movements smooth and almost graceful. His attention fixated on her like a hunter settling on a target.

"That one. She looks breakable."

Heat crept up my neck, but his choice wasn't a surprise. Her calm mixed with her poise, and the shape of someone else's interest already on her skin. Conor liked trophies. The kind of beauty before it shattered, and strength right before it broke.

"Done. We'll keep it clean. She'll be gone like she never existed. No records. No payroll. Nothing to trace. Tomorrow night at closing. Have a car waiting in the alley after midnight."

One of his men cracked a smile that didn't reach his eyes.

"Efficient."

"Always."

"And you might want to send Kael on a job tomorrow," I added. "He's taken a shine to this one. He'll be more compliant if he thinks she just left him."

"Done," Conor replied. "Kael won't be an issue. He knows who signs his pay."

He leaned back in the chair, smug and satisfied.

I stood and adjusted my jacket. "I'll handle the handoff. You keep Kael blind."

He nodded, and his men relaxed.

I walked out of the office feeling lighter. A plan always settled something inside me.

At the bar, Seraphine wiped down a glass and glanced up at me, her professional smile wide on her lips. She didn't realize she had just become a line item on a ledger she never agreed to, and I would need to keep it that way.

I gave her a small nod.

"Take five, Sera. Go for a walk. You deserve it."

Suspicion flickered through her eyes, but only for a moment.

"Alright." She shrugged, tossed a towel over her shoulder, and slipped into the crowd.

I watched her move, measuring the moment the way a man measures a cut. Conor was going to break that sharp mouth of hers, and the thought sent a slow curl of heat through me. I didn't let it linger; I just took another order from a faceless patron and kept my hands steady.

Conor wasn't a patient man, but I was. Patience was where closure lived, and closure was something I could wait for.

Eventually, Kael would learn what happened. He would learn who vanished while he was gone, and when that moment came, there would be a price. Not tonight, though. Tonight, the clock simply kept ticking.

Chapter Twelve

Kael

The next night, the club felt wrong. Not loud wrong. Not busy wrong. Just… off. Like every light was a watt too dim and every shadow knew something I didn't.

I'd been useless all day. Couldn't eat, couldn't sleep. Could still feel her on me, as if a piece of her had wedged itself into my skin. Her pulse, her breath, her mouth tilting up into mine like she didn't mean to give me anything and still gave me everything. One kiss, and she was tattooed on my soul.

I told myself that's why I came early. Told myself I was checking on Conor's interests, checking Michael, checking the crowd. But it wasn't the job that had my boots tracking down the back hallway. It was her. It was always her.

She stepped out of Michael's office right as I rounded the corner. Not dressed up, not made up, just unapologetically her. Hair pulled back, eyes tired, shoulders tight like she'd fought with someone. Or maybe she had been fighting herself. She froze when she saw me, and I swear I stopped breathing. Just for a second. Just for a single heartbeat.

Her lips parted slightly with that same stunned look she had in the alley, like she didn't understand what I did to her any more than I understood what she'd done to me.

"Kael," she whispered.

That was it. That was all it took. I crossed the space before I even thought about it. My hand found her wrist, careful, firm, but not giving her time to talk me down or walk away. Her breath stuttered, but she didn't pull away.

"Come here," I said, voice low enough it barely counted as sound.

I tugged her through the storage closet door, the one barely used anymore, and it clicked shut behind us with a final, absolute sound. The room went dark except for a single sliver of light under the door, enough to outline her face. Enough to make restraint a goddamn joke.

She backed up until she hit a shelf, and the bar towels shifted behind her, and I stepped forward until there was no air left between us.

"About last night," I started, my voice soft and even. I didn't mean for it to sound so fucking stupid, but God, it did.

Her chin lifted. "What about it?"

My body reacted before my mind could. That chin lifting in defiance and that fucking mouth grinning at me like that? Oh, you little brat. She was going to learn how to curb that beautiful mouth of hers, and if not, I'd enjoy teaching her.

"Little Fawn…" The nickname came out as more of a growl than I intended.

Her breath caught, and I smirked and leaned in. Her fingers curled in the fabric of her shirt like she was holding herself together. "Kael, we shouldn't…"

"Oh?" I asked quietly. "I can't pretend when it comes to you, Sera. You're mine, and I've come to collect."

Her pulse jumped, and I watched her artery throb against the skin on her neck. I braced one hand beside her head on the shelf, caging her in without touching her. My other hand hovered just above her waist. All my restraint in not touching, not yet. She looked up at me with those perfect green eyes, wide and locked on mine.

"Everything I've done," I murmured. "From the asshole platinum member to Cameron. Every move has been to protect you, save you… *keep* you."

She exhaled sharply. "I don't need saving."

She tried to push past me, but I caught her waist and pulled her back into me.

"Kael, please…" Her voice cracked softly, but she didn't pull away.

"Tell me you hate me, Sera. Tell me you want nothing to do with me, and I'll walk out this door nothing more than a ghost."

Silence as her throat bobbed and her eyes lifted to mine. Her voice came out soft, just quiet enough to destroy me:

"I can't."

My chest tightened so sharply I had to close my eyes. Because that sound, that simple fucking confession, hit harder than any punch I'd ever taken. When I opened them again, she wasn't backing away. She was leaning in.

"I don't know what this is," she whispered. "But it scares me. *You* scare me."

"Good. I should scare you. I'm the devil's right hand. The one they call when things need to get messy before they get cleaned."

Her lips parted, barely a breath, and my restraint started to crack. I let my fingertips rest on her waist in just a whisper of contact, and she shivered like I'd put my mouth on her instead.

"Sera, you have no idea what I'm trying not to do right now."

"Then stop trying," she breathed.

Her words released a sound from me I didn't know I was capable of making. Something between a growl riding on the back of a need I'd held back for too long. I didn't grab her. Didn't pin her to the shelf. Didn't take the kiss I'd been dying for all damn day.

I stepped in close enough that my forehead touched hers, our breath mingling together in the dark.

"I want you. God help me, I fucking want you. I want to mark your skin and hear you scream my name in the dark. I want to erase any thought you've ever had that didn't include me."

Her hand found my chest, neither pushing me away nor stopping me. Just holding onto me like I was her lifeline, and maybe she was mine.

"Kael…" Her voice was a goddamn balm, and I never wanted her to stop saying my name.

I cupped the side of her jaw with my palm. My touch stayed gentle, reverent, nothing like the man I was supposed to be.

"You're mine. Only ever mine."

"Yours," she breathed in reply.

My lips crashed into hers. A claiming. A surrender. A fucking cataclysm of the inevitable.

She gasped into my mouth, her fingers fisting in the front of my shirt like she was trying to pull me closer and hold me back at the same time. I didn't give her the choice. My hand slid from her jaw to the back of her neck, holding her exactly where I wanted her as I deepened the kiss.

She made a sound. The noise was something soft, wrecked, desperate, and it detonated something inside me. Her other hand slid up my chest, over my throat, into my hair as she tugged.

Christ.

I groaned against her mouth as my restraint unraveled strand by strand. Her body fit against mine like she'd been carved out of the same damn shadow. She arched up on instinct, and my grip on her waist tightened, dragging her against me, letting her feel every hard inch of what she was doing to me. The shelf behind her rattled when I pressed her back into it. She didn't even flinch; she just pulled me closer.

My mouth left hers only long enough to drag down her jaw, to feel the sharp hitch of her breath when my lips reached her throat. She tilted her head, exposing more skin, as if she didn't even realize she was offering it.

"Careful," I murmured against her pulse. "When you offer your throat to a wolf, they take it."

Her fingers curled tighter in my hair. "It's yours."

"Say it again."

I didn't recognize my own voice; the sound was low and hungry, shaking with the effort not to lose myself in her completely.

"It's yours. *I'm* yours."

Fuuuuuck. I growled against her skin, my hands slid lower, gripping her hips, pulling her flush against me until there wasn't a single inch of space left to pretend. She rose up to meet me, breath hot and needy as she trembled in my hold.

Her nails scraped lightly down my neck, and I swore under my breath again, mouth returning to hers in a kiss that was pure hunger. She kissed me back like she'd been waiting her whole life for this moment. As if the fear didn't matter, like the world outside that door didn't exist.

Her leg brushed mine, tentative. Then again, bolder, hooking over my hip like she didn't even realize she was doing it. My hand shot down to catch her thigh, and she froze. Not in fear, but in want. Her breath broke in a way that nearly took me to my knees.

I dragged her leg higher against my waist, feeling her melt into me, the way her body answered mine with instinct, with heat, and with something that felt so fucking close to surrender.

I rocked my hips into her, my cock pressing against her core.

Her mouth opened against mine, and her fingers tightened as her whole body pressed into me like she didn't know how to stop.

"Little Fawn…" I whispered against her lips, voice ruined. "If I don't stop right now, I won't stop at all."

She looked up at me, pupils blown wide, lips swollen, as her chest rose fast against mine.

"Then don't."

The growl I let out at her words was more animal than human. My hands roamed her body possessively, mapping every curve, every dip, committing her to memory. I nipped at her bottom lip hard enough to sting, soothing the hurt with a swipe of my tongue.

"Mine," I growled against her mouth, the word vibrating through her like a physical caress. "You are all fucking mine."

Sera keened, arching into me, desperate for more of my touch, my grip, my everything. Her fingers dug into my shoulders, her nails digging into the fabric of my shirt, anchoring herself against the tidal wave of sensation.

My other hand slid under her thigh, hoisting her up effortlessly. Instinctively, Sera wrapped her legs around my waist like she fucking belonged there. The new position pressed her core directly against the hard ridge of my cock, separated only by the thin barrier of her panties and my zipper. She rolled her hips, grinding down on me with shameless need as towels tumbled to the floor around us, forgotten in the haze of lust.

"Please," she whimpered against my lips.

Her breathy plea made my dick twitch. Her hands fisted in my hair, tugging sharply, urging me closer. She peppered kisses along my jaw, down my throat, biting at my pulse point hard enough to leave a mark. My Little Fawn was claiming me as thoroughly as I was claiming her.

"These have to go."

I hooked my fingers in the waistband of her panties. With one swift yank, I ripped the delicate lace, tossing the shredded remains aside carelessly.

"Now, I need to fucking taste you."

Without saying another word, I gently lowered her legs back down to the floor before kneeling in front of her and kissing upwards along the inside of her thighs.

Her legs spread further apart, inviting me to go deeper; her wordless consent fueled my need higher. I kissed along the apex of her thighs, as her already soaking cunt beckoned me closer.

The moan mixed with a yelp she let out was music to my ears as I lifted a thigh over my shoulder and licked a stripe straight up her middle before nipping softly at her clit.

The sweetness of her hit my tongue, and my eyes rolled back in my head. She was everything I didn't know I had been missing, and I was feasting on everything she was.

My tongue worked her clit in soft circles as I slid two fingers inside her. Her walls immediately clamped down around me as her hips rocked forward. My name falling from her lips was like a siren's call, and I couldn't get enough.

"That's it, baby. Let me hear you," my voice rumbled against her flesh, the vibrations sending shockwaves through her.

"Ride my fucking face like the queen you are. Let the whole club hear you come undone on my tongue."

I sealed my lips around her clit, sucking hard as I curled my fingers, rubbing that perfect spot deep inside her.

My other hand gripped her ass tightly, holding her flush against my face as I worked her higher with wild abandon, determined to wring every last drop of pleasure from her shaking body.

Her fingers tangled in my hair, tugging sharply as incoherent moans spilled from her lips. The wet sounds of my mouth on her cunt filled the room, and the way she whimpered had me desperate.

"Oh god, Kael!" she cried out, her hips bucking erratically against my face.

"Don't stop, don't you dare fucking stop! I'm so close!"

Her thighs trembled, muscles drawing taut as her walls gripped and released my fingers rhythmically. I redoubled my efforts, tongue flicking rapidly over her clit as my fingers drove into her.

"That's it, Little Fawn. Come for me," I breathed against her core.

With a moan that carried into a scream, she shattered beautifully. Her orgasm crashed through her in waves, and I couldn't get enough. Her back bowed off the shelf, toes curling as her release gushed over my tongue, and I lapped up every drop, refusing to let a drop of my perfect, stunning creature go to waste. I kept my fingers pressed inside her, prolonging her high with skillful strokes of my tongue.

"Fuck, Sera." I moaned her name, the vibrations of my voice extending her pleasure.

As she began to come down, I gentled my touch, letting her ease down slowly. I kissed along her inner thighs softly, against her clit, her belly, working my way up her body reverently.

"You have no idea what you fucking do to me," I said, before kissing her deeply and letting her taste herself on my tongue.

My kiss was filthy and a blatant reclaiming of her. I deepened it further, swallowing her mewls and whimpers, staking my claim on every inch of her. My hands mapped her curves, squeezing, kneading, leaving no doubt in her mind about my possession.

"I could devour you for hours," I murmured against her lips, my voice thick with desire.

"Lick every inch of this gorgeous body until you're drunk on pleasure, and the only thing you remember is my name."

I nipped at her bottom lip before soothing the sting with a swipe of my tongue. My hips ground against her, the thick ridge of my cock pressing insistently against her, seeking friction.

Her hands trailed down my chest, teasing along the skin before resting on the button of my jeans. Her eyes looked up at me, seeking permission, even now.

I nodded my head once, and she grinned, her lips curling like the Cheshire cat before her fingers deftly undid my pants. Her hand slid inside, sliding under the waistband of my boxers, and as she gripped my aching shaft, my hips bucked against her.

"Fuck, baby, let me fill you," I groaned, my face buried in her neck.

Her eyes looked up at me, pupils blown and full of desperate need, before she slid my pants and boxers down my legs. She turned around, bending over one of the shelves, and looked back at me, her bottom lip between her teeth.

"Make it hurt," she begged, her hand gripping the shelving tighter as she pressed herself back against me.

My entire body stiffened at her filthy words, and with a feral growl, I grabbed her hips, yanking her back against me.

The head of my cock pressed against her entrance, slick with pre-cum. I teased the tip along her slit, rubbing small circles around her clit. Without warning, I lined myself up and slammed forward, sheathing myself so fucking deep inside her I needed to take a moment, and just feel her around me. Both of us groaned in pleasure.

"Fuck, you feel incredible," I snarled, beginning a punishing pace. Each powerful thrust jostled the shelves, sending various items tumbling to the floor.

The lewd slap of skin on skin echoed around us. I pulled her back against my chest, slamming into her over and over. My teeth found the juncture of her neck and shoulder, biting down hard enough to leave a vivid mark.

"No one else touches you like this again," I warned, licking along the mark of her neck as my hips continued to snap against hers.

"You're mine, Little Fawn."

She cried out loudly, her fingers scrabbling for purchase on the shelf as I pounded into her relentlessly. I changed my angle to hit that place deep inside her with every thrust, stoking the flames of her pleasure higher and higher.

"Yours!" she wailed, pushing back to meet my brutal pace.

Her inner walls fluttered and clenched around my cock as I drove into her, drawing me in deeper. The smell of her filled the air, as both of us chased our release.

My hand slid from her hips, up her chest, before resting against her neck. Her breath hitched as my hand clenched around her throat, tightening and cutting off her air just enough to make her gasps come in short, rapid pants.

"Show me how good you are and cum all over my cock. Mark me in the way only you can," I breathed against her skin, my voice thick with my own impending release.

I gradually tightened my hand around her throat, applying just enough pressure to heighten her arousal without completely restricting her airflow. I relished the feel of her as the dual sensations of my cock pounding into her and my strong grip sent her hurtling over the edge.

"Fuck!" She screamed, another orgasm crashing through her like a tidal wave.

Her walls clamped around me as her knees buckled. I held her tighter to me, not slowing my pace but fucking her through it. Her release rushed out of her, coating my shaft and slickening our thighs.

"Just like that, baby, good girl." I groaned, grinding into her harder.

Her rhythmic clench and release milked my cock, pulling me over the edge with her. I slammed into her, once, twice, three times before stilling, my cock spilling inside her as I groaned into the skin between her shoulder blades.

For a long moment, neither of us moved. I stayed inside her, chest pressed to her back, forehead resting between her shoulder blades as both of us dragged for breath. Her skin was hot under my mouth, and my hands stayed locked around her hips like I needed to hold her together so she didn't slip through my fingers.

Slowly, painfully, my mind started to crawl back into my body. And then it hit me. That kind of clarity that could level a man. I would burn the whole goddamn world for her. I would ruin anyone who tried to take her from me. And if she ever asked for pieces of me in return, I'd hand them over without hesitation. I swallowed hard, my chest rising against her back.

"Easy, baby girl," I murmured, barely audible, easing my grip so I wasn't caging her. "I've got you."

Her body softened in my hold, trusting and pliant. Dangerous to trust a man like me. Nobody had ever trusted me like that. No one should. I eased out of her slowly, and her whimper made me slow further. I already missed the feel of her around me, and I knew in that moment that I was hers as much as she was mine.

I steadied her when her knees threatened to give, and she let out a shaky breath as she leaned into me just enough that my heart nearly split open.

"Stay right here," I whispered.

Reaching blindly to the side, I grabbed one of the towels that had fallen during our chaos. The fabric brushed over my knuckles, soft and familiar. I brought it between her legs gently, wiping her clean, with slow and reverent strokes.

Her breath hitched every time my fingers skimmed her skin. I didn't speak. I couldn't find the words. My throat felt wrecked, and my chest carved open.

When I finished, I pressed a soft kiss to the small of her back. Then another, trailing up her spine, along her shoulders. The motions were quiet, apologetic, and worshipful.

She turned her head slightly, like she didn't know how to look at me without breaking, and I almost kissed her again just to stop the ache.

I helped her step into her clothes, guiding the fabric over her hips and smoothing it into place. My hands shook a little. She let herself melt into my touch.

Finally, when she was steady on her feet again, I reached up and cupped the back of her neck, letting my thumb stroke once along her hairline.

"Look at me." I angled her head up to face me. And fuck, that look. Those green eyes, bright as emeralds, stared back at me like I wasn't the big bad wolf. She was trying not to fall, and I was trying not to break.

"I…" The words jammed in my throat.

I'd just had her in every way I'd ever dared imagine, and still, saying it felt harder somehow than taking her apart.

My phone vibrated in my pocket, shattering the moment. I groaned softly and pressed a kiss to her forehead. Slowly, I reached for it and looked at the screen.

Conor.

A cold, electric dread shot through me so fast it stole the warmth from the room.

"Fuck," I whispered.

Sera's brows pulled together. "Kael…?"

I shook my head, jaw clenching, the war already starting inside me.

"I'm sorry, baby. I have to take this." My voice came out raw and apologetic.

Her face shifted. From fear she tried to hide, to understanding she didn't want to give. I pressed my forehead to hers, just for a beat, breathing her in like it might be the last time.

"I'll be right back," I promised, pulling her fingers to my lips and kissing her knuckles softly.

I didn't know if it was a lie, but I said it anyway. Then I hit *accept*, and everything inside me went cold.

• • •

I stepped out of the storage room and gave her one small glance back before shutting the door. I leaned back against it for half a second like I could hold the world in place even when I knew I couldn't, and I lifted the phone to my ear.

"Yeah."

A beat of silence before Conor's voice slipped through the speaker, smooth as expensive whiskey and twice as dangerous.

"Good lad. Thought you might ignore me."

My jaw tightened. "I was busy."

"Oh, I'm sure you were."

That smile in his voice and that knowing hum. My stomach turned to ice.

"You needed something?" I asked.

"A favor. One that requires your… particular touch."

Dread slid down my spine.

"Name it."

"Couple of lads from the docks tried to move a shipment they shouldn't have," Conor stated, tone still deceptively calm.

"You're going to pay them a visit and have one of your convincing chats."

I frowned. "That's grunt work. You don't need me for that."

"Aye," he agreed. "I don't. But I *want* you to do it."
Something inside me twisted up, and my fist balled at my side.

"What's the real job?" I asked, voice low.

"That *is* the job. Check your messages. The address is there. You leave now."

I looked toward the storage room door. Toward the woman I had just taken apart and put back together with my hands, my mouth, my body. Toward the only thing in this place that felt like it belonged to me, and my heart hammered against my ribs.

"Conor—"

"No."

His tone hardened instantly. "You work for me, Kael. You go where I fucking tell you to go."

My jaw locked so hard my teeth ached as a pulse of irritation flared in my chest.

"You could send anyone."

"I know. But I'm sending you."

That sinking feeling returned, settling deep in my gut. It wasn't panic or suspicion. Just the cold understanding that when Conor wanted something done a certain way, it didn't matter how many bodies it burned through.

"You leave now," he repeated. "Handle it cleanly and call me when it's done."

I ran a hand down my face, fingers dragging over my mouth as I fought the urge to refuse to walk back into that storage room, pull Sera into my arms, and tell Conor he could handle his own damn mess.
But that wasn't how this world worked. I'd made my choices years ago, and men like me didn't get to walk away.

"Fine," I muttered. "Text me the address."

"Oh, I already have. You'll want to be quick, lad. They won't wait around all night." The amusement in his voice was like ice on my teeth.

The line cut off before I could respond. Typical. I stared at my dark reflection on the phone screen, jaw tense, and my heart still thudding too hard in my chest. Then I turned back toward the storage room.

I shouldn't open that door again. If I did, I wasn't leaving at all. I pressed my palm to the wood, just once. Just long enough.

"Dammit…" I whispered under my breath.

Then I forced myself to walk away. The hallway looked different when I stepped away from her. Colder and longer, like the shadows had stretched themselves out just to keep me from turning back.

I moved fast, boots thudding against the concrete, each step heavier than the last. The noise of the club bled through the walls. The bass thumping, glasses clinking, and laughter rising sharply. Normal. Alive. None of it made sense against the cold sinking in my gut.

I adjusted my jacket, forcing my breathing to level out, but it didn't help. Her cum was still on my tongue, and her pulse still throbbed against my palm. Her voice, wrecked and breaking, still echoed in my skull as she offered herself to me. And now I was walking away from her.

I pushed through the back staff door and into the alley. The night slapped me immediately: cold air, wet pavement, mist turning the neon into smeared streaks of color. It felt wrong, the way the world kept moving as if nothing had happened. Like I hadn't just crossed a line there was no coming back from.

A streetlight flickered overhead, buzzing loud enough to grate against my already frayed nerves. My hands flexed at my sides, and I'd never wanted to hit something so badly in my life. She was in there, alone and trusting me to come back.

"You're a fucking idiot," I muttered under my breath.

My footsteps echoed as I crossed to my car, each one a reminder of everything I was choosing, and everything I wasn't allowed to keep.

I unlocked the door, slid into the driver's seat, and gripped the wheel until my knuckles whitened. The interior smelled of leather, rain, and gun oil. Familiar. Steady. Safe. Even when I didn't feel like any of those things.

I grabbed my phone and stared at the address Conor had sent until the letters blurred. I forced myself to breathe past the urge to go back inside, grab Sera, and drag her out of this place entirely.

I hadn't lost control like that in years. I hadn't wanted something like that in even longer, and that terrified me more than any job Conor had ever given me.

I started the engine, and the headlights cut through the misty dark, the twin beams slicing open the alley. The rain picked up, tapping against the windshield in uneven rhythms, like a soft percussion to match the storm building behind my ribs.

I pulled out onto the street, and every inch of me felt wrong. Every instinct screamed that I shouldn't be leaving her behind. That the night had teeth and I'd just turned my back on them. But I drove anyway. Because that's what ghosts like me do. We leave the living behind and handle the darkness for them. Even if it kills us.

Chapter Thirteen

Seraphine

Ten minutes. That's all it had been. Ten minutes wasn't long, not really. Not enough time for anything terrible to happen. Just long enough for the noise in my head to wake up.

I sat on the low shelf where he'd lifted me, where his hands had held me open and shaking, and I tried to breathe past the ringing in my ears. The linen room felt smaller now, like the walls were leaning in, pressing their weight against my ribs.

He said he'd be right back. He said it softly, as if he'd meant it. I twisted the skin beside my thumb until it stung. Then harder. The sharpness helped for a second. Just a second. Then the quiet came rushing back, louder.

Maybe he'd just stepped into the hallway.

Maybe he was grabbing water.

Maybe—

My throat tightened.

Maybe he left.

I shoved that thought away, fast and violently, but it kept scraping up the inside of my skull, refusing to stay buried.

My leg bounced, so I stood up because sitting still felt like drowning. The room was too warm, too dark. The smell of us mixed with clean towels was suddenly suffocating, clinging to my skin like feelings I didn't know how to name.

I paced once. Twice. Three times. On the fourth lap, I stopped at the door, fingers hovering over the handle. He was coming back. He was. I cracked the door open anyway.

The hallway stretched empty, washed in the soft gold of the old factory lights. No footsteps. No voice. No Kael leaning against the wall with that look he got when he was trying to hide how much he cared. My heart heaved with a small, stupid ache, and I swallowed back a lump in my throat.

Maybe he went to the bar. Or the bathroom. Or to check something. Anything. I slipped out of the room, biting my lip so hard it almost bled. Just to check. Just to make sure. Just so my brain would shut up.

My footsteps sounded too loud as I moved down the hallway, every shadow impossibly bright, every silence swallowing me whole.

"Kael?" I whispered once, too soft for anyone to hear.

No answer. My stomach twisted, and I walked faster.

The hallway felt too long, like it stretched farther with every step I took. The bass from the club thudded through the walls in slow, uneven pulses, like a heartbeat that couldn't decide if it wanted to keep going.

I turned the corner toward the bar, where Patrick should be. He was always there. Sharp-tongued, unbothered, steady in a way nobody else in this place managed to be. And he hated Kael enough to glare me back into my senses. Normal, safe, predictable Patrick.

• • •

I pushed through the swinging back door and stepped into the familiar low glow of the bar area. My eyes darted to his DJ booth. His backup DJ was where he should be. She flashed me a grin that was too bright and too happy. I frowned in her direction.

I glanced back over to the bar, my eyes scanning it, desperate for some piece of normalcy, anything to ground me before I spiraled completely.

My eyes landed on one of the new bartenders. A kid with wide eyes and jittery hands who looked at me like he couldn't tell if I was supposed to be there or not. *Fuck*.

My heart dropped straight through my stomach. "Patrick?" I asked over the music, leaning closer so he could hear.

The kid shook his head. "He… uh… he clocked out early. Said he wasn't feeling great."

Not feeling great? Patrick didn't *feel* things. He bulldozed through them with sarcasm and caffeine and sheer spite. He wouldn't have left unless he was actually sick. Or he found some new femdom to leash him and drag him home.

Everything around me was shifting under my feet. I swallowed hard, fingers curling into the edge of the bar until my knuckles ached. The panic rising in my chest was warm and sticky, like honey that had gone bad.

"He didn't say anything else?" I managed.

The bartender shook his head again. "Sorry."

I nodded even though I wasn't okay. My throat felt too tight, and my skin burned too hot. Kael was gone. Patrick was gone. And suddenly the whole club felt like it was tilting sideways, as if gravity had changed without warning.

The crowd pressed in around me. Too much all at once. The bodies and perfume and sweat, the clatter of glasses. Fuck! Every sound felt sharp enough to cut. I needed air. I needed quiet. I needed—

Kael. A stupid and dangerous thought, and one I forced down before it could take root.

I flopped down into one of the barstools, letting the room close in around me. The new kid, Jeremy, I think his name was, poured me a shot without a word, and I gratefully slung it back.

The burn settled in my stomach like molten metal, heat blooming outward in a slow, painful wave. It helped. It wasn't enough, but it was just enough to make the edges blur instead of sharpen. I set the glass down, but my hand didn't stop shaking.

My brain kept replaying it all. Kael's mouth on mine. Kael's breath against my throat. Kael's voice, rough and starving, whispering *mine* like it mattered. Like I fucking mattered. It shouldn't replay like this. It shouldn't ache like this.

It was just sex.

Just a moment.

Just a mistake I let myself fall into because he made it feel like gravity.

My fingers pressed into the bar top hard enough that I felt the wood grain bite my palms. Anything to keep myself anchored. Anything to keep from thinking, but my brain refused to listen.

His hands had been gentle. He didn't touch me like I was something he picked up out of boredom. He touched me like I was something he'd wanted for a long time. Something he was afraid to break. And now he was gone.

Just like every other man who'd taken too much.

Just like every time I believed softness meant safety.

Just like every moment in my life where wanting something was the fastest way to lose it.

I dug my nails into my thigh hard. The pain steadied me for a heartbeat, just long enough to breathe.

Don't do this.

Don't fall apart here.

Not where someone can see you.

But the thoughts kept coming, louder and louder, clawing up the inside of my ribs until they hurt. Maybe he realized what I am. What I'm not. How I break too easily. How I cling when I shouldn't. How I'm not the kind of woman men stay for.

Maybe he walked out of that room, felt the air hit him, and remembered he didn't owe me anything. My throat closed around the thought. It was risky to expect otherwise, and stupid to hope. Insane to think that someone like him, someone dangerous, steady, and terrifying in all the ways that made me feel safe, would actually come back for someone like me. My past curled up in my chest like a cold, familiar weight.

Men don't stay.

Men always leave after they take what they want.

You knew better.

You ALWAYS know better.

I blinked hard, but tears still burned behind my eyes. I pushed my elbows onto the bar and bowed my head, pressing my fingers to my temples like that could quiet the thoughts before they hollowed me out completely.

The club crowd blurred into white noise, but it all felt far away, muffled, like I was underwater and the world was happening above the surface.

My pulse raced, my hands refused to stop trembling, and my breath came in waves, too shallow and too sharp. I could still feel his mouth against mine. I could still feel his hand wrapped around my throat. I could still feel the moment he filled me so completely it felt like all my broken pieces mended at once. And that hurt worst of all. Believing. Trusting. Letting myself crave the feeling of anything more than the broken mess I was.

I sucked in a shaky breath and stared at the empty shot glass like it could tell me what to do next. Like it could fill the hollow chest cavity he'd left behind.

He said he'd be right back. He lied. Or maybe he didn't. I perked up at the thought. Maybe the phone call was an emergency, and he didn't have time to come back.

But trauma doesn't care about reasons. Trauma only knows patterns. And I knew this pattern too well. My voice barely made it out, a whisper swallowed by the music.

"Stupid. You're so fucking stupid."

I blinked again as a tear slid hot and fast down my cheek before I could stop it. I wiped it away quickly, angrily, glancing around to make sure no one saw. No one did. No one ever does.

The thought sat heavy in my chest, sour and familiar. The room felt too crowded again. The music dug under my skin, and the laughter grated. Every breath tasted like sweat and liquor and bad decisions.

I slid off the stool, and Jeremy muttered something I didn't quite catch. I nodded to make him stop talking and turned away, weaving through the press of bodies with my shoulders tight and my head down. Someone bumped into me and sloshed their drink. Cold liquid hit my arm, and I flinched, muttering an apology that wasn't mine to give, and kept moving.

• • •

The staff hallway was a little better. Quieter. The bass turned to a dull thump behind the walls. I pushed through the back door, out into the alley, and the cool air sucked the breath from my lungs. I painfully pulled in a lungful of air that didn't taste like recycled smoke and spilled vodka. It tasted like rain and asphalt and the faint metallic tang of the city. My shoulders dropped a fraction. Not much, just enough that my lungs remembered how to work.

I leaned back against the brick, tilting my head up. The sky was a smear of cloud and light pollution. No stars tonight. Just the distant glow of a world that kept spinning whether I held it together or not.

The door clicked shut behind me as I pulled a cigarette from my pocket, winced at the bright lighter flame, then breathed in and let the smoke curl around my lungs. I closed my eyes and leaned my head back against the brick.

You are fine.

You are not that child anymore.

You are not trapped.

You are not stupid for believing, even if you were wrong.

The reminders didn't help. They never really did. But saying it, even silently, made me feel less like I was just going to unravel and float away. I exhaled and let myself relax another fraction against the brick.

"Rough night?"

The voice came from my right. Smooth. Mild. Familiar enough that my shoulders tensed before I even turned my head. Benjamin.

He stepped out of the shadows near the dumpster, suit jacket unbuttoned, tie loosened. He looked like he had just stepped off a magazine shoot titled "organized crime but make it polished." His red hair was neat. His expression was calm, and his eyes were too sharp. Of course, he was here. Of course, he would be.

He held two cups in one hand, condensation glistening on the sides. The amber liquid inside caught the dim light of the alley.

"I figured the air out here might be better. And that you might prefer this to whatever Jeremy slung into your glass in there."

He held one cup out and my fingers hesitated for half a second before I took it.

"Thanks," I answered. My voice sounded small. Gentler than I liked.

Benjamin's gaze flicked over my face, assessing. Not in the hungry way men sometimes looked at me. Not in the way Kael did, either, like he was memorizing me. This was cooler. Clinical. Like he was running through a checklist in his head.

"You look like you've seen a ghost. Or maybe several."

I huffed out something that wanted to be a laugh and failed. "Just one."

"Ah." He nodded like he understood more than I had let on. "The tall, broody kind with a gun and a death wish."

My fingers tightened around the cup.

"I don't know what you're talking about." The words came out forced and bitter.

Benjamin leaned his shoulder against the wall beside me, leaving a careful bit of space between us. Close enough to talk. Far enough that it did not feel like crowding.

"I watch people. It's an unfortunate habit. Comes with this charming line of work." His gaze slid back to me. "I saw you go into the supply closet with him earlier."

Heat crawled up my neck. "That was none of your business."

"Of course not." He took a sip of his drink. "But now you're standing out here alone, looking like you're about to climb out of your own skin, and while I may be a terrible person, I'm not so far gone that I could ignore something like that."

He let the words hang there, easy and unthreatening. Like he was offering a stool at the bar instead of a conversation.

I stared down at my drink. The ice clinked softly when I shifted my grip.

"I thought he would come back," I heard myself say.

Benjamin didn't react. Not outwardly. His face stayed open and neutral.

"He said he would," I went on, because once the words started, they didn't want to stop. "He told me he would be right back, and then he was just… gone. Patrick is gone. Everyone I usually rely on is gone, and I'm out here talking to you because I can't fucking breathe in there tonight."

"Sometimes things pull people away. Nights like this, in a place like this, there's always some kind of emergency."

"I know that." The words came out too fast and too clipped. I swallowed. Forced myself to slow down. "I know. I just…"

You sound pathetic. Stop. But I couldn't seem to plug the hole I'd ripped in myself.

"I was starting to fall." I swallowed hard, pushing past the lump in my throat. "And he wasn't there to catch me."

The admission scraped out of me, and Benjamin stayed silent for a moment. The sounds of the city filled the space between us. A car passed somewhere down the street. Distant shouting. The muffled thud of bass through the back door.

"You realize how dangerous that is," he replied finally. His voice stayed gentle, but there was something like steel under it. "Letting yourself fall for someone like him."

"I'm well aware," I muttered.

Kael, with his calm violence and broken edges. With the way he uttered, Little Fawn, like it was a prayer and a warning. The way he looked at me, as if I were something worth ruining himself for. And he still left. My chest began to ache again.

Benjamin turned his head, studying me. "He's not the type to play games, you know. If he wanted to hurt you, he'd do it cleanly. Directly. The fact that you're out here alone probably has less to do with his intention and more to do with other people's."

"Is that supposed to make me feel better?" I took a sip of my drink. It burned going down, but softer than the last one.

I took another drag off my cigarette. My head leaned back as I blew the smoke out, watching it swirl and dance in the wind.

He gave a small, almost smile. "No. Just an observation."

I stared out at the alley. The wet asphalt glistened under the security light. The air smelled like rain and exhaust and the faint sour tang of the dumpster behind us. It should have been disgusting. Right now, it felt more real than anything inside.

"I know better. I know what happens when you start thinking someone might stay. I know what happens when you believe you might be more than convenience. I wasn't supposed to make that mistake again." The words landed heavily.

"But you did," he whispered quietly.

I nodded. "Just for a minute."

That was the worst part. That it hadn't even taken long. One night. One kiss. One moment of being held like I wasn't something broken and used. That's all it took to knock down walls that it took years to build.

You're pathetic.

You're naive.

You're nothing special.

You're a warm hole. Easy to touch. Easier to leave.

My eyes burned again, and I blinked hard, staring at the far wall so I wouldn't have to see his face when he realized how weak I was.

Benjamin didn't say anything for a while. We just stood there in the quiet, drinks sweating in our hands, the sounds of the club a distant heartbeat through the door.

When he finally spoke, his voice was softer. "People like us aren't meant for soft things. We get edges, bargains, and survival. Not romance."

"People like us?" I echoed.

He lifted one shoulder in a half-shrug. "You think I ended up working for a man like Michael because I had a wealth of better options?"

I glanced at him. There was something tired in his eyes, just for a second. Something old. It made him look less like a sleazy bartender and more like a man who had been standing in the smoke too long.

"I'm not saying you're wrong to be angry," he went on. "I'm just saying… be careful what stories you let your head write in the quiet. It rarely authors the whole truth."

"It felt real," I whispered.

"Feelings are liars." He tipped his head back against the brick. "Trust me."

I took another swallow of my drink, and the warmth spread faster this time. A little too fast. My fingertips tingled. I finished my cigarette and dropped the butt, stamping it out with the toe of my shoe.

"You sound like you know what you're talking about," I muttered.

He let out a low breath that might have been a laugh. "You'd be surprised."

The alley tilted, just slightly, and as I blinked, it settled again. I chalked it up to the shots. To not eating enough. To the exhaustion that had been building for weeks and had chosen tonight to crash down.

"You shouldn't be out here alone. The vultures love a woman who looks like she has been crying."

"I'm not crying," I snapped back at him, my eyes narrowing.

He didn't call me out on the lie.

"Finish your drink. Then let me walk you to the staff room. You can sit, breathe, and get your feet under you. Patrick would box my ears if he knew I left you out here like this."

The mention of Patrick tugged something in my chest. Familiar and safe-adjacent.

"Fine," I muttered. "But only because I'm too tired to argue."

He smiled, small and satisfied, and lifted his cup in a mock toast.

"To bad decisions," he laughed.

I clinked my cup weakly against his and took another swallow as the world went a little fuzzier at the edges.

"Stronger than I thought," I murmured. My tongue felt thick. "What is in this?"

"Top shelf. Don't stress, Sera. It's me. You're in good hands."

The words should have reassured me, but they didn't. A slow, heavy warmth was spreading through my limbs now, syrupy and wrong. My fingertips prickled. My legs suddenly felt like they belonged to someone else, someone who had forgotten how to stand.

I frowned, looking down into my cup. The ice was melting. The liquid swirled when my hand trembled.

"Benjamin… I feel… weird."

My words slurred as the world began to tilt around me. He moved then. His movements were quick and efficient as he gently took the cup from my hand and set it aside on the low concrete ledge.

"I know. I'd say I'm sorry, Sera, but it's just business." His words sounded muddled, as if he were speaking underwater.

He was closer now. Too close. His hand came to my elbow, steadying me when my knees buckled.

"What did you…?" The words wouldn't cooperate, like my mouth wouldn't shape them right. The alley swam in front of me, light smearing into long streaks.

"Just something to help. You've had a long night. You need rest."

I tried to pull away, but my body wouldn't respond. Panic flared sharply, but it was trapped somewhere behind what felt like a warm blanket covering my brain, unable to reach my limbs.

"I don't…" My tongue felt like cotton. My vision tunneled, narrowing to the crisp line of his jaw, the neat knot of his loosened tie, the unreadable calm of his eyes. "I don't want…"

"I know. Hush, Sera, you'll be fine… maybe."

He chuckled to himself, and the door opened behind us, light spilling out, cutting across the alley. A voice called something I couldn't make out. The sound warped and stretched, as if it were traveling through water.

Benjamin shifted, angling his body as if shielding me from whoever was at the door.

"Got her. You can tell Conor it's done." He called out over his shoulder, his grip tightening against me.

Conor. Kael works for Conor.

The name snagged on something inside me. It didn't make sense. None of this did. What did he want with me?

My head lolled to the side, and the world tilted just as my legs gave up. I would have hit the ground, but Benjamin's arm wrapped around my waist, holding me upright with an ease that made something cold crawl through what was left of my awareness. He was strong. Too strong, and I was slipping further under.

"You'll be alright," he murmured near my ear. "You won't remember much of this. Just let go, it's easier."

Easier. The word echoed, absurd and distant.

The last thing I saw before my eyes slid shut was the sweep of headlights at the mouth of the alley as a car pulled up. The last thing I felt was Benjamin's hand snaking under my thighs as he lifted me and walked toward it. And then? Nothing at all.

Chapter Fourteen

Conor

The girl arrived exactly on time. Not because she fought, or screamed, or tried to run. She didn't have the luxury of panic. Benjamin saw to that. No, she arrived on time because *I* decided she would.

Timing is an art that most men never master. They rush, they grasp, they cling. They choke their opportunities before they even have a chance to bloom. But I've always found that if you want a thing, truly want it; if you're smart, you let it come to you. And tonight, it did.

Headlights swept across the long drive outside my study, cutting through the fog that clung to the grounds like breath on cold glass. I didn't move. I didn't stand. I simply swirled the whiskey in my glass and watched the amber catch the firelight.

The house stayed quiet. Hushed and expectant, and somewhere down the corridor, the front door opened. Footsteps approached. Their sound was steady, measured, and respectful. Benjamin's cadence was unmistakable. Efficient, unhurried, the stride of a man who knew better than to bring chaos into my presence.

The study doors opened, and Benjamin stepped inside first, his head bowed in deference. Behind him, one of my men carried her.

Seraphine.

She was unconscious with her head lolled to the side. Her limbs loose and boneless in his arms. Like a fallen marionette with her strings neatly cut.

Her hair was damp from the mist. A smudge of alley grime streaked the back of her thigh. Her lips were slightly parted, and she looked fragile, making the room feel smaller. Warmer somehow.

Benjamin looked between her and me with a sardonic grin.

"Your requested order."

I took one slow sip of whiskey before responding.

"Set her down."

The burly one who had been carrying her obeyed instantly, lowering her onto the velvet chaise near the fire. Her head tipped slightly to the side, exposing the elegant line of her throat. Such a delicate place to break a person.

I said nothing for a long moment. Benjamin waited, silent as stone, as my men stood at attention. No one dared to even breathe wrong.

Finally, I rose. Taking a single step and then another. The fire crackled as I approached her, its glow painting her skin gold. She didn't stir.

Not even when I crouched in front of her, elbows resting loosely on my knees, studying her like a rare piece of art newly acquired. Something exquisite, yet somehow dangerous. Something worth the trouble she'd no doubt cost me.

"Pretty thing," I murmured, mostly to myself. "No wonder Kael lost his focus."

Benjamin exhaled softly in agreement, amusement, or most likely both. I didn't look away from her.

Kael's marks were still on her, and I frowned. He'd marked my new treasure. That was something I'd correct personally, when it amused me. I should have been irritated. Instead, I found myself rather entertained.

"Fetch the others. We've work to do."

Benjamin nodded and slipped out. I reached forward and brushed a single strand of hair from her cheek. She didn't react. Didn't flinch. Didn't know the world had shifted beneath her. But she would. By morning, she absolutely would. And Kael? He'd burn the city to ash trying to get back what I'd just taken. Good. Let him burn. I've always loved the smell of smoke.

Benjamin returned with the quiet efficiency I paid him for. Two more men followed: Owen and Rourke. Both reliable, both loyal, both too stupid to question the morality of anything I asked. The perfect employees. They shut the doors behind them, and Seraphine still didn't stir.

I stayed crouched before her, elbows on my knees, studying her face the way some men study blueprints. Searching for fault lines and weak spots. Places where the structure was already cracked.

"You got the dose right?" I asked without looking away from her.

"Yeah, she's fine. She'll be out another hour. Maybe two."

"Good." My fingers hovered millimeters from her cheek. "I like them quiet while I take inventory."

Rourke shifted his weight, uncomfortable. Man's got a weak fucking stomach.

"She's smaller than I expected," he muttered.

"Most valuable things are," I acknowledged lightly.

His mouth snapped shut.

I circled the chaise like a wolf tracing the edges of its new territory.

"Any trouble getting her to drink?"

"She trusted me," he replied with a shrug. Not bragging or ashamed. Just stating a fact.

Of course she had. Trauma makes the kind-hearted gullible and the self-reliant blind.

"But she opened up," Benjamin added.

"Oh?" My brow lifted. "What about?"

He hesitated. Not because he doubted whether he *should* tell me, more like he simply knew better than to get the details wrong.

"She said Kael left her. That she was falling, and he wasn't there to catch her."

I chuckled darkly.

"That's the trouble with men like our dear Kael," I smirked, walking back to the fireplace and swirling the last of my whiskey.

"They don't know whether they want to hold something or destroy it. So they end up doing both." I took a sip. "Eventually."

Benjamin nodded in agreement.

"She told me she's been taught her whole life that men leave."

"Ah. A wound and a pattern. A man could build a fucking empire out of something like that."

Rourke swallowed hard. He still wasn't used to how I spoke. How I thought. How honest I was. I set my glass down on the mantle, the soft clink echoing in the quiet room.

"Let's speak plainly," I continued, turning toward them. "Michael is drowning in debt he cannot repay. I gave him one final avenue to clear it. And he—"

I gestured toward Seraphine with a careless hand.

"—has paid the toll."

Owen frowned. "But Kael—"

"Kael," I interrupted smoothly, "is the reason this is interesting."

"He once interrupted my acquisition of another beautiful treasure. But I lost out on that one thanks to his unfortunate timing and an overeager asshole with a penchant for poking holes in my packages."

I strolled back to her again, my footsteps slow, deliberate, the quiet predator pacing his prize.

"Lately, though, he's been losing discipline. Losing focus. Pushing back instead of falling in line like a good soldier."

I brushed my knuckles across the back of her limp hand. "And all for a silly little club girl."

Benjamin didn't flinch, but I saw the glimmer of something in his eye. Anticipation. He enjoyed this. Relished in it even.

"This girl, however," I mused, tilting my head, "is now a lesson."

Owen nodded, and Rourke avoided looking at her entirely.

Benjamin finally spoke. "What do you plan to do with her?"

I smiled. A real one this time.

"I want to see what Kael does without her. What he does when he's forced to make a choice again."

I turned, hands clasped loosely behind my back as I walked the length of the room.

"I want to watch him spiral. I want to see him bleed through the cracks he's tried so hard to patch. I want to find every thread she pulled loose in him and tug."

My eyes slid back to her.

"And when he's on his knees?" Benjamin asked with a wicked grin.

The fire cracked loudly.

"If he kneels, he may survive."

Benjamin stiffened. Just barely, but I saw it.

"You disagree?" I asked, my voice pleasant.

"No," he replied quickly. "Just thinking through logistics."

Lie. A smart lie, but I still noted it and let it sit.

"She's not awake yet," I strolled to the chaise again. "Bring her upstairs. The quiet guest room. Not the basement."

That made Rourke blink. "She's a payment," he reminded gently, as if I'd forgotten. "A trade."

"And?"

My voice cooled. "Do you think I break my toys the second I get them?"

He swallowed. "No, sir."

"Good." I dusted an invisible fleck of ash from my sleeve. "Because the breaking is the best part."

Benjamin gestured, and the men lifted her carefully. She didn't stir, didn't whimper, didn't even twitch. She was beautiful in the way abandoned things are. Still and silent. Just waiting for someone cruel enough to notice.

As they carried her toward the stairs, I spoke again, my voice soft, almost affectionate.

"And Benjamin?"

He paused in the doorway. "Yeah?"

"Not a word of this to anyone. I want him panicked.

Panicked men make mistakes."

I picked up my whiskey again.

Benjamin's brows knit. "Ooh, fun. Make the man bend to your rules. I like it."

"Exactly," I agreed, smiling into my glass. "Let's see how quickly he loses focus when he realizes he left his new obsession alone in the dark."

Benjamin grinned and left, and I was alone again. Alone with a fire, my glass of whiskey, and the delicious beginning of ruin.

Kael thought he knew violence. He thought he understood loss.

He thought he had survived hell. But he'd never been haunted by me, until now.

• • •

I've never understood the appeal of dungeons. Other men, lesser men, think fear requires chains on the wall and drains in the floor. They mistake theatrics for control. They want metal, mildew, and screaming.

I prefer quiet rooms with soft sheets and heavy curtains. A lamp with a warm bulb. Fear ferments better when it has something gentle to contrast itself against.

She lay where they'd left her, on the wide bed against the far wall. Fresh white sheets, her dark clothes stark against them. I'd taken off her boots and jacket, nothing else. There was no need yet. The leather lay folded on the chair in the corner, beside my discarded suit jacket.

I sat opposite her in the armchair by the window, one ankle resting on my knee, a glass of whiskey loose between my fingers.

My own jacket was off, and my tie loosened with the top few buttons of my shirt undone. Comfortable and the picture of civilized.

A single cuff encircled her wrist; a slim band of steel locked to a chain that fed into the headboard. Nothing brutal. Nothing excessive. Just enough to keep instinct from turning into an inconvenience.

The room was quiet except for the faint tick of the old clock on the wall and the whisper of the fire in the small corner hearth. Her lashes fluttered for the first time nearly ninety minutes after we brought her up. Benjamin did good work.

I took a slow sip of whiskey and watched as her brow furrowed, just slightly. Her lips parted on a small, confused breath. Her fingers twitched, testing a world that didn't quite fit her last memory. I let myself imagine the way it knitted together behind her eyes.

She shifted again, a soft rustle of fabric on sheets. She turned her head, and the cuff at her wrist tugged, the chain giving an inch and no more. That got her attention, and her eyes snapped open. Beautiful things are always more striking when fear hits them. The pupils blown wide, the breath catching, the body going very still.

She stared at the cuff first. It's always interesting to see what a person looks at before they look at you. The metal cuff. The chain. The ring that was sunk into the thick wooden headboard.

Panic flashed across her face, gone almost as quickly as it came. She swallowed it down with visible effort. Old habit, that.

Survival. Someone had taught her young that visible fear was an invitation for far worse things.

Slowly, as if she was afraid to startle herself, she turned her head, and her gaze found me in the chair.

We looked at each other for the first time in this new configuration. Her, on the bed, me, in the chair. Prey seeing her predator.

"Evening," I greeted pleasantly, as if she'd just walked in late to dinner. "Sleep well?"

She stared like she was trying to force my face into a different shape. Like if she blinked enough times, I'd turn into someone she trusted.

"Where…" Her voice came out hoarse, small. She cleared her throat and tried again. "Where am I?"

"Home," I answered plainly.

Her shoulders tensed. "This is not my home."

I smiled around the rim of my glass. "No, it's mine, little one. Someone on your salary could never afford windows like these."

Her gaze darted past me then, cataloguing: the tall window with its drawn curtains, the wardrobe, the single door, the soft light. The edges of the room. The distance to everything. She wasn't stupid, my new toy.

Her eyes flicked back to me. "You drugged me," she shuddered. Not a question but a quiet accusation.

"That was Benjamin," I corrected mildly. "Though I did authorize it, if that helps you place your outrage appropriately."

Her fingers curled tight around the sheet, knuckles whitening. "Why?"

"You were tired. Overstimulated. Grieving the loss of your knight in blood-soaked armor." I tipped my head. "And we had a schedule."

"A schedule," she repeated flatly.

I nodded toward the clock. "You arrive. You sleep. You wake. And now we talk. Then, if you behave, we see what happens next."

The chain at her wrist rattled as she shifted, the sound sharp in the otherwise quiet room. Her gaze dropped to it again.

"You're not in any immediate danger," I soothed.

She let out a brittle laugh. "Forgive me if I don't feel reassured by the word immediate."

Smart. So fucking deliciously smart.

I set my glass down on the small table beside the chair and leaned forward, forearms on my thighs, hands loosely clasped. Not looming. Not yet. Just closer.

"What's the last thing you remember, Seraphine?"

She hesitated, lips parting, closing, parted again. The truth was sitting right there on her tongue. Shame crowded it.

"The alley," she answered finally. "Benjamin. And that fucking drink."

"And before that?" I pressed.

Her jaw clenched. "Why does it matter?"

"It all matters," I replied quietly. "I like stories. I like to know where they break."

She slowly inhaled through her nose, nostrils flaring just enough to betray the nerves she was trying to bury.

"Before that… I was in the supply closet," she whispered. "With Kael."

The way she said his name as if it hurt. As if it tasted like blood and honey, sour on her tongue. It made something ignite inside me.

"And how was our Kael?" I asked lightly, my head tilted in amusement. "Gentle? Rough? On his knees for his sweet *Little Fawn*?"

Color rose hot in her cheeks. "Go to hell."

I laughed. Genuine, this time. "Oh, I've been circling it for years. I'm only asking because it's relevant. Men like him…" I waved a hand. "They leave fingerprints. On the body. On the soul. I need to know what he took, so I know what I need to take back."

She went quiet. Her throat bobbed around a hard swallow.

"Why am I here?" she asked again, slower. "What do you want from me?"

Now we were getting somewhere. I sat back once more, letting my ankle drift back onto my knee, my posture relaxed. Everything in the room said civilized conversation. Warm lamp, crackling fire, my shirt sleeves rolled to the forearms.

"Debts. And discipline."

Her mouth twisted. "Michael?"

"Of course." I let my gaze travel over her, unhurried and unapologetic. "He owed more than he could pay. I offered him a choice. Cash. Or collateral."

Her fingers tightened on the sheet again. "And he chose me."

"He offered *a girl*," I corrected. "The choice of girl was mine."

Her face went very still. There it was. That internal drop. The bottom falling out from under her. I watched it move through her like a shadow. She licked her lips, the chain clinking softly when her arm trembled.

"And if I refuse?" she asked. "If I don't play along with… whatever this is?"

"That is the interesting part."

I leaned forward again, elbows on my knees, letting my voice soften. "Refusal is your right," I explained. "But I'm not a patient man. I'd rather not force you; it's always sweeter when you're willing. So, when you break, and you will, I prefer cooperation."

"Cooperation," she repeated. "You're talking about me like I'm furniture."

"Furniture doesn't bleed," I mused. "You're… more of an investment."

Her eyes flashed. The first spark of real anger broke through the fear.

"If I'm an investment, then what does that make Kael?" she snapped. "Your attack dog? Your favorite soldier to make bend to your will?"

I smiled slowly. "There she is," I murmured. "I was wondering how long it would take for your teeth to show."

Her breathing hitched. Not from fear this time, but from the realization she'd given me something I wanted.

"I pay Kael," I continued. "I point him at certain problems. He removes them. Efficiently and quietly. And until recently, he was very good at doing just that and remembering his place."

Something bitter and sharp moved across her expression. "And now?"

"Now," I scoffed, "he's compromised."

I reached for my glass, turning it idly in my hand.

"Do you know what I saw on the cameras at your little club?"

She froze, her eyes wide.

"I saw him watching you," I went on. "Not the doors. Not the exits. Not the threats, but you." I chuckled. "Do you know how rare that is? For a man like him to forget the room, that completely? To forget himself?"

She said nothing, but her silence told me enough.

"I saw you smoking in the alley. I saw the way you leaned into him. The way he bent around you like you were his gravity. I saw," I lifted the glass in a faint toast, "the moment you became my leverage."

A tear slid fast and uninvited down her cheek. She didn't wipe it away. "Why him?" I asked, almost gently. "Out of all the monsters swirling around that place, why attach yourself to that one?"

She pressed her lips together, eyes shining.

"Men like you always ask the wrong questions," she whispered.

"Enlighten me."

"The question isn't 'why him.'" Another tear. Jaw locked, eyes blazing. "It's why was I so easy to choose."

I felt my smile sharpen.

"Oh, pretty thing," I cooed softly. "You have no idea how valuable you are."

She flinched. Not at the word pretty, but valuable. Interesting.

The chain rattled again as she shifted, testing the give, testing herself. I could see the calculations running behind her eyes. What if she lunged? What if she screamed? What if she played along until she found a door?

"You can try to run if you like. The door is locked, and the windows are high. You're welcome to exhaust yourself. I'll still be here when you're done."

She sagged back against the headboard and rolled her eyes.

"I'm not going to scream, there's no point. No one ever comes."

A simple sentence. A history written in twelve words. I finished my whiskey.

"No," I agreed. "They don't. Every scream is a lesson that way."

She closed her eyes for a moment, just long enough to steady, then opened them again.

"What happens now?" she asked.

"Now, we lay down ground rules."

Her laugh this time was hollow. "You kidnap me, chain me to a bed, and want to talk about rules."

"I like order. Chaos is for people who can afford a mess. I don't like wasting good material." I gestured lazily toward her. "You behave, and you eat. You talk; when I ask, and you're left alone to sleep. You make attempts at maiming my staff, you'll find out I can be less accommodating."

Her chin lifted. "And if I put a fork in your throat?"

I grinned. Couldn't help it.

"Then I'll know Kael has excellent taste."

Something flickered in her eyes at his name again. That tiny wince you make when someone presses a bruise.

"He doesn't know, does he?" she asked. "That I'm here."

"No. And I would rather you didn't pin your hopes on him."

Her expression cracked, just for a second. A jagged flash of something like hope and rage and grief twisted together.

"He'll come," she whispered.

"Maybe. Men in love do stupid things."

Her gaze snapped to me. "We're not—"

"Ah ah. Careful. If you lie to yourself too often, that pretty mouth will age early."

She stared at me like she wanted to drive her nails into my eyes.

"You could kill me," she ventured. "You could hurt me. You could sell me. Why keep me here?"

"Because," I rose from the chair finally, "breaking is more satisfying when you understand what you're holding, and I like breaking my precious acquisitions before I share them."

I crossed the space between us at a leisurely pace, stopping at the edge of the bed. Up close, the fear was a tangible thing, humming just under her skin.

I didn't touch her right away. I let my presence do most of the work. The height difference. The angle. The chain's small, subtle pull when she instinctively tried to lean away.

"Here's what you need to know tonight. You are here because Michael chose his own skin over yours. You stay alive because I am a curious man. You stay… intact… because right now I find you interesting."

Her breath quickened.

"Kael has no idea where you are. He will tear apart everything he can see, trying to find you. He will rage. He will threaten. He will beg."

I let my gaze drop to her mouth, then back to her eyes.

"And you, my sweet Seraphine, will learn that no one is coming in time."

Her throat bobbed on a hard swallow. I reached forward, finally, and brushed my thumb over the tear track drying on her cheek. Gentle. Almost tender, and she flinched as if I'd hit her.

"That's the first lesson. Hope is a currency. Spend it too early, and you have nothing left when the real bargaining begins."

She whispered something then, so soft I almost missed it.

"What was that?" I asked.

"You're wrong," she repeated, voice shaking but sure. "About one thing."

"Only one?" My brow arched. "I must be improving."

Her fingers curled into a fist around the sheet.

"I may be collateral. I may be an investment. But I'm not your toy. You don't get to own what you didn't earn."

For a moment, we just looked at each other. Then I smiled, slow and delighted.

"Oh, sweet Seraphine. That's where you and I differ."

I let my hand fall away from her face and straightened, stepping back toward the chair.

"Men like Michael pay in bargaining. Men like Kael pay in blood." I picked up my jacket from the armrest and slung it over my shoulder. "Men like me? We pay in stories. In endings. In who walks out of the room and who doesn't."

I moved to the door, fingers resting lightly on the handle.

"Get some rest. Food will come soon. Water. No drugs in either, I assure you. I want you to be clear-headed when the next lesson starts."

"And what's that?" she asked.

I glanced back over my shoulder, meeting her gaze one more time.

"How to stop waiting for rescue, and start wondering what you're willing to trade to survive."

I opened the door, and a soft pool of hallway light bled into the room.

"And Seraphine?"

She swallowed. "What?"

"Do try not to disappoint me. Kael's about to learn what it feels like to lose everything he loves. It would be a shame if you weren't worth the trouble."

I left her then. Let the quiet close in around her. Let the chain settle. Let the room's softness turn into a cage all on its own.

Downstairs, the house was quiet while somewhere in the city, my guard dog was still driving through the rain, blissfully unaware that his Little Fawn had been led straight into the lion's den. For now.

Chapter Fifteen

Kael

The job made no sense. I tossed my keys onto the counter and stared at the wall like it might explain why I'd just wasted three hours doing something one of Conor's barely-housebroken lackeys could've handled. A pickup. A drop-off. No danger. No point. Nothing had required *me*. Which meant it wasn't about the job at all.

I scrubbed a hand over my face. Her scent was still on my shirt from earlier. I thought back to the linen closet, her breath against my throat, the way her legs trembled when I touched her. I should've been replaying every second of it.

Instead, there was a steady, uneasy weight sitting low in my gut. I unlocked my phone and opened the contact card I'd saved the night I first saw her.

Kael: *I'm sorry about last night. Something came up. Are you home?*

Delivered. Still not read.

Alright. Maybe she was showering. Maybe she passed out early after work. I sat on the edge of the bed, staring at the screen, as if I could will her to answer.

Kael: *Little Fawn…?*

Nothing. The cold trickle down my spine sharpened. I didn't like the job. I didn't like the timing. I didn't like the silence.

I grabbed my jacket and was out the door before I could talk myself out of it. I stopped at a corner market on the way. Stupid, maybe, but I couldn't show up empty-handed after leaving the way I did. I grabbed a small bouquet of white Fuji mums. Not just an apology, but also a promise. That I was hers as much as she was mine.

The clerk bagged them, oblivious, and the world kept turning even though mine stood still.

By the time I reached her building, the unease had calcified into something metallic at the back of my tongue.

Patrick was halfway up the walk when I rounded the corner, a cardboard tray balanced in one hand—two coffees, one clearly meant for her. His hair was damp, his clothes rumpled, and his expression somewhere between exhausted and satiated. He had clearly spent the night in someone else's bed.

He lifted the tray when he saw me. "Are we doing surprise visits now? Because I didn't get the memo."

I held up the flowers. "She's not answering her phone."

Patrick's brows pulled tight in the center. "She told me she'd be home. Like home home."

He wiggled one of the cups. "I even brought her the good coffee. The one she likes to pretend she doesn't like."

We stood there for a beat, both processing the same quiet, ugly thought:

Where the fuck is she?

Patrick unlocked the door, pushed it open, and stepped inside first. We both stopped dead. The apartment was still. Not peaceful. Not normal. Still, like the air had been vacuumed out of the room.

Patrick set the coffees on the island too hard.

"Sera?" he called, voice half-singsong, half-edge-of-panic. "Alright, you're not funny. You hiding? Am I about to get throttled with a wooden spoon again?"

No answer. I crossed the space in a few strides, scanning everything with a soldier's eye. Her jacket—gone. Her boots—gone. Her phone charger was still plugged in. A half-filled glass on the counter. Nothing overturned, nothing was broken. A perfect, intentional kind of absence.

Patrick disappeared down the hall, opening her bedroom door.

"She's not here," he said, but the joke had drained out of his voice. "She wouldn't just leave. Not without telling me. We have rules between us. They keep us both sane."

I already knew. I could feel it in the walls and in the stillness of her apartment. In that gut-deep sense that something had gone very, very wrong. My grip tightened until the flower stems snapped in my hand.

"Alright," Patrick said too loudly, clapping his palms on his thighs. "Cool. Chill. Totally normal that my best friend vanished into thin air. Love this for us."

"Patrick." My voice was low and steady. "Stay here. In case she comes back."

He looked up sharply. "Kael. What are you—"

"I'll find her."

He swallowed hard, sarcasm faltering. "And if you don't?"

I met his eyes. "I will."

Patrick opened his mouth like he wanted to argue, and I shot him a look.

"Stay," I repeated. "If she walks through that door, she should see someone she trusts."

He swallowed hard, throat bobbing. "You are someone she trusts."

"Not enough. Not yet."

I didn't wait for a reply. I stepped out into the hall and pulled the door shut behind me. The lock clicked into place.

The building felt wrong. The street felt wrong. The whole city felt like it had shifted half an inch to the left, and I was the only one who noticed. Fine. Let it tilt. I would set it back when I was done.

• • •

I took the stairs two at a time and cut through the side streets toward the club. Morning traffic hissed past. People walked dogs, carried coffees, and checked their phones. Normal lives. Normal problems. Mine began and ended with a girl who wasn't where I fucking left her.

The club sat dark when I reached it. Front doors locked, and all the lights were off. The sign over the entrance was just dead glass and metal without the glow. I didn't use the front door. Too many prying eyes from the surrounding buildings. Fuck that.

The staff door in the alley was the better option. I had watched bouncers shoulder it open a hundred times. I slid the key I had stolen from Michael's office weeks ago in, leaned my weight into it, and felt the seal give with a wet scrape.

The alarm chirped when I stepped inside, and I punched in a code. Michael was nothing if not consistent. His wedding anniversary. The same one he used for everything. The alarm beeped once, and the familiar space opened around me. Empty. Just the hum of the ancient heating system and the low clank of old pipes.

I moved on instinct. Past the storage, past the dressing room, through the hallway to the office where Michael pretended he ran this place.

The surveillance system was tucked in on one side of Michael's office. The system was old as dirt, but it worked well enough for what I needed to see.

I dropped into the chair and woke the system. A flicker on the screen and then the timestamps glowed in the corner of each feed. I rewound to when I left her.

First to the supply closet in the staff hallway. The time matched the call I had taken. *There you are.*

I tracked her on each camera as she moved. Out of the corridor. Through the swing door by the bar. The overcrowded room made her look smaller than I remembered. She talked to the new bartender. Threw back a shot like she wanted it to burn something out of her. My jaw locked, and I kept following her.

She left the bar, and I clicked to the next camera. Staff hallway, then the back door. The one that led outside.

She pushed through and stepped into the alley. The angle outside was wider. It showed the door, the dumpster, the far mouth of the alley where the streetlights spilled in. Static hissed in the corner like the system was about to give up. She leaned against the brick and lit a cigarette. Tilted her head back and closed her eyes. I bit back the regret that clawed its way up my throat. It should have been me out there with her.

Movement on the edge of the frame pulled my attention from my increasingly dark thoughts. Benjamin slid into view like he had been waiting just out of sight. His shirt sleeves were rolled, and his tie loosened. Every inch of him said harmless, polished, and helpful.

He had two cups in his hands. My fingers curled on the edge of the desk. He offered her one. She hesitated, then took it. Her shoulders were tight. She looked like she was trying not to come apart.

They talked. This camera had no audio, but I knew how his mouth moved when he was charming someone. I had watched him take clients in the bar apart with that expression. Calm and sympathetic. A crocodile in a suit.

She drank. One sip. Two. A third. I watched as her body relaxed too fast. I could almost feel it in my own muscles. The shift in her posture and how her head tipped a little too far when she laughed. Her hand slipped on the cup, and when she swayed, Benjamin moved in. His hand closed around her elbow. He took the drink from her other hand, set it on the brick ledge, and then stepped closer. I watched her knees give out.

If he hadn't been there, she would have hit the concrete. He didn't let her. He caught her under the arms and pulled her against his chest like he was defending her from a fall. It was a good performance. But it wasn't for her.

Her head lolled against his shoulder, and her arms hung loose. The cigarette on the ground near the door still smoked, even after it had been crushed under her heel. Rage pushed up inside me, hot at first, then cold, before it settled low in my gut like ice.

I dragged the footage back a few seconds and watched it again. The way her body went from tense to heavy in less than a minute. The way his eyes flicked to the door behind them. The angle of his mouth when he said whatever he said.

A drug. It had to be. I moved the recording forward. The door opened. Light from inside cut across the alley. Another figure appeared in the frame, just at the edge. Too far to make out a face. A man. Broad at the shoulders. Dark coat. He said something. Benjamin answered without looking away from her. Then he shifted, turning his body so the camera couldn't capture her face. Just her hair over his arm. Her limp hand hung lifelessly. He carried her toward the mouth of the alley as a car pulled up. Big and inconspicuous. The kind you bought when you wanted comfort and no questions about what you carried in the trunk.

It stopped just out of range of a clean shot of the plate. Of course it did. Benjamin opened the back door with his free hand and lowered her inside. Her arm slid for a second, loose and boneless, before he tucked it back against her side. The other man got in from the far side, and the angle hid him well. All I caught was a slice of profile, the cut of a jaw, the edge of a coat. It wasn't enough.

The car pulled away, and just like that, she was gone. I stared at the empty alley on the screen. The cigarette smoked itself out. The door stayed shut. The timestamp marched forward in tiny, indifferent numbers.

My reflection looked back at me in the glass as I rewound and watched the whole thing again. Slower this time. Every frame. Every shift in her posture. Every small tell in his. Fucking, Benjamin.

He had walked her into whatever this was. Not a stranger. Not some drunk from the floor. Not a random threat. Someone on the inside. Someone who worked for Michael.

The chair creaked when I leaned back. It sounded too loud in the quiet room. I printed the frame showing him with her in his arms. Her head on his shoulder and his hand flat on her back with the car door open at his side.

The printer spat out the page. Grainy, but good enough. I folded it once and slid it into my pocket. I checked the timestamp. I compared it to when I left for the job Conor sent me on. The gap was neat. Too neat. He had pulled me away so someone else could take her. I closed my eyes for a second. Just long enough to lock the fury down where I needed it.

When I opened them again, the screens were still glowing. I shut the system down, wiped my trail out of habit, and stepped back into the hallway. The club felt different now. Not like a workplace. Not like a cage. Like a crime scene.

On the stairs down to the alley, my phone buzzed. Patrick. I ignored it.

• • •

Outside, the air hit my face. Cool and damp. The same stretch of alley I had just watched. The same door. The same stain on the concrete where her cigarette had died. I stood in the spot where she had been. I put my hand on the cold brick where her shoulders had rested.

"Benjamin," I said under my breath.

Not a question. No, now he's a target. I took out my phone and finally checked the screen. Three messages from Patrick.

Patrick: *Any luck?*
Patrick: *Please tell me you found something.*
Patrick: *Tell me she is with Michael, or she's drunk in a booth, or anything that isn't what I am thinking.*

I looked down at the photo in my pocket, then at the empty alley, and typed a single reply.

Kael: *I know who took her. I just don't know where she is yet.*

The dots pulsed for a long time before his answer came.

Patrick: *Then we find him.*
Patrick: *And we make him talk.*

A slow, controlled breath slid out of me. Yes. We would. Benjamin had taken someone who belonged to me. He had carried her to a car and handed her to a ghost. I would follow that ghost into whatever hole it crawled back to, and I would pull the truth out piece by piece. One way or another.

I stared at the alley one last time, letting every detail burn itself into memory. From the smell of wet asphalt, to the cigarette butt she had crushed under her heel, to the place where Benjamin had stood while he lied to her.

This was the last place she stood. The last breath she took before the world tilted under her feet. Before someone made the mistake of touching her.

A car drove past the end of the alley. Wrong one. Wrong sound. Wrong everything. I listened anyway, because when you lose something vital, every engine sounds like a maybe. But there was no maybe left here. Just absence. Just the hollow shape of her pressed into the concrete like a bruise.

I pulled the printed photo from my pocket and studied it under the light. Benjamin's hand on her back. Her arm hanging limp over his. The blur of the car's interior. A shadowed figure inside, just out of range. Her eyes were closed.

That did something to me. Not rage. Not panic. Something colder and cleaner.

"I'm coming," I murmured, thumb brushing the grainy line of her shoulder. "Wherever you are, Little Fawn… I'm coming."

I folded the photo once and slid it back into my pocket as my phone buzzed again. Patrick. I didn't open it. Not yet. He didn't need my fear. He didn't need my theories. He didn't need the kind of rage that was sitting in my ribcage like a second heartbeat. He needed me focused.

I walked back toward the car with purpose, the way I used to walk into buildings where I wasn't sure I'd walk out again. Every step writing its own vow.

I unlocked the door and slid into the driver's seat, the leather cold under my palms. The engine rumbled to life, its sound steady and familiar. For a moment, the cabin filled with the faintest echo of her. The scent of her perfume on my shirt. The ghost of her exhaling in the linen closet when she whispered my name like she wasn't afraid. If I closed my eyes, I could still feel her pulse jumping under my thumb.

I didn't close my eyes. I put the car in gear. The city stretched ahead of me; wide, dark, and full of holes to crawl through and men who owed me answers.

Somewhere in that sprawl was Benjamin, thinking he had done something clean and clever, thinking he had chosen the perfect night to disappear with someone I—

I tightened my grip on the wheel.

"Run," I said softly to the empty street. "Run fast. Run far. Because when I find you, and I will, you're going to wish you ran further."

Let the hunt begin.

Chapter Sixteen

Michael

Benjamin was late. He was never late, and tonight of all nights, I didn't have the patience for it. The office felt too small, too hot. Papers were spread across the desk like a taunt and an unwelcome reminder of how much money I still needed to pull out of thin air before Conor came collecting.

I scrubbed a hand over my face and checked the bar area again on the security feed. Still no Seraphine. Still no Patrick. Half my goddamn staff was missing on a Friday night. Unbelievable.

"Useless," I muttered, flipping through the ledger again. The numbers bled together. I'd told Jeremy, the new bartender, to handle shit until the rest of them got here. Kid held his own, but fuck was he green.

Everyone was making my life harder than it needed to be.

The hallway floor creaked, and I looked up as Benjamin stepped inside, closing the office door behind him. His shirt was damp like he'd walked through mist, and there was something off about his expression. Too calm and steady. Benjamin, acting calm, was never comforting.

"You're late," I snapped. "I've called you three times."

He didn't apologize. Just stood there. Which immediately pissed me off more.

"Where the hell have you been?" I demanded. "Sera's a no-show. Patrick called in with a family emergency. I've been waiting on you to bloody well show your ugly fucking mug here. I'm running a circus with no fucking clowns."

Benjamin's gaze didn't move. Didn't flicker. Didn't even so much as blink.

"I handled the situation," he said, his voice flat and toneless.

My eyes narrowed. "What situation, Benjamin?"

"The one involving your debt."

I froze.

"...what about it?"

"Oh, you don't have to worry about that, Mikey. It's taken care of. Simple, clean, and easy."

My annoyance spiked into anger. "What do you mean it's taken care of, Benjamin? How? Start fucking talking, boy."

"It's been handled," Benjamin repeated calmly. "You don't need to worry."

"I *still* owe Conor money, Benjamin!" I snapped. "In case you forgot, we're on a deadline. If I don't get him the rest by Monday, I'm done. Finished. Buried. I need everyone here tonight. Sera's supposed to be working the stage. She's my top earner, and she hasn't bothered to show. What the fuck is going on, Ben?"

Benjamin's jaw ticked once like he was holding something back.

"The debt is no longer an issue."

I stared at him. "Details, Ben. Now."

Benjamin didn't answer. Instead, he placed something on my desk. Something small and metallic with a folded piece of paper beneath it. A chill crawled over my skin.

"What is that?" I asked.

He took a step back.

"You should read it."

I picked up the note with numb fingers. Conor's handwriting was neat, precise, and fucking final.

Payment received in full.

My pulse thundered. "Payment…? Benjamin—what did you *do*?"

His expression didn't change.

"You had a problem that affected me, so I fixed it."

My throat dried instantly.

"Fix my problem?" I repeated. "Benjamin, I didn't authorize any payment. I don't *have* anything to give Conor yet. I haven't—"

He cut me a look. One that was low and sharp, and suddenly, the room felt colder.

"You were never getting the money together. Not in time."

His tone was flat and inevitable.

"You don't get to decide that."

"I did what had to be done."

"Bullshit!" I slammed my palm on the desk. "You don't make moves like that without me. You don't go behind my back. What the hell did you give him? We don't have anything—"

A thought struck me mid-sentence. A terrible, creeping, icy thought that made my tongue stick to my teeth.

"…Benjamin," I whispered, "what did you *use*?"

He didn't answer. He didn't have to. A low buzzing filled my ears like static, like the room had a heartbeat and it was speeding up.

"No," I muttered. "No, no, no. Tell me you didn't. Tell me you didn't give Conor something of *mine*."

Benjamin finally spoke.

"We needed it to be clean. This is clean."

"*What is clean?*" I roared. "What did you give him?!"

Benjamin considered me for a long, painfully calm moment, then said, "Something he wanted. Or, someone, I guess." He shrugged nonchalantly.

My chest seized. Wanted? Wanted. Conor didn't want cash. Conor didn't want booze. Conor didn't want equipment. Conor only ever wanted **leverage**. Human leverage.

"Oh my god," I breathed, stumbling back a step. "Who? Who did you hand over? Patrick? Jenny? Tell me—"

Benjamin's silence hit me harder than the words would have, and my skin crawled.

"No," I whispered. "No. You didn't. You wouldn't."

Benjamin said nothing, just stood on the other side of my desk like a statue. And suddenly I heard my own heartbeat hammering in my skull.

"Sera," I said.

Barely a sound. A hollow breath. Benjamin didn't blink. I rounded my desk and grabbed him by the front of the shirt, slamming him into the filing cabinet hard enough to rattle the drawers.

"You stupid son of a bitch, you gave him SERAPHINE*?!*"

Benjamin didn't fight me. Didn't shove back. Didn't so much as twitch. He only said, cool and quiet:

"She settled the debt."

"Settled the—" My voice cracked. "She's not fucking *currency*, Benjamin!"

"She is now. She was when you traded her for your payment and sold her for a night to that hedge fund asshole. This is no different, Mikey. Except now, you're debt-free."

I hit him. Without warning or second thought. My fist crashed into his jaw, and he staggered, catching himself on the edge of the cabinet. He wiped the blood from his mouth with the back of his hand, examined it like it was uninteresting, then straightened his collar.

"You're welcome," he said sardonically.

"You—" My voice cut off. My stomach turned. The room tilted. "She'll tell Kael. When he finds out—"

"No," Benjamin said mildly. "She won't."

Something in my chest iced over.

"What did you do to her?"

Benjamin's smile was nothing like a smile at all.

"I delivered her," he said simply.

Delivered. The word punched the breath out of me. Delivered. To fucking Conor. To his estate. To the one place Kael would kill me for letting her go.

"Jesus fucking Christ, Ben—Kael will gut us both!"

"Kael won't know," he said calmly. "Unless you tell him."

I felt the floor tilt under my feet. Seraphine. Sera. My top earner. My little wild card. My leverage and my insurance. Gone. Traded like a fucking poker chip. I braced my hands on the desk to keep from collapsing.

"We're dead," I whispered. "Do you understand? We're *dead* when he finds out."

Benjamin's brow lifted a fraction.

"Then don't let him find out."

A bitter laugh scraped out of my chest.

"That's your grand plan?" I snapped. "Just lie to Kael Mercer? Jesus, Ben, maybe you *are* as stupid as you look."

Benjamin didn't rise to it. He just watched me. That same flat, patient stare he turned on drunk customers right before he threw them out on their ass.

"It won't work," I went on, pacing behind the desk because if I stopped moving, I was going to be sick. "You don't know him the way I do. He smells lies. He lives in them, breathes them. He'll walk in here, look at me once, and know something's off."

"Then don't look off. You're good at pretending. You pretend to care all day long. About your wife, your kids, and this bar. Hell, you pretend to care about the whores you parade around the casinos. Keep pretending so he doesn't smell it on you."

I spun on him. "You think this is a joke?"

"No." His tone didn't change. "I think this is survival."

I stared at him. My chest heaving, and my palms slick.

"You think you've got this all figured out, don't you? You think you're clever. You think Conor's going to pat you on the head for delivering his new toy, and we all walk away happy."

Benjamin's mouth twitched. It wasn't a smile. Not really. More like the ghost of one.

"You already did," he replied.

"Already did what?"

"Walk away." He tipped his chin toward the note, still crushed on my desk. "Debt-free."

My stomach turned.

"You don't get it both ways," I hissed. "You don't get to sell my staff, throw them at Conor like meat, and then act as if you did me a favor."

"That's exactly what I did."

"Fuck you."

He laughed, the sound echoing through the room.

"You needed me to fix your problem. You would have lost the bar, then your wife and daughter. Face it, Mikey. I fixed every problem you had. You're back to zero. It's a good thing, man."

"Not like this. Not ever like this. Conor is going to destroy her."

"You needed it however you could get it," he said mildly. "So while you sat in here drinking your problems away as if that shitty whiskey you love could solve them, I fixed every problem irritating that fucking ulcer you whine about. You needed a clean start. I gave you an entire clean fucking slate. Say thank you."

His tone mocked me and grounded me at once.

"You gave him *her*," I snarled.

"*You* gave him *her*," Benjamin corrected, and this time there was a sliver of steel under the calm. "You made her currency the first time you sold her for a night. Don't act pure as snow now."

The words hit like a slap, and I flinched. Images flashed behind my eyes: the hedge fund prick with the too-white teeth and the too-soft hands. Sera walking out after, shoulders tight, eyes empty. The envelope of cash that was supposed to have bought us another month of breathing.

"That was different," I said roughly. "She came back from that night."

Benjamin's gaze didn't waver.

"She may come back from this."

"Or she won't."

He gave a tiny shrug. "Then it's not your problem anymore."

My hands curled into fists.

"You're a fucking monster," I whispered.

"And yet," he said, "I'm not the one Conor wanted to put in the ground come Monday."

My lungs refused to work for a second. He stepped away from the filing cabinet, straightening his cuffs as if this were a staff meeting and not him casually telling me he had just traded a member of my staff for my freedom.

"You owe me now," he added, like he was mentioning the weather.

I blinked. "The hell I do."

"You do," Benjamin said. "Your debt to Conor is gone. He won't come for you. That's my work. My risk. My relationship. You're standing here alive because of me. So yes, Michael. You owe me."

"I didn't ask you to do this," I snapped.

"You needed me to keep you alive," he replied. "Same thing."

"No. No, it isn't. I don't owe you shit."

Benjamin looked almost amused. "You will."

"I'll fire you," I spat. "You think I won't? I can have your ass out of here in ten minutes."

"And tell Conor his new favorite errand boy is unemployed?" Benjamin arched his brow. "Brave."

I swallowed. The office felt smaller. The air was thicker, like trying to breathe syrup.

"I'm still your boss," I said, but it sounded weak even to me.

"For now," he agreed. "And for now, your job is to stay calm, stop screaming, and not hand your head to Kael on a silver platter the second he walks in here."

I scrubbed a shaking hand over my face. It came away damp. I hadn't realized I was sweating.

"I have to talk to Conor," I muttered, more to myself than him. "I have to… I have to clarify. Negotiate. There has to be something else we can—"

"You're not listening. It's already done."

"It can't be done. He can't just take her—"

"He can, and he did."

Panic clawed up my throat. "What if she talks? What if she tells him this was you, not me? What if she gives up the club, my name, everything? He'll—"

"He already knows your name," Benjamin said quietly. "He already owns you. This just gives him something new to play with."

I grabbed my phone. Benjamin stepped closer, gaze narrowing.

"Don't do it, Michael."

My thumb was already tapping Conor's contact.

"I'm serious, man. Don't fucking call him."

"I don't work for you," I snapped, hitting the call button.

The line rang once. Twice. By the third ring, my heart was beating so hard it hurt. Benjamin watched me like he was watching someone step into traffic. On the fourth ring, the call clicked through.

"Mickey. I was wondering when you'd grow a pair and call me."

"I—uh—Conor. Sorry to bother you, I just wanted to—"

"You wanted to bargain for your pretty club girl back," he finished for me.

"Well, not bargain for, but Conor, not her."

He hummed. A soft sound, like he was tasting the words.

"Does my note read poorly?" he asked. "I thought I was crystal clear."

"I got the note," I said quickly, clutching the edge of the desk with my free hand. "I just… listen, there's been a mix-up. I didn't approve any specific… item being sent. I wasn't told which or what, I mean, who you were taking in exchange for—"

"For your bar? For your wife? Your child? I'd say you got the better end of the deal, Mikey. No more smart-mouthed bartender, and you owe me naught. Best to stop diggin' now that I've handed you a ladder."

My mouth snapped shut, and the room spun a little.

"Just, don't kill her, Conor. She's a good kid. Mouthy sure, but still, she'll make you good money."

On the other end of the line, something rustled. Fabric. Sheets. A quiet exhale.

"Does it matter if I do or not?" he asked.

"Yes," I said too fast, too loud. "She's… she's my employee. I need to know that she's…"

Alive? Breathing? Not broken?

"…that she's going to be of use to you," I finished lamely.

Benjamin snorted under his breath. Conor paused. When he spoke again, his voice had gone softer. Almost gentle.

"She's resting for now. But no more frettin' about your ex-employee. She's mine now. Just so we're crystal fucking clear, Mick, your debt is settled. You'll continue to run the club and send me my cut. You'll keep your people in line, and I'll break in my new toy. Everyone wins. Well. Maybe not her."

His laugh rang through the line, turning my insides to liquid, and my grip tightened on the phone so hard my fingers ached.

"Conor, please. She's valuable to me. She makes good money. She's compliant. She's—"

"I'm aware of her value," he interrupted. "That's why I chose her."

I couldn't breathe as the room closed in around me.

"Don't hurt her," I heard myself say. "Please. She's… she didn't owe anything. This was my mistake, not hers."

"Then consider this her… contribution," he replied. "You were never going to crawl out of this hole yourself, Michael. Someone had to take your place in it."

I swallowed hard, bile burning the back of my throat.

"She's not built for your world," I muttered.

There was a soft laugh. Chilling.

"No one ever thinks they are, and yet some of them surprise me."

"And the ones that don't?"

"They stop being my concern," he said simply.

My hand shook so hard I almost dropped my phone.

"Listen to me very carefully," Conor added, voice dropping. "You won't call this number again about her. You will not provoke my patience over a girl you were perfectly willing to rent out to strangers when it suited you. You will, however, be grateful that you're not in her place."

I squeezed my eyes shut. He was right, and I hated him for it.

"I didn't know you would take *her*," I whispered.

"You didn't need to know," he replied. "You only needed to understand the terms. And now ya do."

Something in me snapped. "She has people," I said before I could stop myself. "She has a best friend who's like a brother to her. He loves her. She has staff who rely on her. She has Kael. When he finds out she's gone—"

"Then," Conor said lightly, "you're about to have the most interesting few weeks of your life."

"You can't expect me to keep that man in the dark forever," I said. "He's not stupid."

"I expect you to try," he said. "And if you can't manage that… then at the very least, don't be the one who points him in my direction."

I slumped back against the desk. "What am I supposed to tell him?" I breathed.

"Whatever you like," Conor said. "She quit. She ran. She overdosed. Pick a story. You're good at those."

Tears burned hot at the backs of my eyes, to my absolute disgust.

"Conor—"

"I'm a busy man, Michael."

A faint sound filtered through the line. A door closing. Footsteps. The quiet, muffled sound of breath that wasn't his.

"Your little problem is settled," he added. "Try not to make any new ones."

The call disconnected, and I slowly lowered the phone. Benjamin still hadn't moved.

"Well?" he asked.

"He has her," I said. My voice didn't sound like mine. "He said she's resting."

Benjamin's mouth quirked. "See? Good news."

"Good—" I choked on it. "Good news? Are you insane? He's going to break her."

Benjamin's eyes flicked to the side, to the old photo tacked up on my corkboard. Sera was laughing behind the bar, head tipped back, teeth bared, alive.

"She was already breaking," he said.

I wanted to hit him again, but I didn't. My hands had started to shake.

"I don't owe Conor anymore," I muttered, more to myself than him, clinging to the one sliver of oxygen in the room. "He said I'm clear."

"You are," Benjamin agreed.

"He'll leave me alone."

"For now."

I glared at him. "You're enjoying this."

"I'm enjoying being alive," he said. "And I'd like to keep it that way. Which is why you're going to pull yourself together, splash some water on your face, and go run your club."

"I can't just go out there and pretend everything's normal," I said.

"You can," he replied. "You will. Because the alternative is telling Kael the truth and seeing what color your insides are when he's done."

A tremor ran through me. "He'll know," I whispered. "He'll walk in here and smell it. He always does. Every time I tried to lead him astray, every time I kept something back, he knew. He knows people. He *reads* them, Ben. That's why Conor uses him. That's why no one crosses him."

"Then don't cross him," Benjamin said.

I laughed again, high and thin. "I already did."

Benjamin pushed off the wall and straightened his shirt.

"You've got a head start," he said. "Use it."

"That's your advice?" I demanded. "Lie to him and run?"

"It's what I'll be doing," he said. "You'd be wise to follow my example."

Cold washed over me. "You're leaving."

"Not tonight. I have a shift. But soon, yeah."

"You can't just walk out," I protested. "You're my link to Conor. You're the only reason he—"

"Exactly," Benjamin said. "I'm valuable."

"For how long?" I shot back. "What happens when he gets bored with you? What happens when he decides you're more trouble than you're worth?"

Benjamin's smile finally appeared, sharp and humorless.

"Then I hope I've had time to run far enough," he said.

The door creaked as he cracked it open. The muffled roar of music and voices spilled in—a reminder that the world outside this room hadn't stopped just because mine had.

"Benjamin," I said.

He glanced back.

"What am I supposed to do?" I asked, hating the way it sounded.

He studied me for a long time.

"Don't drink," he said finally. "Don't stare at the cameras. Don't call Conor again. And when Kael comes… lie like your life depends on it."

"It won't be enough," I whispered.

Benjamin's gaze cooled.

"It won't be. But it might buy you an extra thirty seconds, and sometimes that's all you get."

Then he was gone, and the door clicked shut behind him, sealing the quiet back in.

I stood there for a long time. Long enough for the sweat on my skin to go clammy. Long enough for my legs to start aching from how hard I was bracing myself against the desk. Long enough for the word *resting* to turn sour in my mind.

Finally, my feet found themselves again, and I stumbled to the little sink in the corner and turned on the tap, splashing cold water over my face until my skin stung. In the warped mirror, I looked like a stranger. My eyes were too wide, and my mouth was pinched tight.

Not the man who'd walked into this office six years ago thinking he could run a club and dance on the edge of Conor's patience indefinitely. Not a boss. Not a provider. Just a coward with blood on his hands and a girl's name stuck behind his teeth.

"For fuck's sake," I whispered at my reflection.

Saying it didn't make her any less gone. I pulled in a breath that didn't go deep enough and forced myself back to the desk. The ledger still lay open. The note still sat beside it, Conor's handwriting neat and unbothered. *Payment received.*

My vision blurred for a second as I wiped the heels of my hands over my eyes and grabbed my phone again. I scrolled to Sera's name and hit call. It went straight to voicemail, and her voice came through the speaker, bright and amused.

"Hey, it's Sera. If you're hearing this, I'm either avoiding you on purpose or asleep. Leave a message, and I'll see how I feel about you later."

"I'm a fucking dead man."

When Kael put it together… when he realized what my survival had cost… he would burn everything between Conor and us to ash. And I would be the first one he set on fire.

Chapter Seventeen

Seraphine

The first thing I noticed was the clock. Not the bed or the sheets or the expensive ceiling that definitely did not belong in my life. Not the ache in my wrist where the metal bit into the bone. Not even the sour chemical taste at the back of my throat. The fucking clock. A soft, steady tick on the far wall.

Tick. Pause. Tick.

I laid still and waited for it to speed up, the way my heart kept doing. But it didn't. No, instead, the room came back in pieces.

White sheets. Heavy curtains muting the light to a dull gray. The faint smoke-sweet smell of a dying fire. My jacket was folded on a chair in the corner, like I had checked into a hotel instead of being dragged out of my life.

The cuff around my wrist tugged when I moved the wrong way. A narrow band of steel with a locked clasp and a short length of chain. Not brutal, not theatrical. Just enough to remind me that whatever I thought I was before, now I was property.

My stomach rolled. I squeezed my eyes shut and breathed through it. The headlights. Benjamin's hand on my back. The friendly handing over of a glass. *You're tired. Just take a drink.*

The memory of liquid burning down my throat came with a flash of humiliation. I had taken it. I had tipped my head back and swallowed, like a good girl, because I thought the worst thing that could happen was a hangover.

Holy fuck, had I been wrong. I opened my eyes and forced myself to look at the room again. Really look.

The curtains were still drawn, but daylight leaked around the edges in a thin, hazy outline. The fire in the small hearth had burned down to embers, throwing out more glow than heat. My boots were lined up neatly by the chair, laces tucked in. Someone had been in here while I slept.

Or while I lay unconscious, which was not the same thing at all.

I lifted my hand and watched the cuff catch the light. The chain clinked and gave me exactly as much freedom as it had last night. Conor's voice seeped back into my mind.

'Hope is a currency. Spend it too early, and you have nothing left when the real bargaining begins.'

I pulled my hand back in until the cuff bit into my skin and pressed my palm against my chest. My heart beat hard under my fingers.

I tried to remember how many drinks I had served last night. How many songs had played in the club? How many hours had passed between Kael's mouth on mine in the linen closet and Benjamin's hands holding me upright in the alley? It all slid together like wet paint.

What was the last thing I said to Kael? We hadn't said much. Didn't need to. He had said he'd be right back. He didn't come back. He'd left, and I fucking spiraled.

I swallowed hard and stared at the ceiling, counting the cracks in the plaster. One. Two. Three.

He'll come.

The thought slipped in before I could stop it. Soft and treacherous. It wrapped around my ribs with almost physical pressure.

He'll notice. He'll come.

I squeezed my eyes shut again.

"Don't," I whispered to the empty room. "Don't fucking do that."

The clock ignored me with its incessant mocking ticks.

Men leave. That was the rule. Michael had once left me on the floor with my ears ringing and my nose bleeding when I had cost him money. My father left the second he realized I made noise instead of making his friends feel good. Men left. It's just what they do. It was almost funny that I had to be chained to a bed before one of them decided not to.

Footsteps sounded in the hallway outside. Slow and deliberate. Not boots. Softer. Rubber soles on polished wood. The handle turned, and I went very still. I breathed a small sigh of relief when I realized it wasn't Conor.

The woman who entered was older than me, in her mid-forties maybe, with dark hair pulled into a low knot and a face lined from squinting at things she didn't approve of. She wore plain black pants and a gray sweater that probably cost more than my entire closet. A thin gold chain glinted at her throat. Must be house staff, my brain supplied helpfully.

She pushed a cart into the room with the kind of quiet efficiency that never appeared out of nowhere. It was trained, beaten, and bought.

"Good morning," she said, like we were pretending this was normal. Her voice was soft, clipped around the edges with an upper-class finishing-school tone, tinged with resignation.

Morning. So I had lost most of the night.

I swallowed. "What time is it?"

She glanced at the clock. "Eight thirty-seven in the morning, dear."

My chest tightened. How long had I been gone from the club? Twelve hours? Fourteen? Long enough for people to notice I had not rolled in late with a coffee and an apology. Long enough for Patrick to swear at the coffee machine. Long enough for Jenny to check the group chat twice and then stop, because the last message had a read receipt that never changed. Long enough for Kael to… what? I forced my face blank.

The woman lifted a tray from the cart and set it on the small table near the bed. Toast, eggs, and a little bowl of fruit. A glass of water with condensation on the outside, beading slowly.

My mouth flooded with saliva, contrary to the thought of swallowing anything, because it made my stomach flip.

"Mr. Hayes asked me to see that you eat," she said.

Mr. Hayes. So that was how the staff said his name. Man was a pompous, narcissistic prick.

"I am not really in a breakfast mood," I muttered.

"It's not a mood. It's a requirement." She hesitated, eyes flicking briefly to my cuff and back. "It's better to keep your strength up."

Easier for who hung in the air between us.

"What do I call you?" I asked.

Her brows twitched. The question surprised her, and honestly, it surprised me too.

"Margot," she said finally.

"Margot, do you usually serve Conor's kidnapped women, or is this a special occasion?"

She sighed heavily before steeling her features.

"I serve the house, and the people in it."

"So that's a yes," I snapped.

Her gaze landed on my face, really landed for the first time. She looked at me like she was weighing something. Maybe a risk or a cost.

"Eat," she said quietly. "Please."

I glanced at the plate again. My stomach cramped in protest and interest at the same time.

"What if I don't?" I asked.

The chain rattled as I shifted, the metal biting my skin again, making me wince, and her jaw tightened.

"Then he'll come, and he'll stand where I am standing, and you'll have a different sort of conversation. One about control and obedience."

Ice slid down my spine, and I shifted uncomfortably. "Good to know," I muttered.

She hummed in agreement and poured more water from a carafe into the glass, her fingers steady. No tremor. No spilled drop. She had done this a thousand times.

"If you need the bathroom, knock the headboard three times with your wrist," she said. "Someone will come."

Someone. Not her, specifically. *Someone.*

"How many someones are we talking?" I asked. "A whole welcoming committee?"

Her lips twitched, like she wanted to smile and hated that instinct.

"You get privacy, with conditions."

"How fucking generous."

She stepped back from the bed, hands clasped loosely in front of her. The cart waited by the door, neat and harmless.

"Will he be coming today?" I asked, before I could talk myself out of it. "Conor, I mean."

Her eyes flicked to the side, then back.

"Mr. Hayes always comes," she said. "Eventually."

Not an answer and yet somehow exactly the answer I expected.

"Margot," I said. The name made me feel a fraction steadier, like I was still the person who asked coworkers their names and remembered them. "Do you have kids?"

The question surprised both of us. Her shoulders shifted, almost imperceptibly.

"Yes. Two."

"How old?"

"That's not relevant," she replied.

"It is to me." My voice came out gentler than I wanted. "It helps to know what kind of person is watching me starve."

"You're not starving," she said flatly. "You're choosing not to eat in front of a plate I carried up four flights of stairs."

The reprimand landed cleanly as the embarrassment burned under my skin. She adjusted the corner of the tray that didn't need adjusting.

"They are grown," she said then, so quiet I almost missed it. "They don't live here."

I nodded, letting the information settle around me.

"I'll be back in an hour," she said. "If you've eaten, I will ask for the cuff to be removed so you can shower."

Shower. The word landed like a lifeline and a trap at the same time. Clean skin. Hot water. Steam. The illusion of normal. He wanted me to be clear-headed. He had said that last night. No drugs. No fog. He wanted to see what I did with a cage when I could count all the bars.

"I'm not a dog," I muttered. "You don't get to click your tongue and reward me for tricks."

"No," she agreed. "Dogs are rarely used to pay other people's debts."

My breath caught, and our eyes met again. For one heartbeat, I thought she might apologize. For another, I hoped she wouldn't. Apologies were just another kind of lie in a house like this. She walked to the door and paused with her hand on the handle.

"Eat," she said again, without turning. "You'll feel better after you get some food into you."

I didn't answer, and then she was gone. The lock slid shut with a soft click that was somehow louder than a slam.

I stared at the door until my eyes burned, then forced myself to look at the tray instead. At the toast that wasn't burnt, eggs that still steamed, and the fruit cut into careful cubes in a bowl. Nothing fancy, nothing overtly manipulative, but the care in the presentation felt like a hand around my throat.

You are worth arranging things for, it said. *You are worth the time. You are worth the effort. As long as you play your part.*

My stomach growled.

"Traitor," I muttered. Then shifted, testing the chain's length again. I could sit up properly if I moved slowly, but the cuff bit my wrist whenever I pushed my luck. The sheet pooled in my lap, cool air sliding over the bare skin of my arms.

Last night's clothes clung to me. My shirt smelled like sweat and stale perfume, and the back of my goddamn neck itched.

I picked up the glass of water first. The condensation made it slick in my hand. I drank small sips at first, then more, until the glass was nearly empty and the tight ache in my throat loosened.

It helped, yet it made everything worse, as I carefully put the glass down and picked up the fork.

"It is not surrender," I told myself. "This is survival."

The first bite sat like a stone in my mouth. I forced my jaw to move, encouraged my tongue to work, and begged myself to swallow. It hurt. I did it again. By the time the plate was half empty, my hand had stopped shaking.

I kept thinking of Kael. Not the way he had looked in the security footage Conor had described, bent around me like gravity. But the way he had pressed me into the shelves in the linen closet, his hands careful even when his mouth had been anything but, before he had walked away.

He didn't know, I told myself. He couldn't come for what he didn't know was missing.

But Conor was right about one thing. Men like that forgot the room for a reason. Men like that didn't go back to sleep when the thing they had been watching disappeared. He would notice. He had to notice. The clock kept ticking with indifference.

When Margot came back, the tray was empty. I hated myself for that. I hated that the sight of clean plates made something flicker across her face, a quick relief she tried to hide.

"Good," she said. "I'll let him know you ate."

"What does a girl have to do to get coffee around here?" I asked because my mouth always worked faster than my senses.

Her lips twitched again, that almost-smile. "I'll see what I can do."

• • •

An hour later, two men came instead. Two burly men, clearly bodyguards, who were now forced to be my babysitters. Their faces blank in the way you learned from years of being paid to ignore screams.

"Move back," one of them said.

I pressed myself against the headboard and lifted my cuffed wrist. The other man unlocked it, quick and impersonal. The metal fell away. The skin underneath was red and tender. I rubbed it without meaning to.

"Bathroom," the first one said, nodding toward the door in the corner that I had assumed was a closet. "You have fifteen minutes."

"Wow. A whole spa day. Aren't I a lucky girl?"

He didn't bother with a reaction as I made my way towards the door.

The bathroom was bigger than my bedroom back home. White tile, gleaming fixtures, and a tub you could drown a person in without anyone hearing over the echo.

I stepped inside and stopped dead. The sight of my own face in the mirror hit me harder than the cuff ever had. My eyes looked bruised from the inside, and my hair was a mess of knots and tangles. There was a smear of something on my neck I wasn't going to try to identify.

My fingers traced the other side of my neck. Kael's marks were there. Dark against my skin. I bit back a cry as my throat tightened.

He's not coming. You know he's not. Get the fuck over it. Play the game. Live another day.

I turned the water on as hot as I could stand.

One of the men stood in the doorway with his back turned, arms crossed. The other waited outside the bathroom, visible through the gap.

"I'm flattered," I said as I stripped out of my clothes. "All this chaperoning. Normally, a girl has to sit through dinner first."

"Fifteen minutes," he repeated.

I rolled my eyes as steam filled the room. I stepped under the spray and let it pound against my scalp, across my shoulders, and down my spine. Heat crawled over my skin, raising goosebumps. I washed fast, fingers digging into my own flesh like I could scrub off the night and everything with it. The alley. Benjamin's hand. Conor's eyes.

When I closed my eyes, I saw Kael instead. The way his mouth had felt against mine. The way his hands had bracketed my hips, like he was trying to map out where I ended and he began. I shook my head, clearing away those thoughts.

Stupid. All of it. Stupid and reckless and doomed.

I forced myself out when I was sure my time was almost gone. A white towel lay folded on the counter. Someone had brought it in without me hearing. I wrapped it around myself, the cotton thick and unfamiliar.

"Clothes," the man at the door said, handing me a neat stack without looking. "Mr. Hayes's instructions."

I took them with numb fingers. There was a pair of soft black leggings and a long, loose sweater. No bra, and no underwear. Nothing that could be turned into a weapon easily. No strings. No wires. No metal.

"Of course," I sighed.

I dressed quickly and followed them back into the bedroom, bare feet slapping against the wood floor.

The cuff waited on the bed.

I froze. "Again?"

For a second, the man looked almost sorry.

"Rules," he said. "You know how it is."

"No. Actually, I don't. I tend to avoid situations where the turndown service comes with a side of bondage."

His mouth tightened as he picked up the cuff.

I could refuse. I could throw myself at him. I could bite, scratch, or even kick. I could find out exactly how unpleasant it could get and end up with both hands cuffed or worse. My wrist still throbbed from the first round.

I sat on the edge of the bed and held out my hand with a huff. The metal circled my skin again with a small, final sound. The lock clicked, the chain settled, and as they left, the room felt smaller.

I watched the light move across the curtains in a slow, reluctant arc. Somewhere below, I could hear the faint murmur of voices. A door closing. A car engine turning over outside, in the distance. The city kept going without me.

Time stretched and folded. At some point, another tray arrived. Soup this time. Bread. Tea instead of coffee. Margot's face was tighter, her words shorter. I ate again because staying upright seemed like the least humiliating choice.

Eventually, the doorknob turned again, and I knew it was him before I saw him. Something about the air changed. The way it does when a storm rolls in, and the sky can't decide if it wants to spit rain or fire.

Conor stepped inside the room, quiet and unhurried. "Good evening, Seraphine," he said. "You look better."

"Kidnapping really brings out the color in my cheeks," I replied.

He smiled a genuine smile down on me. "The food has agreed with you. I'm pleased."

"Oh, well, as long as you're pleased."

He dragged the armchair a little closer to the bed before he sat. The scrape of wood against wood felt deliberate and unhurried. He lounged there, ankle on knee, as if this were a casual visit to a convalescent friend.

"How's your wrist?" he asked.

"Fantastic. Thinking of starting a new fashion line. Chains for all occasions."

He tilted his head, studying the angry red mark where metal met skin. "You'll live. I've seen you take far worse at Escape. This is… minor."

"Aren't you just a gentleman?"

He ignored my tone, his gaze moving over me in a way that felt more like assessment than leering.

"How did you sleep?" he asked.

"I didn't," I said. "Hard to know what was sleep and what was the drugs your errand boy dosed me with."

"Ah." He nodded once. "The first night is always the hardest. The brain resists new cages."

"How many first nights have you watched?"

His smile sharpened. "Enough to recognize the pattern. You're far more compliant than most."

"That's not a compliment."

"It wasn't meant as one."

He rested his elbows on the arms of the chair and steepled his fingers, watching my face.

"Today is simple," he said. "You eat, you wash, you rest. You pay attention. Your only job is to exist in one room without trying to destroy it. Later, if I'm satisfied, we'll discuss a wider perimeter."

"A wider perimeter," I repeated. "Like letting your new pet walk around the house?"

"If you like," he said mildly. "Though I prefer the word *asset.*"

My mouth twisted. "Feels like livestock from where I'm sitting."

"Livestock doesn't sit across from me and negotiate," he said. "Don't sell yourself short."

"Do you always talk like a self-help book for psychopaths, or am I just the lucky girl?"

"You're one of the interesting ones," he said with a casual shrug. "Usually, I sell the new acquisitions the first night. You're worth holding onto for now."

He leaned back again, gaze flicking to the window.

"It's been an eventful day at the club," he remarked. "Your absence has been noticed."

It felt like someone reached into my chest and squeezed.

"Oh?" I couldn't keep the hopeful note out of my voice. I hated it.

He clicked his tongue softly, like he was debating whether to give a child a toy. "Michael is unsettled. Benjamin reports he's pacing a hole in the office carpet and asking questions with no good answers."

Good, I thought. Let him sweat. Let him choke on the silence he bought with my body.

"And Kael?" I asked, before I could stop myself.

Conor's gaze snapped back to me. There it was again, that spark of interest, sharp and bright.

"Ah, there it is."

"He is just another client," I said quickly. "Another paycheck."

"You say that like you think the distinction matters."

"You said he didn't know I was here. Last night."

"He didn't." Conor's mouth curved. "Last night."

The room tilted around me.

"He knows I'm missing," I whispered.

"Men like him keep track of their assets. Especially the ones that make them forget themselves."

I swallowed hard. My pulse beat against the cuff.

"You're wrong. I'm not his asset. He didn't forget himself enough to stick around. You called, and he left. You sent him away so Benjamin could get me alone in that alley."

Something like approval flickered in his eyes. "You're quicker than Michael."

"That's your big reveal?" I scoffed. "You cleared the board, and now you get to watch the pieces dance? You're a fucking sadist."

"No," he said calmly. "I'm a strategist. You'd be amazed at what people agree to when they're desperate enough to feel like they're choosing."

He rose from the chair in one fluid motion, and I flinched backwards, pressing myself against the headboard before I could stop myself.

"Here is your reality for now," he said softly. "You're here because you were chosen, twice. Once by a man who saw you as a problem he could trade. Once by a man who sees you as a solution he can shape. Everything between those decisions is noise."

"That's not true," I whispered.

"Then tell me, little lamb." His head tilted. "What else are you?"

My mouth opened and closed again. Who was I? I was a bartender and friend. I was the girl who kept pads in the bar's bathroom drawer and the girl Patrick would hug in the alley when the nights got too long. I was the girl Kael kissed like she was something fragile and dangerous at the same time. All of it felt too consequential to hand to him.

"Not yours," I said instead.

"Not yet," he agreed. "Men like Kael always teach their attachments one thing by accident. How to kneel. How to hand over the leash if it means breathing for one more minute."

He smiled then, his face a mask that was too bright, yet cruel. "I'm interested to see which of you breaks first."

I lunged before I could stop myself. The cuff snapped tight, yanking me back. Pain flared in my wrist, and I swore, grabbing the headboard with my free hand to keep from losing my balance.

He didn't flinch. He just watched me, head tilted, fascinated.

"Little lamb's got some teeth after all."

"I won't break for you," I spat.

"Then break for yourself. The result is the same in the end."

He turned and walked to the door, unhurried.

"Sleep, Seraphine," he said as he opened it. "Consider all the ways this could be worse. Gratitude makes people very cooperative."

"Go to hell," I said.

He glanced back, eyes bright. "I brought a piece of it here. No need to travel."

The door closed. The lock clicked, and that stupid fucking clock kept ticking.

I stared at the empty space where he had been and fought the urge to scream just to prove him wrong. The sound would bounce off the walls, soak into the expensive sheets, and die against the heavy curtains. But no one would come. They never did.

Chapter Eighteen

Kael

The second I walked into Escape, it felt all wrong. Not because anyone said anything, nor because the music had stopped or the lights had changed. Not because trouble smelled different in a room like this.

But because she wasn't there.

Sera's absence wasn't a gap; it was a shape. A pulled thread in the fabric of the room that made everything else feel crooked. The bar ran, and the music pulsed. People laughed, drank, and shouted like always. None of it fucking mattered.

My focus dragged across the room the way it always did, checking exits, corners, shadows, and threats. But tonight it snagged on the only thing that was missing.

She wasn't behind the bar. She wasn't on stage. She wasn't weaving between tables. She wasn't anywhere she should've been.

The muscle in my jaw ticked. Fine. Check the back. I already knew she was gone. I'd seen it on the cameras the night before, but it didn't stop me from double and triple-checking.

My boots barely made a sound in the hallway. The dressing room door was cracked open, and it sat empty. Her bag was on the hook. Her stilettos were under the bench. Sera didn't trust this place enough to leave her shit behind.

Bathroom? Empty. Side exit? Locked from the inside.

Fuck.

The itch crept underneath my skin. The kind that had lived there my whole life. The one that meant danger. Loss. That same feeling I had years ago when I watched the light fade from Aryia's eyes and lost her forever.

Like something slipping through your fingers before you even knew you were holding it. I didn't like that feeling. In fact, I fucking hated it.

Patrick should've been here. He wasn't. I texted his phone. No response. Benjamin should've been here. He wasn't. I expected that. The little snake was probably hiding somewhere. I'd find him. I always did.

And Michael—Michael was exactly stupid enough to be here. I headed for the office, the dread settling low and cold in my gut. He'd know something. He always did when it was inconvenient. And tonight? Everything was inconvenient.

The door was closed, and I didn't bother to grace him with a knock; I just turned the handle and walked in. Michael jerked upright from behind the desk like he'd been caught with his hand in a mousetrap. And he had.

"K-Kael," he stammered. "Didn't… didn't expect you back tonight."

I closed the door behind me. Quiet and deliberate.

His throat bobbed around a swallow, and his fear was palpable. Good. He should be afraid.

"Where is she?" I asked.

No raise in volume. No threat. Just the truth. His eyes skittered everywhere but my face.

"Sera? I—I don't know. She probably went home. She wasn't feeling well, said something about—"

"Try again," I said, keeping my voice calm and even. Exactly the opposite of what was thrashing under my ribs.

His mouth opened, closed, and then opened again. Every version of the lie died before he could spit it out. Fear made people sloppy. Michael was inherently a coward. I took another step. Not fast. Not slow. Just enough to make him instinctively back up. He hit the edge of the desk, and his hands flattened against it.

"Kael," he said, voice wobbling. "Listen, man, she—she wasn't feeling good, alright? I told her to take the night off. She left hours ago."

I tilted my head. A tiny movement. Just enough to make sweat bead at his hairline.

"She didn't go home."

It wasn't a question. More of a simple statement of fact.

Michael blinked. "How would you know—"

"Because," I said, stepping closer until he had nowhere left to go, "I already know."

The words settled in the space between us like a verdict, and Michael swallowed hard.

"Maybe she—maybe she went somewhere after—"

"Her jacket's gone," I said. "Her bag is on the hook. She didn't clock out. And Jenny hasn't heard from her."

His pupils shrank. He hadn't expected me to check. He hadn't expected me to notice. He hadn't expected me to care. Fucking idiot.

"What did you do?" I asked.

"I didn't—"

"What did you do, Michael?"

He tried to hold my gaze, and that's when I noticed it. A flicker. Not of fear or guilt, but recognition. A clear understanding of the inevitable.

"Where is she?"

I wanted to hear the words spill from his lips like a confession. I needed to hear him say it.

His breath hitched as he sputtered. "Kael—I… It wasn't me. Benjamin—he orchestrated it. I swear I had no idea!"

I slammed him onto the desk so fast the wood groaned. One hand on his chest. Not pushing, but pinning. The way you'd pin a bug's wings open before you sliced into it.

"What exactly did Benjamin do?" My face was inches from his, close enough to count the beads of sweat breaking out. "Start talking, or I start removing fingers, one at a time."

His whole body trembled as his fingers clawed at my wrist, weak and shaking.

"He traded her," he choked. "He said—said it was the only way. The debt, Kael, the debt—Conor gave me no choice—"

"You had a choice," I said. "You just didn't choose her."

His eyes watered. Not of remorse, just survival. "She didn't fight," he blurted. "She… she trusted him. Benjamin gave her something in her drink."

My vision narrowed to a single point. "She didn't have a chance to fight. You let him hand her over like a fucking poker chip. Like she was nothing. But you were wrong. She's not nothing. She's the line you don't cross."

Michael's voice cracked. "Kael, listen, please, Kael, I'm sorry—"

"No, you're sorry you got caught. You're sorry you took what was mine. But you're not sorry enough. Not yet."

His entire body shuddered.

"Now, where is she?" I asked, each word a blade. "Details, Michael."

"Conor's house," he sobbed. "Benjamin took her there. I… I didn't want to, Kael, please—"

I let go, and he collapsed against the desk, shaking, gasping, and believing he'd been given something like mercy. He hadn't. It was the last easy breath he'd ever take.

I reached into my jacket and threw a stack of papers onto the desk in front of him. They slid across the wood and stopped just short of his hands. A contract. A transfer of ownership that would make Escape mine.

"You want mercy?" I said calmly. "Sign these. Then I own Escape free and clear. No bullshit. No lawyers. No appeals. You walk away alive and breathing, and the club is no longer yours."

He stared at the papers like they were written in another language. "What?" His laugh came out cracked and wrong. "No. No, I won't sign that. That's— that's everything. That's my—"

"—leverage," I finished for him.

I stepped closer and slid a pen across the desk until it bumped against his fingers.

"You lost the right to call it yours the moment you traded her like currency. You don't get to keep the bar *and* your life. Pick one."

He shoved the pen away, panic flashing bright across his face.

"I won't. You can't make me sign—"

"I already have," I said.

His head snapped up.

"You signed Conor's debt note without reading the fine print. You signed away protections when you let him circle your business. You signed the moment you chose survival over her." I leaned down, bracing my hands on the desk. "This is just the part where you acknowledge it."

His hands shook as he looked back at the contract. The pages rustled as he looked at his name written in clean black print, waiting.

"If you don't sign," I went on, voice even, "I walk out that door and let Conor know exactly how much you're worth to him now, and you and I both know what happens then."

Silence stretched around us, thick and suffocating. Michael swallowed hard.

This time, when I pushed the pen back toward him, he didn't shove it away.

"You don't have a choice. Just sign the fucking papers."

His shoulders sagged. Something inside him finally collapsed. With a hand that could barely hold the pen, he signed. Once. Then again. Initialed where I told him to without reading a word. When he was done, he slid the papers back toward me like they could burn him. It was done. Escape was mine.

I straightened, gathering the contract and tucking it back into my jacket.

"Congratulations," I said coldly. "You just bought yourself a piece of my forgiveness."

He looked up at me, hollow-eyed, still breathing like a man who thought he'd been spared. He hadn't, and neither had the club.

"Stand up," I said.

His eyes flashed to mine, but he did it anyway.

"Turn around."

His eyes went wide. "Kael—"

"Turn the fuck around, Michael."

He obeyed. Slow and shaking while he prayed to a God who'd never stepped foot in a place like this.

I reached for him the same way I handled every problem Conor ever put in front of me. With a cold indifference and a calm efficiency. But this time wasn't for Conor. This was for her. And Michael wasn't going to die quickly. He was going to earn every bit of it.

I wouldn't kill him in the office. Not because he didn't deserve it. Because letting him die here would be too easy. Too clean and too public. Conor had eyes everywhere in the club. Cameras. Staff. Drunks with loud mouths. I couldn't risk noise. Not yet. And Michael's death wasn't supposed to be quick. I was going to enjoy every piece of his demise.

"Walk," I said.

He hesitated.

Wrong choice. I grabbed the back of his neck and shoved him forward. He staggered, nearly tripping over his own feet.

"Kael, please… we can talk—"

"The time for talking was before you traded what was mine. Now, fucking move your ass."

I walked him through the back hallway, past the closet where I'd last held her, past the dressing room where her shoes sat untouched. Every room was a reminder, and every empty space scraped against bone. Each step tightened something inside me.

When we reached the alley door, Michael tried to brace himself on the frame.

"I… I can't," he wheezed. "Kael, please! I have a family!"

"You don't deserve them. I'm doing them a favor. Your insurance will keep them going. Don't worry, little rat. They'll survive."

I shoved him out into the cold, and he stumbled against the brick wall, cutting his hand and leaving a smeared print of blood where he caught himself. I took his phone, smashed it against the concrete, and then crushed it under my boot for good measure. His panic spiked so sharply I could almost taste it.

"N-no! Kael, man, come on. Please don't do this. I made a mistake… one mistake! I gave you the club! It's yours. We're even!"

"Even?" I echoed. I grabbed the back of his collar and dragged him toward the car. "Michael, you don't have enough to offer me to make us even after what you've done. You've been making mistakes since the day you crawled out of your mother's womb. It's who you are. A plague. A fucking disease."

"I'll fix it," he gasped. "I'll… Kael, please, I'll help you get her back! Whatever you need!"

"You won't live that long."

I opened the back door of my car and shoved him inside. He landed hard, groaning and clutching his ruined hand, as I slammed the door.

The engine turned over as rain misted the windshield, and Michael whimpered from the back seat.

"Where are we going?"

"Somewhere quiet."

"No! Kael, please—"

I pulled out of the alley, and the city lights fell away behind us, swallowed by the dark stretch of highway. Every mile marker was a countdown. Every passing second tightened the coil inside me.

Michael tried again, his voice shaking.

"W-we can go to the police. Or… or we could go to Conor. He could… he'll fix this—"

I let out a breath of annoyance.

"You're really that fucking stupid."

"Kael! Please!"

"You sold her. You let them touch her. You let them take her. You sat back as she walked into the dark and did nothing."

His breathing turned high and fast.

"I didn't know til it was done! There was nothing I could do, Kael, I swear!"

I met his eyes in the rearview. Dead, flat, and unforgiving.

"You should've come to me first, instead of hiding and trying to forget."

The road narrowed, and the forest swallowed the horizon. Fog pooled low, brushing the headlights. The farther we drove, the quieter the world became. No houses, no lights, and especially no witnesses.

Ten more minutes.

As I turned down a gravel road, the kind that didn't show up on GPS, the kind hunters used when they didn't want bodies found, Michael's fear reached its limits.

"Kael—Kael—WHERE ARE WE—"

"Shut the fuck up, Michael."

Small stones pinged against the metal, and branches scraped the side of the car as Michael started sobbing. My cabin appeared in the clearing. A single dark shape in the trees. The windows were black, and the porch light was dead. No neighbors for miles. No hikers ever came through these parts, and no curious drivers to interrupt me. Just silence. And screaming, soon enough. I parked the car, and Michael began to thrash in the back seat.

"Kael, PLEASE—"

I opened the back door and dragged him out by the collar of his shirt. He hit the ground on his knees, mud soaking through his pants, hands slipping as he tried to scramble backward.

"No! No! Kael, PLEASE, I'M SORRY, I'M SO FUCKING SORRY—"

"You're sorry for the wrong things."

"No, listen! I'LL DO ANYTHING!"

"You've done enough."

I grabbed him by the hair and hauled him to his feet. He cried out, stumbling and slipping as I walked him up the front walk. The cabin door creaked open when I pushed it, and the inside was dark, quiet, and cold. Perfect.

I threw him onto the floor, and he landed hard, coughing and cradling his bleeding hand. I shut the door and slid the lock in place for good measure. Michael sobbed quietly into the floorboards.

I took off my jacket, rolled up my sleeves, and pulled the tarp out from under the sink—the one I used when I didn't want stains. And Michael was a fucking stain. Michael's breathing hitched when he heard the plastic snap open.

"Kael… please…"

I didn't respond. I just dragged the tarp across the floor, smooth and slow, and turned to him.

"Now," I said, voice calm and steady. "We're going to talk. And then you're going to scream. And then you're going to die. Slow."

Michael's eyes went wide. "Why…?" he choked. "Why slow?"

I crouched in front of him and tilted his chin up with one finger. "Because you took the only thing that kept me human, and then you sold her to save your own skin."

He froze. His chest heaved as his breath scraped painfully, his eyes blown wide like prey that finally realizes the hunter isn't bluffing. Beautiful. Cowards always broke in the most spectacular ways. I dragged the wooden chair across the tarp. The legs scraped, and Michael flinched like someone had fired a gun.

"Sit," I said.

He refused, and I grabbed him by the collar and threw him into the chair. His gasp snapped in half as I tied his wrists. First, the ruined hand and then the one that wouldn't stop shaking. Then I moved onto his legs, cinching the knots tight until he whimpered.

"Kael," he whispered. "Please… please, I swear, I didn't know. I didn't know what Benjamin was doing. I didn't know she was being taken—"

"That part is true."

He blinked a startled look up at me as I leaned in close.

"But you knew your debt was due. You knew Conor was circling, and you knew something was coming. And yet, you did nothing to protect her."

His throat bobbed, and I watched the realization, the self-loathing, and the terror knot behind his eyes.

"So far, you've told me nothing," I said as I sat in the second chair, knees brushing his. "Now you're going to tell me everything."

He swallowed hard. "Benjamin didn't tell me his plan until after she was gone," he whispered. "I didn't know he would stoop so low, I didn't think, I couldn't imagine him being so cruel."

"You never think. That's the problem. You react, you panic, you freeze, and now she's paying for your cowardice."

"I didn't choose this! Kael, please! I swear, if I'd known!"

"But even when you did know something was wrong, you did nothing. You could have come to me. Instead, you sat in your office and forgot she was gone."

His breath caught in his throat. "I—I thought she was just missing until he said something. Wouldn't be the first time. She sometimes takes nights off without warning. She didn't seem scared of anything. She didn't… she didn't say anything to me!"

"She didn't know!" I snapped. "And then she was drugged and taken by *your* head bartender in an effort to save your pathetic life."

He crumbled. "I'm sorry," he whispered.

I tilted my head. "Say it like you mean it."

"I'm sorry," he sobbed, louder, throat cracking. "I'm sorry! I'm so fucking sorry!"

"You're sorry now. But you weren't when it mattered."

His sobbing shook the chair. "Kael… please! Please don't—"

"Begging already? And we haven't even started."

He flinched as I stepped behind him and touched his shoulder. Barely a graze, just a ghost of contact. He nearly passed out from fear alone. I laughed at his cowardice.

"Tell me what Benjamin did," I said near his ear. "When he took my Little Fawn."

He shook his head violently. "I can't… Kael, I can't!"

"Yes, you can."

He squeezed his eyes shut. Tears spilled down his cheeks.

"He said that Conor picked her," he whispered. "Because she looked like something he could break, and he wanted to see what she would look like when she did."

My jaw locked tight. "And you didn't come to me then?" I said quietly.

He sobbed harder. "I didn't know!"

"But when you did, when he came to you and confessed his sins, you still didn't tell me."

"I… I didn't know what to do! It was my life or hers, and I fucking chose mine." He spat at my feet; a little fight was left in him after all.

My hand gripped his hair and pulled his head back hard.

"You could've saved her."

His face crumpled. "I couldn't."

"You could've called me."

"Conor wanted to watch you break beside her."

"You could've traded yourself for her."

His sob broke into jagged pieces. "I know."

I crouched in front of him again, taking his face in my hand, rough and steady.

"Look at me. Look at what your inaction bought."

He forced his eyes open, and there was real fear there. A broken man behind the tears as regret ran down his face like blood.

"This isn't punishment," I said softly. "Punishment is for people who have a conscience."

I leaned in until my mouth brushed his ear.

"You don't get punished, Michael. You get erased."

His whole body shook as I took one of my blades from the floor beside me and, without warning, jammed it deep into his thigh. His scream tore through the cabin.

"Kael! No! NO! NONONO!!! PLEASE! PLEASE, KAEL! I'LL DO ANYTHING—"

Without a word, I did the same to his other thigh. His shrieks broke into hoarse, wet sobs.

"Shhhh, little rat. Are you weeping for her… or yourself?"

His sobbing caught mid-breath.

"Mmhmm. Just as I thought." My voice stayed smooth as ice. "Do you think she'll weep for you? Do you think anyone will?"

"No one weeps for the rats who fail to rise above, Michael. No one even remembers them."

His body shook violently, his own mortality breathing down his neck.

"Do you think she's scared?" I asked.

Michael broke entirely. "Yeah," he whispered. "Yes. She's probably fucking terrified."

That was all I needed to hear as I smiled, slow and unhinged.

"Your turn," I said, before dragging him, still tied to the chair, across the floor. I opened the door and walked across the grounds with him in tow. Michael's eyes went wide with terror as we rounded the house and came to a stop.

I let him and the chair tip over. His cry of pain as he hit the ground warmed something dark inside me.

I walked over to the large tractor that held a woodchipper attachment and turned the key, grinning as the engine roared to life.

Michael's breath came in short, panicked bursts now, gasps gripping him as he realized he had no more chances.

"I'd make your peace with whatever God you pray to now, Michael."

I moved the choke lever to run and let the engine warm, rolling my neck until the pops loosened something in my shoulders. I nudged the throttle higher, letting the noise swell and fill the night.

Walking back toward him, I leaned down and plucked my knives from his thighs. His screams spiked as I wiped the blades clean on his jacket. Michael trembled so hard the chair shook against the dirt, and his breath came out in broken, wet gasps.

I crouched beside him, wiped the last smear of red from the blade, and let the silence stretch until he couldn't stand it.

"Kael…" he sobbed. "Please… please… I don't want to die…"

I tilted my head. "And I didn't want her traded into the arms of a different kind of monster. And yet you let her walk straight to him."

His teeth chattered. "I didn't know—"

"You knew enough."

I leaned in, voice quiet, intimate, deadly. "You knew the wolves were circling. You knew Conor's tastes for breakable things, and you still let her walk into that trap alone and thought you were in the clear."

He squeezed his eyes shut. "Please," he whispered. "I'm begging you. Just make it quick."

I hummed low, like I was weighing mercy, and then grabbed his left hand and forced it flat against the ground. He shrieked, jerking, but the ropes held.

"Quick?" I echoed. "Michael, you don't get quick."

My gaze drifted down his trembling fingers, one of them bearing a small, ugly tattoo. The ink was cheap, and the line work was missing in places and blown out. A crude little skull he once bragged about when he thought it made him look like a gangster.

"Ah, yes," I murmured. "This one."

His eyes went wide with terror. "Oh God, please! Please no!"

"This isn't for me to keep. This is a gift for Conor."

Confusion flickered through the panic, and I smiled.

"He likes reminders. So I'll give him one."

Before he could shake out another word, I pinned his palm with my boot, angled the blade, and with no warning at all, carved through skin, tendon, and finally bone. The sound was music to my ears as his scream echoed through the night.

Blood pulsed out in heavy spurts as the severed finger hit the dirt. His cries folded into choking sobs when he vomited down his chest, and I let out a short huff of a laugh.

"You had choices," I said, picking up the finger from the dirt and placing it neatly atop the metal housing of the machine like a gift waiting to be wrapped. "And every choice you made was the coward's one. So now you get a coward's death."

He whimpered, and the sound was small and pathetic. I grabbed his chin, dragging his gaze up until he had no choice but to drown in mine.

"Do you want to know the real reason I'm doing this slowly?" I asked.

His lips trembled, but he didn't answer, so I answered for him.

"Because you claim incompetence. That you didn't know. But when you did, you still let her stay gone to save your own skin."

His eyes filled with fresh terror.

"Innocent men die fast," I murmured. "Guilty men die screaming."

A sob ripped out of him. "Kael… please… don't—"

"Look at me."

He forced his eyes open. I let him see all of the cold, merciless calm I carried.

"You want forgiveness?" I asked. "Fine."

I leaned close enough that he felt my breath. "I forgive you, Michael."

His face lit with the faintest flicker of hope, the kind only a coward would reach for, and then I crushed it.

"But forgiveness isn't freedom."

His whole body sagged.

"It's permission," I said quietly. "To finish what you started."

He made a broken sound. I tapped the metal frame of the machine behind us, its engine snarling steadily and hungrily.

"Say goodbye, Michael."

"Kael—"

"Or don't," I cut in. "Either way, this ends now."

I grabbed the chair and dragged him toward the metal teeth spinning, waiting for its welcome meal.

"Goodbye, Michael," I said, without a shred of remorse, as I angled the chair, legs first, toward the gaping maw of the machine. His screams and the roar of metal teeth that met little resistance ripped through the clearing, rising, peaking, and then—silence.

A wrong had begun to be made right. I killed the engine and stood there for a long moment, breathing in the quiet. One problem erased. I wiped my hands on my jeans, picked the finger off the housing of the machine, turned back toward the car, and finally let my thoughts go where they'd been clawing to get all night. To her. To Conor's house. To the fire I was going to bring with me.

I left the woods behind and drove back toward the city, already planning how to burn a man's world to the ground.

Chapter Nineteen

Conor

The knock came early. Too early for business and too sharp to be a servant with a tray. Far too controlled to be trouble that didn't already know my name. I looked up from the ledger on my desk as the study doors opened a crack. One of my men slipped in, shoulders squared, eyes carefully blank.

"Sir. You've got a delivery."

I arched a brow. "From who?"

He hesitated, then lifted the box into view. White ribboned and perfectly ordinary. I smiled as I recognized the florist's box. I'd used them myself on occasion. Curiosity clung to me as I looked it over.

"Bring it here."

He crossed the rug and set it on the desk, just to the side of my coffee. Steam curled lazily upward, scented with oak and smoke and the faint bitterness I'd grown fond of.

The house was quiet around us as the soft morning light filtered through the tall windows, turning the dust motes into floating stars. Timing, I thought, had always been an art.

I tugged the ribbon loose with two fingers and lifted the lid. The smell hit first.

Rot. Sweet and sour, like someone had left meat on a warm counter. Inside, the carnations were dead. Petals gray-brown and collapsing in on themselves, stems slimy with decay. Maggots writhed lazily in the folds, small white bodies shifting and feeding on the grotesque star of the gift.

A fucking finger.

A small, ugly skull tattoo sprawled across the second joint. The artist had done a poor job. The lines had bled together years ago, turning the already unsightly thing into a smudge across weathered skin.

I recognized it almost immediately. Michael had once been very proud of that tattoo. He'd flashed it in my office as if cheap ink could impress me. The corner of my mouth lifted.

"Ah. So Kael has picked a side."

My man shifted his weight. The smell made his nose flare, but he didn't look away. I hired them for their backbone as much as their aim.

"Do you want it traced, sir?" he asked. "The courier, the florist—"

I plucked the finger out by the twine, ignoring the blood and bloat that smeared my fingers, and held it up before turning it in the light. The bone showed at the base of the cut. Clean work. Efficient.

Kael's work.

"No. I know this handiwork. Taught him myself."

He nodded once. "You want it… disposed of?"

"In time."

I set the finger down on the corner of my blotter, pushing a stack of invoices away to make room for it. The skull stared up at me, pathetic and permanent.

"Tell me," I asked, still studying it, "how many of ours didn't come home last night?"

"Just Michael. Benjamin got back at dawn. The others checked in as scheduled."

Of course Benjamin had. Cockroaches always survived the first sweep.

"And Kael?" I asked.

"No sign of him at the club. Cameras caught him arriving, then leaving with Michael. After that, nothing."

"This is meant to rattle you," the man added quietly, like a suggestion he wasn't sure he was allowed to make. "Sending part of our own like that."

I laughed and shook my head.

"Rattle me? No. This is him remembering who taught him how to write in blood."

The man stayed silent.

"He thinks this makes us even," I said, nudging the finger with a pen until it rolled once and settled, the skull facing me. "Michael, for the girl. One life for one life. A message that he is, as always, still capable of getting his hands dirty."

I smiled wider. "The flaw, of course," I went on, "is that he's still thinking in straight lines."

My gaze flicked to the window, out beyond the glass where the grounds stretched away in manicured rows. Somewhere in the east wing, a very specific problem was waking up and remembering how much smaller her world had become.

"He thinks I will read this as a threat. What it actually is…"

I tapped the finger lightly. "…is permission."

The man frowned slightly, not understanding. He didn't need to.

"Burn the box," I said. "Slowly, so the smell gets into the servants' gossip. I want the whole house to know someone tried to send me a warning."

"And the… rest?" His eyes flicked to the finger.

I considered it. It really was ugly. The tattoo could have been done with better ink and a steadier hand.

"Leave it with me for now. We may find a use for it yet."

He nodded, took the box, and left as quietly as he'd come. The door clicked shut.

I sat alone with my coffee, my paperwork, and the severed piece of a man who had, for a brief and unremarkable stretch of time, believed himself indispensable. Michael, reduced to what he had always been. An easily cut-away part. I sipped from my mug, letting the bitterness settle on my tongue. Kael was moving.

Good. The game was no fun if any one player refused to step onto the board.

I let my mind turn, briefly, to the girl. Seraphine. The way she'd held my gaze instead of sobbing. The way she'd lunged, cuff biting into her wrist, teeth bared. Teeth are interesting on a creature like her.

Most pretty things only ever learn to bare their throats.

I glanced at the clock on the mantle. Margot would have seen to her breakfast by now. If Seraphine had any sense, she'd have eaten.

If she hadn't, I would have to not so gently nudge her until she remembered how to obey. Either way, it was time to remind her that hope, like any other currency, could be managed.

• • •

We found Patrick later that afternoon. Benjamin brought him to me himself, which told me two things: First, that Patrick had been foolish enough to come looking. Second, that Michael and Benjamin had not been as subtle as they believed.

He pushed the man forward into the room. Patrick stumbled, caught himself, and glared.

His lip was split, and one eye was starting to swell. His hands were tied behind his back, his shoulders tight with the strain. Benjamin stood just behind him, smug and alert.

"Found him trying to slip in after Escape closed. Thought he could sneak past us. He was asking questions about her."

Her. As if the building had more than one woman worth this much trouble. Patrick's gaze snapped to mine, full of hatred he hadn't earned the right to wield.

"Where is she?" he demanded.

I looked him over. He was built tall and lanky, but carried a guard's instincts and a dog's loyalty. Useful qualities in their proper place, but fucking annoying when misdirected.

"You're bleeding on my carpet, lad," I said mildly. "It's rude."

He shifted his weight just enough to smear a bit more red onto the rug.

"Good. I hope it stains."

Benjamin's fingers flexed, itching to correct the insolence. I lifted a hand, and he stilled.

"Leave us," I told him.

Benjamin hesitated a fraction of a second too long.

"Sir, I can—"

"Go."

I didn't raise my voice. I didn't need to. His jaw tightened.

"Sure thing, boss."

He left, closing the door behind him.

Patrick and I regarded each other across the room like two men on opposite sides of a line that neither fully understood.

"You're Patrick," I said.

He lifted his chin. "And you're Conor. The coward who couldn't even come for her himself just bought her like stock."

I almost smiled.

"You mistake delegation for cowardice. But then, small men tend to struggle with the concept of scale."

His nostrils flared. "You're not keeping her."

"She's not a set of keys," I replied. "I don't misplace what I acquire."

He took a step toward me before remembering the rope around his wrists, the guards outside, and the distance between what he wanted and what he could do.

"Where is she?" he asked again, quieter this time.

"Here, in my home," I answered. "In a room far more comfortable than the little corner she's been pouring drinks in for the last few years."

His jaw clenched. "She doesn't want to be here."

"Oh, I'm well aware. That's part of the fun."

"You think she's going to stay?"

"I think that people are remarkably flexible when given the right leverage."

Patrick's eyes darkened. "You touch her and I'll—"

"You'll what?" I asked, genuinely curious. "Throw a punch? Look menacing? Bleed on another expensive carpet?"

Patrick exhaled through his teeth. "You think no one's coming for her. You think you're untouchable."

"Think?" I echoed. "No, actually, I know."

I tapped the edge of my desk with one finger, drawing his attention to the severed finger resting beside the ledger. His words died in his mouth.

He knew what he was looking at. Knew whose skin that skull had once been inked onto.

"What did you do?" he whispered.

"Nothing. Yet."

I watched the realization crawl over his face. Kael had moved, and Michael was gone. A message had been sent and received.

Patrick looked from the finger to me with something akin to horror.

"You're not scared of him?"

"He's a valuable piece. He moves with purpose when given the right motivation. Michael served that purpose and now Michael is finished."

"You have no idea what he's going to do to you," Patrick said. "You know that, right? He's not going to stop."

"Yes. That's what makes him useful."

His hands curled behind his back, rope creaking.

"You're sick."

"Possibly. But efficient."

I stood up and moved toward the door.

"Come. We have an appointment."

"With who?" he asked.

"With the girl you're so eager to die for," I replied.

• • •

The walk to the east wing was quiet as my men fell into step behind us, one on either side, their presence more pressure than a spectacle. Patrick stumbled once on the stairs but didn't ask them to slow down. Pride, even when it costs blood, was always interesting to watch.

We stopped outside her door, and I heard her before we went in. The soft scrape of movement. The faint clink of chain against wood. The silence underneath it, heavy and waiting.

I nodded at the nearest guard. He unlocked the door and pushed it open.

Seraphine was on the bed. Not lounging or sprawled. But perched. She was leaning against the headboard, with her knees drawn up, her cuffed wrist resting against her chest. Her hair was still damp at the ends, a mess of dark waves around a face that had seen too much and still refused to dull.

Her eyes snapped to the doorway the instant it opened. They hit Patrick first. The way her expression shattered, then reassembled into something like hope, would have gutted a softer man. I am not a softer man.

"Pat—" Her voice cracked on his name. She swallowed hard and tried again. "Patrick."

He froze just inside the room.

"Hey, Ser," he said quietly.

His mouth tried to smile, but it never reached his eyes.

She took in the swelling at his eye, the split lip, the rope around his wrists, and her hand flew to her mouth.

"What did you do to him?" she demanded, eyes cutting to me like blades.

I almost applauded. Direct and immediate. No attempt at politeness. She was such a little fighter.

"Nothing he didn't volunteer for by being in the wrong place at the right time. You inspire loyalty, and that's inconvenient for me."

Her shoulders rose and fell, sharp with every breath.

"Let him go. He doesn't belong here."

"Oh, but he does. Everyone in this house does, or they wouldn't have made it past the gate."

Patrick shifted, putting himself between us as much as the rope allowed.

"Don't bargain with him," he muttered over his shoulder. "Don't give him anything."

I took a few steps into the room. The curtains were still mostly drawn, letting in a dim wash of gray light. The tray from her last meal sat empty on the table. She'd eaten. Good.

"You misunderstand your position," I said to Patrick. "You don't have anything I want."

He glared. "You sure about that?"

I ignored him, focusing on her.

"This isn't about him. This is about you."

Her cuff clinked against the headboard as she shifted.

"Then untie him. You want me? Fine. You already have me."

"You're here," I agreed. "I don't have you. Not yet."

I gestured lazily to the chair in the center of the room.

"Sit him there," I told my men.

They moved forward, dragging Patrick out of the doorway. He fought them, of course, and he took a fist in the ribs for his trouble. He still tried to angle his body so she didn't have to see the worst of the bruises.

They forced him down into the chair and tied his arms to the armrests. This knot, unlike the one in the hallway earlier, was meant to hold.

"Stop," she said, voice rising. "Please! Conor! He hasn't done anything—"

"He's done exactly what he was meant to! He's gotten in my way. That's his nature. Guard dogs, security men, whatever title you give them. Underneath, they're all the same. Loyal, loud, and fucking expendable."

I moved closer until I could rest a hand lightly on Patrick's shoulder. He flinched but didn't look away from her.

"Don't listen to him, Sera. This isn't your fault. None of this is your—"

A sharp crack cut him off when my fist connected with his jaw. Not enough to knock him out, just hard enough to remind him whose house this was. Silence was required. Not a request.

"Here is what's going to happen," I said, keeping my eyes on hers.

"You are going to listen," I continued. "And you are going to think very carefully before you answer me."

She stared back, jaw tight, fingers digging into the sheet.

"Why is he here?" I asked.

She swallowed. "Because you want me."

"Correct. Because you, Seraphine, are a problem I am in the process of solving. You exist at the intersection of several debts, intricate loyalties, and a variety of fractures within my organization."

I squeezed Patrick's shoulder, feeling the muscle bunch under my hand.

"And he," I added, "is one of those fractures."

"Leave him alone. Whatever Michael owes you, whatever deal you made with Benjamin, it's between you and them. Don't drag Patrick into it."

"Michael is no longer relevant."

I watched as the comprehension flickered across her face.

"This," I said, nodding toward Patrick, "is not about old debts. This is about leverage."

"You're disgusting," she whispered.

"Undoubtedly," I agreed. "But I am also very good at what I do. Which is why we are all having this conversation here… instead of inside a morgue."

I let the next words fall gently, like soot.

"I know you want him to live."

She didn't answer. She didn't need to. It was written in every line of her. In the way she leaned forward, the way her eyes kept darting back to him, and the way her cuffed hand twitched like it wanted to reach for his.

Patrick shook his head sharply.

"Don't. Don't say it. Don't give him anything, Ser. I'm not worth—"

"Wrong," I said mildly. "You're worth exactly as much as she decides you are at this moment. That's the beauty of value. It's fluid, and it bends to my will."

I stepped closer to her side of the bed.

"If you refuse me," I said quietly, "I will have him taken downstairs, I will have him tied to a far less comfortable chair, and I will spend the afternoon finding out exactly how much blood he can lose before his heart stops."

Her face went white.

"And you," I added, not breaking eye contact, "will watch. Every sound, every plea, every useless apology… You will hear all of it. And you will know, with every scream, that you could have stopped it with one word."

Patrick's breath hitched.

"Don't! Seraphine, look at me. Look at me, not him."

She did. Her eyes met his, and I could see the history there. Something far beyond coworkers. A friendship born out of shared trauma and understanding. Years of late nights and early mornings. Movies and coffees and bad dates. Thick as thieves and just as conniving.

"I can handle whatever he does," Patrick said hoarsely. "You don't owe me this. You don't owe *anyone* this."

She shook her head, tears burning in the corners of her eyes.

"Yes," she whispered. "I do."

She looked back at me.

"What do you want exactly? Say it."

Excellent. This was progress.

"I want you to understand that there is no going back to what you were. Not the bartender, not the girl hiding in corners, not the one pretending she could stand just close enough to my world to benefit from it without ever getting her hands dirty."

I lifted my hand, brushing my knuckles lightly along her jaw. She flinched but didn't jerk away.

"I want you to accept," I went on, "that Michael traded you, Benjamin delivered you, Kael lost you… and *I* am the one who kept you breathing."

Her lips trembled. "You kidnapped me."

"Semantics," I said, almost fondly. "So dramatic. I acquired you. There is a difference."

"You don't own me."

"Not yet," I replied. "But ownership, like affection, is a matter of choice."

I let the sentence hang for a beat.

"Here is mine. You give me your loyalty. Fully. No half-measures. No little hidden corners in your head reserved for Kael or Patrick or that sad little club."

Her shoulders stiffened.

"You align yourself with me," I continued. "You stay where I put you. You learn the rules of *my* house. You stop clinging to the fantasy that anyone is coming to rescue you from the consequences of *other people's* choices. You, my little lamb, become mine. Completely and without reservation."

Her throat bobbed as she swallowed.

"And if I do?" she asked. "If I… agree to that?"

"Then he walks out of here alive," I said, nodding toward Patrick. "Untouched from this moment on. He goes back to his life. His bed. Whatever little corner of the city he's carved out for himself. I won't call on him. I won't hunt him. He becomes… irrelevant to me."

Patrick jerked against the ropes hard enough to make the chair scrape.

"You're lying," he snapped. "He's lying, Sera. Men like him don't keep their word."

"When I give it, I do. Lies are for men without power. I prefer contracts."

"This isn't a contract. It's a cage."

"Semantics," I murmured again, rolling my eyes with impatience.

She looked at Patrick, and he shook his head, eyes wild.

"Don't do it," he pleaded. "Don't trade *yourself* for me. I won't be able to live with it."

"You won't be living at all if she doesn't."

"Stop talking," she snapped at me.

The command in her voice made something in my chest tighten. Interesting.

She turned back to Patrick.

"I can't watch him hurt you," she whispered. "Not again. Not for me."

"Ser—"

"Pat. It's ok. It would have always come to this. It was always in the cards. We both knew that."

He stared at her like he was memorizing her face.

"You don't have to do this," he said, voice cracking. "You don't have to save me."

"Yes, Pat, I do. Because you've been the only safe thing I've had for years, and you don't hurt the people who kept you standing. Not when you have the chance to watch them live."

I let them have their moment. Sentiment, when properly timed, is a useful accelerant. Then I stepped in.

"Seraphine, it's time."

She closed her eyes. For a second, just one, I thought she might break in the way most do. Collapse, sob, or beg for alternatives that don't exist. She didn't. She inhaled. Exhaled. Then opened her eyes again and looked straight at me.

"Don't hurt him," she said. Her voice was low and steady, even as it shook. "Let him go. Let him walk out of here and never look back."

"And?" I prompted.

"And I'll stay," she said. Each word cost her something. I could almost see it peeling away inside her. "I'll do what you want. I'll play your games. I'll follow your rules."

She swallowed, eyes burning.

"I'll align myself with you," she forced out. "I'll be yours. Just… leave him alone. Please."

Patrick made a sound somewhere between a curse and a sob.

"Sera, no—"

"Done."

He snapped his head toward me. "You bastard—"

"Untie him," I told my men.

They hesitated.

"Sir—"

"Now," I said.

They moved quickly at my tone, and the ropes came off Patrick's wrists and then his ankles. He sat there for a second, staring, as if he didn't understand what freedom felt like when it came packaged in someone else's sacrifice. Then he surged to his feet.

"Don't touch her," he snarled, stepping toward me.

My men closed ranks, and I didn't bother to move.

"Don't make me regret my generosity, Patrick."

"You call this generous?" he spat. "You just—"

"Walk out of my house," I said calmly. "Right now. With all your limbs attached and your heart still beating. Or stay, and we find out how far her promise stretches under pressure."

He froze. Looked at me and then back to her. She gave him a small, shaky nod.

"Go," she whispered. "Please. Don't make this mean nothing."

His face crumpled.

"I'll come back for you. I swear to God, Seraphine, I'll—"

"Don't. Please. He'll just use you again. Just go be great. Call Jenny. Tell her I'm sorry and let her put you back together."

Our eyes met over his shoulder, and there it was, the broken edge I'd been waiting to see. Not shattered, not yet. But cracked enough and fracturing along the fault line I'd drawn.

"Escort him to the gate," I told my men. "If he turns around before he's off the property, shoot him in the leg and send him limping the rest of the way."

"That's it?" Patrick demanded. "You think this is over?"

"Oh, Patrick. For you? Yes."

He lunged once more, purely on instinct. One of the guards caught him and shoved him toward the door. He dug his heels in long enough to look back at her.

"I'm so fucking sorry," he whispered.

The door closed behind him, and his footsteps faded down the hall. The room fell quiet as Seraphine stared at the door like she could keep him safe by willpower alone.

"You see?" I said softly. "You make the right choices, and your favorite people live."

She turned her head slowly.

"Is that what you call that?" she asked. "The right choice?"

"It was certainly the only one that would have kept him breathing. You can hate me for presenting you with the options. That's fine. But pretend, if you must, that there was a version of today where your refusal didn't cost him something vital."

Tears slipped down her cheeks. She wiped them away with the back of her free hand, angry at them for daring to fall at all.

"I hate you."

"Oh, I expect you will for quite some time, but hate is still a passionate feeling. I can work with hate."

I reached out and gently caught her chin between my fingers, forcing her to look at me.

"Listen carefully, Seraphine. You chose me today. Not because you wanted to. Not because you love me. Because you couldn't stomach watching someone you care about die for your freedom."

My grip stayed light, my tone almost conversational.

"That's the first lesson," I went on. "Freedom is bloody. Ownership is clean."

She tried to pull back, and I let her.

"I'm not yours," she said.

"Not yet," I agreed. "But you will be. Every bargain has a beginning. This was ours."

I stepped away from the bed, smoothing my cuff with one hand.

"Rest. Eat. Think about what you've bought with yourself. Patrick's life, for now. My patience. And the knowledge that Kael is somewhere out there, holding a knife with my name on it, too angry to think straight."

Her fingers tightened on the sheet at that. Let her remember him. Let her cling to him. The higher you build your altar, the more satisfying it is when it falls.

I moved toward the door.

"Conor," she said suddenly.

I paused.

"Yes?"

"If you hurt him," she said quietly, "if you hurt Patrick… whatever you think you're turning me into, you'll never have it. I'll burn before I let you keep it."

I smiled, not bothering to hide it.

"There she is," I murmured. "Teeth and all."

I inclined my head.

"Enjoy your afternoon, Seraphine. You've earned it."

I stepped into the hall, and the lock slid home behind me with a soft, satisfying click.

As I walked away, I thought of the finger resting neatly beside my ledger, and the message Kael thought would land. Let him come, I thought. Let him bring his fire to my door.

I had already taken his asset: his girl, this fragile little piece of his humanity. When the flames arrived, I would be ready to decide which would burn first.

Chapter Twenty

Seraphine

The door closed behind Conor with a click that shouldn't have sounded so final. I sat very still. Not because I chose to, but because my body made the decision for me. My pulse thudded in my ears like something trapped and scraping. My hands wouldn't unclench, and my lungs wouldn't pull air all the way in. Every breath seemed to stop halfway, like my ribs were afraid to expand too far in case something broke.

That something wouldn't be me.

The room felt wrong. The entire place tilted, the walls closing in around me, and everything became too goddamn quiet. I stared at the chair where Patrick had been tied, then at the ropes on the floor and the indentation in the rug. The way the air still held the echo of his weight.

I had saved him. The thought landed where I needed it to, reminding me that I did the right thing. I saved him.

If Conor had dragged that chair downstairs and made good on every threat, if he had peeled Patrick apart piece by piece until there was nothing left but screaming and then silence, I would never have forgiven myself. I would have sat here and rotted around the knowledge that he died because I hesitated.

So I didn't hesitate. I had chosen, and gave myself up for him. And I would choose him again. Over and over, a thousand times. Each and every time. So why did my chest hurt as if I had just made the worst mistake of my life?

Something uncurling under my breastbone whispered that I had traded myself away. That I'd signed something in blood without reading the fine print, and had handed Conor the matches and laid down in the gasoline, all while calling it noble.

My mind knew better, but my body didn't care. My stomach twisted. I pulled my knees up to my chest and hugged them in, my cuffed wrist digging awkwardly against the bone. The metal bit into my skin, and I leaned into the pain, searching for something sharp to focus on.

One, two, three, four…

I started counting the weave pattern in the blanket. Four stitches in each tiny square. Five squares before the seam. Seven seams that I could see from here. Somewhere between four and five, my vision blurred. I blinked, and for a second I wasn't here.

I was ten again, sitting on the edge of my bed, staring at a different door in a different house, listening for footsteps that meant danger.

Counting lines in the wallpaper and counting seconds between creaks in the floor. If you kept the numbers going, nothing bad could slip in.

It hadn't been true then. It wasn't any truer now. But the reflexes years of abuse had taught me didn't know any of that.

I dragged my gaze back to the present. Back to the chair. Back to the empty space that Patrick had left behind when he walked out because I told him to.

He would live.

He would live.

He would live.

The words didn't feel like comfort. They felt like a sentence. Like I had handed Conor a knife and said, here, carve me wherever you like, just don't let him bleed.

A small, mean voice curled its lip in the back of my skull.

You handed yourself over for a man who doesn't even love you like that.

I closed my eyes. That wasn't fair. I knew Patrick loved me. Maybe not the way Kael did, or the way Conor thought everyone should be owned. But he was the only thing in my life that had ever felt unconditionally safe. The only person who stood between me and the world without demanding anything in return.

You didn't weigh that kind of love on a romantic scale. You weighed it against survival. If I had been forced to choose between my heartbeat and his, I already knew which way the scale would tip. Still, the thought lodged somewhere in my throat.

He would go back to the city. Back to Escape. Back to Jenny. Back to the apartment that used to be ours, and would now be his. Back to his stupid favorite mug with the chipped rim and purple handle that matched his hair. He would go back to a life that still had other options, while I had turned my back on mine.

I pulled the blanket tighter around me and made myself smaller, like maybe if I shrank enough, Conor would forget I existed. The cuff clinked against the headboard. The sound zapped up my spine.

One, two, three, four…

The pattern on the curtains this time. Flowers and vines twisted into each other until you couldn't tell where one ended and the other began.

They reminded me of Kael's scars, the ones I'd traced with my eyes when he wasn't looking. Iridescent patterns winding over muscle and skin. Stories written on skin he never offered to explain. Kael.

His name hit harder than the memory of the punch Conor had landed on Patrick's jaw. Harder than the way Patrick's voice had broken when he promised he would come back for me.

I pictured Kael doing his worst to Michael. His hands bloody, and his jaw clenched, while his eyes stayed empty in that way that was somehow worse than rage.

I pictured Michael screaming, begging, bargaining, and Kael not flinching once.

A part of me shuddered. Not because I thought he was wrong. But because I knew that when he found out what Conor was doing here, what had happened in this room today, there would be nothing left of him but ash.

I pressed my forehead to my knees and breathed out slowly. The air tasted like lemon cleaner and expensive linen. Sterile and polished, like the room had been scrubbed of any trace of the last woman who slept in this bed.

I imagined the others. Others who cried in this bed before me. The ones who didn't have Patrick to bargain for. The ones who didn't have a man like Kael carving warning signs out of bone and sending them in flower boxes.

Did they bargain at all? Were they given the chance? Or did they simply vanish?

Stop.

I clamped down before the spiral dragged me under. The point was, I was still here. I chose this, and if Patrick stepped back into this room right now, if Conor replayed the last hour, if I had to stand in that moment again with his life balanced on a single word, I wouldn't change my answer. I would still say yes.

The guilt didn't care. It slunk in around the edges, whispering that I had betrayed more than just myself. In the sense that when Conor held a knife to Patrick's life, I gave myself up without even wondering what Kael would want.

The idea of Kael standing over a dead Patrick because I tried to be noble was unbearable. No. Kael was more than that. He would see that if it had been him here, instead of Patrick, I'd have made the same choice.

My throat tightened again, and I tucked my chin further down, resting it on my knees. My free hand curled into the blanket. The cuffed one gripped the chain, keeping count of the links just to have something to do.

One. Two. Three. Four. Five.

I lost track and started again. There was a shape in my chest that felt a lot like regret. It pressed against my ribs, heavy and wrong. If I poked it, it shifted into something else. Grief. Fear. Rage.

It wasn't regret for saving him. It was grief for the version of me that thought I might get out of this life without repeating my past. For the girl who swore that if anyone ever tried to cage her again, she would burn the place down before she let them turn the key. Now I had put the chain around my own wrist, and it felt like a betrayal I didn't have a name for.

My brain kept trying to spin it into weakness.

You chose to stay.

You let him win.

You let them all be right about you.

I knew that voice. I'd grown up with it. It sounded like every adult who ever told me I should have screamed louder, run faster, known better. The ones who thought a child could out-think a monster.

I breathed in and out, slow and shallow, until the feeling loosened a fraction. I didn't let anyone win. I had looked a monster in the face and bought someone's life with my own. That was not a weakness. It was the only kind of strength I had left.

A sound slipped out of me. A noise that wasn't quite a laugh, too soft to be a sob. Something in between.

"If Kael were here," I whispered into the empty room, "he'd tell me I did the right thing."

He would have said it in that rough, quiet way, like the words scraped his throat on the way out. He would cup my face in those big, careful hands and tell me I chose mercy, and that that was the part of me he never wanted to lose.

Then he would go commit atrocities, so I didn't have to. The thought soothed and terrified me in equal parts. Because Kael wasn't here.

Conor was. Conor, with his ledgers and his fancy whiskey, and his calm, amused eyes. Conor, who had looked at my choice and seen not sacrifice, not bravery, but leverage. Another string to pull. Another way to reshape me into something that fits on his shelf.

Footsteps passed in the hall again. Different this time. Lighter. The measured rhythm of someone carrying a tray, perhaps. Or someone who had done this walk enough times that their body took over while their mind went somewhere else.

I went still until the footsteps faded. I told myself I was being dramatic. That he had better things to do in the middle of the day than come back here and pry at my cracks.

Then I remembered the way he had touched my chin in that last moment, the way his eyes had lit when I snapped at him, the soft, delighted '*there she is*'.

He wasn't done with me.

I shifted, uncurling just enough to stretch my legs out on the bed. The movement felt clumsy, like my limbs belonged to someone else. I smoothed the blanket over my thighs and stared at my hand.

The cuff was stark against my skin, shiny and neat. Not a rough rope or a rusty chain. A pretty prison. I twisted it once, testing the give I already knew wasn't there as my mind reached for old tricks.

If you don't look at the door, it won't open.

If you act small enough, quiet enough, empty enough, they get bored faster.

If you float your head somewhere else, they can't really touch you. Not all the way.

I hated that I remembered these things so easily. I hated that my body was already lining them up like tools. I swallowed hard and made myself lift my chin.

This is not then. I am not ten years old anymore. I am not powerless. I have people who love me now. A man who was sending fingers in flower boxes. A best friend who walked out of this house alive because I told him to. A woman back at the club who would put Patrick back together again and then start quietly planning how to burn all of this down if I gave her half a chance.

I wasn't alone, but the fear didn't vanish. Instead, it settled lower. Thicker and heavier, filling the emptiness with something worse. I sat there and let it exist. Let the panic roll through in waves instead of pretending it wasn't there. Every time it peaked, I counted.

Stitches. Seams. Links in the chain. My breaths.

By the time it ebbed, my muscles trembled with exhaustion, and I lay back against the headboard and stared at the ceiling. There was a crack in the paint near the light fixture; a tiny, crooked line the painters had missed. I fixed my gaze there, as if it were the center of the universe.

Somewhere deep in the bones of the house, a door closed. A male voice laughed. Another answered.

I didn't catch any words. I didn't need to. I felt it. The shift and the way the air tightened when someone dangerous was moving closer.

I dragged one last breath into my lungs, slow and controlled, and uncurled my fingers from the blanket.

"Okay," I whispered. "Okay. You're here. You chose this. You can survive it."

My heart didn't believe me. My body remembered too much. I kept my eyes on the crack in the ceiling and waited for the footsteps I knew were coming. The soft ones. Measured and unhurried. The ones that never rushed, because men like Conor never needed to.

• • •

The days that followed passed in a blur. Margot came and went with her trays of food, and approving smiles when she would return to carry the empty plates away again. Time felt like it had forgotten me. Left me here to simmer in the choices I made. To save Patrick. To save myself in a way.

It was early in the evening when the sound of footsteps stopped outside my door. Not hurried or angry. Just purposeful in their intent. The kind of steps someone took when they already knew what the room looked like. What I looked like. How this would end.

My pulse climbed high into my throat, thick and hot. I couldn't tell if I was breathing too fast or not at all. My hand tightened around the chain again—*one, two, three, four*—counting like it might build a wall between me and what was coming.

The door opened, and Conor stepped inside as if he lived here. As if this wasn't my cage but his parlor. He shut the door behind him, and the soft click of the lock slid down my spine.

"Good," he said, voice warm in a way that made me want to curl away from it. "You're awake."

I didn't answer. I couldn't move.

His gaze skimmed the room, moving from the rumpled blanket to the empty tray and the chair Patrick had occupied like a ghost still pressed into the fabric of the air before finally settling back on me.

"You look exhausted," he observed, crossing the room without being invited. "You should rest. The body suffers when the mind carries too much."

My fingers dug harder into the blanket, and I pressed the metal cuff into my skin for something to anchor me.

He stopped beside the bed.

Close.

Too close.

"I've been patient with you. I've given you time to grieve. Time to mourn the life you traded so he would live. More patient than most men in my position would be."

His hand lifted, and this time I didn't flinch. I forced myself not to. His knuckles brushed my cheek. Barely a touch, a whisper of contact that felt like a command. My stomach dropped, heat and cold colliding under my ribs in a way that made it hard to stay in my skin. His thumb traced the corner of my jaw.

"You're trembling."

"I'm not—" My voice cracked.

"Seraphine." His tone smoothed into something dangerous. "Don't lie to me. We're building something stronger than that."

I pulled my head back a fraction, but the headboard stopped me. The cuff clinked in the quiet. He watched the movement with a slow smile, like he enjoyed the reminder that escape wasn't an option for me in particular.

"You made a choice. A loyal one. A brave one, despite what you tell yourself."

He sat on the edge of the bed like he had every right to. The mattress dipped under his weight, and my body reacted before my mind did, curling in tighter as my chest constricted.

A familiar sensation crept through me, its reminders old, unwanted, and fucking instinctive. The same one I used to feel when footsteps came down a hallway I didn't want them in. When doors opened that I had prayed would stay shut.

Float.

Don't think.

Go somewhere else.

Conor noticed the shift. Of course he did.

"Ah," he murmured. "There it is. The part of you that survived by disappearing."

My throat closed.

"Don't," I whispered.

"Don't what?"

"Don't talk like you know me."

"But I do." His hand slid to the side of my face again, tilting it up. Gentle rather than cruel, which somehow made it worse. "People reveal themselves when they are most afraid."

I wanted to pull away, but I still couldn't move. My body wasn't listening to me anymore.

He leaned in, breath brushing my temple.

"This isn't punishment," he said quietly. "This is acclimation. You chose me, and choices have… rewards."

I shut my eyes, just for a second. Just to get one breath that didn't feel like broken glass. The room swayed, and the sound stretched around the edges.

His fingers trailed down my arm. Slow, unhurried, while laying claim to pieces of me I refused to give.

The weight of his body pressed into the mattress as he pressed me down. His hand skated up my inner thigh as I tried in vain to recoil from him. But there was nowhere for me to go.

His palm settled high on my thigh, fingertips grazing the hem of my skirt he'd had brought to me after my earlier shower. I should have known then what was coming. The heat of his touch seared through the thin fabric, branding my skin. My breath came in short, panicked gasps as his hand began to creep higher, mapping the contours of my leg with deliberate slowness.

"This is just the beginning," he murmured, his lips barely brushing the shell of my ear.

"I'm going to unravel you piece by piece until there's nothing left but what I've made you." His other hand found my free wrist, pinning it above my head with a grip that was just shy of painful.

He used his body weight to keep me pinned to the mattress, the hard planes of his chest crushing against my body.

The air grew heavy with a suffocating sense of inevitability, and I could feel the last pieces of my agency slipping away, replaced by a rising tide of helpless dread.

His hand drifted to where I least wanted him, fingers ghosting over skin that had never been his to touch.

"You're trembling again," he observed, a note of dark satisfaction coloring his tone.

"Anticipation or fear? Perhaps a delicious mix of both. It doesn't matter. Your body knows who it belongs to now."

He caught my chin, forcing me to meet his gaze. In the shadowed depths of his eyes, my own reflection looked back at me. Small and trapped in eyes that held no softness for me. A silent scream built in my throat, but I swallowed it down, knowing it would only spur him on.

"This is your new reality," he whispered as his thumb brushed over my lower lip in a mockery of tenderness.

I felt myself shift under him, letting myself retreat into that place I had built in my mind as a child. Where the monsters couldn't get me. Not safe. No, never that. Just… gone. Pulled up and out of myself like I used to when the world got too loud, too sharp, too unavoidable.

Count.

Focus.

Stay small.

Stay still.

If you were quiet enough, sometimes the moments passed more quickly.

"Such a good little lamb for me," he murmured. His voice wasn't kind, not gentle, but triumphant. "You're learning."

My stomach twisted. The words hit somewhere raw, somewhere that didn't belong to him.

He reached for the cuff. Not to free it. To test it. To make sure the metal held.

"You're mine," he said.

The bottom dropped out from under me.

"Conor, please don't," I whispered. Not pleading or bargaining. Just to name the danger in front of me. The way a child named a shadow to prove it was real.

He smiled, and the mattress shifted as he pressed closer, making sure there was no part of me that could forget how much he was enjoying this.

I kept my eyes on the ceiling, on that tiny crack near the light fixture, and I pulled into my mind, somewhere higher, somewhere quieter.

The world narrowed to three sounds:

The chain, his breath, and the bedframe creaking.

Fade.

Float.

Survive.

The darkness wrapped around me like a welcome shroud as everything else faded into the background. He could take my body, but my mind would always be mine.

• • •

The door closed behind him with a final click that shouldn't have been so loud. It shouldn't have been the thing that made my stomach fold in on itself. But the sound carried through the room, and I dry-heaved the instant his footsteps faded. Silence spilled into the space he'd left. Thick and slow. Heavy as wet wool.

I didn't move. My body stayed where it had been. I was curled on my side, one arm tucked under me, the cuffed wrist angled in a way my joints would hate later. My cheek pressed into the pillow, and my hair clung to my skin, damp with sweat I wasn't ready to feel.

For a long time, I didn't breathe. I think my body forgot how. The house creaked somewhere outside the room. A pipe hummed.

Someone laughed on a distant floor. Life went on in a place where mine had just split along a fault line I felt through to my bones.

I stared at the duvet pattern. One branching line. Another. And another.

My mind tried to count them and tried to find the repetition again. The rhythm. The quiet mathematical truth that had held me together earlier. But the numbers wouldn't come. Everything in my head felt muted. Like I'd been submerged underwater, sound warping as thoughts drifted in slow, disjointed pieces.

I tried to lift my head. My muscles felt numb and heavy, like they belonged to someone else. The cuff slipped against the metal bracket on the headboard when I finally managed to move. The noise, as small as it was, cut something deep inside me. I flinched so hard it jolted pain up my arm.

I froze again. My breathing stuttered, then rushed back into my lungs before stuttering again. I pushed myself upright in small increments, like each motion needed permission. Sitting hurt in ways I didn't want to think about. An ache where it wasn't welcome. And then everywhere all at once. In the hollows and the in-between places. In the parts that weren't meant to be touched by someone like him.

My legs shook when they slid out from under me, and I pulled the blanket over them quickly. I didn't know why. Instinct, or shame maybe. Or just the need for something between me and the air in the room. My throat ached when I swallowed, like I'd been holding back sound for too long.

The clock on the dresser ticked. I stared at it for a long time without seeing it as the minutes passed.

Or maybe they didn't. Time felt stretchy, unreliable. I lifted my hand. Not the cuffed one, my free one, and pressed my fingertips to my chest. My heart thudded under my palm, fast and uneven. Too loud in the quiet room.

Stop.

Stop shaking.

Stop thinking.

Just fucking stop—

But thoughts leaked in anyway. Patrick's face came first. The way he looked back at me before the guards dragged him away. The promise he tried to make, even when he knew he couldn't keep it.

I saved him. The words rose again, but they didn't settle the way they had before. They twisted. I had saved him, and now I get to live in what was left of me. A sharp inhale cut through my chest before I even realized I was breathing in again.

I hugged my knees. Not tightly, but just enough to feel the pressure. Enough to keep myself anchored so I wouldn't float away.

My free hand gripped the chain again, the links cold and hard and real. Real felt better than the alternative. I counted them. I didn't mean to. I didn't consciously start. My fingers moved on their own.

One.

Two.

Three.

Four.

Five.

Six—

I lost my place and started again.

One. Two. Three—

Somewhere under the numbers, something hot pressed up behind my eyes. My throat tightened. My breath hitched around a sound that almost escaped.

Not yet.

Not here.

Not where he would be waiting for a reaction.

I pressed the heel of my hand against my mouth. Hard. Enough to force silence. I sat that way for a long time.

My thoughts sank into small details. The coolness of the headboard. The weight of the blanket.

The faint lemon smell the cleaner left behind. The way my hair stuck to my neck. The tremor in my fingers I couldn't stop. The distant hum of something cutting through a silence that refused to swallow me.

The steadiness of it.

Steady. I needed steady.

But my vision blurred again, the edges of the room going soft. I blinked once and then twice. The third blink dragged a tear free, and it hit my knee.

I didn't realize I was crying until the second tear followed, warm and slow. Then another. And another. They didn't come with sound. No sobs, no shaking breaths. Just silent tears rolling down my face, slipping off my chin, soaking into the blanket pooled around my legs.

My shoulders folded forward, and my body swayed. The tears kept coming, quiet as snowfall. Grief, not for Patrick. Not for Kael. For me. For the version of myself I'd hoped I'd never have to be again. For the girl I'd promised I would protect. For the woman I was now, sitting on a stranger's bed with a cuff around her wrist, counting metal links to stay conscious inside her own skin.

I wiped my face with the back of my hand. The gesture felt clumsy, like my arm belonged to someone else.

I hiccupped as I pressed my fingers to my eyelids until colors burst behind them.

Stop.

Stop.

Stop.

The tears didn't listen.

I curled forward until my forehead touched my knees, my whole body folding in on itself like I could make myself smaller than the memory of his touch. Smaller than the room. Smaller than the moment. If I could get small enough, maybe none of this would stick.

But it already had. A sound escaped me. Thin and broken. Barely a whimper. I clapped my hand over my mouth again, instinctively and sharply.

He could come back.

He could be listening.

He could hear—

The panic spiked like a flashfire, hot and blinding, stealing the air from my lungs. My breath quickened, too fast, too shallow, the edges of the room warping like heat haze.

Not here.

Not now.

Not now.

I forced myself to sit upright. My spine protested. My ribs felt too tight. I pressed one hand against my sternum like I could hold myself together.

Just breathe.

It's fine.

You're fine.

I wasn't fine, but I inhaled anyway.

One breath.

Two.

Three—

The fourth one caught and broke. I pressed both hands to the bed, grounding myself against the mattress, the headboard, the weight of the cuff.

Here.

You're here.

You're here.

Gradually, with great slowness, the panic began to ebb, leaving me trembling and hollow. I wiped my cheeks again. The tears had slowed to a trickle. The pressure behind my eyes began to dull.

I sat for a long time in the quiet aftermath, staring at nothing. Then, carefully and deliberately, I pulled the blanket around my shoulders and leaned back against the headboard.

Exhaustion settled over me like a second skin. My body felt bruised everywhere, even where no hands had touched. My throat burned and my chest felt scraped raw.

But I was alive. Patrick was alive. And somewhere out in the city, somewhere drenched in rain and gasoline and fury, Kael would feel the shift in the air.

He would feel the loss of me. He would come. The thought didn't comfort me; it scared me in a different way. Because whatever Conor started in this room? Kael would finish with fire.

I pulled the blanket tighter and let my eyes focus on the crack in the ceiling again. Just a line. Just paint and plaster. Just something to hold on to. I sat there until my breathing steadied. Until the tears dried. Until the trembling quieted. Until the silence stopped feeling like a threat.

And then, when the house had gone still around me, and the light through the curtains began to fade, I whispered, just for myself:

"You survived this. You can survive everything that comes next."

I didn't believe it yet. But I needed to hear it. Even if the only person listening was me.

Chapter Twenty-One

Benjamin

I hadn't slept. Not a minute. Not a second. My mind kept scraping itself raw while my body refused to shut down. Every tick of the clock felt like a drop of water in a torture cell.

I should have fucking run. I should have packed a bag the second I saw that goddamn message about Michael. I should have been a hundred miles away by sunrise. But instead, I'd holed up in this shitty apartment like it was some kind of fortress. It wasn't. It was a coffin waiting for the lid to close.

My hands shook so badly that I dropped things just trying to make coffee. The mug shattered, and I didn't bother to pick it up. The shards glittered on the floor like little promises.

Michael was dead. Not missing. Not simply gone to ground to hide. Dead. And not cleanly. No one needed to say it. The way everyone spoke his name, as if they were afraid of waking something, told me enough.

Kael had done it. Which meant I was next.

Fuck!

I paced the kitchen, my breath catching in my throat, as the sweat crawled down my spine. My heart kept lurching in my chest like it was trying to escape me. A floorboard creaked in the living room, and I jumped as if a gun had gone off.

"Calm down," I whispered to myself, even though calm wasn't an option anymore. "He won't get this far. Conor has eyes everywhere. He'll protect—"

I stopped mid-sentence. Conor didn't protect people. Conor used them. And I knew **too much**. Worse, I had **done too much**.

Especially a few days ago.

Dropping Patrick at the estate had been routine. Easy. Normal. Conor barely looked at him. Owen, one of the guards, had winked at me as if Patrick were just another fucking package.

God, I was stupid. So stupid. My throat tightened, and I rubbed my face hard enough to sting, trying to scrub the panic out of it.

The floor of the hallway creaked again.

"Get it together," I hissed.

I grabbed a kitchen knife. It was dull and useless, but it made my hand feel less empty. I edged toward the sound. Nothing there. Just dark corners and old drywall. I sagged back against the table, shaking.

Then my phone buzzed, and I screamed when it slipped from my fingers and hit the counter before bouncing to the floor. I froze, staring at it like it was a snake.

Unknown Number.

"No," I whispered. "No, no, no—"

I forced myself to crouch down and pick it up. My thumb trembled as I accepted the call and pressed it to my ear.

"H-hello?"

Silence. Then—

"Benjamin."

His voice was low and calm, and I almost threw up right then.

I dropped the phone, and as it clattered on the tile, I backed away so fast I tripped over my own feet and hit the floor.

He was here. He had to be here. He was watching. Listening. Waiting.

"Kael," I gasped. "Kael, please—"

My voice cracked apart on the words.

I scrambled to my feet, knife brandished like it mattered. I ran to the window and yanked the curtain. Nothing outside jumped out at me, just the empty street loomed dark and uninviting.

I turned in a circle, chest heaving, and then I saw it. On the rug by the front door. A shape, small and red. No. No, please—

A spider lily. Its bright color was a stark contrast to my dreary rug. Death had come for me, and its horseman was Kael.

My legs gave out. I fell back against the wall and slid down it, shaking so badly it felt too wrong to be real.

A shadow moved across the floor.

"No," I whispered, but it came out strangled.

I looked up.

Kael stood in the doorway. Not breathing hard. Not sweating. Not even rumpled. He looked like he'd taken a peaceful walk.

"Hello, Benjamin," he said.

The knife fell from my hand, and a broken sound tore out of me. The sound was humiliating, small, and terrified.

"Kael! Please! I didn't know what Conor planned. I swear, I didn't know!"

Kael didn't react. He didn't blink. He just crouched down in front of me, calm as a priest hearing confession.

"Yes you did, Benjamin. Lies do not become men like us."

My breath hitched.

"Michael actually didn't know. Not really. But he still died screaming."

Something inside me split, and I broke. Sobs ripped out of me. Not normal crying, no, horrible, gagging sobs that shook my whole body. Kael tilted his head slightly, studying me.

"You have something you want to tell me?" he asked quietly.

"I… I can help," I babbled. "I know the estate. I know the guard rotations. I know the codes! I can help you get her out—"

Kael smiled down at me.

"I know the place, Benjamin. I know the codes. I know Conor. You have nothing left to offer me when it was you who traded the one thing I actually fucking care about to the man with the iron fucking leash."

My blood turned to ice.

"Kael! No! I never meant for her to get hurt!"

He stood up smoothly, and I curled into myself like a dying insect.

He looked down at me with that terrifying stillness he had. Anger was an emotion, and Kael never did emotion. This was purpose.

"You drugged her," he said. His voice was eerily calm, as if he were recounting my sins before pronouncing his judgment.

I shook my head wildly. "It was just business! Doing what I was told—"

"You carried her." Another sin. Another charge. Another reason I wouldn't make it out alive.

"I didn't know—!"

"You handed her over."

"I HAD NO CHOICE!"

Kael knelt again, and he wiped a tear from my cheek with his thumb, and I threw up in my mouth. He looked at the moisture on his thumb, then wiped it casually on my shirt.

"You always had a choice, and now you're just afraid of the consequences," he observed.

I nodded so hard my vision went blurry.

"You should be."

The lights flickered. Once. Twice. Then all at once. Darkness swallowed the apartment. I sobbed, scrambling backward until I hit the wall.

"Kael—please—please, I can—don't—"

His voice came from somewhere in the dark. Close. Too close.

"She was trembling too," he whispered. "But she didn't get the luxury of begging."

My lungs seized as something brushed my ankle, and I kicked wildly, screaming. Then a fist tangled in my hair, gripping at the root. Pain shot through my scalp as he dragged me across the floor.

I screamed. I begged him for my life. Promised him everything I didn't have. Lied to the man who held my fate in his hands. I cried, desperate to get out of this alive.

He didn't reply. He didn't grunt. He didn't even break a sweat. Just dragged me to the center of the room, smooth and patient.

In the dark, I heard one faint sound: A long, slow exhale.

Then nothing. Silence. I didn't feel the blade open the skin on my neck. Didn't notice the way my blood began to pool around me. A quiet calm washed through me, lulling me under with far more care than I deserved.

Kael stepped over me, and the front door opened, closed, and locked from the other side.

His footsteps faded down the hallway as if he'd just finished taking out the trash. He was already gone. Heading for Conor. Heading for her. Heading for the end of this.

And I—

I was finally still.

Chapter Twenty-Two

Kael

Benjamin's blood was already drying under my nails by the time I stepped out into the open air. A cold night and a quiet street. Nothing dramatic. Just another evening in a city that didn't care how many bodies I fed it.

I wiped my hands on a rag I'd taken from his kitchen. Useless. Nothing short of fire would get the stain out of fabric like that, but it didn't matter. I wasn't hiding anymore. Conor would know long before I reached him.

He'd changed the codes. Of course he had. Michael disappears. I disappear. A finger arrives in a box.

Any half-intelligent man would rotate his security. Conor wasn't stupid. He was arrogant.

I pulled Benjamin's phone from my pocket and looked at the blood smeared across the cracked screen. I thumbed it awake, and there it was on the main screen, in an encrypted group thread: Rotation update. Shift assignments. Codes and patrol points. The kind of updates a man sent when he thought he still had control. Men like Conor always forgot who trained their dogs to heel.

I memorized them in one pass, then snapped the small device in half. A small, pointless act of violence, but it steadied something in me.

The estate wasn't far. Fifteen minutes driving with care. A climb up a long, winding hill, and I knew every inch of it. From every blind spot to every shadow, and every camera that Conor trusted more than the men he kept on his payroll.

I'd walked those hallways a hundred times. Guarded his doors and stood for hours outside Conor's study while he talked in circles. And now she was upstairs in his house. The thought didn't burn. It fucking froze inside me and festered.

Benjamin had begged. Michael had bargained. Conor wouldn't get the chance to do either. He'd taken something from me. No. Not something.

Someone.

Someone who trembled in my arms like safety wasn't something she could register. Someone who went quiet in a way that made me want to pluck out my own heart, hand it to her, and let her take what she needed from it. Someone who had looked at me like she needed me as much as I craved her.

Conor had taken that, and he was going to die for it. Not quickly. Not like Benjamin or Michael. His would be a slow, exact, and measured death, and I wouldn't lose a minute's sleep over it.

I crested the hill and the estate rose out of the dark like a cathedral built for monsters. There were lights on in the windows, guards lining the perimeter, and cars lining up along the drive. Reinforcements in the form of men answering a summons they thought meant safety. He had no idea the kingdom was already burning.

I flexed my hand once, wiping off the last of Benjamin's blood. "Alright," I murmured to myself. "Let's end this."

• • •

The gate loomed ahead. A gaudy wrought iron thing, tall, and ornamental. There was a brand-new keypad with brand-new guards, but none of it mattered.

I moved through the tree line instead, my boots silent in the underbrush. The shadows here were familiar. I'd stood in them dozens of times, waiting for Conor's signal, or his cousin

Cillian's report, or the next order to fall out of someone else's mouth. Tonight, they would all answer to me.

Two perimeter guards stood by the rear corner of the estate. They weren't relaxed tonight. They were rigid and scanned the dark as if they expected a ghost. They weren't wrong.

I waited for the wind to rise, and the second it did, I stepped out behind the first guard and clamped a hand over his mouth. He bucked once, a sharp inhale, before my blade slid cleanly into the base of his skull. I lowered him to the ground without a sound.

The second one turned, but his movements were too slow and too unsure as he reached for his radio. I grabbed his wrist midair, twisted until his bone cracked, and drove the same blade across his throat in a single, practiced sweep. He dropped to his knees; his hands pressed to the wound as if he could hold in the life spilling between his fingers.

He couldn't, and neither of them survived long enough to know I'd already taken off their radios, their earpieces, and their weapons.

One set of Conor's guards down, and no alarms sounded. So far, so good.

I slipped around the side of the house. Gravel crunched under the tires of a car pulling into the front drive. Two men climbed out, laughing like the world wasn't about to snap in half beneath their feet.

They didn't matter. Not yet.

I headed for the service entrance tucked beneath the stone archway that most people forgot existed, but I never had. I'd smoked half my teenage years beside that door while Conor decided whether he needed my fists or my silence.

The keypad blinked red, and I typed in the updated code from Benjamin's phone. The light turned green, and I almost smiled.

Inside, the air was colder and sterile, thick with lemon cleaner and the faint undertone of expensive meals. The place always smelled like someone trying to mask rot with polish.

I stepped into the narrow service hallway, with its concrete floors, low ceilings, and storage closets lining both sides. Voices echoed from the kitchen at the far end. Too many to take cleanly, which was fine. I didn't need the kitchen, I needed shadows.

Two guards stood at the bottom of the stairwell leading up. Leaning on the railing, talking in low tones.

"Conor says nobody in or out until he gives the word."

"Because of the girl?"

"Because of Kael."

The first guard laughed nervously. "You think he's really coming here? Tonight?"

"He cut a man's finger off and mailed it in a flower box. What do you think?"

I waited until their laughter overlapped and then moved. The first man didn't even see me before my hand clamped over his mouth as my knife angled beneath his jaw into a swift downward slice that opened everything that held him together. He collapsed without a sound.

The second reached for his gun, but I was quicker, slamming his head into the wall. Once. Twice. On the third, his head left a smear of blood trailing down the wall as he went down boneless.

I stepped over them and started up the stairs to the second floor. The west wing, where the guest rooms were. They would be empty tonight. Conor never housed his sins near his visitors.

I moved through to the third floor and the staff quarters. Lights spilling under the doors muffling conversations as footsteps paced, nervous and restless. They knew something was wrong. Good.

I kept climbing.

The fourth-floor landing was quiet. This wing was off-limits to everyone except Conor's inner circle and me. I'd spent years stationed outside his office door, listening to the scratch of his pen across his ledgers, the quiet hum of classical music he never admitted to enjoying.

Tonight, that same door stood cracked open, and a thin line of light spilled across the hallway floor.

Voices murmured inside. One deep, and one agitated. Cillian's voice.

"...you're overreacting, Conor—"

"No," Conor replied to his cousin, his second-in-command. "I'm preparing."

Preparing for me. Smart man, I thought as I slipped past the door before either of them sensed the shift in the air.

My footsteps carried me toward the far end of the hall, where I crossed into the east wing to where her room waited.

I'd guarded this hallway. Walked it. Patrolled it. Memorized every squeaky board, every shadow, and every blind angle the cameras didn't quite reach. That was Conor's mistake. You don't build a prison and then give the layout to the wolf.

Two guards stood outside her door. Both of them were armed, alert, and tense. Excellent. Fear made people sloppy.

I stepped into the nearest alcove. A decorative niche where an expensive painting hung. The kind of place no one looked twice at while the guards talked quietly.

"All this trouble for one fucking girl."

"Must have a golden fucking pussy or something."

The guards laughed among themselves, and I saw red. A cold, focused red that didn't wait for permission. I took two breaths. Measured and even before I stepped out of the shadows.

The first guard barely had time to register movement before my blade slid across his throat. He dropped instantly, knees buckling under him as his blood darkened down his clothes and onto the expensive carpet.

The second reached for his gun. Quick, but not quick enough. I slammed him into the wall, elbow pressed to his windpipe, my knife poised beneath his ribs.

"Not a fucking sound," I growled.

The guard choked. "O-okay, man! Please, I've got a kid."

His choked whisper caught in his throat with his pleas. I knocked him out clean with a single hit. He slumped to the floor, unconscious. I didn't kill him. Didn't need to. The alarm would come either way. Conor was waiting for me, and I wasn't wasting precious time on fear.

I turned toward her door, and her scent hit me first. Not the smell of her perfume or shampoo. Just her, warm skin, and adrenaline, mixed with the specific laundry detergent from the linens that Conor preferred. My throat tightened as I touched the doorknob lightly.

Cold metal. Predictable and locked. That wasn't a problem. I slid a thin pick from my jacket. The lock clicked open in seconds. I exhaled once before pushing the door open.

• • •

The room was dim, lit only by a thin strip of dying daylight leaking through the curtains. And it was too quiet.

I scanned the room and saw her. Curled up on the bed, a blanket wrapped around her shoulders, and her knees pulled up. Her head was bowed, and her arm was cuffed to the headboard. My vision went black around the edges.

"Sera," I breathed.

She didn't move. Not even a flinch as I stepped inside, and shut the door behind me without a sound.

The air felt wrong and heavy. Like someone had wrung the life out of it with their bare hands. Her shoulders trembled once. The movement was small and involuntary. It was the only sign she was even conscious.

"Little Fawn..."

I called, softer this time, but the edges stayed rough. I didn't recognize my own voice.

Her head lifted a fraction, and her eyes found me. The look that hit me wasn't fear. It was something worse. It was hollow. Like a part of her hadn't come back yet. Something in my chest cracked clean in half. I crossed the room and dropped to my knees beside the bed.

"It's me, baby," I whispered. "I'm here."

Her lips parted as a small sound spilled out, nothing like a word, everything like a wound reopening. She leaned back against the headboard like she needed the support just to stay upright.

"Kael?"

Barely a breath. Barely real.

"Yeah," I said, voice breaking. "I've got you."

Her eyes widened as she looked at me. Not with wild panic, nor with shock. This was something quieter and devastating. She shifted her hand, and the cuff clinked. Her breath stuttered, and that sound… I'd never forget it. Not even when I was dead.

"Conor did this to you."

It wasn't a question. It was an execution sentence dressed as a whisper.

She swallowed hard. Shook her head.

"Kael—don't—just get me out—please just—"

"I will."

The promise left me before I could think it through.

"I'll get you out, but I need to know what he did."

Her face crumpled, and my heart shattered. She didn't say a word and somehow said enough. I exhaled slowly, viciously.

"Okay," I said quietly. "Not now. Not here."

My hands shook once before I forced them steady.

"But he's going to pay for all of it."

Her gaze darted to the door, a look of fear slicing through her expression.

"He's down the hall," she whispered, voice cracking. "He said he'd come back. Kael, he said—"

"I know," I murmured. "I know, baby. I've got you."

I reached up, brushing a strand of hair off her cheek, and she flinched. Not at me, but at the movement itself. At the memory of hands that hadn't been gentle, and it gutted me in a way I would never recover from.

"Don't touch me," she said suddenly, her voice sharp and panicked. "Please. Just don't."

I pulled my hand back instantly.

"Okay," I whispered. "Okay. I won't. My hands are off."

I stayed exactly where I was, keeping my hands open and palms up.

Her breathing evened out. Barely. But it was enough to keep her upright. I lifted the blanket around her shoulders, careful not to graze her skin.

"You're safe. I'm right here. Nobody's laying a hand on you again."

A tremor ran through her, and her jaw tightened as her eyes flicked to the window. Her movements were calculating and desperate.

"He's not alone. There are guards. And someone else. Conor's cousin. Cillian. He watches everything. Kael, you can't—"

A cold, vicious smile pulled at my lips.

"I can, and I will."

Her eyes filled again.

"Kael," she whispered, shaking her head, "please don't die for me."

"I'm not dying. I'm the one doing the killing."

I pulled the cuff key from my pocket. The one stolen from Benjamin two hours ago, before his blood even stopped spilling, and her breath caught.

"How did you—"

"He had it on his key ring." My eyes darkened. "He didn't need it anymore."

The cuff clicked open, and she pulled her hand to her chest instantly, cradling her wrist like a wound. I didn't reach for her. Didn't grab her. I just waited for her to be ready.

"Can you stand?" I asked.

She hesitated. Then gave a small nod.

I rose first, giving her space.

She slid her legs off the bed slowly and carefully. The moment her feet touched the floor, her knees buckled.

I grabbed the bedpost instead of her. Grounding myself so she could brace against the mattress without my hands anywhere near her. Fuck, I wanted to hold her. To grab her, hold her close, and never let her go again.

She looked up at me. Her body was shaky and exhausted, trying so hard to be strong, and it made my throat burn.

"I'm okay," she whispered.

She wasn't. But she was still here. Still fighting, and that was all I needed to see.

"Stay behind me and do exactly what I tell you. Don't run unless I say run."

Her lips parted.

"Conor… he's—"

"Conor's not a problem." My voice was devoid of emotion. "He's a corpse waiting for me to decide where to dispose of him."

A small, broken sound escaped her. Not fear, but pure, shaking relief.

I stepped toward the door, my hand steady on the knob, and took one breath in and let it out.

The house was still around us. The air felt thick with tension, with danger, and with the promise of blood. I glanced back at her once. Just once.

"I'm getting you out of here," I said softly. "And then I'm burning this place to the ground."

Then I opened the door and walked her straight into the war waiting on the other side.

• • •

The hallway was dim and silent. There were no footsteps, no murmured guard chatter, just silence.

No shifting shadows. Conor wasn't being careless. He was waiting.

I stepped out first, my body angled to shield her without touching her. Sera followed tight to my side, the blanket wrapped around her shoulders like armor she desperately needed.

"Stay with me."

She nodded and kept her breathing quiet and controlled. Fragile in a way that made something in me snarl for blood.

The two guards I'd left unconscious still lay crumpled where they'd fallen. One was bleeding, and the other was stirring lightly, but nowhere near conscious.

Sera's breath caught, but she didn't look away. Let her see the carnage I would wage to get her to safety.

We reached the end of the hall, to the final turn before the grand staircase. Before Conor. Before the last line between us and fire.

I slowed and lifted a hand for silence. Listened. There—

Voices drifting up from the lower landing.

One familiar. Conor. Smooth. Controlled. Mildly irritated, like he was discussing wine pairings and not the collapse of his entire kingdom. And another. Lower and rougher with an Irish lilt sharpened into iron.

Cillian. Conor's blood, his shadow, and his favorite weapon.

"—I'm telling you, he'll come through the west wing," Cillian said. "Kael was raised in those shadows."

A quiet hum from Conor. "And where would you wager he is now?"

"Close," Cillian replied. "Men like him always circle the door before they breach it."

Sera stiffened beside me, and I touched her elbow lightly before hating myself immediately for it. It was enough to guide, but I'd crossed her line just the same.

We moved down one step and then another. Soundless. The second-floor landing opened below us, wide and polished, chandeliers dimmed to a gold haze. Conor stood near the base of the stairs, hands in his pockets, his posture relaxed as if he hadn't orchestrated a nightmare.

Cillian stood beside him. The younger cousin was tall and broad with his dark hair tied back. The tattoo creeping up the side of his neck looked like a warning, but I've never cared for warnings I didn't make myself.

He didn't scan the house lazily like the other guards. Instead, he watched the shadows.

Where Conor was brazen, Cillian was calculated and predatory.

My eyes narrowed as he looked up. Not to me. To *her.* Sera inhaled sharply, freezing mid-step.

Cillian's expression changed, just barely, but I saw it. The flicker of recognition and the immediate understanding of what had been done to her. And the quiet, simmering fury he began to aim at Conor because of it. Interesting.

Conor noticed us, too. His head turned, eyes lifting to the staircase and right to me. He smiled. Cold. Like a man greeting a guest who'd arrived precisely on schedule.

"There you are," Conor said. "I was beginning to think you'd gotten lost."

I stepped down another stair, placing myself fully in view, my body blocking Sera from his line of sight.

"I don't get lost. Just delayed sometimes."

Conor's gaze flickered from the blanket wrapped around her to her hand gripping the railing before it landed on her swollen wrist, where the cuff had been.

He didn't smirk. He looked pleased. Like he'd carved something into her and was admiring his handiwork. Something inside me tightened at his look. I was going to enjoy snuffing him out.

Cillian stepped forward slightly, his gaze shifting between us. Not hostile. Just assessing.

"Conor," Cillian murmured, "this isn't—"

"Necessary?" Conor finished. "Of course it is. Everything tonight is necessary."

He clasped his hands behind his back like a teacher addressing unruly children.

"Kael, you've always had a… flair for dramatics. The finger was a touch excessive, but I admit, it was surprisingly effective."

"Effective or not," I said flatly. "Michael is no longer a problem."

"Mm." Another soft smile. "Well. You've made your move."

"I'm here to finish it."

"Of course you are." He tilted his head. "But she's not yours to take anymore."

My pulse slowed, and my breathing evened out as an eerie calm took over every part of me.

"She was never yours. You just have a habit of taking what doesn't belong to you."

Conor's jaw tightened. Only slightly, but I saw it.

Sera flinched behind me at the raised voices. I felt how her breath caught, and her fingers trembled against the railing.

Cillian's eyes flicked to her again. There was no hunger there or cruelty. Just calculation as he stepped forward another inch.

"Conor," he said quietly, "look at her. You didn't have to—"

"Stay out of this," Conor snapped, more sharply than I'd ever heard from him.

Oh. So the cracks were showing. Well that's new. I kept my voice low.

"You touched what's mine, and that's all the reason I need to kill you."

Conor laughed. The sound was light, gentle, and fucking amused.

"You say that like I didn't train every single step you've taken," he replied. "Like I didn't teach you where to put the blade."

"That's exactly why you should be afraid."

A heavy silence fell. Thick and suffocating, and it crackled with the promise of violence.

Conor lifted a hand in a small gesture of bored indulgence.

"Come on, Kael. If you want her, take her. If you want my blood, come earn it. But don't hide on the stairs like a petulant child."

I took one deliberate step closer as Sera pressed behind me, her breath shaking, and her fingers knotting in the blanket.

Conor's eyes flicked upward.

"You really think you can walk out of my house with her?"

"Yes, actually. And you're going to watch me do it."

Cillian exhaled, the sound low and sharp. The first hint of a real reaction. Conor's composure cracked, only for a split second. But it was enough. His voice shifted into a cold steel beneath velvet.

"Kael."

I tightened my grip on the railing.

"No. I'm no longer the man you pulled out of an alley and sculpted into a weapon. He left the moment you touched her. The moment you thought you could keep her."

The air snapped tight as wire, and Cillian took a slow step backward. Sera whispered, barely audible:

"Kael..."

And before I could answer, before we could take our next breath, the security alarm shrieked through the house. A second later, the lights cut out, and darkness swallowed the staircase. A muzzle flash bloomed from below and then—

Gunfire.

Chapter Twenty-Three

Seraphine

The alarm hit first. A screaming, mechanical wail that sank its claws into my skull and shook everything loose. Then the lights died. One second, there was a staircase, a chandelier, Conor's face tilted up toward us like we were an amusing inconvenience. Next, the world snapped to black.

The sound of gunfire that followed was loud and close. Too fucking close.

I didn't see where the first shot landed. I just felt Kael slam into me, hard enough to knock every thought straight out of my head. My back hit the wall as his weight drove the air from my lungs and turned me into something small. My frame was pinned beneath him, shaking.

Plaster dust rained down, and something cracked above us. The sharp, ugly whine of bullets chewing through wood made my stomach turn.

I tried to breathe, but couldn't catch a breath. The alarm shrieked, setting my teeth on edge.

"Stay down," Kael growled in my ear.

I wasn't exactly thinking of standing up. My knees were jelly, and my hands had a death grip on the blanket around my shoulders, as if that thin layer of fabric were the only thing keeping me from coming apart.

More shots rang out in short, controlled bursts. This wasn't wild panic or random shots. Someone knew where they were shooting.

Kael shifted, his body a solid wall between me and the rest of the staircase. I felt the flex of his muscles, the bunch of his shoulders, and the way he leaned into the dark as if it were a familiar friend.

He belonged in this. I didn't. I was a club girl in bare feet and stolen linens, trying not to throw up while men killed each other over who got to own me. The thought almost made me laugh. As if a broken thing like me warranted all of this.

A flash of emergency light sputtered to life below, bathing the foyer in a sickly red glow for half a second before cutting out again. It was just enough to burn an image into my brain.

Guards moved, and Conor stepped back, cool and collected, while everyone else scrambled. And Cillian. He hadn't moved toward a gun. Hadn't grabbed cover. He was watching the stairs. Watching us. His gaze locked on me.

Then darkness swallowed everything again. Something loud and metallic hit the floor below with a crash. Someone swore, and the alarm kept screaming.

"Kael," I rasped as my throat burned. "What is happening?"

"Nothing you need to see." His voice was steady and calm in a way that made me want to cling to it with both hands. "Keep your head down."

My head was already down, but it was full of things I didn't want. Conor's voice. His hands. The bite of the cuff. The feel of the mattress when it dipped under a weight that wasn't supposed to be there. My stomach lurched. I swallowed hard, tasted bile and metal and lemon cleaner.

One, two, three, four…

I dug my nails into my palms and held on.

Another shot. This one hit the wall near my feet. A hot sting licked across my calf, sharp and searing. I sucked in a breath that almost became a scream. Warmth began to trickle down my leg, sticky against my skin.

Kael tensed. "Sera!" His voice cut through all the haze in my head.

"I'm okay," my voice shook. "I think it just… grazed me."

There was a pause, the weight of his attention dropping to where the bullet had carved its path in my flesh.

"Can you put weight on it?" he asked.

"I'm standing, aren't I?" I said, even though my knee wanted to buckle. "It's okay."

With ringing ears, shaking bones, and a now steady throb in my calf pulsing with every heartbeat, I steadied myself against the wall beside me, careful not to put too much weight on my left leg.

Someone shouted from below.

"Cease fire! You'll hit her, you idiots."

Cillian. I know that voice now. Steel wrapped in Irish whiskey. Nobody listened as another volley of gunfire tore through the dark.

"Useless," Kael muttered.

He shifted his weight again, then pushed off the wall and dragged me with him, backing us upward, away from the open line of the stairs. His hand found my arm through the blanket, as his fingers closed firm but carefully.

I flinched anyway. He paused. I felt it. That tiny, hitching hesitation.

"I'm sorry, Little Fawn. But right now I need you alive more than I need you comfortable."

My laugh came out broken. "That's a low bar."

"Baby." He exhaled. I felt it against my forehead, warm and rough and so real it hurt. "We're revisiting comfort later. Right now, we need to get out."

We. He kept saying we like I was part of something other than the problem.

I tried to move with him. The first step sent a bolt of pain up my calf, white-hot and blinding. My leg wobbled, and Kael tightened his grip just enough to keep me steady, adjusting without comment, while he matched his pace to my limp.

A brighter glow cut through the dark behind us. Emergency lighting finally kicked on properly, as the strips along the baseboards flickered to life in a weak yellow wash. It made everything worse.

Now I could see the bodies on the landing below and the smear of blood from the guard whose head Kael had bounced off the wall. Conor's men were moving like insects, ducking behind pillars, and shouting over the alarm.

Conor himself stood in the center of it all. Untouched and composed. Like the gunfire was an orchestra and he was just waiting for the right swell in the music.

His gaze climbed the stairs and found us again. Even with half his face in shadow, I saw the satisfaction there. I heard his voice in my head. *Very good, little lamb. You break so pretty for me.* My lungs locked, and my legs threatened to give out.

Kael squeezed my arm, light but grounding. "Hey. Breathe for me."

I tried, but my chest refused. The edges of my vision were already starting to gray, and the alarm dug its claws deeper.

"You can't get out," Conor called up, raising his voice over the chaos like this was some kind of civilized debate. "The perimeter is locked down. Every door, every gate, and every guard knows your face."

"Then they'll fucking die knowing it," Kael shot back. But his tone didn't change. He didn't yell. He didn't posture. He just sounded like a man stating the weather.

Cillian stepped in closer to Conor, his shoulders tight, and his jaw clenched. I watched them talk, their words lost to the distance and the screaming alarm, but I saw the tension in Cillian's posture and the way his hand cut through the air in a sharp, frustrated gesture.

He pointed up the stairs. To us. To me. Conor's lip curled. Whatever Cillian said next made him freeze, before Conor slapped his hand away, sharp enough to echo off the marble. Not so loyal after all. Not really.

My body swayed again, and the blanket slid down my shoulder, exposing skin that still remembered Conor's grip too vividly. I pulled it back up with numb fingers. The movement tugged at the torn skin on my leg and sent another pulse of pain through me.

If Kael died here because of me, I was going to come back and murder every motherfucker in this house myself.

"Kael," I whispered. "You can't win a war on a staircase."

"Good thing I'm not trying to win." His mouth twitched. Not a smile, but something harder. "Just trying to change the rules."

He let go of me, and my heart stopped. For one awful second, I thought he was leaving. That he'd hand me back like a damaged package and decide I wasn't worth the cost.

He stepped away, just far enough to pull something from the inside of his jacket. A small, matte black device no bigger than his palm.

"What is that?"

"A contingency plan."

He thumbed something. A small red light blinked once on the side of the thing, then went dark.

"Kael." My voice went quiet. "Please tell me you didn't bring a bomb into the same building as me."

"Relax." He said with a grin as he slid it back into his pocket. "It's not in *this* building."

His words did nothing to relax me, but before I could argue, the entire house shuddered. Deep and low, like the foundation itself had just taken a hit. The alarm stuttered, and dust sifted down from the chandelier. Somewhere far below, glass shattered in a long, screaming cascade, and the gunfire stopped.

Every head in the foyer turned toward the sound echoing up from the lower levels. Shouted voices rose in a confused wave.

"What the hell was that?" one of the guards yelled.

Another guard swore. "The garage. That came from the garage."

I tightened my grip on the blanket, and through the roaring in my ears, through the alarm and the shouting, I heard something else. Faint and in the distance. A car engine. No. Several car engines.

Kael smiled, and this time it looked real, terrifying, and so fucking beautiful.

"Conor should have locked this place down better."

"Who is that?" I breathed.

"That would be the cavalry."

"You have friends?"

"Not exactly."

He took my arm again, carefully, and tugged me higher up the stairs, back toward the upper landing. The motion dragged my injured leg up each step, and every rise burned. I bit the inside of my cheek until I tasted blood rather than give Conor the satisfaction of hearing me whimper.

"Wait," I hissed. "Up is the wrong direction. I don't know much, but I know that."

"We're not going up." He nodded toward a side hallway, half hidden in shadow. "We're cutting through there."

The corridor he led me into was narrower, lined with heavy framed paintings and a runner that muffled our footsteps. The alarm was slightly less deafening here. Only slightly.

I tried to keep my breathing even and not think about how the carpet scratched the bottoms of my feet or how every brush of fabric against my skin felt too much like a hand. I begged myself to ignore the cool wetness of blood on my calf.

"Kael." My voice shook. "If they catch us again…"

"They won't."

"You can't promise that."

"I didn't say I was promising. I said they won't."

Infuriating fucking man.

We reached a heavy door at the end of the hall that wasn't ornate or obvious. Just solid wood with an old brass handle. Kael pushed it open and ushered me through. The smell of cold air, oil, and damp concrete hit first.

Another set of stairs appeared, and I groaned. These ones at least went down, spiraling tight and close, with walls that pressed in on both sides. A service staircase, hidden behind staff corridors and decorative nonsense for guests.

"Where does this go?" I asked.

"Everywhere that matters." His hand hovered at my back, never quite touching. "Keep your hand on the rail. It gets darker after the second turn."

He wasn't wrong. The emergency lighting barely reached past the threshold. Within a few steps, the world narrowed to the circle of space right in front of me, and the sound of our footsteps slapping down concrete.

Somewhere above, the alarm still screamed. Muffled now and distant. The gunfire started again, farther away. Toward the back of the house this time. Whoever had hit the garage was drawing fire, and my chest loosened by a fraction.

"If someone dies to get me out of here…" I muttered, mostly to myself. The thoughts in my head were growing louder again.

"Later. Not here," Kael said, squeezing my hand just enough to pull me back. "At home, where you're safe."

At home. Safe. The words didn't feel real, as if he were talking about someone else's life.

We dropped down another flight, and my legs started to shake from more than fear. I wasn't built for this. My body ached with a thousand small, ugly protests. My wrist throbbed where the cuff had bitten in, and my calf burned with every downward step, each impact sending a jolt up my spine. Every step felt like walking through wet cement.

I misjudged the bottom stair and stumbled. Pain flared bright in my leg as it took my full weight, and my knee buckled. Kael caught me by the elbow before I could hit the ground.

"I've got you. Keep close to me." He didn't let go of my arm this time, his hold keeping me upright and moving, taking just enough of my weight that I could keep going.

At the bottom of the stairs sat another door. This one metal, with a push bar and a small wired-glass window that showed nothing but black.

Kael paused and tilted his head as he listened. There was a new sound now. Barely there, underneath the alarm and the distant shouts. A low, constant rumble like more engines moving closer.

"Ready?" he asked.

No. Absolutely not. My whole body wanted to curl up on the step and never move again.

"Yes," I replied instead.

He pushed the bar, and the door swung open into the cold night and chaos surrounding Conor's opulent grounds.

The back lot spread out before us, with a row of expensive cars parked along one wall. The far end of the garage bay was a twisted mess of metal and flame where part of the gate had apparently exploded inward.

Beyond that, through the skeletal remains of the security fence, headlights cut through the dark. Three cars with their engines idling and doors open.

Men moved between them and the hole in the fence. Not Conor's men. Their suits and their stance didn't match. Their guns were leveled at the estate, laying down a controlled curtain of fire.

"Who are they?" I asked.

"The kind of people Conor shouldn't have pissed off," Kael said.

He stepped out into the open, pulling me with him long enough to angle his body in front of mine again. Shouts snapped our way as we appeared. Guns shifted, and a few muzzles swung up toward us.

"It's us," Kael barked. "Hold your fucking fire."

One of the men by the fence straightened. He lowered his weapon and squinted through the dark at us. Even from here, I could see the scar cutting across his cheek, the mark pale and opalescent against his skin.

"Mercer?" he called. "You look like shit."

"Have you checked a mirror lately?" Kael laughed darkly. "Cover us, we're coming through."

Another shout cut across the yard from a different angle.

"Kael!"

Conor's voice rang out, closer now.

I looked back over my shoulder.

He'd followed us. Or calculated where we'd come out. It didn't matter. He stood framed in the open mouth of the service door, flanked by two guards with rifles. Cillian was behind him, half in shadow, his expression carved out of stone.

Conor's gaze slid over Kael and landed on me.

"Going somewhere?" he asked.

I had nothing left to give him. No fear. No begging. No polite little tremble to soothe his ego, so I stared back.

"Yes. Anywhere you aren't."

His mouth tightened, and his eyes flicked past me. To the cars. To the men at the breach. Calculation flashed there, quick and sharp.

"If you leave, Seraphine," Conor said quietly, "I will find you. I will kill everyone you love and make you watch before I finish what I started. I will fucking break you, little lamb."

A jagged laugh ripped out of me. The sound was unhinged, ugly, and the last sound he expected.

"Fuck you, Conor. Try it, and I'll kill you myself."

I heard Kael stifle a sound that sounded like a half-laugh, half-something dangerously close to pride, before his hand brushed my back. Not pushing. Not rushing. Just there. Solid and present and mine to lean on. He took a step sideways, angling us toward the hole in the fence.

My leg screamed with every step now, each shift of weight a raw scrape of pain, but I kept moving. I would drag myself if I had to.

The alarm shrieked, and the engines idled as the cold air cut through the thin blanket and straight into my bones.

"Last chance," Conor said.

He wasn't talking to me this time. He was looking at Cillian, and his cousin didn't move. Time stretched forever while the men at the fence shifted restlessly. One called out something in a language I didn't know, and the scorched metal of the gate creaked.

Then Cillian stepped forward. Not toward Conor, but past him as he planted himself between Conor and us, his body turned just enough that his shoulder brushed Conor's arm and pushed him a half step off balance.

"Think you misread the room, cousin," he said calmly. "Tonight, you're the one who doesn't walk back inside."

I should have been relieved, or at least felt grateful. Instead, all I could feel was the way my leg shook, and how every man with a gun here was still deciding whether I walked out or bled out.

Conor stared at him, and the world around us held its breath.

Then everything broke at once, and chaos detonated.

Conor lunged first. His movements were fast and vicious, a flash of polished teeth and rage, but Cillian was already moving. He caught Conor by the front of his expensive jacket and slammed him into the metal doorframe with a crack that echoed across the entire back lot.

The guards behind Conor shouted, guns rising. Kael didn't wait as his hand locked around my arm just tight enough to keep me upright as he pulled me into a low sprint toward the breach in the fence.

My calf flared in protest on the first step, nearly buckling. Kael tightened his grip, taking more of my weight, and turned my stumble into something that almost felt like running.

Gunfire erupted again, bright streaks of muzzle flash tearing open the dark. The men by the cars answered with their own barrage, covering us with a precision that made the hairs on my neck stand up.

"Keep your head down," Kael barked.

I ducked, and my bare feet slapped cold concrete, with each step sending pain shooting up my legs, but adrenaline burned through it. My injured calf felt like it was on fire; every stride was a raw, open nerve.

Behind us, there was a shout, then a scuffle, followed by a scream. I didn't look back. I couldn't.

Kael urged me on faster, guiding me in quick, sharp movements that kept us behind overturned crates, car frames, and pillars. Anything that could stop a bullet. When my leg faltered, his arm hauled me that extra half step, as if he'd already factored my limp into his calculations.

We were almost to the fence. Ten feet. Five. A shape barreled toward us from the right. One of Conor's men who'd circled around, gun raised, face twisted with desperate fury.

I didn't even have time to scream. Kael was lightning fast. He pivoted, shoving me behind him with one arm while the other hand flung a knife so fast I barely saw it leave his hand. It lodged in the man's throat with a wet, squelching sound.

The guard collapsed before his gun even hit the ground.

Kael grabbed my hand and pulled me through the twisted metal gap in the fence. My calf clipped the ragged edge; pain ripped up my leg, and I hissed, but I held on. I stumbled into the dirt, caught myself on my palms, then pushed up again as headlights washed over me.

"Get her in!" someone yelled.

Hands reached out for me, open and ready, and I let them take me. When my leg tried to fold, one of them caught me under the knees for a second before I found my balance again, the blanket tangling around my ankles.

Kael vaulted through behind me, landing like a predator, eyes scanning, his chest rising and falling in slow, controlled breaths, even though the world behind us was on fire.

The man with the cheek scar stepped forward. "We've got the left flank. The road's clear for five minutes, maybe less."

"Plenty," Kael said, already moving around the hood of the nearest car. "She goes with me."

"No shit," the scarred man muttered. "She's all yours, Mercer. And now we're even."

A bullet pinged off the metal behind us.

"GO!" he shouted.

Kael threw open the passenger door and guided me in with a gentleness that made my throat tighten. My leg protested as I climbed in, but he steadied me with a hand under my elbow, careful of the mess below my knee.

I slid into the seat, trembling too hard to pull the blanket over my knees. My breath fogged the window, and blood from my calf smeared against the floor mat, a dark, ugly reminder that I hadn't gotten out unscathed.

Kael got in on the driver's side, and the engine roared to life.

"Seatbelt," he said.

My fingers shook, useless on the buckle. He reached over, careful not to touch me, only the metal latch, fast and mechanical. His arm brushed mine, and I froze. He froze too. A heartbeat stretched between us, and he pulled back slowly, deliberately, eyes flicking to my face, checking.

"You're safe, Sera."

The words shouldn't have made me want to cry, but they did.

He slammed the car into gear, and the tires squealed while the back lot blurred as the car shot forward.

Through the smoke and the remnants of the horrors I'd just crawled out of, shots followed us into the night. I didn't look back. Not until we cleared the hill. Not until Conor's estate was just a disappearing smear in the distance. Only then did I let out the breath I'd been holding since the lights went out.

Kael didn't look away from the road, but his voice came low and rough.

"You're out," he said. "You hear me? You're out, and you're safe now."

My throat bobbed, and I nodded. And for the first time since all of this began, since the glass in the alley, since the handcuffs, since the bed, I believed him.

Chapter Twenty-Four

Seraphine

The world narrowed to the sound of the engine and the shudder deep within my own bones. Streetlights smeared past the window in thin orange streaks that got swallowed by the dark every few seconds. My breath still hadn't found a normal rhythm, and it scraped in and out of my chest like it had to fight for every inch.

Kael drove like he murdered. Calm and exact, with never a single wasted movement. His knuckles sat easy on the wheel, not white-knuckled or tense. He kept his eyes forward and his jaw set, like he had done this a thousand times. Like he hadn't just walked me out of a war zone with blood under his nails and a kingdom burning in the rearview.

I kept waiting for the chase. For headlights to appear behind us. For the crack of more gunfire. For Conor to materialize out of the dark like a nightmare that refused to follow normal rules. But nothing came.

Just the hum of tires on asphalt and the soft rattle of something loose in the glove compartment, mixing with the tinny ring in my ears where the alarm had set my ear canals on edge.

My calf throbbed in time with my pulse. Every heartbeat was a hot, insistent ache where the bullet had ripped open my flesh. The blanket stuck to the back of my leg, damp and tacky.

I stared straight ahead. I knew if I looked down, if I saw the blood, if I saw my bare feet on the floor mat of a stranger's car, my brain was going to snap in half.

"You still with me, Little Fawn?"

Kael's voice cut through the noise, and I swallowed before trying to speak.

"Yeah," I said. "I think so."

"You're quiet."

"Newsflash, big bad wolf. I came this close to getting shot in the fucking head." I lifted my hand and put my pointer and thumb super close together, mimicking how close I had come.

His mouth twitched.

"Close only counts in horseshoes and hand grenades. You're still breathing, and that's what matters."

Easy for him to say. His body hadn't been someone else's plaything for hours.

The thought hit, and my stomach rolled. I pressed the back of my head into the seat and stared harder at the road, trying to keep the inside of the car from tilting. The air inside the car smelled like leather and the faint metallic tang of my own blood.

"Talk to me," he said.

"About what?"

"Anything. Tell me what you see out the window."

"Darkness," I muttered.

"What else?"

"A sign just went past. I didn't read it."

"Try the next one."

It was so stupid I almost told him to shut up. But his voice was a rope, and I was so goddamn tired of drowning. The next sign came up fast. A big, reflective green rectangle, with its letters smearing until I forced my eyes to focus.

"County Road Twelve," I said. It felt like I had to drag each word through wet cement. "Speed limit eighty."

"Good. What else?"

"There was a yellow sign with a deer on it."

"Fitting."

I snorted, but it came out shaky.

"You doing your therapist voice on me now?"

"Do you want me to?"

"No. Yes. I don't know."

"It's shock." He didn't sound offended. Just matter-of-fact. "Your system's still running hot from the house, and your brain's trying to catch up. It'll hit harder when we stop."

"Oh, goodie, something to look forward to."

"You won't be alone when it does."

The words landed heavier than they should have, but I didn't have space for them. Didn't have room for anything that felt like comfort. It sat on top of the panic and the nausea and the bone-deep exhaustion, waiting.

My hands had stopped shaking at some point, and I unclenched them from the blanket and stared at my fingers. There were faint half-moons where my nails had dug into my palms. No blood there. Just marks. Ghost bruises that would fade.

"Your leg. How bad is it?"

"Fine."

"Seraphine."

I closed my eyes.

"It hurts," I admitted. "A lot. But I can move my toes, so that means it's not, like, hanging off or anything."

"Any numbness?"

"No."

"Good."

He went quiet for a few seconds as the car ate up more distance. We turned off the main road onto a narrower road, the tires bumping over rougher pavement. Trees crowded closer, branches knitting overhead into a tunnel that swallowed the sky, and my chest tightened.

"Where are we going?" I asked.

"Somewhere Conor doesn't know about. You'll be safe there."

The word still sounded foreign in my head. Like a language I'd heard once in a movie but never learned to speak.

"You have a safehouse?"

"I have several."

"Of course you fucking do."

He glanced over at me then. Just long enough for his eyes to skim my face, as if he was checking for something I couldn't dare name.

"I'm not taking you anywhere I can't keep you safe. Can you trust me? Even just enough to let me catch you when you fall?"

"I don't even know how to catch myself, Kael."

"So don't. Let me do the heavy lifting for now."

I let my head tip toward the window. The glass was cold against my temple, and I watched the trees streak by, just dark shapes and deeper shadows.

My body started to catch up to what had happened. The trembling came back first. Not the adrenaline shake from the stairs, but a deeper one. It started in my chest this time, a fine, quivering hum that spread out to my arms, my jaw, the muscles in my back. Like my bones were buzzing.

My throat felt tight, and I tried to swallow around it, but that made it worse. I lifted a hand to my face and realized I couldn't feel my fingers properly. They got fuzzy at the edges when I looked at them.

"Kael," I said. It came out quieter than I intended.

"Yeah?"

"I feel… weird."

"How?"

"Like I'm… far away. And here at the same time. I know I'm in the car, but it's like I'm watching us drive from outside my own head. That makes no sense."

"Breathe, Little Fawn. You're dissociating on me."

"Fuck."

"It's your brain trying not to shatter. It's doing the best it can with what you gave it."

"That's rude."

"Accurate, but I need you with me a little longer. Can you do that?"

"I can try."

"Good. Look at me."

I forced my gaze away from the trees, and it felt like moving through molasses. When I finally focused on him, he was already looking back, just for a second, before his eyes shifted to the road again.

"What color are my eyes?" he asked.

"Seriously?"

"Yes. Just answer the questions."

"Gray. Like storm clouds over the ocean."

"What color is the dashboard?"

"Black."

"And the blanket?"

"Off-white." I hesitated. "It's honestly kind of fucking ugly."

"Good," he chuckled. "Name five things in the car."

"You and me," I muttered. "That's two."

"Three more."

"Steering wheel. The radio and the floor mats."

"Four things you can feel."

"This is stupid."

"Do it for me anyway, please."

I sucked in another shaky breath.

"Blanket. The seat under me and the door against my shoulder. My leg. It hurts."

"Three things you can hear besides my voice."

"Engine. The road. My heart trying to pound out of my chest."

"Two things you can smell."

"Smoke," I said immediately. It was in my hair, in my lungs, mingling with my sweat. "And… you."

"What do I smell like?"

"Metal. And soap. And something like… rain."

He was quiet for a moment.

"One thing you can taste," he said finally.

"Blood," I whispered. "I bit the inside of my cheek."

"Spit it out."

"What?"

"Into the blanket or out the window. Either way, you don't need the reminder."

I stared at him. Then I turned my head, rolled the window down, and spat red into the dark. It was disgusting, and yet somehow it helped.

The buzzing in my bones didn't stop, but it got quieter. The car felt a little more solid around me. My leg hurt too much to ignore now, every throb a sharp, insistent signal that I still had a body and it was not okay.

"Better?" he asked.

"A bit," I admitted.

"Good. We're almost there."

• • •

Within minutes, we were deep in an industrial part of the city. The sewer grates billowed steam into the cool night air as we made our way down roads lined with abandoned factories, heavy with years of neglect.

A building rose out of the dark ahead. Two stories of weathered brick with no sign and no porch light. Just another unremarkable building with boarded windows and a rusted metal door in a city filled with them. Kael didn't hesitate for even a beat. This place was his.

It didn't look like safety from the outside. It looked like every abandoned warehouse in every late-night crime documentary I'd watched with Patrick. But there were no other cars, no men with guns, and to my own surprise, no Conor. That counted for something, and I was glad for it.

Kael killed the engine, and the sudden lack of noise made the ringing in my ears roar back to life.

For a second, neither of us moved. The quiet wrapped around us both before he turned in his seat to face me fully.

"I'm going to get you inside," he said. "Your leg won't like it, but it needs looking at sooner than later."

"I can walk," I said on reflex.

He raised a brow. His gaze dropped to where my calf had soaked the blanket, leaving it a dark, ugly red.

"Maybe, but you don't have to."

The words lodged somewhere under my ribs. I had been carrying myself for so long, I didn't know how to put the weight down. He watched my face, just waiting for me to be ready.

The buzzing under my skin climbed higher, and my throat burned, and there was a pressure behind my eyes that was building higher.

"Okay," I said, barely more than a breath. "You can carry me. Just don't fucking drop me."

"I won't," he promised, without a flicker of doubt in it.

He got out first and came around to my side. The cold wind slammed through the car as he opened my door. I hadn't realized how hot the air inside had gotten until the chill hit my damp skin and made me shiver.

"Ready?" he asked.

"No, but do it anyway." I didn't want to waste time thinking about it.

He leaned in, and for a heartbeat, my body panicked on instinct, some buried part of me bracing for hands that hurt and a voice that lied. Then his arms slid under me, one behind my back, the other under my knees, being so careful of the ruined muscle in my calf. He moved slow enough that I could track every inch, slow enough that I could pull away if I needed to.

He lifted me like it was nothing. Like I weighed no more than a bottle in his hand. My arms went around his neck before I could think better of it as my fingers fisted in the collar of his shirt, needing something solid, something that wasn't spinning. He was warm, and solid, and real. His heartbeat thudded steadily against my shoulder.

"I've got you," he murmured against my hair.

The words wrapped around my chest and settled there like a balm as he stepped back from the car and nudged the door shut with his foot. Gravel crunched under his boots as he carried me toward the building. Each jolt sent another throb through my leg, but his hold didn't waver.

"Keys are in my left pocket," he said quietly. "Can you get it, or do you want me to set you down?"

I nodded against his chest, my fingers fumbling at the outside of his jacket until I found the outline of the key ring. The metal jingled as I fished it out and held it up.

"Top key, love. The big silver one."

The lock protested like it hadn't been used in years, then gave way with a grudging click. Kael shouldered the door open and stepped us into the darkness.

The smell inside hit me first. Dust and old wood with a faint undernote of oil and coffee.

He kicked the door shut behind us, and the sound echoed up into the high ceiling. His shoulder brushed against the wall as he reached out with one hand and found a switch by memory, and the lights hummed to life.

Not too bright, just a few overhead fixtures and a floor lamp in the far corner, bathing the room in a soft, yellowed glow.

It wasn't a warehouse inside. It was something adjacent to a living space. There was a big open floor area with an old couch, a scuffed coffee table, and a small kitchen area off to one side with mismatched cabinets and a stained sink. A metal spiral staircase in the corner led up to a loft where I could just make out the outline of a bed.

It wasn't pretty or polished, but it looked lived-in and trusted.

"You have a bachelor pad for murdering people," I said, voice wavering and slightly hysterical.

He huffed something that might have been a laugh.

"Safer than a hotel, and there are no neighbors to hear you scream."

My body flinched and he froze.

“Shit, I’m sorry! Not you! I just meant in general. Fuck!” He looked down at me sheepishly and shook his head.

I let out a bit of a huff and tried to give him a half smile back.

“Maybe save those jokes for when I’m not bleeding and trying to keep my brain from vacating, yeah?”

He gently kissed the top of my hair and muttered another apology as he carried me to the couch and lowered me down like I was made of glass. The cushions sagged under my weight, swallowing me in the best way. The second his arms left me, the buzzing rushed back. Air felt wrong against my skin again. Too much and not enough at the same time.

He crouched in front of me, bringing us eye-level. His hands stayed on his thighs, nowhere near me.

“I need to look at your leg.” His voice was careful, and threaded with remorse. “Can I?”

My throat was tight again as I stared at him. The careful way he phrased it, and the way he left silence there for me to say no and mean it. I nodded.

“Yeah,” I whispered. “You can.”

“Tell me if anything feels wrong. We stop when you say stop.”

He reached for the blanket, and his fingers brushed the fabric near my ankle, slow and deliberate. He didn’t tug or reveal anything further until I gave him another nod. Only then did he ease the blanket back from my calf.

The cool air hit the wet, torn skin, and I hissed between my teeth. The graze was ugly. A long, angry stripe carved across the side of my leg. Blood had crusted in places and smeared in others where the blanket had stuck and shifted. It wasn’t deep enough to see anything important, but it was deep enough to make my stomach twist.

Kael’s jaw clenched.

“Could have been worse,” he said, his voice low. “Bullet just kissed you, but luckily missed the artery.”

“It has terrible fucking aim,” I muttered in reply.

"I'll be sure to send a strongly worded letter on your behalf."

My mouth twitched, and I hated that he could easily pull that out of me.

He stood up and moved to the kitchen, and my lungs tightened again at the loss of him in front of me.

I watched him as he moved quickly and with efficiency. Cabinet doors opened and closed. Water ran. A drawer clattered. He came back with a bowl of water, a roll of gauze, a small first-aid kit that had seen better days, a clean dish towel, and what looked like a bottle of clear liquor.

"You're going to drink that?" I asked faintly.

"It's for your leg."

"Oh."

He set everything down on the coffee table and knelt again.

"This is going to sting," he warned. "A lot. You want something to bite down on, or you want to hold my hand?"

The answer should have been neither. I wasn't a child or a damsel. I had teeth and a spine and a whole lifetime of white-knuckling through worse than antiseptic. My hands were trembling again.

"Your hand," I heard myself say.

His fingers slid into mine, careful and warm, his grip firm enough to anchor but loose enough that I could pull away whenever I wanted.

"You ready?" he asked.

"No, but do it anyway."

He poured the liquor over the wound, and fire raced up my leg. I choked on a cry and squeezed his hand so hard my knuckles ached.

"Breathe," he murmured. "In. Out. That's it. You're doing so good."

"I hate you," I gritted out.

"I know."

He dabbed gently with the dish towel, wiping away blood, dirt, and whatever else had gotten in. Every touch burned, but his thumb stroked the back of my hand in slow, calming circles that gave me something else to focus on.

Tears blurred my vision, and I blinked them away, angry at them. They just came back, thicker.

"Stop," I rasped.

He did. Immediately.

"Too much?" he asked.

"I just…" My voice cracked. "I need a second."

He nodded and sat back on his heels, still holding my hand. His other hand braced on the floor, steady and solid, like he was ready to take my weight if I tipped.

The tears I'd been fighting slipped free. Just a few at first in silent, hot trails that streaked down my cheeks. Then more. They came in a rush, like someone had ripped the dam out of me.

I bowed my head, free hand flying up to cover my mouth as the first sob tore its way out of my chest. It was ugly and loud. Nothing like the neat, quiet crying I'd perfected over the years in bathroom stalls and dressing rooms.

This was messy. Open and raw. I tried to swallow it back and tried in vain to shush myself. It didn't work.

"Hey," Kael said softly. "Look at me."

I couldn't. His fingers tightened around mine.

"Seraphine," he said, low and steady. "You're not in that room anymore."

Another sob hit, harder than the last, and my shoulders curled in. The blanket shifted around me, threatening to slide off. I clutched it tighter with one fist and his hand tighter with the other.

"It's over," he reminded me. "He's not here. He's not ever going to touch you again. It's just you and me in this room."

"He'll find us," I choked out. "He always finds a way. He said—"

"I don't give a damn what he said." There was steel in his voice now, sharp enough to cut. "Conor's power ends where my promise begins."

"That's not how the world works."

"It is tonight."

"You can't know that."

"I can. Because I'm the one who built the kind of fear he's feeling right now. His house is on fire, his people are bleeding, and his cousin turned on him in front of a dozen witnesses. He's got bigger problems than chasing the girl who got away."

The girl. Me. I sucked in a shaky breath that almost stayed down this time.

"He hurt me," I whispered. The words tasted like acid.

"I know."

"He… he…" The rest of it jammed in my throat like broken glass.

"You don't have to say it. Not tonight. Not to me. Not ever, if you don't want to."

"Someone should know."

"I know enough to kill him for it."

A broken laugh hiccupped out of me.

"You were going to kill him anyway."

"Yes," he said simply. "Now I'll get to enjoy it more."

It should have horrified me. It didn't. Instead, I felt almost like a small piece of the cracks in my soul slipped together. Like his words began stitching all the things Conor had broken.

He shifted closer, slow enough that I could track every inch. His free hand came up, hovering near my face, fingers open, waiting.

"Can I touch you?" he asked. "Just here."

I nodded before my brain caught up. The idea of not being touched, yet also being touched, scared me. He brushed his thumb under my eye, catching a tear before it could fall. The gentleness hurt worse than the liquor. More tears came, and I let them. It didn't feel like I had a choice anymore.

He stayed there on the floor, solid and unmoving and entirely mine to lean on. He didn't fill the silence with platitudes. Didn't tell me it was okay, that it could have been worse, that I was strong. He just stayed.

My breathing slowly dragged itself out of panic and into something closer to human. The sobs tapered off into shivers. My head ached. My throat felt raw. My eyes burned like I'd scrubbed them with sand.

"I'm sorry," I said eventually. It came out hoarse.

"What for?"

"Falling apart all over your murder couch."

His mouth twitched as he suppressed a smile.

"That couch has seen worse, and you're allowed to fall apart."

"I don't have time for it."

"Then we make time," he said, as if it were that simple. "You don't have to be okay right now. I just need you to breathe."

I dragged in another breath, just to prove I could. He watched my chest rise and fall like it was the only thing in the room worth paying attention to.

"Can I finish your leg?" he asked after a moment. "Quickly this time."

"Yeah, just do it."

He went back to work, cleaning the last of the blood, then opening the first-aid kit. The antiseptic wipes made me hiss again, but the worst of the fire had already burned through. He wrapped the gauze with careful hands, neither too tight nor too loose.

"There, all finished. You'll scar, but you'll keep your leg."

"Lucky me."

He sat back, studying his work, then tilted his head to look up at me.

"How's your head?" he asked.

"Like someone used it as a drum."

"Concussion-level bad?"

"I don't think so. Just… used."

He nodded. "You should drink water. Then sleep."

"You say that like you think I can."

"You will." His mouth firmed. "Your body won't give you a choice much longer."

As if on cue, a wave of exhaustion washed over me so hard I almost slid sideways off the couch. The adrenaline that had been propping me up all night finally decided it had done its part and left. My limbs felt heavy, and my eyelids even heavier.

"If I fall asleep," I said slowly, "and I wake up, and this is all gone…"

"It won't be."

"Men like Conor don't just lose."

"Men like Conor don't think they can. That's their first mistake."

I studied his face. The lines at the corners of his eyes. The set of his mouth. The faint smear of dried blood near his hairline, he hadn't bothered to wipe away.

"You're really gonna kill him?" I asked.

His eyes darkened.

"Not yet. I want him to sit in his panic first. Let the suspicion marinate."

The way he said it made something deep in my chest go very still.

"I don't want him dead just because of me," I said. "I don't want that on my head."

"His death was written the second he put his hands on you. Everything else is just timing."

I should have argued. Should have told him it was not that simple, that people didn't get to rewrite the rules of the world just because someone hurt them. Maybe it was time for someone to do it for me.

"Are we…" I hesitated, the word thick on my tongue. "Are we safe?"

He didn't lie just to placate me.

"For tonight, at least. No one knows this place. Nobody followed us. I'll stay up so you can sleep."

"You're not sleeping?"

"I will later."

"That's not fair."

He shrugged one shoulder. "Fair is a luxury we can't afford right now. You're tired."

"I don't want to close my eyes."

"I know, but close them anyway."

I wanted to argue. I really did, but instead, my body betrayed me again, and I sank back into the couch, adjusting the blanket around my shoulders. The cushions cradled me, swallowing all my sharp edges. Kael stood long enough to grab another throw from a chair and drape it over me, double-layering the warmth.

"Is this okay?" he asked.

I nodded, my eyes already half-lidded.

He moved away then, just far enough to drag a worn armchair from the corner and position it a few feet from the couch, angled toward me. He sat, elbows on his knees, hands loosely clasped, watching the door.

"Kael?" I mumbled.

"Yeah?"

"If he comes…"

"He won't," he said.

"If he does."

His jaw tightened. "Then he dies on the doorstep."

I should have been horrified. Instead, for the first time since Conor's hand closed around my throat in that room, I felt something that might have been the beginning of real, fragile safety.

My eyes drifted shut. The last thing I saw was Kael's outline in the dim light, solid and still as stone. The last thing I heard was his voice, low and certain, threading through the dark like a promise.

"I'm not letting anyone take you again," he said. "Sleep, Little Fawn. I'll be right here when you wake up."

Chapter Twenty-Five

Kael

I'd forgotten how loud silence could be. The safehouse settled around us as I watched her sleep. Old pipes echoed softly through the walls, every small sound bouncing back louder than it should have. The low hum of the fridge. The faint wheeze of the heater kicking on and off.

And under it all, there was one sound I kept counting, the only one that mattered. Her breathing. Slow and sometimes uneven, but hearing it settled me in a way I had no words for.

Seraphine slept curled on the couch, swallowed in blankets, with one leg stretched out, and the other bent slightly. The bandage around her calf was already stained in places, the pale gauze turned an ugly dark brown. Her hair was a mess of knots and tangles, and her eyes were swollen and red even at rest.

Her jaw was tight, like she was holding on to something even in her dreams. She didn't look peaceful. She looked like someone whose body had finally knocked the power out as a last resort.

I sat in the armchair across from her, elbows on my knees, and my hands loosely clasped. The position looked relaxed from a distance, but it wasn't. Every muscle in my body was running on a thin electric wire that refused to stop buzzing.

I looked toward where I kept a pistol on the coffee table within easy reach, and another one was tucked at the back of my waistband. I still had my knife in my boot and one more inside the cushion where I was sitting. Old habits coupled with keeping the woman on the couch safe, by any means necessary.

I checked the door again, making sure the front lock was engaged and the deadbolt set. The extra slide lock I'd installed three years ago was thrown into its position. No alarm was ever set up in this place. I didn't need a siren to tell me if I failed her.

A soft sound pulled my attention back to the couch. She made a noise that wasn't quite a whimper as her fingers twitched against the edge of the blanket.

"Easy," I muttered under my breath. "You're alright."

She didn't wake up, but her face pinched for a second, then smoothed itself out again as the smallest bit of tension bled away. Good. Let her brain sand some of the edges off tonight. Tomorrow would cut new ones.

I let my gaze trace the line of the bandage again. The wound was still seeping. She would need a doctor, but that would be tomorrow's plan. Tonight, she needed sleep.

Better a few stitches in her leg than a hole in her skull, and I had seen more than enough of those.

Something in my shoulder pulled when I shifted, and I ignored it. I had a slice along my shoulder from a lucky guard's bullet, a bruise on my ribs where a rifle butt had tried to make a home, and what would probably be a matching set of scratches and bruises along my back from the fence.

Minor. My body knew the difference between pain and a problem, and my real problem lay on the couch, wrapped in blankets, and sleeping under my roof. Somehow, after everything, she still trusted me. I wasn't built for this anymore, or so I thought. Not since Aryia.

Her lashes fluttered, and for a second I thought she was waking, but she only shifted, rolling slightly onto her side. A small wince crossed her face when her bad leg moved, then faded when the blanket cushioned it.

"Careful, Little Fawn," I murmured. "You're hell on my control."

I pushed up out of the chair, grumbling as my legs complained. They could align with everything else. I didn't have time for muscles that wanted to rebel.

Up close, I could see the way she held herself even in sleep. Shoulders hunched and her hands pulled in tight, as if ready to shield her throat. The leftover tremor in the muscles around her eyes. Her breathing caught every now and then, like she hit a bad memory and had to fight her way past it.

I reached for the edge of the blanket near her chest and tugged it up higher, tucking it around her shoulders. She flinched in her sleep at my touch, and I stilled my hand.

"It's me," I said quietly. "Just fixing the blanket."

Her fingers uncurling was the only answer I got.

I checked the bandage again, touching only the gauze. My brows furrowed as I noticed more fresh blood seeping through. The skin around it was hot, but not angry red. I would clean it again in a few hours.

Something soft skirted against my leg, and I looked down. Her hand had slid just far enough that her fingertips brushed the inside of my calf. Barely there. A whisper of contact.

She hadn't reached for me. Not consciously. But my body reacted like she had, and I swallowed, taking a slow step back, breaking the contact before I could read too much into it. There would be time later to indulge whatever this was turning into. If we survived it.

I crossed to the small kitchenette and grabbed my phone off the counter. Hairline cracks webbed across the screen from where I had slammed it into a concrete post earlier in the night, but it still worked. I wiped a smear of dried blood off the corner with the heel of my hand and checked the time.

3:12 a.m.

No missed calls, but one unread message on the encrypted app tucked behind an unremarkable calculator icon. I opened it and clicked on Rafe's contact.

A grainy photo took up most of the screen of Conor's estate. Taken from the tree line, probably with a zoom older than the man holding the camera. The front lawn looked like a crime scene. Blood trails. Glass. A broken statue. Smoke was rising from the direction of the garage.

The text under it was short. Rafe never liked wasting words.

Rafe: *House still standing. Barely, but there. Cousin put him into a wall in front of half the guards. Last seen bleeding and screaming orders. You made friends tonight. You made enemies, too.*

No kidding.

A second message came in while I was still reading the first.

Rafc: *Price on your head already. And hers.*

My jaw clenched, and the phone creaked faintly in my grip. Of course, Conor would throw money at the problem he couldn't beat. That's what men like him did when fear finally found them. They hid behind dollar signs and hoped the world would get bored before their luck ran out.

He was going to learn some new things about luck, I thought as another line appeared.

Rafe: *You owe me.*

I snorted and typed back a quick reply.

Kael: *You owed me a favor. We're even.*
Stay away from the house for a few days. The stench will draw flies.

The typing bubble flickered, then vanished, then came back.

Rafe: *You good?*

I glanced at the couch. At the small, curled figure under my blankets. At the bandage I had wrapped with my own hands.

Kael: *Yeah.*

Rafe sent back a single thumbs up and a skull. His sense of humor had never been subtle.

I locked the phone and set it face down on the counter.

So, Conor was alive, but hurt and cornered. Cillian had shoved him into a wall in front of his own men. I replayed the moment on the stairs. The shift in the air when Cillian stepped forward, and the calm way he had said you're the one who doesn't walk back inside.

Men didn't make moves like that without an exit strategy. Cillian wasn't afraid of Conor. Not enough, anyway. That made him dangerous and possibly useful. I would have to decide which way to tip that scale. But not tonight.

I looked back at Sera. Tonight, my priorities were simpler. Keep her breathing. Keep the world out. Give Conor enough time to wonder where the cracks had come from, long enough for paranoia to eat his sleep, his trust, and eventually his sanity. I didn't want him dead while he still believed he was in control. A quick death was mercy. He had forfeited that right the second he put a cuff on her wrist.

• • •

A soft sound dragged my attention back to the couch.

"Kael…" she whispered.

The word was shredded by sleep, more of an exhale than actual speech. It still hit like a sucker punch to my heart, as I crossed the room before I registered that I had even moved.

She had rolled halfway onto her back again, with her head tilted toward where the armchair sat. Her eyes were still shut, and her brow furrowed. Her hand had crept higher on the blanket, fingers flexing on empty air.

"I'm here," I said, voice low. "Right here."

Her breath hitched, then steadied. Somewhere deep in her head, that landed in the right place. Her grip on the blanket loosened, and the lines around her eyes softened.

Kael. God, the way she said my name made something inside me long locked away stir against the bars. Everyone else saw a weapon. She saw the man holding it, and I desperately wanted to be worthy of that.

I moved back to the armchair and forced myself to sit again. The springs gave a tired groan. I shifted until I could see both the door and the couch without turning my head. I wouldn't let her wake up to an empty room.

Sleep tugged at the edges of my vision, and I let it circle without succumbing. My body had done far worse nights. I had gone forty hours on less. There was a familiar pattern in the exhaustion. Your muscles get heavy, thoughts begin to slow, all while your skin buzzes like a speaker turned low.

I cataloged it and then put it aside. Later. Another time.

My head tipped back against the chair for a second. Just enough to unkink my neck. The ceiling stared back at me, a stain in one corner catching my eye where the roof had leaked years ago. I remembered patching it myself one winter afternoon with a cheap ladder and even cheaper tar. Rafe was on the ground, laughing at me while I swore at the cold. I had bought this building so no one else could use it against me. A place that was off the books with no lease. Paid for in cash only, so it didn't cause a paper trail.

Now it had a better use. I looked at Sera again. She was the worst decision I had ever made, but also the only one I would never regret. I replayed the night for the thousandth time. The stairs and the alarm. The shot that had grazed her leg and the way she had pressed herself into the wall and tried to disappear. The way she had pushed past her own fear and still found a way to look Conor in the eye and tell him to go to hell.

'Fuck you, Conor. Try it, and I'll kill you myself.'

My mouth tugged, more instinct than humor. He had no idea what kind of problem he had just made for himself. He had taken a girl he thought was a toy, put a leash on her, and then tried to break her. Maybe he had a little. But I had spent my life building nightmares for the people he wanted gone, and now I'd get to build one for him. And it would hurt; I'd make sure of it.

I checked the corners of the room again, and my gaze snagged on the spiral staircase and the loft bed above. I should move her up there. The couch was fine for tonight, but the mattress would be better for her back. Less draft and less chance of her leg stiffening into something more painful.

I pictured carrying her again, the way her arms had gone around my neck. How she had buried her face in my shoulder and tried to make herself smaller, as if she could take up less space in the world, and that would keep it from hitting her.

She had trusted me to hold her weight. I didn't fucking deserve it. I didn't deserve her. But I was going to spend the rest of my life trying anyway.

A buzz at the counter pulled my attention back to the phone. Another message on the encrypted app. This time, it was a different contact and a whole other problem. The name at the top of the thread was Silver, someone I'd asked to keep eyes inside the club.

Silver: *Cleaning up after the alley took longer than expected. Dumpster handled. No cameras. No loose end*s.

Good. No evidence and no footage of what I had done to Michael. No proof of me taking him from the club and throwing him in the back of my car. For now, the story would stay clean. Michael had run and disappeared like a man too far under to crawl out.

I typed back a short reply.

Kael: *Good work. Lay low. Tell Patrick I will be in touch as soon as I can.*

The answer came back almost immediately.

Silver: *He has questions.*

Of course he did. I had dragged his best friend out of hell without him there to help. Patrick would never forgive himself or me for that. I sent a short reply, just enough for now.

Kael: *She's safe, and she's resting. She's bent, but not broken.*

I set the phone down again and scrubbed a hand over my face. My fingers came away with a smear of blood from along my cheekbone. I licked my thumb and wiped it off, then gave up on the rest. I would shower once she woke up, and I knew she could keep water down. Once I had watched her look at the walls and remember she wasn't locked in that room anymore.

Until then, I was not leaving this spot. A creak from the couch made me look up as Sera shifted again, rolling onto her back. Her arm slid out from under the blanket and fell toward the edge. Before it could drop, I was already there, catching her wrist gently and guiding it back onto the cushion. Her skin was warm. Softer than it had any right to be after the life she had lived.

Her eyes cracked open. Just a sliver.

"Kael?" she mumbled.

The word was barely audible; more air than anything.

"Yeah. I'm here, baby."

Her gaze found my face, and her eyes were unfocused and heavy. The panic I had grown used to seeing there was dulled now, blunted by exhaustion and whatever thin safety her brain had started to believe.

"You're still here," she whispered.

"Where else would I be?"

Her lashes fluttered as she opened her eyes, as if the effort was almost too much.

"People leave when it gets hard."

"I don't."

She studied me as if she could see all the ways that was a lie, all the exits I had taken in my life, all the times I had walked away from people before they could do the same to me. Then she gave the smallest nod.

"Okay," she breathed.

And just like that, I cracked a little as she trusted me with one more piece of her. It felt like someone had set a weight on my chest. Heavy, solid, and welcoming. But still terrifying.

"Go back to sleep, Little Fawn," I said softly. "You're safe."

"For tonight," she murmured, echoing my own words from earlier.

"For tonight," I agreed. "Tomorrow I'll make sure it stays that way."

Her eyes slid shut, and her breathing evened out again. My hand hovered near her wrist for a second longer, then I stepped back and returned to the chair.

I settled in, guns within reach, my eyes on the door, and my mind already moving pieces on a board only I could see. Conor had put a price on her head. On ours. He had no idea how expensive that would be for him. No one was ever putting their hands on her again. Not while I was still breathing. Not while I could put myself between her and them.

And if the world had a problem with that? I would burn it down along with anyone else who tried.

Chapter Twenty-Six

Seraphine

The first thing I noticed was the smell. Not smoke, or expensive cologne. None of that awful lemon cleaner. Coffee. Real, cheap, burnt-at-the-edges type coffee. For a second, my brain refused to believe it. My eyes stayed shut, and my body stayed perfectly still, waiting for the couch to dip under another weight. For fingers to close around my throat, and for Conor's voice to slide into the dark like oil.

But the couch under me was lumpy and old, not the expensive mattress of a prison I never thought I'd escape. The blanket scratched against my skin, and the air tasted faintly like dust and stale heat. Somewhere nearby, something ticked, steady and soothing.

I opened my eyes, and the room looked the same as it had before sleep dragged me under. With its high brick walls and scuffed floors. The battered coffee table by the couch and the metal staircase curling up to the loft in the corner. Morning light crept around the edges of the boarded windows, turning the dust in the air to slow-moving glitter.

I was still on the couch, still wrapped in the blanket cocoon, and my leg was still wrapped and throbbing. He hadn't moved me.

The armchair across from me was empty, and panic snapped awake in my chest before I could stop it. I shoved myself upright too fast. The world tilted hard left, and stars burst at the edges of my vision as the sudden change in blood pressure made my head roar. My calf screamed in protest. A small sound slipped out of me as I gripped the blanket.

"Easy, baby."

His voice came from my left, and I jerked my head toward the sound. Kael stood in the kitchen area, one hand braced on the counter, the other wrapped around a chipped mug that steamed in the cool air. He still looked like he had walked out of a crime scene, without bothering to clean up. His shirt was wrinkled, and dried blood cut a thin line near his hairline, while a bruise blossomed along one forearm. He had taken his holster off, but the imprint of it still marked his shoulder.

His eyes were on me, clear and alert as if he'd been awake the whole time anyway.

"Didn't mean to startle you."

I swallowed, trying to shove my heart back down out of my throat.

"You weren't in the chair," I said. My voice sounded rough. "I thought…"

You left. The words tangled on my tongue, and I dug my nails into the blanket instead. His mouth tightened like he heard the rest anyway.

"The bathroom is behind that wall," he said, taking my attention off my panic and nodding toward the far side of the room. "And for the record, I was trying not to be a creep and watch you sleep for eight hours straight."

"How long was I actually out?" I asked.

"Six hours, give or take."

Six hours. My body believed it. I ached in places I didn't know could ache. My eyes felt sticky, and my throat was raw. My muscles were stiff and heavy, like I had been poured in concrete and left to set.

"Did you sleep?" I asked.

"Some."

Which, in big scary murderer speak, meant probably not at all.

He moved away from the counter and crossed to the coffee table. The limp in his stride was barely there, more a hint than a real hitch, but I saw it anyway. Something had caught him in the hip somewhere in the mess that I didn't remember clearly.

He set the mug down within my reach and straightened up again.

"This is for you, if you want it, of course."

The smell of it hit me fully. Cheap coffee that was made too strong and slightly burned. The sight of it was so fucking perfect, it almost made me cry.

"I thought you said I should drink water," I said, trying for something close to normal.

"There is water," he said, nodding at the bottle on the table. "The coffee is purely for emotional support."

I let out a sound that might have been a laugh, but it came out cracked and wobbly. My hands shook when I reached for the mug. Not as violently as in the car, but just small tremors that made the surface of the coffee shiver. Kael noticed. Of course he did.

"I can get you a straw, if you need it."

I rolled my eyes because the alternative was falling apart again.

"I'm not that fragile," I muttered.

He tilted his head like he wanted to disagree, but let it go.

The first sip was too hot. It burned my tongue and scraped all the way down. It was perfect. Something normal, something ugly and bitter and simple.

"How's the leg?" he asked.

"Still attached."

"Pain level?"

"High enough. Depends what it does if I stand up."

"You're not testing that alone," he said. "You said yes to me carrying you once, and the world continued to spin. We can repeat the experiment."

Heat crawled up my neck, and my brain flashed an image of his arms under me, his chest solid against my side, and the way my fingers had curled into his shirt without permission. I took another too-hot sip to chase it away.

"I want to try it. But on my own. I just… need a minute."

"Take two. I'm in no hurry."

We sat in the quiet for a few breaths, as the coffee warmed my hands, then my chest. My leg throbbed in time with my pulse while the bandage itched under the blanket. My skin felt both numb and too tight, too aware.

I could feel the grime of the last few days clinging to me, in the form of smoke in my hair and the faint feel of sweat dried on my neck. Someone else's hands still ghosted over my skin if I let myself dwell on it for too long.

I swallowed hard and set the mug down before I dropped it.

"I need a shower," I said quickly, chasing away the thoughts.

The words fell into the room like bricks. Kael's jaw tightened for half a second. His eyes flicked over my face, down to the blanket, then back up. He didn't linger on my exposed skin, not even a little.

"I can get the water running for you. Make sure it heats up. Towels are in the cabinet above the toilet. There's nothing fancy, but I can find you something clean to wear."

Something clean. The idea almost made me weep more than the coffee did.

"Clothes would be good, thank you," I said quietly.

He nodded once.

"Do you want help getting there?" he asked. "Or do you want to try walking and use me as a wall if you need it?"

"Wall," I said.

I didn't know if I meant it or if I was just saying it to prove something to myself. It didn't matter. He nodded like it was a tactical choice and not me being stubborn.

He moved to the small dresser near the stairs, opened a drawer, and rummaged around. When he came back, he had a black T-shirt and a pair of sweatpants in his hands.

"They'll be big, but you can pretend it's a fashion choice."

I gave a snort and pretended to look offended.

"Do I look like the kind of girl who cares about fashion?"

He let his gaze sweep me once, slow and deliberate, without touching anything that would make me flinch.

"You look like you could make anything work," he said softly.

The compliment landed oddly, fusing itself somewhere between my ribs and my throat. I didn't know what to do with it, so I pretended it bounced off as he set the clothes beside me on the couch, then stepped back.

"Ready to try standing?" he asked.

"No, but let's do it anyway."

He moved to my side, not close enough to touch, but close enough that if I tipped, I knew where I would fall.

"Hand on my arm, if you want it. Not my shoulder, though, that will pull."

I nodded, then slowly peeled the blanket back from my legs. The air hit the bare skin of my thighs, and I fought the urge to drag the blanket right back up. Dark bruises bloomed there in ugly, finger-shaped smudges. My stomach lurched. If I looked higher, I knew I'd find worse.

Kael's gaze didn't follow mine. He kept his eyes level, waiting. I put one hand on the couch, and the other on his forearm. His skin was warm under my fingers, and the muscle there tensed, ready to take whatever weight I threw onto it.

"Slow," he warned.

I shifted my uninjured leg first, getting my foot under me. The movement pulled at my calf, and fire licked up the back of it. I hissed and sucked air through my teeth.

"Breathe for me. In and out. That's all you're doing right now. Nothing else."

I did what he said. One breath. Then another. Then one more. My vision steadied again, and the edges of the room slid back into place.

I pushed myself up, and for a second, it felt like my body had forgotten how to be vertical. My knees trembled, and my leg screamed. The couch creaked like it wanted to keep me and let me lie there forever.

But then I was standing, barefoot on the cold floor and wrapped in stubbornness and someone else's blanket. Alive. His arm under my hand didn't move. He might as well have been part of the building.

"You good?" he asked.

"Define good," I said through clenched teeth.

"Not currently falling. That counts for something, Little Fawn."

"It fucking hurts."

"I know. Lean on me as much as you need. I promise I can take it."

The words almost broke something inside me, so I clung to his arm instead. One slow step. Then another. Every shift tugged the wound. My leg felt too tight for the skin that held it, and the room swayed but didn't tip.

He kept pace with me without rushing. His hand hovered near my waist, never quite touching, a steady presence there if I wanted it.

We made it to the short hallway that led to the bathroom. The door was open, showing a small, utilitarian space. A toilet, a sink, and a narrow shower stall with a cheap curtain. No windows and white tile that had seen better days.

The sight of it made me want to drop to my knees and give thanks, but before I could, the panic hit hard and fast. Four walls with no exit except back the way I came. The water, too much noise in the tiny space. All of it made my lungs stutter.

"Hey," Kael said quietly. "Stay with me. It's my bathroom. Not a cell in that house."

I forced my gaze away from the shower and up to his face.

"Easy for you to say," I said.

"No," he said. "Not easy. Not for this. But I can promise you something."

"What?"

"I won't come in there unless you tell me to. Not for any reason. If you want me nearby, I'll sit on the floor by the door. If you want me on the other side of the room, I'll move. You choose."

Control. And he handed it to me like it was the easiest thing in the world.

"I want you close," I said before I could think better of it. "Not in the room. But… here. Where I can hear you."

"Done," he said.

He helped me with the last step to the door, then let me go, making sure I had the frame under my hand.

"Towels are above the toilet," he said. "The water should be a good temperature, but double-check before you get in."

"You have shower preferences for me now?" I asked weakly.

"Only that you don't pass out in there and crack your head open. It would one hundred percent ruin my morning."

It was such a stupid line that I almost laughed, and it actually helped a bit. Humor always did when it got too dark around me.

Once he knew I was in and not in immediate danger of falling apart all over again, he closed the door most of the way, leaving a small gap in the frame, and his shadow fell across that line, a dark bar of certainty.

I gripped the sink and forced myself to look up. The mirror above it was streaked, and the light overhead was too harsh. I almost didn't recognize the woman staring back at me.

My eyes were bruised, with purple and red shadows smudged beneath them. My skin looked too pale, except where it didn't. Finger-shaped marks stood out on my throat, my shoulders. The faint red ring around my wrist from the cuff glared back like a brand. I touched it with the fingers of my other hand. The skin there ached at the contact.

"You're not there," I whispered to myself.

The girl in the mirror didn't look convinced as steam began to fog the edges of the glass. The sound of the water filled the room, bouncing off tile and porcelain, and my chest tightened.

I turned away from the mirror and fumbled with the blanket. Dropping it felt wrong, like peeling off armor, but the thing smelled like blood and sweat and Conor's house, so I let it slide to the floor and kicked it aside.

As the air hit my bare skin, goosebumps raced over my arms and legs, and my stomach churned. Bruises were everywhere. Some older, some far too new. The kind that didn't belong to accidents or wild nights or anything I had chosen. For a second, I forgot how to breathe.

"Little Fawn? I'm still here," he called from the other side of the door. Not too loud. Just close enough.

I swallowed hard. "Yeah," I said. My voice shook. "Me too."

"Talk to me. Tell me what you are doing."

"Trying not to throw up."

"That's progress. Anything else?"

"I'm… getting in the shower," I said.

My hands didn't seem to understand the instructions I was giving them, and it took longer than it should have to pull the curtain aside and step in. The tile was cold under my feet as I tested my weight on my bad leg. It held, though it screamed the whole time. I kept it out of the water the best I could as I stepped under the stream.

The water hit my shoulder, and I flinched. Not because it was too hot. Because it was a touch of something on my skin, sudden and unseen. My body didn't care that I had stepped in on my own, or that I knew where it was coming from.

I pressed my back to the opposite wall, let the spray hit my chest instead, and sucked in air.

"You alright?" Kael asked.

"I'm in, and still upright, so that is… something."

"Good. Can you name five things you feel right now?"

"Seriously?" I asked.

"I promise it helps, Sera. Humor me."

I shut my eyes, letting the water run over my skin. It tracked over bruises and grazes; the bulk of them over places I didn't want to think about.

"Tile under my feet, and the water on my shoulders. Air on my face. The wall against my back. My leg. It fucking hurts."

"Four things you can hear," he continued.

"Water. You. The fan and my breathing."

"Three things you can smell."

"Soap," I said, reaching blindly for the bottle and popping the lid. The scent hit me. Not lemon cleaner or some asshole's cologne. Just cheap, generic soap. "Blood. Coffee from the other room."

"Two things you can taste."

"Metallic. From the cuts in my mouth," I said. "And… water."

"One thing you can see."

I opened my eyes. "Tile. It's white and cracked in the corner."

"Good," he said. "Stay with the tile if you need to."

It was ridiculous, and yet it helped. The ebb and flow of anxiety began to bleed out of me and down the drain with the dried blood from my skin and the water.

I squeezed shampoo into my hand and worked it through my hair. The movement made my shoulders protest, but I gritted my teeth and kept going. Dirty water slipped down my back, turning the drain into a swirling little storm.

It should have felt cleansing. Some of it was. Some of it felt like I was scrubbing at something that had been ground too deeply to come off in one go. When I worked the soap over my arms and over the bruises there, my breath hitched. My hand hovered over my ribs, over the worst of the marks, and refused to touch.

The room seemed to shrink. The sound of the water grew louder, enclosing, blanketing. My skin crawled, and my vision tunneled. I was no longer at the safehouse. Not in an old brick room with a spiral staircase and a man who had killed to get me out.

I was back in Conor's house. Back in the dark. Back in that bed. Hands on my wrists. Weight on my chest. A voice in my ear telling me how pretty I sounded when I broke. My lungs forgot how to work.

I pressed my back harder into the tile, and my fingers dug at the grout. The water hammered at me. My heart slammed against my ribs like it wanted out. Somewhere, far away, I heard my own voice.

"Stop," I whispered. "Stop, stop, stop."

The tap didn't turn itself off. The water just kept coming.

"Seraphine."

Kael's voice cut through the roar.

I couldn't answer. The sound of rushing in my ears drowned everything out as my body shook against my will.

"Little Fawn," he said. "Are you with me?"

I sucked in air, but only half of it. The rest stuck in my throat.

"I can hear you breathing," he said. "That's good. Can you say something for me?"

"I… can't," I gasped.

"Okay," he replied, voice still calm. "You don't need to say much. Just one thing. Tell me where you are."

My hand slapped the wall blindly, searching for something solid. My palm hit tile. I focused on that. Cold. Ungiving. Here.

"Bathroom," I forced out. "Safehouse."

"Good," he said. "You're in my bathroom. Not his. What do you see?"

"Tile," I whispered. "Cracked in the corner."

"The water is really loud. Do you want me to come in and turn it off?"

The offer made my stomach flip. Another body in this room. Another presence in this small, closed space.

"No," I gasped. "No, don't… don't come in. Please."

"I won't," he said immediately. "I'll stay where I am. I promise. You are the only one in that room."

I squeezed my eyes shut, and the water kept beating down. I slid slowly to the floor, my bad leg screaming as I bent it, until I was sitting under the spray with my arms wrapped around my knees. I felt ridiculous. Pathetic and broken wide open.

"Breathe with me," Kael said. "In for four. Out for four. I'll count."

He did, and I tried to follow.

One inhale. Two. Three. Four.

One exhale. Two. Three. Four.

My chest fought it at first. The breaths came shaky and uneven. I choked on one and almost lost it again. He didn't rush me. Didn't get impatient as I faltered. He just kept counting and kept talking me through it.

"You're not weak, Sera. Your brain is doing what it needs to keep you alive with what it remembers. That is all."

"I hate it," I rasped.

"I know, but hating it won't make it stop. Breathing will."

Little by little, my lungs started to cooperate again. The buzzing in my vision stopped, and the water felt less like a wall and more like… water.

My skin still crawled, and my stomach still knotted, but the urge to claw my way through the tiled wall had eased.

"I'm sitting on your shower floor," I said after a minute. "Like an idiot."

"Like someone whose legs need a break," he corrected. "You can stay there as long as you want. I promise the water doesn't care if you stand or sit."

A small, broken laugh slipped out of me. I scrubbed my hands over my face, wiping away soap and tears and everything else.

"I still don't feel clean," I whispered.

There was a pause on the other side of the door, and when he spoke again, his voice was softer.

"That will take time. More than one shower. More than one night. But this is a start."

"I want it off. All of it. Every part he touched. I want to peel it off."

My fingers dug into the skin on my upper arms.

"Hey," Kael said, a little sharper. "Easy, love. Don't hurt yourself to erase him. That gives him space he doesn't deserve."

My hands loosened.

"I don't know how to be in my own skin anymore. It feels fucking wrong."

"Then we go slow. You don't have to like it today. You don't have to forgive it. You just have to stay in it. That's enough for now."

It didn't feel like enough yet. It still felt like drowning. But the water temperature had cooled slightly, and the sound had faded into something manageable. My heart had downgraded from a constant explosion to just pounding.

"I'm going to turn it off now," I said.

"Alright. I'm still here. Take your time."

I reached up and twisted the tap. The sudden quiet when the water stopped made my ears ring. The leftover droplets ran down my shoulders in thin rivulets, collecting at the hollow of my throat. My skin prickled as the cold came in fast now that the heat was gone.

"Clothes?" I croaked.

"Already here," he said.

Something soft nudged the bottom of the door, then slid through the gap. I looked down and saw the T-shirt and sweatpants.

I wrapped a towel around myself first and dried off as quickly as my screaming leg would allow. Every brush over a bruise was a jolt.

Seeing them made my chest tighten all over again, so I kept my eyes on neutral ground. Tile. Towel. The clothes were in a small pile by the door.

Getting dressed hurt more than I thought it would. Pulling the sweatpants over the bandage took careful maneuvering that lit up every nerve in my leg. By the time the shirt was on and hanging almost to my mid-thighs, I was shaking again. But I was covered, and that helped quiet the screaming in my brain.

"Good?" Kael asked.

"Yeah," I said. My voice sounded smaller in the tiled room. "Can you… back up. I'm coming out."

"I never got any closer, but I'll give you space."

His shadow shifted, and I cracked the door and looked out.

He was a few steps back, as promised. His hands loose at his sides and his eyes on my face. Not my legs. Not my bruises. Just on me. On the cotton of his shirt that swallowed me, and the sweatpants bunched at my ankles. I felt ridiculous. I felt like a kid playing dress-up. But I still felt safer than I had in days.

"How is the leg?" he asked.

"Annoyingly painful, but functional."

He nodded once. "Water?" he asked. "I can make you something light to eat. Crackers. Toast. It will help more than coffee."

"I don't think I can."

"Half a slice, please. We negotiate, like functional adults."

"You're bossy."

"You're alive, and eating is how you get to repay me."

I rolled my eyes again, but the fight had gone out of it.

He moved ahead of me toward the couch, giving me room to follow without feeling watched. I made my way back slowly, each step a careful test of balance and pain. When I sank down onto the cushions, my whole body sighed in relief.

He came back from the kitchen a minute later with a glass of water and a plate. Two triangles of toast sat on it with butter already melted into the surface.

He set them on the table and then took his place in the armchair again. Not hovering over me or crowding my space, just there. Exactly where I needed him to be.

I stared at the toast like it might bite.

"One bite," he said. "Please. Just to see how it sits."

I picked up a piece with shaky fingers and took a small, mechanical bite. Chewed and then swallowed while my stomach rolled in protest, and then begrudgingly accepted it.

"See?" He smiled, small but real. The first one I could remember seeing. He was beautiful when he smiled, and I let my brain catalog the image.

"You're very proud of yourself for this," I laughed softly, taking another small bite of toast.

"I'm very proud of you."

His words landed in a way I didn't know what to do with, and rather than unpacking all that, I took another sip of water.

We sat like that for a while as the morning light crept higher along the wall. Somewhere outside, a car drove past, and the safehouse settled around us, the old bones of it creaking and sighing.

"I had a panic attack in your shower," I said eventually.

"Yes," he said.

"I cried on your couch."

"You did."

"I'm a fucking mess."

"For very good reasons."

"I don't know how to come back from this," I admitted. "I don't know how to be me again."

He studied me, his gaze steady.

"Maybe you don't need to. Maybe you can build something new out of what's left. Seraphine version 2.0."

"More like Seraphine version 174.0 at this point," I deadpanned.

"So then you've had 173 versions to practice. But just know, you're not going to have to do it alone."

His voice calmed pieces of me I never thought would feel calm again. But the other voice always came back.

"People leave when it gets hard," I said quietly, looking down at the floor. Anywhere but at him.

"Some do, yeah. Luckily, I'm not one of them."

"You can't promise me that. People leave. Especially when it comes to me."

He tilted his head.

"Never you," he said quietly. "Never again."

I looked at him. From the bruises on his arms to the dried blood near his hairline, and the exhaustion in the lines at the corners of his eyes. The way he still sat like a guard dog at a door.

"Why?" I asked. "I'm not… I'm not easy. I'm not soft. I'm definitely not worth a fucking war with the likes of Conor."

His jaw tightened before he spoke. "You don't get to decide your worth based on the worst thing that ever happened to you," he said. "I'm starting a war with Conor because his time was coming anyway. You were the line he crossed that made it personal."

"That doesn't sound any better," I said.

"It's not meant to, Sera. It's meant to be honest."

Silence settled between us again. Not comfortable, but not entirely painful either. Just real.

My leg throbbed in a slow, steady ache, and my skin still crawled in places. The shower hadn't magically washed anything away. It hadn't fixed the way my stomach flipped when I caught sight of a bruise or felt the ghost of fingers on my throat.

But I had stood. I had walked. I had sat under the water and breathed my way back from the edge. Small achievements.

I curled my fingers into the fabric of his sweatpants bunched at my knees.

"Kael?" I asked quietly.

"Yeah?" he answered.

"Thank you," I said. "For not coming in. And for not leaving."

His face changed at that. Just a fraction. Something in his eyes sharpened, then softened again.

"You don't owe me thanks for the bare minimum, but you're welcome."

He leaned back in the chair, eyes sliding to the door again.

"Sleep if you can, Little Fawn. I'll keep watch."

"I just woke up," I grumbled, finishing the last bite of toast and washing it down with water.

"You survived a garage bombing, a kidnapping, a bullet, and my cooking," he said. "You're allowed to sleep twice in one day."

It was ridiculous. But it was also so fucking tempting.

I shifted sideways on the couch, easing my bad leg into a less painful position. I tossed the blanket from Conor's house on the floor like a rag, the thought of it touching me again making my stomach curl.

Instead, I pulled up the clean blanket Kael had placed on me last night around my shoulders and nestled myself into the warmth. My eyes were heavier than I wanted to admit.

"Will you be here?" I asked.

He didn't look away from the door.

"Right here. Until you tell me to move."

I let my eyes close, not because I trusted the world, but because there was one man in the room who was ready to set it on fire if it tried to touch me again. It wasn't peace. Not yet. But it was enough to drift on. For now.

Chapter Twenty-Seven

Kael

The light came in gray and too bright the next morning through the cracks in the blinds, cutting the room into narrow bands. The heater coughed to life somewhere in the corner, rattling like it was ready to retire. The old pipes ticked inside the walls as a car rolled past outside. The city was doing what it always did. Pretending like the night before never happened.

I sat in the armchair facing the door, gun on the table beside me, my neck stiff, and my eyes burning. At some point, my body had stopped being tired and slipped into that uncomfortable place beyond it, where everything felt a fraction louder, and edges caught a little sharper.

Just off to the side of me, Sera slept. Still on the couch, and still wrapped in my blanket and my clothes. Her hair was a dark snarl around her face, and the bruises on her throat had come up ugly and stark, as the blue and purple fingerprints stood out against her pale skin. Her calf was propped on a pillow, the new bandage was clean on top, but already faintly shadowed where the blood underneath was trying to soak through again.

Her breathing wasn't pretty. It stuttered sometimes, caught, then dragged itself back into rhythm. But it was there, and that was all I needed from her, for now.

My body had started to file its own complaints. My shoulder throbbed where a guard's bullet had grazed the skin. My ribs were sore in a familiar way, while a deep ache settled down the center of my spine from the scratches of the fence and sitting too long in one position.

It didn't matter. Not right now. Pain meant I was alive, and being alive meant I was useful. To her. For her.

The clock on my burner phone said 7:39 a.m. when my eyes slipped shut. Just for a second. Just a blink. My chin hit my chest, and I slipped into that space where there were no dreams and no images. Just a black drop, like someone had cut the power behind my eyes.

Forty-five minutes later, my body ripped me back, and I jolted awake like I'd been shot. My heart beat hard against my ribs as my breath stuttered in my chest. My hand was already closing over the grip of the gun while my eyes locked on the door before my brain caught up and remembered the room.

I catalogued the space quickly: the old brick, the spiral staircase leading up to the loft, the worn-in couch, before landing firmly on her. I shifted my focus and checked her over without moving.

She hadn't moved much. A little deeper into the cushions, and the blanket had bunched higher over her shoulder. Her face was turned toward the back of the couch now, and her cheek was pressed into the fabric. A faint crease cut into the skin between her brows. But she was still breathing.

I let my fingers ease off the gun and scrubbed my free hand over my face. My neck cracked, and my shoulder protested, while my brain tried to shove me back down into sleep. No. Forty-five minutes was a luxury. Anything more was indulgence.

The burner chirped in my lap, the noise short and sharp. The sound it made when a specific app lit up.

Rafe.

I picked up the phone, slid my finger across the cracked screen, and opened my messages.

Three messages. All in the encrypted thread. No attachments. No emojis. He wasn't in the mood.

Rafe: *Conor's losing it.*

I opened the thread fully.

Rafe: *Been up all night. The house is burning down without flames.*
Rafe: *Guards walking. Others holed up in the staff wing and refused to follow orders.*
Rafe: *He put a hole in a door with someone's head around three a.m.*

I could see it. Conor's calm was finally slipping. Years of careful posture cracking under the weight of fear. Good. I scrolled again

.

Rafe*: Cillian is still missing. Rumor says he took something out of the office before he went ghost. Ledger, phone, or a thumb drive. Nobody knows.*
Rafe: *Conor's having people strip rooms. Screaming about "loyalty" and "betrayal." It's a whole shit-show.*

My jaw clenched, and my teeth scraped together. So Cillian had not only put him against a wall in front of the guards. He'd robbed him blind on the way out. That tracked. Cillian was a lot of things. Stupid had never been one of them. If he had a ledger or a phone, that was leverage. Names. Numbers. Deals Conor couldn't afford to let daylight see. Conor would tear his own house apart brick by brick to find it. He'd tear the rest of the world apart to find anyone connected to it. Including us. Let him come.

My thumb hovered over the keyboard for a second before I typed.

Kael: *How fast is the word spreading?*

The reply came almost instantly.

Rafe: *Fast. Underground's buzzing. Your name's in a lot of mouths. Hers too.*
Rafe: *But that's not the part you're going to hate.*

A second bubble popped up before I could ask.

Rafe: *He put a price on Patrick, too.*

Everything in me went still except my pulse. That sped up. Everything else around me slowed to a crawl. I breathed in once, slow, trying to calm myself before I did something extra stupid.

Kael: *Explain.*

There was a longer pause this time. Ten seconds. Twenty. I pictured Rafe chewing his lip, watching the screen, and choosing his words.

Rafe: *Word from one of the collectors. Conor's offering good money for Patrick, alive. No damage to the face, no holes in the head or chest. He wants him breathing and able to talk.*
Rafe: *Bonus if he gets delivered within a week. Bigger bonus if the courier can confirm "the girl" hears about it.*

There it was. Patrick wasn't leveraged for me. He was bait for her.

Conor had watched it once already on the night she'd given herself over to him to save Patrick's skin. He was her Achilles heel, and Conor knew it.

Sacrifice was a pattern with her, and Conor was counting on that. If she heard about a price on Patrick's head, if she got even a whiff of him being in danger because of her, she'd do something stupid. No. Not stupid. Fucking loyal. Stupid was what people who didn't know the cost called it.

She knew the cost. She calculated it and let it be weighed and measured against herself. My fingers tightened around the phone hard enough to make it creak

.

Rafe: *I don't think he's been grabbed yet. No one is bragging about a delivery. No footage of a snatch.*
Rafe: *But with that price? It's only a matter of time.*

I looked at the couch. Sera's hand had slipped free of the blanket, resting palm-up on the cushion. Her fingers curled slightly in sleep, like she was still holding on to something that wasn't there. The last thing she needed was another body on the line because of her. The last thing she was going to get was a choice between herself and Patrick. Not again. Not on my watch.

Kael: *Anyone close to taking the job?*
Rafe: *Plenty talking. A few are scouting the club. I've got eyes nearby.*
Rafe: *Patrick's jumpy. Hasn't gone home. Sleeping at random places. Locked doors. Panicked but smart.*
Rafe: *He knows something is off. Probably knows more than he should.*

Of course he did. Patrick had a nose for wrong. It was how he kept his nose mostly clean in the dirtiest parts of town. He'd feel the pressure building. He'd know Conor was going to want something from him. He'd already walked away from Sera once; there was no universe where he'd do it again.

Which meant his only real play would be to try to protect everyone else himself. Martyrs. Fuck. Everywhere I looked, someone was trying to die for someone else.

Kael: *Keep your eyes on him.*
Kael: *If anyone makes a move, you get me a plate, a face, and a direction. Fast.*
Rafe: *You going to tell her?*

My gaze flicked to the couch again. Her lashes fluttered, and her lips parted on a small exhale. She tucked her chin in tighter, shoulders curling like she was bracing against something even asleep. She'd given up everything to keep Patrick breathing the first time. She'd walk straight back into hell if she thought he was standing where she should be. And that was exactly what Conor was banking on.

I typed back slower this time.

Kael: *Not yet.*
Rafe: *She's going to find out.*
Kael: *Not. Yet.*

There was a pause.

Rafe: *Fine. My conscience is clean.*
Rafe: *But the clock's ticking, Mercer.*
Rafe: *Conor might be spiraling, but he's not stupid. He's scared. Scared men gamble big.*
Kael: *Then we stop giving him chips.*

I locked the phone and set it face down on the counter. The room felt smaller, even though it was still the same brick, same couch, same dust in the light. Same rattling heater in the corner. But the weight was different.

The other night had been raw survival. Get in, get her, get out, don't die. This was something else entirely. The game had shifted.

Conor wasn't just trying to drag us back into his orbit. He was widening the circle. Pulling other people onto the board. Any runner who thought they could make a quick payday. Anyone who would be stupid enough to think they could stand between him and what he wanted and walk away.

He was turning the city into a hunting ground. He thought I'd keep running with her until we were exhausted, then force her to choose. He had no idea what I was doing. I flicked a glance at the door.

We needed a different safehouse. This one could be compromised, and now it had something more important than problems in it. It had her. Not because anyone knew we were here yet, but because if anyone ever did, I'd blow the whole building sky-high before I let them walk in.

Too much heat would be gathering around my usual haunts now. All the corners I leaned on. Storefronts that looked the other way under the protection I offered. The same alleys I parked in too often.

We needed something further out and off-pattern. One of my other addresses. The old warehouse toward the harbor, the one with the broken windows and the condemned notice that never made it through the system. Or the converted workshop tucked behind a junkyard on the edge of the industrial district.

We needed more distance, more choke points, and fewer neighbors. Easier to secure meant easier to defend. Fuck.

Supplies first. Then, a new safehouse location.

The medical supplies I had here would hold for a day or two. Maybe three if I stretched it. But her leg needed more than my half-stocked kit and cheap liquor. She needed a better wrap, proper antiseptic, and probably antibiotics. I had a doctor on the books who didn't ask questions, if the money was right. He'd patch her up, look at my shoulder, and forget we were ever there.

If I could get her there without waking up every ghost she had in her skin. My jaw clenched. We'd cross that bridge when we had the car started.

Third problem: Patrick. I knew I could trust him to stay upright and out of trouble. He would do the right thing, even if it hurt, and he'd never sell her out just because a price tag got waved in his face. But I also knew I couldn't trust him not to do something suicidal if he thought someone else was going to pay the price for him. Especially her. He wouldn't let her again.

I needed someone close to him on my leash. Someone who could get him out if this went bad, or at least buy him enough time for me to do something worse somewhere else.

I picked up the phone again and switched threads. Another encrypted contact. No name, just a symbol. Lightning bolt on a dark background.

I typed.

Kael: *Need ears on Patrick. Around the clock. Discreet.*

The reply came quickly.

Unknown: *I'm not a babysitter.*
Kael: *You are when I'm paying.*

A beat.

Unknown: *What am I listening for?*
Kael: *Anyone sniffing. New faces. Tension. Cars that don't belong.*
And if he leaves the club, you follow.
Unknown: *Leash length?*
Kael: *As long as it takes.*

No more questions, and that was why I paid her as well as I did.

I set the phone down again and let my shoulders drop a fraction. The outline of the next few moves was clear now.

Move her, have the doctor patch her up. Rig the game and surround Patrick with people who weren't on Conor's payroll. Start tightening Conor's options until he had nowhere to point his panic but at me.

Then give him a target he couldn't resist. Not Sera. Me.

• • •

"Kael?"

Her voice was barely there. Rough and sounding like it was dragged up from somewhere halfway down a well.

I turned to look and saw she'd shifted onto her back without me noticing. One arm lay over her stomach, fingers curled in the blanket. The other hung slightly off the edge of the couch. Her eyes were open now, blinking in the morning light, trying to focus.

I crossed the room before she could push herself upright.

"Morning," I said quietly.

She huffed something that might have been a laugh.

"Already," she murmured.

"How's the leg?" I asked.

"Still attached. Still hates me."

"Any numbness? Tingling?"

"Only in my pride."

Her voice was steadier than I expected. Raw still, but less shattered. The breakdown from last night had managed to bleed off some of the pressure.

She shifted, then winced as the movement tugged the wound.

"Okay," she amended. "It hates me a lot."

"Good. Pain means it's not dead, and neither are you."

Her nose wrinkled. "That's your medical opinion?"

"Comes with the scars."

She searched my face for a second, then pushed herself upright with a low sound of effort. I slid a hand to the back of the couch, close enough to catch her if she tipped, but not touching unless she reached. She noticed that too.

"You slept?" she asked.

"Some," I said.

"How much is some?"

"Forty-five minutes."

She stared.

"That's not sleeping, Kael. That's blinking in slow motion."

"It's enough."

"For a robot, maybe."

"I'll upgrade later."

Her mouth twitched. That tiny flicker of humor looked wrong on her bruised face and exactly right at the same time.

Then it faded, and the rest of it came back. She pulled the blanket tighter around herself and glanced around the room, orientation passing behind her eyes. Safehouse. Spiral stairs. Kitchen. Me. Not the house. Not the bed. Not his hands. Her shoulders dropped a fraction.

"How bad is it?" she asked.

The question sounded small but heavy.

"Define it."

"Everything."

I could give her the sanitized version. Tell her it was handled. Tell her Conor was licking his wounds and we were ghosts. Or I could tell her enough of the truth to keep her from stepping into traffic.

"Conor's bleeding resources. His people are scared, and some are walking. Some are hiding. Cillian screwed him over and vanished. His kingdom is in chaos."

"That sounds… good," she said slowly.

"For us, yeah," I said. "For the city? Not yet. Men like him don't go quietly. They flail. They make messes. They take hostages, and they throw money at the problem and hope someone else dies before they do."

She swallowed hard. "Anyone… hurt because of us?" she asked.

Because of me, she meant. Because she'd breathed near Conor and he'd decided she was his favorite way to break things.

"His guards, mostly. Men who signed up for the paycheck. Men who looked the other way."

"Anyone I care about?" she asked.

Patrick. Jenny. Staff at the club. Not yet.

"Not so far. I've got eyes near the club, so if that changes, I'll know."

Her gaze held mine for a beat too long, like she was weighing the words on some private scale.

"And us?" she asked. "Do we have a target on our backs?"

"Yes, Little Fawn. We had one the second I walked you down those stairs. You had another one the second you looked him in the eye and told him you weren't coming back."

Her jaw tightened.

"I don't regret it," she said.

"Good. Regret's a waste of a spine."

She snorted softly.

"You're full of inspirational quotes today."

"Must be the coffee."

She paused.

"Do we need to run?" she asked. "Again?"

"Not run. We move. There's a difference."

"In what universe?"

"In mine. Running means scared and sloppy. Moving is choosing better ground."

She looked down at her hands, twisting the edge of the blanket between her fingers.

"I'm tired of being the fucking problem," she said quietly.

"You're not a problem, Sera."

"I feel like it."

"No. You're the reason he's slipping. He had a whole machine built, and you jammed yourself in the gears when you refused to break clean. He doesn't know what to do with that."

She huffed.

"Glad my trauma is finally useful," she said.

"Sera," I warned.

She shrugged one shoulder, small and sharp.

"What? You said no regret."

"No regret doesn't mean you get to use yourself like a punchline."

Her throat bobbed, and the humor bled out of her eyes.

"What do we do next?" she asked. "In your universe, where we move instead of run."

We. Her words settled into my chest like a weight and like a promise, and I took a pause before continuing.

"We get you out of here before anyone knows this place exists. We get your leg looked at somewhere that isn't my couch. We keep your name off the streets as much as we can. And we make sure the people he could use against you aren't easy targets."

Her gaze sharpened at that.

"Patrick," she said.

I kept my face still.

"Among others. He's on Conor's radar, whether we like it or not."

She flinched. Guilt flickered across her face like a shadow.

"He shouldn't be," she whispered. "This isn't his problem. I dragged him into it."

"No. Conor did that when he decided everyone around you was a tool he could use to his own advantage."

"It's because I traded myself to him. He knows Patrick's my weak spot."

"You traded yourself, and I took you back. The scales are balanced."

Her jaw clenched. She looked away, breathing a little too fast.

"Is Patrick okay?" she asked again.

"For now. He's jumpy. Hasn't gone home. Sleeping wherever he thinks Conor can't find him. I've got someone nearby keeping an eye out."

"Should we warn him?" she asked.

"We will. But not over an open line, and not before I've moved you. I'm not painting a path between you and him that anyone else can follow."

Her eyes flashed.

"So I'm a liability now," she sighed deeply.

"You're an asset I'd like to keep breathing," I replied calmly. "Conor knows you'd bleed yourself dry for the people you love. He's counting on that. I'm not giving him a neat map labeled 'more of her weak spots.'"

She stared at me. The worst part was that she didn't argue. Because she knew I was right. The knowledge sat raw in her eyes, turning the hurt into something wary and tired.

"Can I do anything that isn't just me hiding?" she asked.

Her voice was small when she said it. Smaller than I'd ever heard it. No sharp edges or teeth. Just a woman who'd had her world carved open and handed back to her in chunks.

"Yes."

"What?" she asked, her eyes lighting up a little.

"Breathe. Eat. Walk when I tell you to. Let me get you somewhere better than this. That's it. That's the job."

"That's not a job."

"It is now. You're not bait. You're not currency. You're not a message. Not for him. Not for anyone. Not anymore."

That was the part she didn't understand yet. Not completely. For Conor, she had always been a message. Proof of control. Proof of reach. Proof that he could lay his hands on anything he wanted and keep it.

For me, she was something else. A line. One I'd decided in the back of that alley without really understanding it. No more hands on her. Not his. Not anyone's without her say so. Not even her own when they turned on her.

She frowned.

"You can't keep me wrapped in blankets in abandoned buildings forever, Kael."

"Fucking watch me."

She shot me a look that said we'd be revisiting that later, and I softened my look a little.

"Can I at least help you pack or something?"

"Yes. Absolutely."

She blinked like she hadn't expected me to agree that fast.

"I can't lift anything heavy. Or walk fast. Or—"

"You can sit there and tell me if you feel dizzy. You can tell me if the leg feels worse, or if your head goes fuzzy, or if you need water. That saves me from having to check every thirty seconds, and that helps."

It was a stretch, but not entirely a lie. I watched as her shoulders eased a fraction.

"Okay. I can do that."

"Good. Start now. How's your head?"

She tipped it back against the couch and thought about it.

"Less like it's full of bees. More like it's full of cotton."

"Vision? Any blurring? Light hurting?"

"Light always hurts. But that's nothing new."

"Chest? How's your breathing?"

"It stings every now and then if I breathe too hard," she admitted. "Like something pulled."

"Probably bruised ribs. From when he…"

I stopped as her mouth tightened. We let it sit there for a second, and then she nodded once.

"Bruises I can live with," she said.

You already did, I thought. Too many fucking bruises.

"Drink some water, please."

She made a face but took the bottle when I handed it to her, sipping without argument. I moved around the room as she drank, letting muscle memory take over.

I put the spare mag in the small duffel. Grabbed the cash from the lockbox under the sink before checking the blade in my boot. I tucked an extra knife into the lining of my jacket. Palmed the burner phone and then found the second one in the drawer.

Her eyes followed me, tracking the sequence.

"You're really moving us," she said quietly.

"Yes."

"Where?"

"Further out."

"That's not an answer."

"It's the only one you're getting until we're in the car."

Suspicion flickered across her face.

"Are you always this bossy, or do I just bring out the worst in you?"

"Best, Sera. You bring out the best in me."

That startled a small huff of breath out of her. Almost a laugh. Almost a sob.

"You're really not going to tell me?" she pushed.

"Later."

Later, when she couldn't walk away and do something noble and suicidal at the first mention of Patrick's name tied to a bounty. Later, when she was behind thicker walls with fewer doors. Later, when I had my hands around the throat of whoever thought Patrick was a good way to get to her.

She studied me, eyes narrowing.

"You're keeping something from me."

"Yes."

Her mouth opened and then closed. Her nostrils flared.

"You're not even going to deny it?"

"You don't want me to start lying to you now. It's a bad habit and one that's hard to break."

"Then tell me the truth."

"Fine. I'll tell you what I can. Conor's scared. Scared men lash out. You and Patrick are both leverage. I'm not putting that weight on your shoulders when you can barely stand without swearing."

Her jaw flexed.

"That's not your call."

"Actually, Little Fawn, right now it's exactly my call. You've had to make too many decisions for too many people for far too fucking long. You don't get to make this one."

"I should."

"Maybe. But you're not going to. Not this time."

She looked like she wanted to argue until her lungs burned. Instead, she sagged back against the cushions and pressed the heel of her hand into her eyes.

"You're fucking infuriating."

"Yeah, I get that a lot."

Silence slipped in for a few seconds. Not heavy or comfortable. Just there.

"Will you at least promise me something?" she asked finally.

"Depends on the something you're asking."

"If Patrick needs help, you don't let him go down alone. Please. I can't..."

Her throat closed around the rest, and I let her breathe through it.

"I can't lose him because of me," she finished.

"You won't."

She let the words sit and finally accepted them as if they were clean, even though they weren't. They were already stained with what I hadn't told her.

I checked my watch out of habit. Time felt like it was moving faster now. Rafe's messages would keep coming. The bounty talk would spread. Collectors would start sharpening their knives. We had a window. Not a big one, but enough.

"This is your job for the next hour. Drink. Breathe. Don't pass out. I'll do the rest."

She snorted softly.

"Bossy," she quipped.

"Focused."

I turned away before she could see the rest. Before she could see the part of me that was already miles away. The pieces of me that were mapping routes, picking a second safehouse, and running through supply stops while lining up contingencies around Patrick. And somewhere underneath all that, making a decision I wasn't going to share with her.

Not today. Probably not ever. If Conor wanted to use Patrick to pull her back into reach. Fine. If he wanted a target, I'd give him one. But it wouldn't be her. This time it would be me.

Chapter Twenty-Eight

Seraphine

The world outside the safehouse felt too big. Too open. Too exposed. Just too fucking much. The door shut behind us with a clank, and the morning air slid under the collar of Kael's shirt on my shoulders, cold enough to bite my skin and leave me shivering.

I already knew we were leaving. We had talked about it. Agreed. First, the doctor, then a new place. One with safer walls and better sightlines, Kael had said. But knowing it and being in the thick of it were two different things.

I stood on the cracked concrete for a second, swaying as my fingers fisted in the fabric at my sides. The street was mostly empty, except for a few cars in the distance. A pigeon was picking at something near the curb, and a man across the way was smoking, his gaze fixed on something that wasn't us.

Nothing special or dangerous about any of it, but my body didn't seem to care. Every shadow looked hungry, and every sudden sound made my nerves twitch.

Kael stayed just behind me, close enough that I could feel the heat of him at my back. Not touching. Not even hovering. Just there. A solid weight in my peripheral, the kind of presence my nervous system had already started cataloguing as safe, whether my brain liked it or not.

"Slow," he said quietly. "We're not in a race."

I let out a breath I didn't remember sucking in and took a step, and my calf pulsed in protest. Not the sharp, searing pain of last night. A deeper, angrier throb. The bandage pulled, and my ribs ached with the simple effort of staying upright. But my feet moved. One after the other. Off the step and toward his car, and toward whatever came next.

I wasn't in that house. I wasn't on that bed. I wasn't ever going to be there again. I repeated it silently until the words sounded less like a lie and more like a reckoning.

We reached the curb, and he opened the passenger door with an easy swing, then stepped back just enough so I had room to move.

"In," he said gently, gesturing with his hand.

I braced a hand on the doorframe and tried to lift myself, but the motion pulled at my leg, and a streak of white-hot pain flashed up my calf. I hissed and froze, my breath catching. Before I could fold in on myself, his hand slid under my thigh, the other steadying the door. He didn't grab or pull, just held enough to support and shift my weight.

"Good. That's it. Breathe through it."

His voice smoothed over my panic. It didn't erase it, just put something else in the room with it.

I sank into the seat and let my head tip back for a second, closing my eyes as my chest grew tight. The car smelled like leather and something that was all him underneath it. The door closed with a soft click, and a moment later, the driver's side opened, and the balance of the car shifted as he got in. The engine rumbled to life, and he checked the mirrors, the street, and the rearview. Always scanning. Always counting exits.

"Ready?"

"Do I have a choice?" I muttered.

"Yes. You always do. They might just all be shit."

That pulled a humorless huff out of me.

"Then sure, big bad wolf. I guess let's pick this particular pile of shit."

His mouth twitched, and he pulled away from the curb.

The safehouse shrank in the side mirror. First, the rusted metal door, then the boards, and finally the brick all disappeared with distance and the turn of the corner.

A curl of panic rippled under my ribs as I watched it fade. The place had been ugly and uncomfortable and echoing, but my brain had just started to catalogue it as safe. Leaving it felt like yanking a bandage off half-healed skin.

"You're quiet," Kael said after a minute.

"So are you," I replied, my temple resting against the cool glass of the window.

"I'm thinking."

"About what?"

"How to keep ahead of him. And how many idiots I'm going to have to erase to make that happen."

I turned and stared at the side of his face. At the faint bruise starting along his jaw that I hadn't seen in the dim light before. At the dried smear of blood near his hairline, he hadn't bothered to wash away.

"Anyone ever tell you your bedside manner needs work?" I asked softly.

"Often. And yet here you are. Alive."

He pulled one hand from the wheel long enough to nudge the bottle of water wedged in the cup holder closer to my leg.

"Drink. Your body will revolt and throw a tantrum with that leg if you don't."

"Stop cataloging me."

"No."

I let out a sigh and took the water. Drinking it down in one go, before unceremoniously crushing the plastic and placing it back in the cup holder with a bratty grin.

"Happy?" I asked, smugness radiating off me, if only for a minute.

"Yes, actually."

I leaned back in my seat victoriously and laid my head against the window, watching as the city shifted around us.

The squat brick houses of neighborhoods gave way to taller, dirtier buildings. More chain-link fences. Empty lots filled with rusted metal and weeds. I caught a glimpse of water through a gap between a warehouse and a row of shipping containers.

"Waterfront?" I asked.

"Back side of it. The doctor's near the docks."

"Of course he is," I said under my breath. "Where else would you keep your on-call crime physician?"

"He's not my crime physician. He's a retired trauma surgeon with a flexible moral compass."

"Tomato, tomahto, Kael."

We turned down a narrow side street that looked more like a sidewalk than a road. The asphalt was cracked and buckled, and graffiti crawled up the side of a building in bright sprays of color. A dog slept under a broken sign, its starving form a testament to the area's condition.

At the end of the block, a small one-story building hugged the corner with faded white paint and bars on the tiny windows. A metal door stood in the center, its facade rusted and weathered. Kael pulled into the alley beside it, parked near a back entrance with peeling blue paint, and killed the engine. He didn't open his door right away.

"If at any point in there you need to stop, you say it. Out loud. You don't grit your teeth and eat the pain because you think I expect you to. Are we clear?"

My throat tightened.

"You're very pushy about consent for a man whose job description is professional people eraser," I said.

"Consent is where everything starts. Everything that matters, anyway."

My chest did a weird, painful little skip, and I looked away before my eyes could do something embarrassing like water.

"Yeah. We're clear." My voice felt small but steady.

He nodded once, then got out and came around to my side. The air outside was colder. Damp. It smelled like the lake, exhaust, and old oil. The air clung to my skin and chilled me through to the bone.

He offered his arm, and I took it. For once, my body didn't twitch at the contact. Progress I noted, smiling a little to myself.

• • •

Inside, the hall smelled like antiseptic and metal. Fluorescent lights buzzed overhead, casting everything in a washed-out haze. The floor was stained, and the walls were scuffed. It could have been any back room in some mechanic shop if not for the metal cabinets lining one side and the exam table bolted to the floor.

A man in his sixties stepped out from a back room, drying his hands on a towel. His once dark hair had gone all the way gray, and his jaw was rough with half a day's growth. His bright blue eyes were sharp, though, missing nothing as they scanned over the two of us.

"Mercer. Thought I might see you sooner or later. You collect trouble like bottle caps."

His gaze slid to me, assessing in a way that felt more clinical than cruel.

"Is this her?"

Kael nodded.

"She needs her leg cleaned. A fresh wrap and antibiotics. Anything else is secondary."

"Mm." The doctor's eyes flicked from my face to my throat, to the blanket of bruises disappearing under the collar of Kael's shirt. He took it in, but said nothing about it. That made something in me unclench a fraction.

"And you?" he added, looking back at Kael. "You're leaking, again."

"Later," Kael said.

"Now, Kael. If you pass out on my floor, I'm charging extra to mop your insides up off the linoleum."

Kael's jaw flexed once before he let out a sigh.

"Her first. Then you can stop me from ruining your precious flooring."

The doctor and Kael had a staring contest that I was ninety percent sure had been an ongoing thing for years.

"Fine," the doctor sighed. "Help her onto the table. Let's take a look at this leg."

Kael guided me to the exam table, his hand warm and steady at my elbow. Climbing up felt like scaling a mountain. My calf screamed, and my ribs pinched. By the time I sat, my breathing was too fast again.

"Lie back," the doctor said.

I shook my head on instinct.

"I can't. Please. Not… not like that."

There was a flicker of something almost like understanding in his eyes.

"Then sit how you need to. I can work around you."

Kael shifted closer, positioning himself between me and the rest of the room in case anyone else magically sprouted from the walls.

The doctor cut through the old bandage, and the gauze peeled away from my skin with a wet stickiness that made my stomach turn. Cool air rushed over the exposed flesh, followed a second later by a burn that felt like someone had poured acid into the wound.

I flinched so hard the table creaked.

"Easy, Little Fawn," Kael murmured. "You're okay."

"Define okay," I gritted out.

"You're not dead. That's still the bar for today."

The doctor hummed under his breath as he worked, cleaning away dried blood and dirt. I stared at a spot on the wall over his shoulder and counted cracks. *One, two, three, four, five.* When that stopped working, I counted my breaths.

"You're lucky," the doctor said eventually. "The bullet grazed you and kept going. No fragments. No deep tissue damage. You'll limp for a bit, and then you'll just have a story with a scar to match."

"Ten out of ten would not recommend the experience," I muttered.

The corner of his mouth twitched with a small smile as he kept going.

The doctor used some skin glue to close the wound on my leg before wrapping the leg in fresh gauze, tight but not choking, and taped it off.

"You can walk, but you listen when your body screams. Pain is information. Don't be stupid."

"She has help for that," Kael said.

"From you?" the doctor snorted. "That's rich."

He turned to Kael.

"Shirt off."

"No," Kael said.

"Yes," the doctor said.

"I'm fine."

"You're bleeding through the fabric."

"Nothing important."

The doctor crossed his arms. "You want antibiotics for her? Stitches? Clean bandages? That doesn't come with a free pass on your stubborn bullshit. Shirt off. Now. I won't ask again, Kael."

I shouldn't have enjoyed watching Kael lose an argument, but I did. Just a little.

He peeled his shirt off with careful movements that made my ribs ache in sympathy. Underneath, his body was a map of old violence. A symphony of scars, some faded and some fresher. A puckered circle sat near his shoulder, and a pale notch ran along his side in a long, jagged line low on his ribs.

It was almost enough to distract me from the new damage. Almost.

Bruises bloomed across his torso. Purple and sickly yellow, some were already spreading. A long graze crossed his shoulder, raw and angry where a bullet had skimmed him. The skin along his back looked scraped, like he had bounced off something hard, maybe that fence, maybe the floor, maybe both.

"You're an idiot," the doctor muttered. "Hold still."

"No stitches," Kael said again.

"Glue then. You like scars. This will give you a nice one."

He cleaned the wound with efficient, impersonal hands. Kael's jaw locked, and while his breathing never changed, a vein jumped in his neck.

He kept looking at me. Every few seconds, his gaze flicked over, checking my face, my posture, my breathing. Like he couldn't let go of the idea that if he blinked too long, I might vanish back into the dark.

"You done?" Kael asked when the doctor stepped back.

"For now. You rip that open, and I'm charging you double. She rips hers, I'm charging you triple."

Kael dug into his pocket and dropped a folded stack of cash on the small metal tray by the wall.

"You always overpay," the doctor muttered, scooping it up.

"You always pretend you don't like it," Kael replied.

He moved to my side again, offering his arm. It felt wrong and right at the same time to take it. But I did, grateful for the leverage.

• • •

Outside, the air hit me like a slap. The alley felt narrower, and the sky seemed lower. My leg hurt in a cleaner way while the rest of me ached everywhere else. I took two steps toward the car, then paused. For a brief second, his hand wasn't on the small of my back. He had let go to scan the street, checking corners, mirrors, and rooftops. My lungs seized as the panic that hit was instant and vicious, rising before I had a chance to shove it down. My head filled with white static.

He's leaving. He's leaving you here. He's done. He's—

"Seraphine."

His voice cut through the noise immediately, and I blinked. He was right in front of me. One arm extended, his hand hovering just this side of touching my shoulder.

"I'm not going anywhere without you. Not now. Not ever. Not even by accident." His voice was low and comforting.

The words lodged in my throat like splinters.

"I know."

It still took my muscles a second longer than it should have to uncoil.

He opened the passenger door, and I eased myself in. The new bandage made the motion hurt in a different way, less jagged, but still there. By the time he slid into the driver's seat, I had both hands clenched in his shirt as it hung over my knees, twisting the fabric tight. He started the engine and pulled us back onto the street, merging with the thin line of traffic like nothing about us was unusual.

I watched the city go by. Warehouses gave way to low buildings. Those turned into blocks of apartments, then small shops with metal grates. People. Buses. Bikes. Ordinary life moved in loops and patterns, while my life felt like it had been kicked off the map.

"You're a little quieter than usual," he said after a while.

"You say that as if quiet is new for me."

"You're loud in all the ways that count. Haven't heard you tell me to go to hell in at least ten minutes. I'm starting to worry."

"That was terrible. Do you practice this material, or is it spontaneous?"

"I'm versatile. Now answer the question."

I stared at my fingers for a second, nails digging half-moons into his shirt.

"I feel like my brain is three steps behind everything. Like I'm… watching myself move around in a body that doesn't fit."

"Dissociation. Again, that tracks."

"I know what it is," I snapped. "Doesn't make it less awful."

"I never said it did."

A light turned red, and he eased the car to a smooth stop. The pause made everything inside me feel too still.

"I keep thinking. About… who I was. Before all of this. Before Conor. Before you. And I don't know how to get back there."

He was quiet for a moment.

"You just don't."

The words hit harder than I expected.

"Great. Love that for me."

He glanced at me, then back at the light.

"You don't go back. You go forward. Different doesn't automatically mean worse."

"It feels worse," I whispered. "I feel… ruined. Like he wrote himself on my skin and I can't scrape it off."

His hands tightened on the wheel.

"He didn't make you. He doesn't get credit for who you are. He only gets the blame for the damage."

"I don't feel like me. I don't know who this version is. The one who cries on couches and panics in showers and can't walk across a fucking room without counting her breaths."

"The version who walks across the room anyway. The version who told Conor to his face she'd kill him herself. The one who still wants other people alive when she has every excuse to stop caring. That one."

Tears stung my eyes, and I blinked hard until they retreated.

"I don't want this to be all there is. I don't want to be just… what he did to me."

"You're not. You're allowed to break and still be more than the breaking."

"Does it ever stop? Feeling disgusting? Dirty? Like my own skin is the place where all the worst things happened."

He was quiet long enough that I realized he was choosing his words instead of reaching for a pretty lie.

"It gets quieter. Some days more than others."

I turned my head slowly.

"You sound very sure for someone who doesn't know what it feels like," I said.

His mouth twitched, humorless.

"You think I've only ever hurt people? You think I've never had someone's damage on my hands and wished I could crawl out of my own body because I failed them?"

My chest ached with his words.

"That's not the same," I said.

"No. It's not. But I know what it is to live with the thing you wish you could outrun. To hate the space you take up because of it, and to think the worst thing that happened to you, or the worst thing you did, is the whole story."

The light turned green, and the car rolled forward.

"You said once I was Seraphine two point zero," I said, voice thin. "Joking. Sort of."

"Not joking. Updating. Doesn't mean the old code vanishes, it just means it gets rewritten around what you survived."

"What if I don't want to be a new version?" I whispered. "What if I just want to be the girl I was before I ever met him?"

His jaw clenched.

"Then I'd tell you she was headed toward him whether she knew it or not. And I would rather have you now. Angry. Messy. Breathing. More than whatever version of you he would have built."

That cracked something deep within me. A long, thin fracture that let in a little light. I stared out the window for a while, and the city blurred past. My thoughts didn't get gentler, but they stopped clawing at me as hard.

"Patrick," I said quietly.

His knuckles flexed again.

"What about him?" he asked.

"You're dancing around something. In there. At the safehouse. Now. Every time I say his name, you get this look."

"What look?" he asked.

"The one that says you've already made a decision I'm not going to like," I said.

He exhaled once through his nose. Not quite a sigh. Not quite a curse.

"Conor put a price on him."

"I know there's a target. You said he was on Conor's radar."

"That was the gentle version. The real version is that he put a bounty on Patrick's head. Alive."

Everything inside me went cold.

"And," Kael added, his voice flattening, "there's an extra bonus if whoever grabs him can prove you know about it."

The car might as well have hit a wall.

"He wants me to hear," I whispered.

"He wants you to come running. He watched you trade yourself once. He thinks you'll do it again."

My heart hammered against my ribs hard enough to hurt. Images flashed behind my eyes. Ones of Patrick's face, white and strained; Conor's hand on his shoulder; my own feet walking back toward that house like I was walking into a grave.

"He's right," I said numbly.

"No. He's betting on you walking into the fire alone."

I turned on him.

"And you think I wouldn't?" I demanded. "If it was Patrick? If it meant he didn't die because of me?"

"I think that you would throw yourself into anything to keep the people you love breathing. I also think you're in no condition to crawl across a parking lot right now, let alone take on Conor's men. Loyalty doesn't change physics."

"That's not an answer. If someone grabbed him today and I knew where he was, you really think I would just sit in whatever safe little hole you picked and do nothing?"

He didn't look away.

"I think it's my job to make sure you never have to make that choice again."

Anger and grief tangled so tight in my chest that I could barely tell them apart.

"I won't hide forever," I whispered.

"You're not hiding, Sera. Fuck, you're healing. You're learning all the ways you can exist that don't involve bleeding for someone else's ego."

"It feels like hiding. It feels like doing nothing while he keeps hurting people."

"He's hurt people for a long time. That doesn't become your responsibility simply because he made you one of them."

"I want him dead. I want him gone. I want to wake up and not feel like he's still in the room."

"I know, baby. I do."

The words felt too big for the car as my fingers curled into fists in my lap.

"Are you going to kill him for me?" I asked.

His shoulders went still.

"For you. For Patrick. For me. For every girl he's touched and every man he's broken and every body he's buried so he could feel bigger than he is."

He took one hand off the wheel, flexed it once, then set it back.

"I was always going to kill him. He always had a death note. Just now, you're the reason I'm going to enjoy it a little more."

His words settled something in me before I could register what it was.

"And I'm just supposed to sit and wait for the news? Like a good girl tucked away in a tower?"

"You're supposed to breathe. Eat. Sleep. Let your body remember it's not in danger every second. You're supposed to be alive when this is over. That's the job."

"That's still not a job…"

"It's whatever you need it to be so you can keep moving forward, Sera."

I swallowed hard and looked out the window again.

"What if I can't stand it?" I whispered. "What if I can't stand feeling like he's still winning while I'm sitting still?"

"Then you tell me. And we find something you can do that doesn't involve walking straight into his teeth."

A bitter laugh scraped out of me.

"You really think there's a version of this where I don't get chewed up?" I asked.

"I think there's a version where you come out the other side. Changed and pissed off, but still you."

The city outside had thinned into fewer buildings and more gaps as a row of warehouses slipped past.

"Holy fuck. You're going to use yourself as bait," I said suddenly.

His eyes flicked to me. Just once. That was all it took.

"I know that face. That's the 'I'm going to do something reckless and call it strategy' face."

"You don't know my faces that well."

"Please. I'm also the reckless girl who would step in front of a bus to save someone I love. I don't have to know your specific faces when it's the same one I wear."

One corner of his mouth twitched a little before he smoothed it out.

"Conor wants a target," I went on. "He wants movement. He wants someone to chase."

"Good. Then he won't be looking at you."

Fear flared in my chest, sharp and sudden.

"If you die because of me," I said quietly, "I will never forgive you."

"If I die, Sera, it won't be because of you. It will be because I spent too long in a world that was always going to cash in on what I do for a living."

"That doesn't make it better."

"I'm not trying to make it better. I'm trying to make it so you don't die with me."

"That's not your decision," I snapped.

"Today? It is. You've been making impossible decisions for everyone else for a long time. You get to lay some of that down on me."

I looked at him. At the bruises and the fresh bandage under his shirt. The exhaustion in the set of his mouth and the way he still drove like nothing could touch us while planning for every way it might.

"Why?" I whispered. "I'm just a girl from a club. I mean, yeah, I have a great ass, but that doesn't explain murder and mayhem over me."

His jaw ticked twice. "I'm not starting a war because you're fragile. I'm finishing one because he crossed a line that should never have existed."

"Me. I'm the line."

"You," he said simply.

Silence fell between us. Heavy. Strange. Not comfortable. Not entirely painful either. A thought slid in through the cracks.

"If Patrick gets taken," I said quietly, staring at my hands, "you do whatever it takes to bring him back. I don't care if you light Conor's world on fire, so long as you both come back to me."

"Sera…"

His voice came out almost pleading. As if he had already resigned himself to the fact that he wouldn't get out of this alive.

"Promise me."

He swallowed.

"I will do everything in my power to keep him breathing. Same as you."

"And you," I said, my eyes narrowed on him.

"And me. But if it comes down to Patrick or me…"

"Then you shift your plans and bring you both back. Period. I don't care what it takes."

The air in the car shifted as Kael let out a long sigh. As if what I had said took more of a toll than he'd been expecting.

"I will do my best," he said, softer than I'd ever heard him before.

It wasn't the neat promise I wanted. But it was an honest one, and that mattered more to me.

The road curved, and buildings rose again in the distance. I could see the hint of an overpass ahead, and the expanse of the city beyond it. My body was still shaking inside. My skin still felt too tight, and my chest still ached. But under all of that, something else had started. Small. Quiet. Stubborn.

Not hope. Not yet. More like resolve. I let my head rest back against the seat, eyes on the way his hands stayed steady on the wheel.

"You're really going to kill him?"

"Yes."

"For me."

"For you. So you never have to hear his voice in your head again and think he's still deciding what happens to you."

My throat burned.

"And I'm going to live long enough to see it."

He exhaled slowly.

"That is the plan."

The city rose up ahead of us.

Conor was somewhere in it, spiraling. Patrick was somewhere in it, hunted. The version of me that had been taken to that house was gone. The version in this car was bruised, shaking, furious, and very much not finished. For the first time since the glass in the alley, since the cuffs bit into my wrist, since the bed, I let myself believe there might be a tomorrow with my name on it.

Not his. Not theirs. Mine. And as the car carried us forward, the only thing that felt solid in all of it was the man beside me and the simple, terrifying truth of what he had said.

He was going to kill Conor, and I was going to live to watch the world learn what it meant when a man like Kael picked a target and refused to stop.

Chapter Twenty-Nine

Patrick

I'd always hated mornings. They always felt too bright and too honest for someone like me. Today, though, it was worse. Everything felt off, like the city knew something I didn't.

I stayed at the club again last night. Not because I wanted to, but because every time I tried to go home, my insides would turn to jello. I missed her. I needed her around, and without her, sleep wasn't coming. Every time I closed my eyes, I saw her face that night. I saw Sera's face etched in fear, her jaw tight and set as her eyes begged me to let her go, and I had. I'd done what she asked and watched as she traded herself for my freedom. So yeah. Sleep wasn't really on the menu.

I did the usual: checked cameras, did the cash drops, checked the back doors, and the alley. Routine was my fucking life raft. Routine had gotten me through worse shit than this. Mia hovered around, asking questions she didn't really want the answers to. Jenny brought me food I didn't eat. People stared at me like I was slowly turning into a ghost, and honestly? They probably weren't wrong.

By early afternoon, the pressure in my chest felt like someone sitting on my ribs. So I went outside to take out the trash. Because apparently that's where my life was now. Temporary club manager, glorified janitor, walking panic attack. I wondered if I could fit all that on a desk nameplate.

The alley was quiet as I stepped out of the back door to Escape. Almost too quiet. As if the birds had somehow lost their voices, and even the traffic seemed to disappear. I set the trash bag down and wiped my hands on my apron.

As I turned around, I nearly ran face-first into a wall of denim and bad cologne.

"Hello, Patrick," the man said, smiling like a shark who'd just caught himself the perfect fish.

My stomach dropped straight out of my ass, and my heart followed it. Behind him stood another guy, taller and meaner, with eyes like dead light bulbs. Collectors.

"Hey, guys. If you're here for bottle service, the club opens at nine."

The tall one didn't laugh. "Boss wants a word."

"Boss who?" I said even though I already knew, because sarcasm is a survival tactic. My survival tactic.

"Don't make this difficult," the short one said, flashing just enough of the gun at his waist to make his point clear. "No holes and no broken bones. He wants you pretty and perfect just as you are."

"Pretty is subjective."

Then they moved. Fast. Too fucking fast. One grabbed my arm, the other grabbed my collar. I jerked back and caught the tall one in the ribs with my knee, but the short guy shoved the barrel into my side so hard it felt like getting punched by steel.

"Walk."

So I fucking walked. They shoved me into a van, slammed the doors, and the engine roared to life. My voice came out higher than I wanted as I took in my surroundings.

"You boys at least gonna play music back here? It's fucking rude to kidnap someone and not offer a bit of ambiance."

"Shut up," the tall one said, turning halfway in his seat. "You're lucky he wants you alive."

"Not sure that makes it any fucking better."

We drove forever. Or maybe ten minutes. Time didn't know what the hell it was doing. When the van slowed and the angle changed, my body tried to move in any other direction. The hill to Conor's house. My stomach grew bats instead of happy little butterflies as I looked over the house that had almost claimed me once. I wasn't sure I'd be lucky enough to survive it a second time.

They dragged me out of the van and across the gravel. My shoes skidded under me, and I tried not to look at the windows. I tried not to think about what had happened behind them just a few days prior. Tried not to see Sera tied to some asshole's bed like his prisoner and prize all in one.

As they dragged me through the doors, everything smelled like expensive whiskey and disinfectant.

Conor sat in a chair like he'd rehearsed for this. The perfect posture to match his perfect suit. But the bruise that bloomed along his jaw was actually perfect. I secretly hoped Sera had given him that pretty addition.

"Patrick, mate. You look tired."

"Rough night. Couldn't stop playing with my dick."

He nodded once to the collectors, and they shoved me into the seat across from him.

"You disappointed me," Conor said.

"Aw, pumpkin."

"You should have brought her back to me, boy."

"I kept my girl alive. Didn't realize I owed you."

"Benjamin had brought me something valuable that I requested, and you helped someone else steal it back."

"You don't own her, asshole, and I didn't help anyone. If Kael took her from you, it would reflect on you, and your ugly ass goons here."

One of the bodyguards clamped his hand tight onto my shoulder, keeping me firmly in place as Conor continued.

"She was fucking mine. I bought her. I bought her time, her obedience. All of it was mine."

Anger flared deep inside me at his words.

"You really believe that shit? Fuck, man. Get a hobby."

Conor ignored me and rambled on.

"But you still have your uses."

"Oh, good. I love being useful."

"You matter to them. To Mercer. To the girl. You matter. And that makes you bait."

Every part of me went cold as I looked anywhere but at him.

"Don't bother. She won't come."

"She will. She caved to save you once. She'll do it again."

"She won't," I repeated. My voice shook, and I hated that it made me feel weak. "He won't let her."

Something flickered in Conor's expression. Annoyance. Just a touch.

"Take him downstairs. Let him fucking rot down there."

The collectors yanked me to my feet, and I felt my legs try to give out.

"Face intact. Mostly. And no holes that can't be fixed. She won't come if he's fucking dead."

"Yeah, it's always better to fish with live bait."

They dragged me down the basement stairs, and the cold, damp air hit me, sharp enough to sting.

My eyes danced around the room. Nothing but concrete walls, a metal chair, and a fucking drain in the floor.

I winced as they tied my wrists behind the backrest. The knots were tight enough to sting but loose enough that I knew it wasn't meant to kill me, just keep me compliant.

Bait needed to stay alive, even when trapped.

They left me alone with a slam of the door, and the silence tasted like ash in the back of my throat.

I sat there, strapped to a chair in the dark, and whispered into the room:

"Sera… please don't come here. Not for me. Not again."

My chest ached. If anyone could stop her, it was Kael. If anyone could burn this place down? It would also be Kael.

For the first time in my life, I prayed she wouldn't try to save me. Again.

Chapter Thirty

Kael

The new safehouse didn't look like safety and that was exactly the point. From the street, it was just another dilapidated building in a dead strip of the industrial district. Two stories of tired brick slumped between a junkyard and a warehouse that had been "For Lease" so long the sign's phone number was half peeled away.

Boarded windows and faded graffiti gave the place a kind of anonymity, while the rusted metal door with no handle served as a muted warning, with only a deadbolt to keep it sealed. You didn't look twice at it unless you knew where to look. Luckily, I knew.

I eased the car against the curb, kept the engine idling low, and scanned the street. No parked vehicles that didn't belong. No unfamiliar silhouettes at the corners. No eyes where there shouldn't be eyes.

Beside me, Sera watched the building with a wary frown, like it might decide to spontaneously combust at any moment.

"This is it?" she asked.

"Yeah."

"Charming."

"It grows on you."

She snorted softly. "So does mold."

I let my lips twitch at that, but my attention stayed on the surroundings. Two exits on the block. One way out behind the junkyard and the camera's three streets over that nobody remembered to fix. No solid sightlines from the main road if you weren't looking for them.

This place had kept me alive more than once, and it would keep her alive, too. I killed the engine and unbuckled my belt.

"Stay put."

"Not happening," she muttered, already fumbling with her seatbelt.

I caught the strap with two fingers before she could shove it off. Not hard. Just enough to make her stop and look at me.

"I'm checking the door. Then I'm going to come back to walk you in. You try to prove a point on that leg and face-plant on the sidewalk, I will laugh first and help second."

Her nose wrinkled. "You're an ass."

"But I'm *your* ass," I winked and gave her a cheeky grin. "Now, give me two minutes to make sure there's no wild raccoon in there waiting for you."

I stepped out into the cold without waiting for her to say another word. The air tasted like metal and exhaust. Somewhere down the block, an old sign creaked and groaned in the wind.

The front door stuck the way it always did in the cold, so I leaned my shoulder into the metal, felt it give, then caught the weight of it before it slammed and echoed. Inside was dark, stale, and utterly familiar.

I stepped into the dark space and keyed in the code on the small box hidden behind the torn insulation panel, listening.

Nothing.

I flipped the first breaker. Emergency strips along the floor hummed to life, low and dim. Enough light to navigate. Not enough to silhouette anyone in the windows.

The place looked exactly the same as I remembered. The extremely worn couch and the old table still sat where I left them, but there were no new footprints on the dust track near the back hall where pipes sweated against exposed brick.

Perfect. Just as I left it.

I left through the same door and went back for her.

She already had her belt off. One hand braced on the door. Stubborn as ever and just as adorable. Fuck. This girl would be the death of me, but what a way to go.

"This would be easier if I just grew wings," she muttered.

"You're enough trouble with two feet, Ser. One step at a time."

Her fingers tightened on the doorframe as she eased herself out. She sucked in a sharp breath and froze halfway up. I slid in beside her, arm hovering.

"Can I?"

She nodded, jaw clenched.

My hand closed around her waist. I took as much of her weight as she'd let me and helped her stand.

"You good?"

"Define good," she said through her teeth. "If good means 'not currently screaming,' then sure, yeah, I'm good."

"We'll make that the working definition for now."

We moved slowly across the cracked sidewalk and up the short concrete step. Each shift of her weight sent tiny vibrations up through my arm where it braced her. Her body was a list of complaints; ones I could read from the hitch of her breath to the way her fingers dug into my forearm.

But she moved. And she kept moving.

Inside, the air hit her like it always hit people the first time they crossed this threshold. I watched as she looked around with her whole body.

From the high ceilings and exposed beams, the skeleton of what had once been an open-floor workshop before someone gave up and walked away. One corner held the makeshift living space I'd carved out for myself on bad weeks. Couch. Coffee table. Small kitchen area with a fridge that hummed louder than it should.

Stairs toward the back rose up to another loft area with a mattress and more secrets.

"This is less murder-y than I expected," she chided, but her voice was soft.

"You didn't get to see it before I vacuumed."

She gave me a look, but some of the tension in her brow eased.

I got her to the couch and lowered her down slowly. She sank into the cushions like her bones were made of sand, and the moment the pressure came off her leg, her shoulders slumped.

"How's the head feeling?"

"Buzzing. More bees than cotton, though, so better, I guess."

"Any dizziness?"

"A little."

I watched her pupils for a second. They tracked fine. No lag or rolling.

"You're going to rest."

She made a face. "I slept earlier."

"You closed your eyes in the car for six minutes. That's not sleep. That's blinking aggressively."

"You are very judgy about my resting habits for a man who survives on forty-five-minute power naps and spite."

"Spite works for me. You, however, need more than spite right now."

She opened her mouth, probably to argue, then winced and pressed a hand lightly to her ribs instead.

"Ribs still hurting?" I frowned a little as I looked her over.

"Breathing is overrated."

"Lie back and keep a pillow under your leg. I need you to drink some water, and then you can glare at me until you pass out."

"That's manipulative," she muttered, but she moved herself deeper into the couch anyway.

I helped shift her calf onto the cushion, careful not to jar the gauze. Her face pinched, but she didn't make a sound. I shoved a folded blanket under her ankle to keep the leg elevated and then handed her the bottle from my pocket.

"Small sips."

"Yes, sir," she muttered, giving me a small, mocking salute.

The word did something strange in my chest, but I decided to ignore it for now. I could revisit her calling me 'sir' when death wasn't stalking us both, and we were both completely healed.

I stood a step back and let myself look at her properly for a second. She looked wrong on my couch. Wrong in the way, there was nothing in this place that deserved to have her in it.

Her hair was a tangle around her face. The bruises at her throat had gone from red to dark purple overnight, blooming into ugly fingerprints that made my hands itch. The cuff mark around her wrist was an angry ring. My shirt, she wore, swallowed her, draping off one shoulder to show more damage she refused to look at. She looked like hell. But she looked like she was still here. Still with me. Still fighting through it all.

"That look on your face is illegal," she said quietly.

"What look?"

"The one where you're building a murder plan and a guilt complex at the same time."

I huffed out a breath. "I don't do guilt."

"Liar," she said, eyes slipping half-closed. "You're full of it. Guilt and caffeine and homicidal tendencies."

"Go to sleep, Little Fawn."

Her lashes fluttered as the fight in her shoulders loosened.

"You'll be here when I wake up, right?" she asked.

"Always."

My phone buzzed in my pocket, and her eyes flicked to it, then back to me.

"See?" she whispered. "Trouble has your number on speed dial."

"Sleep, Ser. Fuck."

She let out a breath that might have been a laugh and let her head tip sideways against the back of the couch.

Her fingers were still curled around the water bottle when her breathing evened out. Not soft or pretty, but steady.

I waited a full two minutes, watching the rise and fall of her chest, before I stepped away and pulled the phone free.

The screen showed the lightning bolt icon. The contact who had been shadowing Patrick.

Striker: *He's gone. Two men in a van, no plates. Took him out of the alley. Club staff didn't see till it was done.*

My jaw clenched as I typed a reply.

Kael: *Faces? Descriptions? Got a direction they were heading?*

It took forty seconds for the reply to come through. Long enough for my pulse to settle into something that was not quite calm and not quite panic. Just focus.

Striker: *One short, stocky, denim jacket. Bad ink on the hands. The other was tall, with a shaved head and a coat too nice for the block. Gun flashed, but no shots. Headed east. Hill direction.*

Of course. I didn't need a map to know where they were going.

Striker: *He fought. They hit him twice but followed the rules. No face, no holes in his body. He was standing when they shoved him in.*

Rules. Conor's rules. Alive, pretty, and transportable. Fucking bait to catch a Sera-shaped fish. My hand tightened around the phone as the next message came from Rafe.

Rafe: *Heard it. Patrick's in the wind. Word is two of Conor's collectors got a "package" for delivery.*

My thumb hovered for a minute before I typed.

Kael: *Basement?*

Rafe: *Yeah. Same house. One of the kitchen staff saw them take him down. Concrete room. Metal chair. You know the one.*

I did. I knew it in too much detail.

Rafe: *He's alive. Conor wants him talking, not dying. Yet.*

Yet. There was always a yet.

Rafe: *He's telling people it's a message. "No one touches what's mine." Might as well put your names on the invitation.*

The anger inside my ribs stretched and clawed against me. Not a new feeling, more like something that had been waiting for this since that night in the alley when I was a teen, and was finally being handed the right excuse.

The room around me sharpened, and I looked over at her. She slept like someone whose body had hit a wall. Her muscles were slack, and her mouth was gently parted. A faint line between her brows, as if even unconscious, she still braced for impact.

Conor had taken Patrick. Fuck. Of course he had. It was the move I'd been waiting for and the one I'd hoped he was too arrogant to make. He wasn't. He'd watched her trade herself once. He'd seen where her fault lines were. He'd put her in a cage and tossed the key, so I had to steal her from his grasp. I'd made myself a target, and instead he'd changed tactics.

If she wouldn't come for a bounty, he'd make it more personal. Take the man she loved like family, tie him to a chair, and wait to see how long it took for the news to get to her. Wait to see how long she could stay away. He thought he knew her, but he really didn't know me.

Kael: *How long till he moves from leverage to lesson?*

Rafe's answer was blunt.

Rafe: *Depends on how fast he hears from the street that she knows. That's the whole point.*

My gaze slid back to Sera's sleeping face. She didn't know yet, and that wouldn't last. Information had a way of seeping through cracks.

She had ears in half the clubs in this city. Girls who liked her more than they liked their bosses. Runners who owed her favors. Staff who would bend rules because she once slipped them an envelope on a bad week and told them to pay rent instead of paying her back.

Somewhere in that network, someone would hear, and they'd text her, or call, or hell, even walk right up and say the wrong words if they ever caught her on the street. I couldn't let her find out. Not when she was finally trying to relax, even in the smallest increments.

Kael: *I'm going to get him.*

Rafe didn't waste time.

Rafe: *I know.*
Rafe: *You want eyes?*
Kael: *Perimeter only. No one else goes inside. He'll expect that.*
Rafe: *You want him or just the boy?*

I let that sit for a second as Sera's voice came back to me, quiet, shaking, and fierce.

'Are you going to kill him for me?'
'For you. For Patrick. For everyone he's broken.'

Kael: *Both.*

A skull emoji popped up after a beat. Then:

Rafe: *I'll start a pot. Loser buys drinks. Try not to bleed out on the marble.*

I snorted once, humorless, and locked the phone. The plan was already there. I always had a plan for nights like this. I moved through the space on autopilot, letting the two halves of my brain do their separate jobs. One cataloguing, one calculating.

In the small kitchen, I opened the false bottom of a cereal box that had never held cereal. Pulled the spare burner and two extra mags from the hidden compartment under the sink. I checked them over. Good, they stayed loaded and ready.

From the cupboard above the fridge, I took the small black pouch with the backup cash and the pills. Painkillers, just in case. Sedatives, in case I had to knock someone out who wasn't meant to die. Like Patrick, if I had to drag him out half-conscious and screaming. Whatever it took. I would bring him to her, alive and as unscathed as possible.

In the back corner of the room, the metal locker I had bolted to the wall years ago still waited. The key was where I always kept it, tucked in the crack behind the old fuse panel. Inside it, the rest of my toys waited. Another handgun. Two knives. A thin roll of flexible plastic strips. Gloves. A clean black shirt.

I set them on the table in an ordered line. Gun. Ammo. Blades. Restraints. Fabric.

Simple. Obvious. Effective. I wasn't going in blind. I wasn't going in loud, not at first. You didn't walk into a nest like Conor's swinging, not if you wanted to make it out in one piece. You walked in like a shadow, and then you decided which lights to cut.

I shrugged out of my shirt and hissed under my breath when the movement pulled at the glued graze along my shoulder. The doctor's voice echoed in my head, annoyed and fond.

You rip that open, and I'm charging you double.

He wasn't going to get the chance.

I swapped the shirt for the clean one. Dark. Fitted. Easier to move in. Easier to hide blood on, his or mine. My shoulder pulled, and my spine ached, but the pain that mattered wasn't mine.

"Kael?"

Her voice came from behind me. Sleep blurred and small and too damn soft for this room. I turned to look at her.

She had pushed herself upright on the couch, and the blanket had slid into her lap. The water bottle rolled onto the cushions beside her. Her hair fell in messy, knotted waves around her shoulders. Her eyes were unfocused for a second, then sharpened as she took in the table. The gun. The knives. The change of shirt. I watched as the color drained from her face.

"No," she whispered.

"Sera…"

"Don't. Don't you dare say my name in that voice. That's the voice you use when you're about to do something we both know I'm going to hate."

"You're awake, and you should be sleeping, love."

"Too bad," she snapped, swinging her legs over the edge. "What are you planning?"

I watched her for a second. Her leg shook when she tried to put weight on it. Her body was screaming for rest, and she was ignoring it. I crossed the room and caught her before she could stand.

"Sit."

"Tell me what's happening," she shot back.

I stared at her, and she stared right back. Her pupils were blown wide with fear, exhaustion, and something like fury. I could lie. I had before. I could tell her it was a precaution, that I just wanted to be prepared, that she didn't need to worry.

She would know. Somehow she always knew. Not about the details, maybe. Not about the angles and the exits and the numbers I ran every time we walked into a room. But about me. About where my temperature sat. About when it changed.

"Patrick," I said simply.

All the air went out of her lungs, and her hands flew to the edge of the couch like she needed something to hold on to.

"What about him?" she whispered.

"They took him. Conor's men. They got him in the alley behind the club."

For a moment, her face was blank. Then it cracked.

"I told you," she whispered. "I told you he would use him. I told you he—"

"You told me, and I listened. That's why I have eyes on him.

That's why I know where he is."

Her head snapped up.

"Where?" she demanded.

"In *Conor's* house. He's being kept in the basement."

She made a sound somewhere between a sob and a curse.

"No! No, no, no. He can't be there. Stupid. Stupid. I should have made him leave town, I should have—"

"Sera…" I warned.

"He'll hurt him," she choked out. "He'll hurt him because of me. Because I—"

"He won't get the chance."

She dragged in a ragged breath.

"I traded myself once. He knows I'll do it again. That's the whole game. That's all this is. He thinks I'll walk right back through those doors and hand him my throat if it means Patrick gets to live."

She looked at me with wild eyes. "He's right. I can't let Patrick die because of me. I won't."

"No."

"Yes," she snapped. "You can't stop me from making that choice."

"Watch me."

She glared daggers through me as her voice danced between fear and anger.

"Don't you dare. Don't you dare cage me and go play hero while he kills my family."

"I'm not playing anything."

"Yes, you are. You're comfortable in this. The violence and blood. You do this. This is where you live. I'm just the problem you're dragging around."

"That's not what you are."

"Then what am I?" she demanded, voice cracking. "Because from where I'm sitting, I'm the reason Patrick is in that fucking basement."

"You are the reason Conor is scrambling and scared. Don't confuse the two."

"Semantics," she snapped. Tears gathered at the corners of her eyes, and she blinked furiously, like that would send them back where they came from. "He took him because of me. He's going to hurt him because of me. I have to go."

"You're not setting foot in that house again."

"You can't stop me."

"You can't walk across this room without swearing! You couldn't stand up just now. What are you going to do, limp dramatically into his foyer and hope he dies of secondhand embarrassment?"

"You're not fucking funny, Kael!"

"I'm not trying to be."

She dragged a hand through her hair, fingers shaking.

"This isn't your decision. It's mine. It's my life. My friend. My mess."

"Yes, and now I have a say too."

"In what?" she demanded.

"In whether I drag you back into the place that broke you when you can barely breathe without remembering what he did. Whether I hand Conor exactly what he wants and hope I'm fast enough to stop him when he decides to show you what 'punishment' really looks like. In that, and in keeping you alive and with me, I absolutely have a say."

Her eyes went glassy. "You don't understand," she whispered. "You don't know what it's like to watch someone suffer because of you. Because you made a choice and they paid for it."

"Yes actually, I do."

She flinched.

I let the silence sit for a second.

"You think I haven't watched the light go out of someone's eyes and knew it was because of a call I made? You think you're the only one who feels like their hands are dirty every time they look at someone they care about?"

Her mouth opened, and she shut it again. Nothing came out at first.

"You said once I wasn't currency anymore," she whispered. "Not for him. Not for anyone. I felt like maybe you meant that."

"I did mean it."

"Then why does it feel like the only way to keep Patrick alive is to put myself back in his hands?" she said.

"Because you've been trained your whole life to think that way. People made your world so small that the only options you could see were sacrifice or silence. That doesn't mean those are the only options."

Her laugh came out jagged. "You really think there's a version of this where we all walk away? You? Patrick? Me? Conor is just dead and buried, and the world is somehow better for it?"

"Yes."

She stared at me like I'd grown another head.

"Do you hear yourself?" she asked.

"I've not gone deaf, Little Fawn."

"How?" she demanded. "How do you think that is even remotely possible?"

"Because I've seen worse men fall. Because his house is already cracking. His cousin stole his secrets, and his guards are walking. And before all that, he had to kidnap the pretty bartender to get my attention instead of just sending a text."

Her mouth trembled.

"You're really going to go," she whispered.

"Yes."

"And you're going without me."

"Yes."

"You're going to walk back into that place where he—" her voice broke, "—and you're going to leave me here. Alone."

The last word was small. Smaller than anything I'd heard from her. I felt it like a punch. I sat on the edge of the table facing her, close enough that she had to tilt her chin up to meet my eyes.

"You won't be alone."

"That's what everyone says right before they walk out the door," she shot back.

"I'm not everyone, and I'm not *them*."

"How do you know?" she whispered.

"Because I'm still here. Because I walked into that house and took you out instead of leaving you where it was easiest. Because I'm standing in front of you right now planning how to break a man I've been paid to tolerate for years."

Her throat bobbed hard around a swallow. "You've left people before," she said.

"Yes."

"You'll leave again."

"Maybe. But not you. Not like that, and not like this."

She searched my face, looking for the seam in the lie. I let her look.

"You can't promise," she said.

"I can. And I am."

"If you die," she whispered, "I will never forgive you."

"If I die, you'll be alive to hate me. I can be happy in the afterlife with that."

"That's not funny," she said.

"I wasn't trying to be."

She dragged another shaky hand over her face.

"I can't sit here and do nothing. I'll crawl out of my own skin. I'll go crazy."

"You're not doing nothing. You're doing the hardest part. You're staying put. You're not throwing yourself into the first fire that sparks. You're trusting someone else to walk into the dark for once."

"I don't like that part," she said.

"I know."

She stared at the floor for a long moment.

"What if he hurts him before you get there?" she asked, voice so soft I almost missed it.

"He might."

"What if he kills him?" she whispered.

"He might try."

Her head snapped up, and anger flared through the tears.

"Then what is the point?" she demanded. "What is the point of all this planning and moving and hiding if he still gets to win?"

"He won't."

"He has Patrick in a chair in his basement!" she shouted. "He has my best friend strapped to a piece of metal like some kind of warning sign, and he is waiting for me to hear about it so he can drag me back. How is that not winning?"

"Because I'm going to take his warning sign. I'm going to cut it loose and walk out with it breathing. And then I'm going to knock his whole life down around him."

She stared at me for a long minute before letting out a ragged breath. "You sound very sure," she said.

"I am."

"What if you're wrong?" she whispered.

"I'm not."

Silence fell between us again. Her fingers twisted in the hem of my shirt, still pulled over her knees.

"I made you promise something once," she said slowly. "In the car."

"I remember."

"Say it again," she whispered.

"Which part?"

"The part where you said you would kill him."

"For you. For Patrick. For every girl, he's turned into a message. For every man he's put on a leash and for the city he thinks is his hunting ground."

I held her gaze.

"Yes, Sera. I'm going to kill him."

Something in her eyes flickered. Not relief. Not even satisfaction. This was something older. Something like a long, thin wire inside her was finally hearing the note it had been waiting for.

"And you're going to bring Patrick back," she said.

"Yes."

"Swear it," she said.

"I swear."

"Swear it on something that matters to you," she said.

"On my own hands. On the blood that's already on them. On whatever is left of my soul. Take your pick. But beyond all that. I swear it on you."

Her lips trembled. "Come back to me," she said quietly. "Both of you."

"We will."

"You promise a lot for a man who keeps telling me the world is cruel."

"Maybe that's why I can promise. I know exactly what I'm walking into."

Her shoulders slumped as some of the fight leaked out of her, leaving something raw in its place.

"You know I hate this, right?"

"I know."

"I hate that he keeps making the rules. I hate that we're still moving around his stupid little board like chess pieces. I hate that my choices are either to break myself to save someone or sit still while you risk yourself instead."

"Those aren't the only choices. They're just the ones he wants you to see."

She laughed once, bitterly. "You're so sure of what I can and can't do."

"You can do whatever you want. I'm just not letting you walk back into his hands while you can't even stand up without shaking."

Her mouth twisted. "That's the part that hurts the most. If he hadn't done this. If I wasn't…" She gestured at herself. "If I weren't like this. I'd be there with you."

"No. If he hadn't done this, you'd be at the bar, minus a bullet graze, and I'd be ordering a whiskey."

She stared at me.

"You're so fucking infuriating."

"So you keep reminding me."

She let out a breath that sounded more like defeat than surrender. "What do you need me to do?" she asked finally.

The question pulled at something deep in my chest.

"I need you to stay here. I need you to lock the doors when I leave. I need you to drink water. Eat something if you can. Take the pills I set out if your leg starts screaming. Listen to your body if it says lie down. Don't open the door for anyone who isn't me or someone who says the right words."

She narrowed her eyes. "What words?"

I went to the kitchen, opened the drawer with the random tools, took out a marker, and walked back.

"Give me your hand."

Suspicion flashed, then faded under something else. She slowly extended her left hand, palm up.

I wrote on her wrist. Three words in looped letters.

She frowned at them. "Really?" she said.

"Yes."

"'Bad Bishop Falls.' You're so fucking dramatic."

"It's obscure, and no one's guessing it. If you hear those words from the other side of the door, it's safe. Anyone else knocks, you don't move."

"How will I know it's not someone forcing you to say it?" she asked.

"You won't. Which means if anything feels off, you still don't move."

She nodded slowly. "What about you?" she asked.

"I'll know you're on the other side of this door breathing. That's all I need. It's enough."

It wasn't. But it had to be. I pulled my extra burner phone and one of the knives off the table. Not the heaviest, but the narrow one with a clean balance. I flipped it in my hand and then held both out to her. Her eyes widened.

"What is that for?" she asked.

"Pretend it's decorative if you need to. But keep it on you. Under the cushion or under your leg. Wherever you want. You don't open the door, but if someone makes it through anyway, you don't freeze. As for the phone, it's so that if anything goes sideways, you'll know."

She tightened her lips as she took it slowly, and her fingers curled around the handle. The weight shifted her posture slightly. Something old and feral stirred in the way she held it. She let her thumb move over the phone softly.

"I thought you said no hands on me," she said quietly.

"That rule doesn't apply to you. Anyone who tries to take something from you again, you introduce them to the pointy end."

A ghost of a smile flickered across her mouth. "You got a lot of faith in the girl from trauma island."

"Just reminding you you're not helpless."

She looked down at the knife, then at the words on her wrist, then back at me.

"Who's watching the watchers while you're gone?" she asked.

"Rafe will be. Outer ring only, and he doesn't know this address. He just knows the general area."

"Someone's going to be nearby?" she asked.

"Yes."

"Do I want to know where?" she asked.

"You can ask, but I'm not going to tell you."

"You've got it all figured out, huh?"

I nodded once. It would give her something she didn't know she needed. A thread tying her to the rest of the world while she sat inside, counting breaths.

I picked up the gun and slid it into the holster at my back. Checked each knife and its place. Left one on the table where she could see it, then moved it closer to her side. She watched every movement as if she were memorizing it.

"How long?" she asked.

"Depends on how stupid he is. Stupid means fast. Clever takes longer for me to navigate."

"Which one do you think he is tonight?" she asked.

"Panicked. That's when men like him make the worst choices."

She swallowed. "Do you need me to do anything else?" she asked.

"Stay awake for an hour if you can. The first hour is the danger zone. After that, if you crash, let it happen."

"You're really just leaving me… here," she said, glancing around the room. "With my thoughts."

"You have a knife and my shirt. You'll be fine. Keep the phone close. I'll call when we're clear."

Her eyes flicked to me.

"I'd feel better if I had your gun," she said.

"I'd feel fucking worse, Ser. I've watched you throw darts at Escape. No way I'm letting you hold my gun."

She huffed out a breath.

"Always have to have the last word," she said.

"If it keeps you alive, yeah."

I moved toward the door. She didn't call out at first. Didn't move. Then, just as my hand touched the deadbolt, her voice came, small and sharp.

"Kael."

I turned. She had pushed herself to the edge of the couch again. Her injured leg stretched out, the other bent, toes digging into the floor. Her hand fisted in the hem of the shirt. The knife lay beside her, blade glinting in the low light, and her eyes were glassy.

"Come here," she said.

I did as she asked, moving toward her like she was once again the moon, and I was the helpless tide. She caught the front of my shirt in both hands and hauled herself up just enough that her forehead met my chest. The movement pulled a pained sound out of her, but she didn't let go. My hands hovered for a second, then settled at her waist, careful of the bruises.

"I still hate this," she whispered into the fabric.

"I know you do, Ser."

"I hate that he still gets to decide what my life looks like. That he takes people, and I just… have to survive him."

"He doesn't get the last word."

"Who does?" she asked.

"I do. If I have to carve it into him with my bare hands, and hopefully, I will."

She let out a shaky breath that might have been the start of a laugh and died halfway. Her fingers twisted tighter in my shirt.

"Come back to me," she said again. "Don't make me learn how to exist in a world where you're not in it."

The words did something to me I didn't have language for. I tilted her face up with a thumb under her chin. Her eyes were blown wide. Scared. Furious. So full of fight, she didn't know what to do with it. I bent and pressed my mouth to her forehead.

"I'll be back," I whispered against her skin.

"With Patrick," she said.

"With Patrick."

"And Conor dead," she said quietly.

"Yes."

She closed her eyes for a second, soaking something in that I couldn't see. Then she let go of my shirt and sank back into the couch like her bones had given up.

"Go," she said hoarsely. "Before I change my mind and tackle you. Bad leg and all."

"You'd miss."

"I'd still try."

"I know."

I stepped back. Memorized the way she looked in that moment. My shirt. My knife. My ugly couch. Here, in all her fury, alive and well. I turned toward the door and locked eyes with her one more time.

"Remember the words," I said, nodding at her wrist.

"Bad Bishop Falls. Got it."

"Don't open for anything else."

"Even if it sounds like you," she said.

"Especially then."

She swallowed.

"Okay," she whispered.

I turned and walked to the door, the weight of knives and promises settling into their places. The deadbolt slid back with a solid chunk.

• • •

Cold air rushed in when I opened it. The city waited outside. Gray sky. Empty street. A horizon painted with all the wrong men in all the wrong places. I stepped over the threshold and pulled the door shut behind me. For a heartbeat, I stood there, my hand still on the metal, feeling the faint vibration of the building settling around her.

The anger I had kept caged settled into something colder as I walked down the short set of steps and across the cracked pavement. Not rage or frenzy. Just a decision that had finally reached the end of its patience.

I slid behind the wheel and started the engine. Checked my mirrors. Front. Back. Side. No tails. Not yet.

The road toward the hill unwound ahead of me. The familiar turns moving into familiar intersections. The path to a house where too many bad things had happened to people who didn't deserve them.

Conor thought he understood how tonight would go. He had taken Patrick and strapped him to a chair. He had sent a message to the streets. He wanted the girl brought back to him on a silver platter of fear and guilt.

He thought that was control. What he had actually done was give me something simple. A fixed point. A reason that wasn't money, or obligation, or old debts. I tightened my hands on the wheel.

Tonight I wasn't his cleaner or his quiet solution. I wasn't the man who smoothed out his messes and disappeared before the credits rolled.

Tonight, I would make the mess. One more job. Not for a contract. Not for my reputation. But for her. For Patrick. For everyone who had ever walked into that house and never made it out again.

Chapter Thirty-One

Kael

The hill looked different when you were coming to burn something down rather than burying it. From the outside, it was the same winding road with the same clean asphalt and the same expensive houses pretending they weren't built on rot. But the closer I got, the quieter everything felt, like the city was holding its breath and waiting to see how bad this was going to get.

My hands sat easily on the wheel. My stomach didn't twist, and my pulse didn't spike. It wasn't calm. It was the steadiness that came when there were no versions left except one.

The house rose out of the fog the way it always did; too big, too polished, with glass and stone etching the estate into light and dark. Lights glowed warm behind expensive windows like the world's most tasteful haunted house.

I pulled off before the main drive, into the line of perfectly manicured trees that edged the property. I killed the engine and let the dark swallow me.

The burner in my pocket buzzed once.

Rafe: *Perimeter set. One car at the bottom of the drive, one up past the bend. We've got eyes on movement. No one is coming down yet.*

Kael: *House?*

Rafe: *Usual guard pattern, lighter than it usually is. He's bleeding people faster than he can replace them. You're clear to go knock.*

Kael: *Hold the road. Nothing in, nothing out.*

Rafe: *Copy. If you die, I'm stealing your car.*
Kael: *You touch my car; I will haunt you.*
Rafe: *Fair.*

I slid the phone away and stepped out into the cold.

The air up here always tasted cleaner. Less like exhaust and more money. Tonight it tasted like rain that hadn't decided if it was coming or not, and the faint, distant bite of woodsmoke from some other rich asshole's fireplace.

I checked my weapons, committing their placements to memory. The gun at my back and a knife at my hip. A smaller blade in the sheath at my ankle, while the plastic restraints sat coiled in my pocket. A backup mag inside my jacket. My ribs were tight but holding, and my shoulder ached, sore but not useless.

Every scar on my body hummed with the memory of nights like this, but I pushed it down and started walking.

I didn't take the drive. The driveway was for people who were meant to be seen. I curved wide into the trees, my boots silent on the damp ground. The house loomed to my left, a slice of brick and glass against the gray sky.

I walked until I could see the back corner of the property, where the hill dropped off, and the foundation shouldered into rock. Security lights haloed patches of wet lawn. Cameras blinked lazily at the eaves.

I knew where the blind spots were; I'd helped design them. Conor liked to know when the wrong people came. He'd never even considered the possibility that one day, I'd put myself in that category.

I waited in the shadow of a tree until the nearest guard finished his slow sweep along the back patio. He was bored, his posture was loose as his gun hung too low on his hip. He glanced at his phone once, thumb flicking, face lit blue from the light for half a second.

I moved when his head tipped down, my movements quiet and deadly. My hand clamped over his mouth as the other yanked his gun hand down and away. He jerked, too slow, too surprised. My knife slid in under his ribs and up, fast and clean. His eyes went wide as he tried to make a sound. Air hissed through my fingers.

"Shh," I said against his ear. "Retirement's expensive."

His knees buckled. I eased him down onto the grass, rolled him onto his side so he wouldn't gurgle, and pulled his jacket over the worst of it. From the patio, in the dark, he'd look like he'd sat down and taken a break. I wiped the blade on his shirt and moved on.

The basement access sat where it always had. Tucked half under the hill, half under the house. A recessed metal door, more like a service entrance than anything glamorous. No handle on the outside, and a keypad on the wall beside the door.

I pulled the memory of codes I'd seen on Benjamin's phone and pushed the keys in order. The light blinked green, and the lock shifted open. I cracked the door just enough to listen.

The hum of the furnace sounded through the floor grates, and distant footsteps echoed, not close enough to matter. I slipped inside and let the dark close over me.

The corridor smelled like lemon cleaner and spice. The kind of smells that never really left the walls of a place like this.

I kept my steps light, staying in the sliver of shadows. One door to my left was a storage room. Another to the right, laundry. Ahead, the hallway curved right toward the cold room and the cellar. Left, toward the room with the drain in the floor. I went left.

Voices drifted under the hum. The tone of their words said they were more bored than alert.

"—told you, man, the odds are shit. Mercer's not stupid enough to walk in here."

"You wanna bet? He went in once to steal a girl; he'll do it again for the DJ. Guy's got a type."

"His type is 'trouble.'"

A snort.

My jaw ticked, and I stopped just short of the corner. I pulled the smaller knife from my ankle sheath and swapped it to my left hand.

One of them laughed, short and sharp.

"You think the boss really lets the kid live if she doesn't show?"

"Doesn't matter. We get paid either way."

Hot, pulsing anger slid through my ribs, and I stepped around the corner as if I belonged there.

The first man was leaning against the wall, thumb scrolling his phone. The second sat on a folding chair by the basement door, foot propped on the rung, chewing gum with his mouth open.

Both looked up. For a beat, there was nothing. Just three men in a hallway, the universe waiting to see who would admit the truth of what this was.

"Evening, gentlemen."

The guy with the phone blinked. His brain made the connection first as his hand jerked for his gun, but he was too slow.

The knife left my hand in a flick. The throw was short and tight. The blade buried itself in his throat just under the jawline. His hand flew up, fingers clawing at the handle. He gagged and sagged against the wall.

The one in the chair shoved to his feet, scrambling for his own weapon, but his legs tangled and the chair skidded. He stumbled, and I was already moving.

I slammed into him, shoulder to chest, driving him back into the wall. His head cracked against concrete while his hand fumbled with the holster as my forearm pressed against his windpipe. My other hand stripped him of his gun and shoved it into the back of my belt before he had the chance to use it.

"Keys. Please."

He clawed at my arm, and I pushed into his throat harder.

"Okay. Fuck! Keys, now!"

His hands scrambled in his pocket with the last of his coordination. Metal flashed. I eased the pressure just enough for him to get them out. They hit the floor with a clink.

"Good boy."

His face darkened, and his eyes rolled.

I let him go when he was about to tip past useful. He dropped to his knees, wheezing, grabbing at his throat. I grabbed his jaw in one hand, braced, and slammed the back of his head into the wall once. He went out like someone hit a switch, and silence rushed in.

The other man lay on the floor, blood soaking his collar, eyes glassy. His phone screen glowed beside his hand, some casino app open and sending off fireworks and bright lights across the screen. Apparently, he had won. Oh well.

I picked up the keys and the phone, powered it off, and slid it into my pocket. No point in giving anyone a notification they didn't need yet.

I stepped over the bodies and went to the basement door. Same metal, same heavy handle. Same sense of the world changing on the other side. I unlocked it and swung it open.

The musty air spilled up from the stairwell. Concrete steps. Bare walls. No rail. The kind of descent that had never been meant for guests. I went down, counting the twelve steps out of habit.

At the bottom of the stairs was another hallway, this one shorter. The door on the left? Cold storage. The door to the right was a cell. The light was on under the farther door. Voices faint and curling through the damp air. One of them, raw and hoarse, I knew.

My fingers tightened around the knife at my hip as I opened the door. The room was exactly as I remembered it. Concrete floor, concrete walls, and a drain in the center. One metal chair bolted in place, and Patrick was strapped to it.

His wrists were bound behind the backrest, and his ankles were tied to the legs. His face bore a bruised, split lip, and one eye was half-swollen shut. Blood crusted at his nose, and he was breathing fast and shallow through his mouth, his jaw set as sweat dried on his skin in a dull sheen.

He looked up when the door opened, and for a split second, I saw the flicker of fear, hope, and resignation twisting together. I watched as he registered it as me.

"Oh, thank fuck it's you. I was about two minutes away from pissing myself just to make a point."

I snorted once, and the relief hit so fast it almost made my knees unsteady.

"Nice to see you too."

"You're late," he rasped. "I was starting to think you broke your murder alarm."

"Traffic was a bitch."

He huffed a broken laugh that turned into a wince. Up close, the damage was clearer. Dark bruises along his ribs where his shirt had ridden up. Scrapes marred his knuckles where he'd clearly swung at someone and connected a few times before they tied him down. The raw, chafed skin around his wrists was red and abraded.

I stepped in, knife in hand, and he flinched a fraction, then rolled his eyes at himself.

"If you're here to kill me," he muttered, "you have the weirdest bedside manner I've ever seen."

"I don't kill her best friends. Wrong way to build a relationship."

"You kill everyone else," he croaked.

"Only when they deserve it."

He swallowed as I stepped behind the chair. The restraints weren't complicated. Simple ropes, not locked cuffs. Whoever had tied him knew what they were doing. There was almost no slack as I slid the knife under the first knot, felt the tension, and cut. The rope split, and his breath hitched. One wrist free.

"Don't move yet."

"Not really in the mood for interpretive dance anyway," he muttered.

The second rope came free more easily now that the first had loosened. Blood rushed back into his fingers, and he hissed, flicking his hands out a few times.

"That— ow— fuck me. Okay. Not dead. That's good."

I crouched to deal with his ankles.

"Anyone else come down here?"

"Two dudes. One punched me for calling him a dick. They were bored. Kept talking about bonuses and what Conor was going to do when she showed up."

My jaw tightened.

"She's not coming."

"Good," he said immediately. "Good. She better not. I swear to God, Kael, if you give her any details that make her think this is her fault, I'll—"

He cut himself off, closed his eyes, and swallowed hard.

"Is she okay?"

There was no hesitation or bargaining from him. The first thing out of his mouth wasn't 'am I going to die' or 'what's the plan.' He just needed to know she was safe, and I watched his shoulders drop just slightly when I replied.

"Yes. She's safe."

He breathed out, and it shook with the weight falling from his shoulders. The rope around his ankles gave way. He slumped forward a little, arms hanging, fingers flexing like he wasn't quite sure they were attached.

"I don't feel safe," he muttered. "Does that count?"

"You're alive, and that's what counts right now."

"You're so fucking dramatic. You know that, right?"

"So I've been told." I chuckled softly.

He started to stand, and his legs began to tremble. I grabbed his shoulder and hauled him back enough that he didn't faceplant into the concrete.

"Easy, Speed Racer. You're not walking out of here on pride alone."

He sagged against my grip, panting.

"Where are we going?" he asked.

"Out. Then down the hill. Then to a doctor who's going to yell at me again."

"Oh, good. Can't wait to meet someone who yells at someone like you."

He tried to straighten, but his knees buckled. I shifted, getting my shoulder under his, wrapping an arm around his back.

"We'll do this my way."

"And your way is—?"

• • •

The door clicked behind us, and every muscle in my body tightened.

"You always did like an entrance, Mercer."

Conor's voice slid into the room like a snake as Patrick went rigid under my hand. I tightened my grip slightly, took a steadying breath, and turned.

He stood just inside the doorway, arms crossed as he leaned casually on the frame. His tailored suit was clean and his tie slightly loosened, as if this were just another late night at the office. The bruise along his jaw had gone from a light blue to a devastating deep purple over the last twenty-four hours. His eye held a crescent of red at the edge from a burst vessel.

Two guards flanked him, guns at a lazy low ready. Not the cheap help from the hallways. These were better dressed, better armed, and held their posture tighter.

Conor took us in with one sweep. The cut ropes on the floor. Patrick half off the chair with my arm around his back, and he smiled.

"See? I told them you'd come."

"Your security needs work."

He chuckled.

"Considering you designed half of it, I'll take that into consideration."

His gaze slid to Patrick.

"You look terrible. I hope they didn't damage anything essential. I still need your tongue."

Patrick rasped out a laugh that had no humor in it. "Sorry, mate. You're not my type. I prefer my partners to be dominating and less kidnappy."

Conor's mouth thinned as he looked at me.

"Is this what you do with your free time, Mercer? You walk into a man's home, dismantle his plans, and you convince his favorite people to turn on him."

"You call that a plan? Snatching DJs in alleys and hoping word gets around?"

He shrugged lightly.

"It worked. You're here aren't you?"

"I'd have come for you anyway. You just made it personal when you put your hands on what's mine."

Something flickered in his expression. He stepped farther into the room as his guards followed, spreading just enough to give themselves angles.

"You've always been sentimental. I thought it was just a quirk. Something I worked out of you after Ariya. I thought I trained you for what you're good at and you'd ignore the rest. But you keep surprising me."

"You keep underestimating me."

He smiled again, but the lines of his mouth were thin and humorless.

"Do you really think this ends the way you want it to? You and the DJ walk out while the girl waits in some little hole. I disappear. You live happily ever after in whatever fantasy you've built in your head?"

"I don't believe in happily ever after, but I do believe in people getting what they've earned."

"And what have I earned?"

Patrick made a small, broken sound. I didn't look at him. Not yet. Instead, I watched Conor's eyes. The way they lit when he thought he'd found a seam.

"Ah. You're not angry because I took Patrick. You're angry because I broke your toy."

The word hit like a slap.

"Careful, Conor."

He didn't stop.

"You think I don't see it? The way you look at her? The way you talk to her? You took my asset and decided you could build something better out of her. You think she's yours now."

"She was never yours," I said.

"She's not yours either, lad, and you hate that."

My jaw locked as he stepped closer, hands spread, like this was a negotiation and not the lead-up to a bloodbath.

"You have such talent, Mercer. You see value where other people see noise. You saw it in me when you took your first job. You see it in her. But you're still a man who takes orders. You're still a piece on someone else's board. You don't know how to exist without a boss."

"Is that what this is? A recruitment speech to try and bring me back into the fold?"

"Why not? We could fix this. Clean the mess. Send the boy home in one piece. Let me have the girl, and you stay with me. We reset the clock. You keep doing what you're good at. I keep the city and the girl. No one has to die tonight."

Behind me, Patrick's breath hitched.

"You're really offering him his old job back? After all this? You're either desperate or delusional."

"Desperation is just motivation with less time. And I am a very motivated man."

He looked at me.

"You walk away from this, Kael, and what do you have? A broken girl who thinks she owes you, a DJ full of guilt, a handful of burned bridges, and a target on your back from whatever scraps of my organization you don't manage to kill. You think that's a future?"

"More than I have here. More than I've ever had here."

He laughed. Genuinely.

"Then you're more sentimental than I gave you credit for. And that? That is going to get people killed."

"You already did that. You made sure of it the minute you decided a girl's body was a message you got to write."

His mouth tightened. He flicked a glance at Patrick.

"You know what the boy said? When I asked him why you'd risk everything for her? He said you were bored. That you needed something to believe in so you wouldn't drink yourself to death."

Patrick turned his head slowly to look at him.

"I said you were an egotistical prick with a god complex. Nice try though, dickhead."

Conor ignored him and stepped closer.

"You think this is about her. But this is just who you are. You burn things down. You break systems. You can't help it. You walk into people's lives, and you leave bodies behind."

"Yes. I know."

He blinked, thrown off for a second by the lack of denial. I let the silence stretch.

"You're right. I do burn things down. I break systems. But there's a difference between you and me."

"And what's that?"

"I know what I am, and you still think you're some kind of hero."

His eyes blazed, and the air in the room shifted. The guards' fingers tightened on their weapons, almost imperceptibly. Patrick sucked in a breath through his teeth.

Conor's smile didn't return.

"You walked in here alone. You really think you walk out again?"

"I don't think, friend. I plan."

Then I moved. The gun at my back cleared the holster in one smooth pull, but Conor was ready for me. His hand went for his own weapon even as he stepped sideways, putting one of his men between us.

The guard on my right raised his gun. I shot him twice in the chest before he finished the motion.

The second guard dove for cover, firing as he went. Concrete dust exploded off the wall where my head had been a heartbeat before. I twisted, pulling Patrick with me, shoving him toward the entrance. He stumbled and landed hard, his hands scrambling to open the door.

"Stay down!"

"Not arguing!"

Conor fired once, wildly, more to create noise than to hit anything. The bullet ricocheted off the far wall, and the room filled with echoing gunshots and smoke. I dropped low and moved sideways, using the chair as partial cover, counting shots in my head out of habit.

One from him. Two. Three.

The remaining guard had stopped firing. That meant he was moving. Trying to flank. Old habits again. I let my ears do what my eyes couldn't. The scuff of a boot on concrete. The slight hitch of breath from my left. I shot through the middle of the chair.

There was a grunt that cut off short before the sound of something heavy hitting the floor. Silence rushed in around the ringing. One guard down for sure. One bleeding, maybe dead. That left Conor.

He exhaled slowly, toward the back of the room.

"This doesn't have to end like this," he called.

"It really does, Conor."

I shifted, putting myself between him and Patrick, body angled to give as small a target as possible. Another shot cracked. White heat lanced through my upper arm, and my fingers went momentarily numb. I bit back a curse and dove behind the chair.

"You're slowing down," Conor said. His voice had that ugly edge now, the one that came out when the façade slipped. "You're not as careful as you used to be. She's making you sloppy."

"She's making me honest."

"I don't need you, honest! I just need you fucking obedient!"

A bullet chewed a divot out of the concrete an inch from my boot, and Patrick flinched from the doorway.

"Okay," he croaked. "Just going to say it. This is not my favorite day."

"Shut up, Patrick," Conor snarled.

The snarl was useful. Anger made people predictable. I used the edge of the chair to lever myself up just enough to angle my gun around the metal back.

Conor was edging toward the door, trying to hit the frame so he could grab Patrick. I shot the wall an inch from his head, and he jerked back instinctively.

"That one was a warning."

He laughed, breathless.

"You don't warn people, Mercer. You kill them."

"Sometimes I like to be dramatic."

He fired again. The shot went wild. He was panicking now. The control he worshipped so much was slipping between his fingers.

Good. I moved, fast and low, using the chair as a springboard. My shoulder slammed into him before he could correct his aim. We hit the floor hard. His gun skittered away, clattering under the storage shelves.

We grappled on the floor. A fist in my ribs, and my fist to his jaw as we rolled.

He was much stronger than he looked. He always had been. Lean, wiry muscle under expensive suits and civilized smiles. He knew where to hit. The ribs, kidneys, and all the places that stole your breath.

Pain flared hot along my shoulder where his fingers gripped into the healing graze. The glued skin tugged and then ripped. I felt my blood, wet and warm, ooze under my shirt.

I snarled and slammed his wrist into the concrete until his fingers spasmed and went slack. He tried to go for my eyes. I caught his hand, twisted, and felt something give with an ugly crack. He screamed, and it almost made me lose focus. I'd never heard him make a sound without control over it before, and I liked it more than I should have. He bucked under me, trying to roll. I let him get just enough traction to think he was winning, then drove my forearm across his throat and my other hand into his broken fingers.

His eyes bulged.

"Here's how this ends. You aren't leaving here in anything but a body bag tonight, Conor."

"You think killing me fixes anything? You think the people I answer to just… disappear? There are bigger men than me, Mercer. Men who like their pet monsters on shorter leashes."

"I'm counting on it. You're not the only house that needs cleaning."

His lip curled. "You arrogant son of a—"

I slammed his head into the floor, and his words dissolved into a grunt. I could have taken the clean route. Gun to the head. Quick. Efficient. The way I'd done it a hundred times for men who meant nothing but a number on a page. Except he wasn't just another number.

He was every bruise on Sera's skin. Every finger-shaped mark on her throat. Every twisted thought in her head that said she was currency and not a person. He was the chair and the cuffs and the bed and the way her voice had sounded when she said I want him dead.

"You think you own people. You think you get to decide what they're worth. You don't know how to exist in a world where you don't get to make that call."

"I built this goddamn world," he spat.

"You built a fucking cage. I'm just here to break the locks."

His eyes burned into mine.

"Even if you walk away from this, you'll still be what I made you. You'll still be the man who kills for a living. You think she'll ever really look at you and not see my hands in it?"

The words hit. He knew where to aim, too. I felt the echo of them down old fault lines. Every job, every body, every time I came home and washed someone else's blood off my knuckles and sat in the quiet and pretended it didn't matter.

He smiled, small and vicious, when he saw it land.

"She'll remember the way I broke her," he whispered. "And she'll remember you walked into my house and did the same thing to me. Don't you see it? You and I, we're—"

I broke his nose with one sharp punch. Bone crunched under my knuckles, and blood exploded over his face. The smile on his lips vanished.

"You don't get to write her story. Not anymore. Not ever again."

He choked, coughing thick, red streaks onto the concrete.

"You think killing me gives her closure? That's not how this works, Kael. Trauma doesn't end just because you put a bullet in the man who caused it."

"Oh, I know."

"Then why—"

"Because this isn't for closure. This is for fun. For penance. For her and every other girl you decided to trade like currency."

His eyes widened, and for the first time since I'd met him, I saw it. Fear. Cold and written in every line of his face. I pulled the smaller knife from my belt and pressed the flat of the blade against his throat, just under the jaw. Not enough to cut. Enough to get his full attention.

"You used her body as a message. You made her pain a billboard. Every bruise meant to say 'this is what happens when you forget who owns you.'"

He swallowed, and the blade shifted against his skin.

"You don't own her. You never did. You just borrowed her fear."

He spat blood up at me.

"She'll never be free of me," he hissed. "Every time you touch her, she'll hear my voice. Every time she closes her eyes, she'll see my house."

I leaned in close, the stench of sweat and blood permeating the air.

"Maybe. But she'll also know you died for it and that it was me who made sure of it."

His breath stuttered.

"You're doing this for her," he said.

"Yes. And for Patrick. And for me. And for every person who ever walked out of here carrying something they couldn't put down. And for Ariya."

His gaze flicked past me, toward the doorway where Patrick lay half-curled, watching, chest heaving.

"You really want him to see this?" Conor croaked. "You want him to watch you become exactly what you pretend you're not?"

Patrick's voice cut through the room, rough and shaking.

"Do it," he rasped. "Don't you dare stop now."

Conor's mouth twisted.

"See?" he whispered. "You corrupt everything you touch."

"Maybe."

Then I shifted the blade, and he realized what I was going to do a heartbeat before I did it. His eyes flared, and his body bucked.

"No—"

My hand moved quick and the knife slid in, clean and deep, just to the side of his Adam's apple, angled back and up. Not the dramatic throat slash he'd used on men he wanted to make an example of. This was precise. Clean. Personal.

His breath hitched, and he clutched at my wrist, his fingers slick as blood welled up around the steel, hot and dark.

I held his gaze.

"You'll never get to touch her or anyone else again. Not even in the story you tell yourself about how this ends."

His lips moved, but no sound came out. The fight went out of his hands first. Then his shoulders. Then his eyes, as the light faded and fucking finally, went out.

I pulled the knife free and sat back on my heels. The only sounds left in the room were Patrick's ragged breathing and the slow drip of blood onto concrete. My own pulse roared in my ears. It didn't feel anything like triumph. Just an absence. Like a noise that had been humming beneath everything for years had finally cut out.

My shoulder throbbed, my ribs burned, and my arm bled down to my wrist. I wiped the knife on Conor's silk shirt and slid it back into the sheath. Behind me, Patrick let out a shuddering breath.

"Is he—"

"Yeah."

"Thank fuck," he whispered.

I shoved myself to my feet, and the room tilted for a second, then steadied. Pain flared behind my eyes, but I shoved it down with everything else.

"Can you stand?"

He swallowed hard and tried.

"With help."

"Good enough for me."

I crossed over to him and hauled him up again, slower this time. He grunted, knees trembling, one hand grabbing the back of my shirt like he was afraid his body was going to keep going without him.

"You alright?"

He gave me a look. "Define, alright."

"Alive. That works for me right now."

"Then yeah. I'm there. Barely."

On the way out of the cell, I grabbed the broken folding chair and jammed it sideways under the basement door handle from the inside. It wouldn't hold serious pressure, but it would make anyone trying to come down in a hurry trip over themselves.

We climbed the stairs one slow step at a time. My shoulder screamed, and his breath came out in heavy pants.

When we reached the top, I eased the door open an inch and listened. Nothing. The two men I'd left in the hallway were still where I'd put them. One slumped. One sprawled. Neither moved.

"Jesus Christ," Patrick muttered. "You work fast."

"We can have a performance review later. Right now, we need to move."

We pushed out into the hall as every nerve I had was screaming for speed and quiet at the same time. The house overhead felt like it held its own breath, waiting to see if it was all over. We made it ten feet before my burner buzzed and I froze.

Rafe: *Movement at the house. Two cars just pulled up. More men going inside. You on your way out or do I start writing your epitaph?*

Kael: *Almost. Keep the road shut. If anyone gets past you, make them regret the trip.*

Rafe: *Copy. Try not to die. I really don't want your car.*

My chest tightened.

"You're texting at a time like this?" Patrick hissed weakly.

"Multitasking."

We moved again and cut through the service corridor instead of heading for the main stairs. My feet knew the pattern of this place better than most men knew their own kitchens. Laundry room. Storage. Back stairwell. We reached the door to the outside, and I paused with my hand on the bar.

"Ready?"

"No, but fuck it. Go anyway."

I pushed the door open, and the cold air hit us full in the face. The dark curve of the hill and the faint glow of the drive beyond it.

Three men stood between us and the trees. They turned as the door opened. One of them swore.

"Well, shit. The boss said Mercer might try this way."

"Your boss is dead."

They didn't flinch. Right. That news hadn't traveled yet.

"Put him down, and maybe we only break your legs," the one in the middle said, pointing his gun at my chest.

I let out a slow breath. "I've had a long night. I'm fucking tired. Walk away, and I'll let you pretend you never worked here."

"Can't let you do that. He owns us."

"Not anymore. The dead can't own anything."

They didn't get it. Of course they didn't. People like this rarely saw the man behind the curtain fall until the floor gave out under them.

They spread out instead, trying to bracket us. Patrick's hand tightened on my shirt.

"Do your thing," he muttered. "I'll be over here trying not to die."

"You're doing great so far, keep it up."

I shifted my weight and threw us sideways, dragging him down behind the low concrete lip of the stairwell as the first shots rang out. Bullets sparked off the brick above us as Patrick yelped.

"You okay?"

"I would like to opt out of this part," he groaned.

"No refunds or returns on my saving you. Sorry."

I popped up, fired twice, and dropped back down. One of the men went down clutching his shoulder. He screamed as the others scattered, trying to find angles. I did quick math in my head, the way I always did. Distance. Cover. Ammo. Patrick's ability to move. We didn't have the luxury of sitting here and trading shots until someone got lucky. More men would be coming. Rafe's perimeter was tight, but not impenetrable.

"We're running for the trees."

"Terrific. Let's do it."

I grabbed his arm and counted under my breath.

"On three. One… two…"

On "two," I hauled him up and shoved us out of cover. We ran. Or something similar to it. His feet scraped, and my shoulder screamed. The grass underfoot was slick and uneven as more shots cracked behind us.

A hot line seared across my side as another whizzed past my ear.

"Fuck!" Patrick yelped. "Did you just get shot?"

"Keep moving!"

"That's not a no," he gasped.

We hit the small dip at the edge of the lawn and half-slid, half-fell into the line of trees. Branches whipped at our faces. The darkness swallowed us.

"Here!" a voice shouted from the drive. "They're cutting through—"

Another voice cut him off with a grunt. Distantly, I heard the thud of a body hitting gravel. Rafe, I thought. Or one of his. We pushed deeper into the trees, lungs burning. When we were far enough that the house was more suggestion than shape, I slowed and finally let Patrick sag against a trunk. He clung to it like it was a lover.

"Okay," he panted. "Status update. I am ninety-nine percent sure I peed a little."

"Occupational hazard. You'll survive."

He laughed weakly, then winced and held his ribs.

"Is he really dead?" he asked after a second, voice quieter.

"Most definitely dead."

"Good. He doesn't get to own the end of this."

"No. He doesn't get to own anything else, ever again."

We moved more slowly after that. Making our way downhill and through the trees toward the spot where I'd left the car.

By the time we broke out of the cover and hit the shoulder of the road, my vision was fraying at the edges. The wound on my arm had gone from sharp to throbbing. My side felt wet and slick under my shirt where the graze had opened up again.

Patrick squinted at me.

"You don't look great," he said.

"I feel fucking worse."

"On a scale from one to 'Sera is going to kill you,' where are we?" he asked.

"Somewhere past she's already digging my grave."

He snorted.

"Worth it," he murmured.

The burner buzzed in my pocket.

Rafe: *You clear?*
Kael: *Out. Package in hand.*
Rafe: *Confirm boss status.*
Kael: *Conor's dead. By my hands.*

There was a longer pause this time.

Rafe: *About fucking time.*
Rafe: *Streets are gonna lose their mind when this filters down. You want me spinning a story?*
Kael: *Not yet. Let it simmer. Keep the boys' mouths shut. No one mentions the girl.*
Rafe: *Copy. What about Patrick?*
Kael: *With me.*
Rafe: *Tell him he owes me a drink for the trouble.*

I slid the phone away and looked at Patrick.

"Rafe says you owe him a drink."

"Rafe can have the whole fucking bar," he muttered.

We made it to the car, and I got him into the passenger seat first this time. He hissed as he sat, one hand braced on the dash.

"You're bleeding all over your shirt," he said, squinting at me.

"Not the worst thing that's happened to me today."

He studied my face.

"She's going to be a mess until she hears from you," he said quietly.

"I know."

"Call her," he murmured.

"I will."

"Now, Kael."

Bossy, for a man who'd been tied to a chair half an hour ago, but he wasn't wrong. I slid into the driver's seat. The motion pulled at every injury I had as the pain washed over me in a hot, dizzy wave. I rode it out. Then I pulled my phone again with fingers that weren't as steady as I wanted them to be.

The burner phone's contact sat at the top of the list, glaring at me as I stared at it for a second. She'd be sitting in that ugly couch in the old workshop, my shirt hanging off her shoulders, my knife under her leg, the words Bad Bishop Falls written on her wrist in my hand.

Counting breaths and waiting.

Fuck. I hit the call button, and it rang twice.

"Kael?" Her voice was raw. Thin. Too many miles in it for how close we were.

"It's me, Little Fawn."

The breath she let out sounded like it had been held since the moment I walked out.

"Are you—" She cut herself off and tried again. "Are you okay?"

"Mostly. We're on our feet. Still on the right side of the dirt."

"We," she echoed. "Patrick?"

I looked over. He was watching me, his eyes tired and bright.

"Hey, Ser," he croaked. "Next time you decide to get kidnapped, maybe make sure I'm on vacation or something."

She made a broken sound that tried to be a laugh and failed halfway.

"Oh my God," she whispered. "You're okay."

"No. Definitely not ok, but I'm alive. Mercer did his thing."

Silence for a beat and then very softly:

"Conor?"

I met my own eyes in the rearview mirror.

"He'll never lay hands on you or anyone, ever again."

There was no cheer on the other end. No sigh of relief. Just a quiet, shaking inhale.

"Okay," she whispered. "Okay."

"We're coming home. Keep the door locked. Don't open it for anyone but me."

"Say it."

"Bad Bishop Falls, baby."

Her breath hitched.

"I'll see you soon."

The line clicked, and I let the phone drop back into my lap and put both hands on the wheel. Patrick tipped his head back against the seat and closed his eyes.

"Did we win?" he asked after a minute.

I started the engine.

"No. But we survived. Winning comes later."

He huffed something that might have been a laugh.

"Okay. Let's survive somewhere that doesn't smell like Conor's cologne and bad decisions."

"For once, we agree."

I pulled the car onto the road and pointed it away from the hill.

Behind us, the house sat full of dead men and old ghosts. Ahead, the city waited. For the first time in a long time, I felt something under the pain and the exhaustion and the years of doing the wrong things for the wrong people.

Not hope. Not yet. Just the faintest sense that the board had been flipped and we weren't the ones scrambling to pick up the pieces anymore.

Conor was gone. Sera was alive. Patrick was breathing in my passenger seat. I'd deal with the rest. One consequence at a time.

Chapter Thirty-Two

Seraphine

Waiting was almost worse than being in that house. Almost. Worse than the cuffs. Worse than the shower. At least those had walls I could see.

The safehouse felt too big and too small at the same time. Every sound was either nothing or everything. The hum of the fridge. The tick of the heater. The occasional car passing on the street outside. They all scraped along my nerves like dull knives.

I sat on the couch where Kael left me, his shirt hanging off one shoulder, his knife tucked under my bad leg, the words on my wrist starting to blur.

Bad Bishop Falls.

I had read it so many times that the letters stopped looking like words and began to look like some strange little map.

> If someone knocked and didn't say it, I wasn't supposed to open the door.
>
> If someone knocked and did say it, I didn't know if that made it better or worse.

I tried not to look at the door and failed. Every few seconds, my gaze slid back to the metal, waiting for the rattle of the lock, the shadow under the crack, the sound of a voice that may or may not belong to him.

My leg throbbed in a slow, mean rhythm. My ribs pinched every time I took a deeper breath. The couch smelled faintly like dust and him. My fingers kept finding the knife hilt even when I wasn't thinking about it.

At some point, I realized I was counting. Not seconds. I had lost track of those. Breaths. In for four. Out for four. The same way he had counted me away from the edge of a panic attack in the shower.

Tile. Water. Soap. Coffee. Now it was a couch. A knife. His shirt. My wrist. The fucking door.

My phone lay on the table where I'd set it after the call. The screen was dark and mocking. No new messages. No missed calls. He had told me Conor was dead and that Patrick was alive. My brain kept replaying those two facts over and over, like maybe if I ran them enough times, they would feel real.

Conor is dead, Patrick is alive.

I could almost see it. The house. The basement. The concrete room. Patrick tied to a chair, cracking jokes with his mouth full of blood. Kael walking in with that steady walk that meant adrenaline had already moved into the background, and something colder had taken over.

I could imagine the sound of it when Conor died. I thought I would feel more of something like joy or relief. Something sharp and clean. Instead, there was just a low, strange ache. Like a tooth had been pulled, and my tongue kept going back to the empty space, surprised it was gone.

I wanted to throw up. I wanted to sleep for a week. I wanted to get up, walk out the fucking door, and go find them myself. Instead, I sat. I drank water in small sips he had told me to. Ate half a granola bar that tasted like cardboard and regret. Checked the lock three times even though I hadn't heard anything.

Time kept creeping by. My body was exhausted. My muscles shook with tiny tremors that had nothing to do with movement and everything to do with nerves burned out from the last thirty-six hours. My eyes stung, and I couldn't close them. Every time my lashes dropped, I saw two things.

The room in Conor's house, and Kael walking out of this one. The memory hit the same way each time. The feel of his shirt under my fingers when I grabbed him. The press of his mouth against my forehead. The way his voice had sounded when he said he would come back. With Patrick. With Conor dead. It felt like ripping a piece of myself out and handing it to him.

Here. Take this. Try not to die with it.

I didn't know how long it had been when the knock finally came. Three sharp raps. Bone on metal. The sound shot through the room like a gunshot, and I froze. My heart slammed into my ribs so hard I thought they might crack. My hand went for the knife without permission. My leg screamed as I shifted, but I barely felt it.

Another knock. Slower this time.

"Seraphine."

His voice. Or something that wore his shape. It slid under the door and wrapped around my spine.

"Bad Bishop Falls."

I exhaled so hard it almost hurt. My fingers still didn't loosen on the knife.

"Prove it."

The words came out strained, too high. Outside, there was a short pause.

"You're going to make me do this now?"

"Yes. Absolutely. If you are you, tell me what you did the first time I saw you in the alley."

"Which time? The one where you told me you weren't scared of me, or the one where I told you to get home safe and you lied about what that meant?"

My throat tightened at his words. "Get inside, you infuriating asshole."

I pushed myself to my feet, and the room swayed while my leg protested. The knife stayed in my hand, blade held low the way he had shown me once, weeks ago, behind the bar when the club was quiet, and my biggest problem had been drunk men who didn't take no as an answer.

I limped to the door. Every step felt like walking into a memory I couldn't trust. The lock was cold under my fingers. I turned it and pulled hard; the door dragged in the frame and then finally gave out. They filled the doorway like a memory I was terrified to keep.

My eyes landed on Kael first. He looked worse than I'd ever seen. His shirt was darker in patches that weren't its original color. His sleeve was torn, fabric stiff with blood. The line along his shoulder where the doctor had glued him was blooming red again. His jaw was shadowed with stubble and bruises. His eyes were tired, like the night had taken a little more than it needed to.

Patrick stood half behind him, mostly held up by his shoulder.

He looked like someone had decided his face was a piñata and then got bored halfway through. One eye was completely shut, and his lip was split and crusted over. His nose was swollen and crooked in a way that said it hurt to breathe through it. The way he held his middle told me he was bruised, maybe broken under there, but he still managed to grin at me.

"Hey, trouble," he rasped. "You look better than me, and I kinda hate you for that."

Whatever dam I had been trying to build against my own emotions snapped. The knife clattered to the floor. I grabbed the door with one hand and the frame with the other because my knees forgot how to hold me.

"You fucking idiots."

"Hi, sweetheart."

Kael's voice was raspy and filled with exhaustion, and it made my eyes burn.

"You're bleeding. Both of you are bleeding everywhere, and you call me sweetheart?"

"Would you prefer buttercup?"

Something like a laugh tore out of me. It sounded wild and half hysterical.

"Get inside. Before I scream and bring the whole neighborhood down on us."

He nudged Patrick forward first.

"Watch the step."

The two of them shuffled in like some kind of broken two-man parade. I closed the door behind them and shoved the lock back into place, then leaned on it for a second, my breath shaking. Being near them made it worse. The smell of blood, mixing with sweat and gun powder, was second only to the sharp metallic edge of adrenaline that still clung to them like a second skin.

Patrick sagged toward the couch. I limped ahead and grabbed the back of it with both hands.

"Sit," I ordered.

"Look at you," he croaked. "Giving orders now."

My hands shook, but my voice didn't.

"Sit," I repeated.

He sat and groaned as his body remembered it had bones. His head tipped back. He shut his eyes. I turned on Kael. He was still standing in the middle of the room. Watching me. Taking everything in at once.

"Close the door and lock it," he said softly.

"Already did. Now sit down before your arm falls off."

"It's still attached."

"For now," I snapped. "Sit."

Something flickered in his eyes, but he sat. Opposite Patrick, in the chair he had been brooding in earlier. The gun was gone from the table. The knives were gone. Only the faint, ghostly outlines in the dust showed where they had been.

My body wanted to crumple between them. To slide down onto the floor and press my forehead to the cool boards and let my brain finally stop running worst-case scenarios.

Instead, I went to the little kitchen area, grabbed the first aid kit, the bottle of cheap antiseptic, three clean cloths, and the remaining painkillers Kael had left for me earlier. When I turned back, both of them were watching me. It made something warm deep inside me.

"You first," I told Patrick.

He blinked back at me.

"Seriously? The man is leaking from at least two places."

"Yes. He is also the one who dragged you out of hell on earth. He can wait thirty seconds."

Kael's mouth twitched.

"Listen to your nurse, Patrick."

"I hate both of you," Patrick muttered, but he didn't argue when I scooted closer and knelt beside the couch. My leg screamed at the angle, but I ignored it.

"Let me see."

He cracked his good eye open.

"You do know this isn't your fault, right?" he asked.

"Shut up."

"Just checking," he muttered.

I studied his face. It was worse up close. Bruises that sat in that ugly in-between stage, already swelling but not yet fully bloomed. I sighed at the split skin mixed with dried blood.

"Did they break your nose?"

"Feels like it. But the doc will tell me later if I need a new face."

"You don't get a new face. I like this one. Even when it is stupid."

He snorted, then winced and pressed his tongue against his teeth.

"Ow," he grunted. "Okay. Soft jokes only. Nothing that uses my whole head."

I dampened a cloth with water, then added a little antiseptic.

"This is going to sting."

"Everything already stings. It's a fucking party."

I cleaned the worst of the blood from his lip and nose. He gritted his teeth but didn't pull away. At some point, I realized my hands were steadier than I expected. They shook more when I reached for my own water bottle than when I dabbed at his bruises.

"This is going to look worse tomorrow."

"Excellent. I can guilt customers into buying me pity drinks."

My throat tightened.

"Patrick…"

He opened his eye fully and looked at me.

"I'm so fucking sorry."

His brows pulled together.

"For what?"

"For this," I said. My voice broke around the word. "For him taking you. For putting you in his sights. For the basement. For the chair. For everything."

He stared at me like I had grown an extra head.

"Sera, no."

"Yes. If you didn't know me. If I hadn't been in that club. If I hadn't been so stupid with Conor, you wouldn't have been there."

"If I didn't know you, I would probably be dead from something else by now," he shot back. "Bad drugs. Worse people. A dumb bar fight. Something."

"That doesn't make this better."

"You think I got dragged into your orbit by accident? You think I stumbled into your world one day by some cosmic chance? No. I made choices, and I'd follow you into hell any day, just to hear you yell at me one more time."

"That doesn't mean you deserved a concrete room and rope burns."

His jaw flexed. "I didn't say I deserved it. I'm saying I had a say. Same as you. You're not the only one who gets to claim fault here, Seraphine. You don't get to hoard the guilt like it makes you noble."

I flinched, and he softened his words just a little.

"I knew what this life was. Long before you ever stepped into Escape. I knew what could happen in this kinda place, and I stuck with you. Through thick and thin. We're homies. Besties. Platonic soul mates, through mob bosses and shady club owners."

"Still, I wouldn't have survived if you hadn't."

"It's they who have to worry about surviving us, Ser."

"You could have died. Because of me."

"Maybe. But you don't get to sit there and tell me this is all on you. That is what your parents and every other shitty human in your life have taught you. That everyone's pain is your price to pay. I'm not letting you foot that bill."

Tears stung behind my eyes. "I traded myself for you. And I would again. As many times as I had to."

"And I would do the same for you. That doesn't make either of us currency. It makes us idiots who love each other."

A broken laugh slipped out of me.

"I fucking hate you."

"Love you too, Ser."

"You are never allowed to get kidnapped again. Got it?"

"If I do, I expect you to keep your ass put wherever you are. If you trade yourself to someone like that again, I will haunt you."

"You aren't dead."

"I'm not. But I'll still haunt your ass."

I sniffed and wiped at my nose with the back of my wrist. The words there were smudged a little more.

"Okay. Deal."

He smiled even though it hurt his face. "Can I pass out now? Or do you need more emotional catharsis first?"

"Sleep, Pattykins."

His eyes slid shut, and I watched him for a minute. He was breathing, and that was enough.

I pushed myself upright, every muscle complaining, and turned to face the other problem in the room.

Kael watched from the chair, elbows on his knees, hands clasped loosely. He looked worse now that he was not trying to stand.

Adrenaline had clearly left the building. His skin looked grayer, and the line of his mouth was tighter. A dark patch spread slowly on the side of his shirt where the fabric clung to his ribs.

"You're next."

"I am fine."

"You're bleeding onto your shitty old murder chair. You're anything but fine. Sit still."

He didn't argue, but I saw the flicker of resistance in his shoulders. The need to do, to move, to be the shield. I knelt down beside him instead of standing over him.

"Take the shirt off."

His brows lifted that fraction he used when he wanted to make something dirty and was holding himself back.

"If you make a joke right now, I will stab you with your own knife and make sure it sticks."

"You're the only person I want stabbing me, Little Fawn."

He pulled at the hem of his shirt, and the motion tugged at his injuries. His jaw clenched as he peeled the shirt up carefully, over the bandage on his ribs, over the fresh wound on his arm.

He was a canvas of old violence and new damage. Bruises bloomed across his chest and side. Purple, blue, and yellow in places. The graze along his shoulder that the doctor had glued was open again in spots, the edges raw and angry. A new furrow marked his upper arm, just shy of his shoulder. Not deep enough to be instantly deadly. Deep enough to need more than my shaky hands and cheap supplies.

I sucked in a breath.

"I told you to be careful."

"I was."

"This is your version of careful? What the fuck does reckless look like?"

"We're all still breathing."

"That is a low bar."

"It's the only one that matters right now."

I wanted to hit him, but I also wanted to hug him so hard his ribs screamed. Instead, I poured antiseptic onto a clean cloth and pressed it gently around the edges of the worst wound. He didn't flinch. Of course he didn't.

"Patrick told you to call me."

"Yes."

"Did he also tell you to get shot twice and reopen your stitches?"

"Naw. That was freelance work."

"Don't ever phrase it like that again."

A ghost of a smile tugged at his mouth.

"How bad is it? Really."

"You look like you went ten rounds with a truck and lost."

"Well good news. The truck is dead in his own basement."

"Not funny."

He watched my hands as I worked.

"You are steadier than you think," he said quietly.

"I'm pretending we're on a beach somewhere and you spilled a Bloody Mary on yourself."

"Flattering."

"If I think about you as broken, my brain starts supplying helpful little flashbacks. So shut up and let me delude myself." He quieted, and for a while there was only our breathing and the sound of cloth on skin. The antiseptic smell burned my nose, and my leg shook under me. The room felt both very small and very far away all at the same time.

"You killed him," I said finally.

"I did."

"How?"

"Efficiently. Not slowly. Not like he did with other people. Quick, but painful. He had time to think about it before he was gone."

I swallowed back a lump in my throat.

"I thought it would feel different. Knowing he's gone. I thought I would feel this… release."

"Do you?"

"No. I feel like my brain has misplaced something. I keep expecting him to walk through every door."

"That's going to take time."

"Time," I repeated. "Everything is time. Time to heal. Time to process. Time to figure out who the hell I am now."

"You have time now."

"Because you killed him."

"Yes. And because you're safe to do so now."

My throat burned as I let his words settle around me.

"Do you regret it?"

"Not even a little. Do you?"

I thought about it for a minute. Really thought. About the chair. The bed. His hand on my throat. His voice in my ear. About Patrick being strapped to a metal chair and used as a lure to force me back into my own personal living nightmare.

"Not even a little."

I smiled a little, just enough to let myself feel anything other than the oppressing panic.

"I don't regret him being dead. The world is a better place without a man like him in it. I just wish it made everything else vanish with him."

"It won't."

"I know. And I hate that I know that."

"You're allowed to hate it, but not to dwell on it."

"Do you feel guilty?"

"For him?"

"For any of it."

He was quiet for a moment as I wrapped gauze around his arm, focusing on keeping the tension right. Not too tight. Not too loose.

"I feel responsible for bringing you into his orbit. For not cutting ties sooner. For every job I did that kept him strong."

"You didn't bring me to him."

"I worked for him. He used the stability I gave him to build the cage he put you in. That's on me as much as anything."

"You were there to do a job. I just happened to be there too. Same club, same time, same need for something more than I should be allowed in this life."

"That doesn't erase it. I should have stayed away from you. Not let him see what you did," he paused before continuing. "No, what you *do* to me."

"No. It doesn't erase it, but it also means you don't get to hoard the guilt either."

His mouth twitched.

"Patrick rub off on you?"

"Apparently, we are all idiots who love each other."

"I do, you know." He caught my eye for a second before tilting my chin up with his fingers. "Love you, I mean."

"Tell me again when you're on less pain meds, more sleep, and not suffering mass blood loss."

"Deal, but I promised you something else."

"In the car. I know. And here. And a lot of other places, actually. You keep promising things."

"I promised you he wouldn't touch you again."

"Yes. You did."

"I kept that one."

My chest tightened and ached at his declaration.

"You did."

"And I promised I would bring Patrick back."

"Yes," I said, my voice cracking softly.

"I kept that one too."

I looked over my shoulder at Patrick. He had drifted sideways on the couch, one arm thrown over his eyes, breathing shallow but even. He was here, and he was hurt, but he was alive. My eyes stung with tears I'd been holding back too long.

"You keep promising things you can't control."

"I promised I would try. That's the best any of us get."

The words settled around us.

"So, what happens now?"

"Now, we get him and me patched properly. We'll move again when you're ready. We make some calls. There are people who need to know he's gone. There are holes that will open up in the city, and I intend to make sure the wrong men don't rush in to fill them."

"And me?"

"You get to decide what your life looks like when it is not shaped around someone else's threats."

"I don't know how to do that."

"We figure it out together. One piece at a time."

"I can't hide forever."

"You're not hiding. You're regrouping."

"Feels a lot like hiding."

"That's because every time you stopped moving before, you got punished. You're allowed to be still without waiting for someone's hand to fall."

His voice gentled on that last sentence. Something in me shrank away from it and leaned into it at the same time. I sighed softly and leaned into him. His hand softly gripped my wrist as I rested my head on his knee.

"Little Fawn, I'm gonna fall asleep."

"Is that a promise or a threat?"

"Probably both, to be honest. There is a limit to how much blood you can lose before your body files a complaint."

"We should get you both to the doctor. Tonight."

"We won't make it in one piece if I drive now or if he tried."

I glanced at Patrick. He was out cold.

"Okay. So we stay. Just for tonight."

"Just for tonight."

"Then what?"

"Then we take stock, and we make it official. Conor's gone. The debt chains he wrapped around people go with him. The club isn't his anymore."

"Escape."

At the word, something loosened in my chest and tightened somewhere else.

"Who owns it now? With Conor and Michael both gone, it's just in limbo."

I felt the panic start to rise inside me again. "Oh god, I don't have a job to go back to. Neither does Patrick. The fuck are we going to do?"

Kael tipped my chin up to look at him again.

"Breathe, Ser. You still have a job. And the club is yours if you want it."

I looked at him as if he had sprouted horns. "What do you mean it's mine if I want it? What did you do?"

Kael smiled. His eyes were tired, and he was barely hanging on to his last thread of consciousness.

"Michael signed it over to me before his unfortunate logging accident. I'm going to sign it over to you. You decide what happens next. You make the rules."

I let out a soft gasp.

"It's mine?"

"Yours."

Fear churned in my stomach.

"What if I don't want it? What if it's too big, too much, too soon?"

"You love that club. You just don't want what it was."

He was right. Of course he was.

"I want it to be safe. For the girls. For the patrons who aren't assholes. For people who don't have anywhere else to go when the world is too loud."

"That sounds like a really good plan."

"You seem very confident in my abilities."

"I've seen what you do when you build worlds in small corners. You did it before. You can do it again."

Emotion clogged my throat.

"I'm so tired."

"I know, baby."

"Every part of me hurts."

"I know that too."

"I am scared it'll always feel like this. Like I am holding myself together with duct tape and spite."

"Spite works. We'll upgrade to Gorilla Glue later."

A broken laugh slipped out of me.

"You and Patrick are a terrible influence."

"You love us anyway."

"Yes. An infuriating amount."

His eyes softened.

"Come here, Little Fawn."

I hesitated and then moved, curling into his lap, moving slowly to be careful of his bandaged wounds, and my own broken pieces as his arm wrapped around me. I rested my head on his shoulder and breathed him in. They were safe. They were alive. The world could go back to spinning again.

From here, I could reach both of them. Patrick's hand hung limp off the edge of the couch. I could touch his fingers if I wanted.

Kael's shoulder was a warm, solid line against my cheek. His fingers traced slow circles against my skin. It felt ridiculous and dangerous and safe all at once.

"Do you ever sleep?"

"Sometimes."

"You should try now."

"So should you."

"I'm scared to close my eyes."

"I know, but do it anyway."

"You're fucking bossy."

"I'm focused."

The room hummed around us. The heater clicked, and the fridge rattled. A car drove past outside, the sound fading into the distance. My body was finally starting to shut down, whether I wanted it to or not. Every blink lasted a little longer, and every inhale took more effort.

"Kael?"

"Yeah."

"Did it hurt?"

"Killing him?"

"Yes."

He thought about it.

"Not the way you're asking. The hitting, the knife, that's just work. The part that hurt was knowing I should have done it sooner."

"Would it have made a difference?"

He was quiet for a moment.

"Probably not."

"Then maybe you did it exactly when you could."

He huffed out something like a laugh.

"You're fucking dangerous when you start making sense."

"And you're still a bad influence."

My eyes slid closed for a second, and for the first time, the room didn't twist into his house. When I opened them again, I saw the underside of the table, the edge of the couch, the faint ink on my wrist where his fingers still rested.

"Do you think we'll get a tomorrow?"

"Yes."

"How do you know?"

"Because I am too stubborn to let it end tonight."

"That's not how time works."

"Probably not, but it's how my time works."

I believed him, and that was the wildest part. Patrick snored once, softly, like some bizarre punctuation mark at the end of the night. My mouth curved into something that was almost a smile.

"You did it."

"What?"

"You killed him. You brought Patrick back. You came back. You kept your promises."

"I only make the kind I can keep."

"Don't make a habit of making new ones. My heart can't take it."

"No more tonight, at least."

"Good."

I let my eyes close. This time, when the dark moved in, it didn't feel like a hand over my mouth. It felt like a room with the door locked, my two favorite men breathing beside me, and the faint, impossible shape of something waiting on the other side of sleep.

Not a house on a hill. Not a basement.

A club with a new name on the deeds. A life that hadn't been written yet.

It was fragile and tentative and full of sharp edges, but it was mine. And no one was going to take it from me again.

EPILOGUE

Three Weeks Later…

Escape didn't smell like fear anymore. It smelled of whiskey and industrial floor cleaner and cheap glitter spray, the way it used to back when it was just a club and not a hunting ground. The lights were softer now. The music was lower. The staff were louder, laughing with each other between shifts instead of glancing at the doors for shadows that didn't belong there.

Conor's fingerprints were gone. Scrubbed out. Burned and buried. Some days, I still woke up expecting to hear his voice. Most days, I didn't hear it at all.

I stood in the middle of the back office, my office now, leaning a hip against the table as Patrick flipped through paperwork with exaggerated disgust.

"This is disgusting."

"What, the forms?"

"No," he said, stabbing a finger at the top page. "This part where it says I'm an employee."

"You *are* an employee."

"Rude."

I chuckled as I took stock of his old wounds. He was healing well. His bruises had faded, and the doctor straightened his nose again. He told everyone that a raccoon had attacked him. No one believed him, but it made the girls laugh, and right now, laughter was the only thing that mattered.

"So," he said, leaning back in his chair and grinning. "You're now the proud owner of Escape. How's it feel?"

I looked at the stack of documents. Then at the club. Then at my hands.

"Strange," I admitted carefully. "But good."

He watched me for a beat.

"You're doing it, Ser. You're actually fucking doing it."

A breath I didn't know I was holding loosened in my chest. "Yeah," I murmured. "Maybe I am."

A soft knock landed on the doorway, and for once, I didn't tense. That was new, and I was trying to get used to it.

Kael leaned against the frame, arms crossed loosely over his chest. His bruises were mostly gone, and his stitches had been removed two days ago. The only sign of what he had done was the tired set of his shoulders and the new scar that would sit along his shoulder forever.

Patrick groaned dramatically.

"I swear he appears every time I start feeling important."

"Coincidence," Kael replied dryly.

"Lies," Patrick said, standing. "Anyway, boss-lady. I'm going to grab the cases from the back. Try not to ruin the new furniture while I'm gone."

I flipped him off, and he saluted back before he wandered off, humming.

When it was just the two of us, the silence between us felt different. Not brittle or loaded. Just full of possibilities.

Kael pushed off the doorframe and crossed the room toward me.

"You ready?"

"For what?"

He tipped his head toward the front of the club.

"Reopening night. The first night it's officially open and yours."

Nerves fluttered up my spine, and I smoothed my hands down my thighs.

"Do you think people will come back?" I asked, looking up at him softly.

"You could open the doors and sell nothing but tap water and bad choices, and they would still come."

I bit the inside of my cheek to keep from smiling too widely. He stepped closer. His presence grounded me, making my knees weak rather than causing panic. Three weeks ago, that kind of closeness would have made my lungs ache. Now it made something in my ribs settle into place.

"You look different," he murmured.

"How?" I asked quietly.

"Like you're not waiting for the world to hit you. Like you're getting ready to hit back."

A shiver slid down my spine.

"And you? How do you look?"

"Like a man who kept his promises."

Emotion pinched inside my chest, causing my eyes to sting.

"You did. Every single one."

His eyes warmed. "Not all. Not yet."

Before I could ask, Patrick's shout carried from somewhere near the front hallway.

"Doorbell. I got it."

I frowned slightly. "When did we get a fucking doorbell?"

Kael's head tilted, just enough that I saw the change in him. The way his attention sharpened.

"Probably a delivery," I said, more to myself than to him. "We've been getting flowers and stupid baskets all week."

He didn't relax, because of course he didn't.

I stepped closer, catching his sleeve.

"Wait."

He looked down at me. The noise from the club faded for a second, dulling down to just the hum of the lights and the low thump of bass through the walls from the sound check out front.

I turned my wrist so the ink caught the light. The fresh tattoo sat just over my pulse. His handwriting was looped and careful.

Bad Bishop Falls.

"You hate that I did this, don't you?"

"I don't hate it. I'm just very aware of what it means."

"What does it mean?"

"That you plan on surviving long enough for it to fade."

My throat tightened as I reached up and curled my fingers in the fabric of his shirt.

"Because of you, Kael. Now, say it, please."

"Seraphine…"

"Say it anyway."

His hand came up, warm and steady against the back of my neck.

"You're safe, Little Fawn."

I closed my eyes for a heartbeat. Let it sink in. Let it land somewhere deep and settle.

"I know."

For the first time, it felt completely, painfully true.

"Ser, you want this one?" Patrick's voice floated back toward us, closer now, tone lighter. "It has your name on it. Like… handwritten. Pretty little package and everything."

My eyes snapped open.

"What package?" I called.

There was a pause. Too long for something simple.

"I don't know. No return address. Just a card," he said. His voice sounded further away, like he had stepped outside or into the vestibule. "Relax. I'm just going to crack it open. Maybe it's more cookies. Or one of those ugly fruit baskets you love."

"I don't fucking love them," I muttered.

Kael's hand slipped from my neck. His body had gone very still.

"Patrick. Don't open anything until I see it."

The music from the front cut out mid-beat. Someone must have hit the wrong switch. The sudden silence made every sound carry. There was the squeak of hinges. Chairs scraping against concrete.

A muffled curse.

"What the hell. There's no—"

The rest of his sentence vanished in a white-hot crack that tore through the floor.

The world jumped, and a blast hit like a fist from underneath. The air punched out of my lungs as the walls buckled with a sound like an animal being torn in half. Lights exploded and then shattered, raining glass.

Kael slammed into me. One second I was standing, and the next my back hit the table, and his weight folded over me, his arms locking around my head and ribs as heat rushed through the doorway.

Somewhere ahead, where the entrance and the bar and Patrick were, something roared. Metal screamed, and wood snapped while voices all mixed together in a haze of panic and terror.

The floor lurched sideways, and my teeth clicked together. I tasted dust and smoke.

A second, smaller boom chased the first, and the whole building shuddered. A crack raced up the far wall like a jagged black vein. Bottles shattered in the bar. The emergency lights tried to kick on and died halfway, bathing everything in a low, hellish glow.

"Patrick!" I screamed.

I couldn't tell if he answered. I couldn't hear anything except the ringing in my ears and the deep, ugly groan of Escape as something heavy gave way in the room beyond.

Kael's mouth moved near my ear. I couldn't make out his words. His hands were still on me, solid and unshakeable as the ceiling dust rained down around us and red light from the front of the club flickered against the walls. For a heartbeat, all I could see was that.

I shouldn't be able to see the sky, I thought as Escape, the club I had just started to call my own, began to come down around us.

*****End of Book One: ESCAPE*****

RED LIGHTS

BOOK TWO OF THE
DARKNESS IN DEVOTION SERIES

Coming Soon

www.ingramcontent.com/pod-product-compliance
Lightning Source LLC
LaVergne TN
LVHW041056080826
845145LV00007B/1597

* 9 7 8 1 0 6 9 9 9 3 1 3 7 *